Ghost of Sonora

MORGAN HILL

Sage River Books *Sisters, Oregon*

This is a work of fiction. The characters, incidents,
and dialogues are products of the author's imagination and are not to
be construed as real. Any resemblance to actual events or persons,
living or dead, is entirely coincidental.

GHOST OF SONORA
published by Sage River Books
© 2003 by ALJO PRODUCTIONS, INC.

International Standard Book Number: 1-59052-134-X

Cover illustration © 2003 by Rene Milot. All rights reserved.

Printed in the United States of America

For information:
Sage River Books, Post Office Box 1720, Sisters, Oregon 97759

Library of Congress Cataloging-in-Publication Data
Hill, Morgan.
    Ghost of Sonora / by Morgan Hill.
        p. cm. -- (Legends of the West)
    ISBN 1-59052-134-X (pbk.)
    1. Murieta, Joaquin, d. 1853--Fiction. 2. California--Fiction. 3. Outlaws--
Fiction. I. Title.
PS3608.I435G47 2003
813' .6--dc21   2003005447
        03 04 05 06 07 08 09 — 10 9 8 7 6 5 4 3 2 1 0

PROLOGUE

Wherever the *mariachis* gather in old Mexico, they often sing "The Ballad of Joaquin Murieta." A national hero of well over a hundred years ago, Murieta is still remembered with deep affection by the Mexican people. The ballad is analogous to Washington Irving's tale of the Headless Horseman.

In California, from the Mother Lode country of Calaveras County all the way south to Cantua Arroya near Coalinga reports are still made today of a mysterious headless night rider wrapped in a black serape, who wails, "I am Joaquin Murieta, and I want my head!" Sometimes the apparition is not seen, but only the sound of hoofbeats, followed by a forlorn cry that echoes throughout the passes of the Coast Range where Murieta roamed from 1849 to 1853. Though Murieta is revered as a hero in Mexico, he is thought of as an infamous outlaw in California, where mothers still control their disobedient children with the intimidating words, "Joaquin Murieta will get you if you don't be good!"

There is much history and a great deal of legend surrounding Joaquin Murieta. I have blended the two, along with the use of my own imagination to bring you this story. If you find it interesting and enjoyable, my purpose for writing it will be served.

CHAPTER ONE

Puffy white clouds riding southerly winds scudded across the blazing face of the noonday sun in the azure California sky, casting fleeting shadows over San Diego's Union Station.

An engine pulling a coal car, eight passenger cars, and a caboose chugged its way into the railroad yard, made a full circle, and drew up parallel to the platform, facing northward. Billows of steam hissed from the engine's bowels as it ground to a halt with the bell above the cab clanging loudly. A crowd of eager people waited on the platform to greet friends and relatives.

The first passenger to leave the rear door of the car in front of the caboose was a tall, well-dressed man with blond hair. When he reached the platform, he set his small suitcase down and took the hand of an elderly woman who followed him, helping her from the car.

The woman smiled. "Thank you, Mr. Bartlett. Sitting next to you has made the trip very pleasant."

Bartlett touched the wide brim of his gray Stetson. "Same for me, Mrs. Wilkins. I hope we will meet again some time."

At that moment, a young couple approached, and embraced her. She introduced her daughter and son-in-law to Bartlett, telling them how nice he had been to her all the way from San Francisco, then walked away, happy to be with her loved ones.

Bartlett, who was in his early forties, ran his gaze around the depot, then entered the large waiting room and approached the ticket window. Two middle-aged couples were ahead of him. He waited patiently while they purchased their tickets and walked away chatting, then moved up to the window, looked at the agent through the small bars, and said, "I just came in on the San Francisco train, sir, and will be leaving on it when it pulls out. Will it be leaving on time?"

The agent was a wizened old man whose false teeth seemed too big for his mouth. Cocking his head, he grinned. "Yep, it'll pull out

4

at one-thirty sharp." After a brief pause, he added, "You must really like to ride."

Furrowing his brow and loosening the hat on his head, the tall man smiled. "What do you mean?"

"Well, with only an hour and a half between stoppin' and pullin' out, you couldn't do much business or visitin' here in San Diego…so I figger you must just like to ride."

Broadening his grin, Bartlett said, "I guess it *does* look like that, doesn't it? Truth is, sir, I rode all the way down here from San Francisco in hopes of riding all the way back with a particular individual. I checked with the railroad office in Frisco, and they told me that Señor Don Miguel Gonzales was booked on the train leaving at one-thirty this afternoon, along with a companion. Could you check and see if he is still booked?"

"Sure," nodded the clerk, turning toward a telegraph key nearby and picking up a yellow sheet of paper that lay next to it. Running his finger down a long list of names, he said, "Yep, here it is. Mr. Don Miguel Gonzales. Next name is Don Pablo Gonzales. That has to be the companion you mentioned. Probably related, wouldn't you think?"

"I'd say so."

"And what's *your* name, young fella?"

"Bartlett, sir. Allen Bartlett."

It took the agent only a second to find the name on the sheet. "Yep, here you are. Guess you're gonna connect with this Mr. Gonzales as planned, Mr. Bartlett."

Bartlett thanked him and headed for a newsstand nearby. He bought a copy of the *San Diego Sun*, found an empty bench within sight of the station's front door and sat down to read the newspaper. It was dated Tuesday, April 17, 1906, and was hot off the press.

At precisely 12:50 P.M., a carriage rolled to a halt in front of the station. Two Mexican men alighted from the vehicle. The younger—twenty-seven-year-old Don Pablo Gonzales—stepped down first, helped his seventy-six-year-old grandfather from the carriage, then paid the driver. Lifting two suitcases from the carriage, the younger man walked beside the other as they headed for the door. A cool ocean breeze gusted along the street as they entered the depot.

Allen Bartlett spotted them immediately, and laying the newspaper down, followed them to the ticket window. Remaining a few feet away, he observed as the younger Mexican told the ticket agent his name and the name of his grandfather, saying they had reservations on the train to San Francisco. He spoke in perfect English with no accent.

"Oh, yeah," cackled the elderly agent past his mouthful of false teeth, "your grandfather's friend, Mr. Bartlett, has been waitin' for him."

"Pardon me?" said the younger Mexican.

Pointing with his chin, the agent looked past the two dark-skinned men at the tall, blond man who stood behind them. "Your grandfather's friend, Mr. Bartlett. He's right there."

Bartlett's face tinted as he stepped up. "I'm sorry. I didn't make it clear. I have never met Señor Gonzales before, but I certainly want to."

"Oh, 'scuse me," said the agent.

To both Mexicans, the tall man said, "My name is Allen Bartlett, gentlemen. I will explain after you have purchased your tickets."

When the transaction was finished, the Gonzales men turned toward Bartlett. "I am a writer for the *California Police Gazette*, gentlemen. You have heard of my paper, perhaps?"

While the elderly man was shaking his head, the younger said, "I have read it on a few occasions, sir."

"Good!" exclaimed Bartlett. "I live in San Francisco, and I learned last month that you, Señor Don Miguel Gonzales, are to appear before the annual convention of the California Historical Society on Thursday."

Don Miguel's dark eyes were friendly as he responded in accented English, "That is correct, Mr. Bartlett."

"I understand, sir," proceeded Bartlett, "that you are going to lecture to the Society on the Ghost of Sonora."

The old man nodded with a weak smile. "I do not know if it should be called a lecture, but I am going to tell them about my friendship with Joaquin Murieta." The old man's face was cracked with lines, fascinating Bartlett as the crevices deepened and occasional flat planes appeared while he spoke.

Don Pablo said, "Mr. Bartlett, you say you are from San Francisco. What is your business here in San Diego?"

"Only to meet your grandfather," replied Bartlett. "I came all the way from San Francisco on the same train you will be riding, hoping that he will allow me to sit with him."

"How did you know I was going to be on this train?" queried Don Miguel.

"Well," said the reporter, clearing his throat, "when I read in the *San Francisco Times* that you were coming to speak at the convention, and that you now live near San Diego, I figured you'd come up by train. So I checked with the railroad office and they told me you would be on this particular train today."

"I assume you want an interview for your paper," said the old man.

"Not quite, sir," said Bartlett. "You see, on the side I am writing a book I hope to publish on the life of Joaquin Murieta, who as you know, is California's legendary headless horseman. I am ready to write the last chapter of the manuscript, but with all the mystery surrounding Murieta's death, I would like to have an interview with you that would furnish me with some facts that are not available anywhere else."

"This I will be glad to do, Mr. Bartlett," said Don Miguel, "but I may not be able to give you much more than you already know— at least about Joaquin's death."

"Anything you can tell me will be of help," Bartlett assured him. "You see, I have been traveling California for the past nine years in my spare time, gathering information about Joaquin from his friends and foes. A year and a half ago I traveled to Sonora in Mexico to gather additional information. Since Joaquin had been gone from his birthplace for quite some time before he died—or disappeared— most everyone who had known him in Sonora is now deceased. Some of the older people, however, told me that you had moved to somewhere in California and were possibly still alive."

"I see." Don Miguel nodded. Looking toward the train, he said, "Let us board the train and sit down."

The three men chose seats positioned so Don Miguel and Don Pablo could sit side by side, facing Allen Bartlett. Other passengers were boarding a few at a time.

When they were seated comfortably, Bartlett said, "I desperately wanted to interview you before I even started writing the manuscript, but since the people in Sonora had no idea where you lived in

California, there was no way to find you. So I went ahead and began writing. I had just finished the next to the last chapter in March when I read in the *Times* that you had been located near San Diego, and had consented to appear before the California Historical Society during its convention. I…I hope this interview won't be too much for you."

"Not at all." Don Miguel smiled. "It will make the time pass more quickly as we travel."

At that moment, Bartlett spotted a young mother entering the car with two small children and a babe-in-arms. Excusing himself, he hurried to her aid and helped her get situated in a seat with the children. She thanked him warmly, and he returned to his seat. Taking a deep breath, he smiled at the two Mexicans. "She's a brave young woman to travel alone with those children. They can be a handful."

"That is for sure," agreed Don Miguel, smiling.

Don Pablo asked, "Do you have children of your own, Mr. Bartlett?"

"Yes," he said, "but they're really not children any more. My son is nineteen and my daughter is seventeen. They grow up fast."

"Indeed they do," spoke up Don Miguel. "It still seems that Don Pablo's father should be a little boy."

Don Pablo laughed. "Grandfather still thinks of me as a small child sometimes, too."

At that moment, the conductor passed through the car, greeting the passengers and assuring them that the train would be pulling out on schedule.

Getting back to the business at hand, Allen Bartlett said to the older Mexican, "Señor Gonzales, the newspaper said that while at the convention you are going to view the famous Head in the Bottle and settle once and for all whether it is the head of Joaquin Murieta."

"Yes." The old man nodded. "I understand it is on display in one of San Francisco's saloons."

"Yes, sir. The Silver Slipper. It's on the Barbary Coast."

"You have seen the head, Mr. Bartlett?"

"I have."

"It is still intact?"

"Yes, sir. The brine is changed periodically to make sure there is enough salt to keep it preserved. It looks like the man died only recently."

"The facial features are still quite clear?"

"Very much so," replied Bartlett. "But I am wondering…"

"Yes?"

"It has been so many years since you saw Joaquin Murieta, Señor. Your friends in Sonora told me about the last time you saw Joaquin…and I have written about you in my book. After all this time, can you really be sure that you will remember what he looked like?"

Don Miguel smiled. "My memory of Joaquin's facial features is still quite clear, Mr. Bartlett. Such a uniquely handsome face is not easily forgotten."

"So many others have written and spoken of his good looks," said Bartlett. "He must have been a fine specimen of a man."

"Yes, indeed. He was strikingly handsome. He had thick, curly hair that was black as midnight—just like his eyes. He wore his hair reasonably short, and he had a thin mustache. His sideburns were clipped at the middle of his ears. His teeth were pearl white, and he had a very warm smile."

"I have him in my book as just under six feet in height. Is that correct?"

"Si. Pardon me…I mean, yes. He towered over me. I am only five feet eight. Or, at least I used to be. I think maybe age has shortened me a little more. Joaquin—" a dreamy look came into the old man's eyes. "Joaquin had a healthy, slender, muscular body. He was very tough. You are no doubt aware that he was a trained conquistador fighter, and that he fought in Mexico's civil war."

"I am," replied Bartlett.

"Grandfather was a conquistador too, Mr. Bartlett," put in Don Pablo. "I know he won't tell you that, so I will. He was very tough in his day."

"I don't doubt it," said the reporter. "I've understood that as adept as Joaquin was with weapons and his own two hands, he had a quiet nature and avoided violence as much as possible."

"Yes. He only became violent when he was forced to do so."

Don Pablo adjusted himself on the seat. "The California gringos treated him and our people so bad, they turned Joaquin into a virtual killing machine, Mr. Bartlett."

"I've depicted it that way in my book," responded Bartlett. Turning to Don Miguel, he said, "I assume you and Joaquin were close to the same age, sir."

The old man smiled. "We were both born the same week in the same town, Mr. Bartlett. Joaquin was born February 8, 1830. That was a Monday. I was born on Thursday, February 11. He was three days older than me. We grew up together, fought in the civil war together, and courted our girls together. We were very good friends. Joaquin left Sonora with Rosita before he turned nineteen. He returned once when he was twenty-one. I never saw him again. But if it is Joaquin's head in that bottle, Mr. Bartlett, I will know it."

"Yes," said Bartlett. "Then the mystery will be settled, and I can finish writing my book. I'm so excited I can't stand it, but since I've been working on it for nine years, two more days won't matter."

The car was filling up. Bartlett pulled a pocket watch from his vest, noted that it was one-twenty, and slipped it back in its place.

Don Pablo asked, "What got you so interested in Joaquin Murieta, Mr. Bartlett?"

The blond man rubbed his chin. Meeting Don Pablo's curious gaze, he replied, "I don't know for sure. I guess it was just because whenever I journeyed into the San Joaquin Valley to pick up different stories, somebody was always talking about him. The idea of the ghostly headless horseman finally got its claw in me, and I couldn't leave it alone. It holds a powerful fascination over me."

The conversation went into a lull for a moment, then Bartlett looked at the old man. "Since you have not yet seen the head in the bottle, Señor Gonzales, what is your opinion at this moment? Do you think you will find your old friend's head there, or do you think he pulled off one of the greatest escapes in history and lived out his life in the Sierra Madres of Mexico as some believe?"

Don Miguel held the reporter's gaze, but did not answer. Growing a bit uneasy by his grandfather's silence, Don Pablo spoke up. "If the latter is true, Joaquin could still be alive, even as Grandfather is, Mr. Bartlett."

"Yeah, I know," said Bartlett. "That possibility makes my blood race. Wooee! Wouldn't it be something if El Patrio was still alive somewhere up in those mountains?"

Don Miguel tilted his head and holding the reporter's gaze with jet black eyes, said slyly, "I believe you are aware that many historians have called the legend of Joaquin Murieta a folk tale."

"Yes, sir. I've met some personally who say Joaquin never existed. They believe he is only a composite of several Mexican patriots who became thorns in the sides of the California gringos."

"You perhaps have heard about the 'Ballad of Joaquin Murieta' that is sung by our people."

"Yes, sir. I have heard the ballad, itself. I've heard it sung several times in the Silver Slipper Saloon, and I heard it when I was in the Mexican town of Arizpe. The mariachis there sang it for me."

The aging man nodded. "Many earnest historians claim that the ballad is based on nothing but myth. They say we Mehicanos made up the story only that we might have a hero to love and admire. That is foolishness. Aside from we who knew him, there are many gringo graves in California soil that hold his victims."

Bartlett chuckled. "Well, those historians may be earnest, but they also have their heads in the sand. Besides the great number of gringo graves, there is too much historical evidence that Joaquin existed to ever honestly claim that he is a myth. Now, the headless horseman that is supposed to ride the canyons of San Joaquin Valley crying for his head is certainly a myth. The idea, of course, is captivating. I'm even calling my book the 'Ghost of Sonora.' The title should cause it to sell well, but as far as believing it, I don't. I certainly—"

"Don't be too sure that it is a myth, Mr. Bartlett," cut in young Don Pablo. "On several occasions I have visited relatives who live in San Joaquin Valley. They are responsible and intelligent people. They tell me that from Coalinga in the south to Grizzly Flats in the Mother Lode country of the north, sane and sensible people still report the spine-tingling night appearance of a headless horseman dressed in black. They say the apparition rides the dark hills and canyons and through the forests, wailing, 'I am Joaquin Murieta! I want my head!' Sometimes the ghostly specter is not seen, but they say the thunder of hoofbeats is heard, and the same haunting, forlorn cry echoes through the passes where the fearsome young bandito once roamed."

Bartlett shrugged his shoulders. "Who am I to argue with that?"

"There is no argument, Mr. Bartlett," Don Pablo said evenly. "The Ghost of Sonora exists."

Allen Bartlett ran a hooked finger around his shirt collar and straightened his necktie. "If that is true, then the head in the bottle *has* to belong to Joaquin Murieta." Swinging his gaze to the old gentleman, he asked, "Isn't that true, Don Miguel?"

There was a strange look in Don Miguel's eyes. He only looked at Bartlett, but again, did not commit himself. Allen Bartlett felt an inexplicable chill slither down his spine.

Don Miguel ran a gnarled finger across his silver mustache. "You spoke a moment ago that some believe Joaquin lived out his life in the Sierra Madres of Mehico."

"Yes."

"As my grandson said, if this is true, Joaquin might still be alive."

"Yes."

"But in your research, have you not come upon the story that many of my people in Mehico tell?"

"Which one is that?"

"They say that Joaquin did indeed return to Mehico. That he built a cabin in the Sierra Madre mountains so he could live alone. He wanted only to cling to the memory of his beloved Rosita. They say he died of loneliness for her and is buried in a Jesuit cemetery in the mountain village of Cucurpe."

"Guess I only heard part of the story," replied Bartlett. "I knew about the supposed grave in Cucurpe. I inquired about it when I was in Mexico, but no one would tell me much about it. When I asked how I could find Cucurpe, they seemed reluctant to tell me. I never did find out. I figured they wanted to keep as much mystery around Joaquin as possible."

"Some are like that," said Gonzales.

"But the part about Joaquin dying of loneliness for Rosita I have not heard," said Bartlett. "This, of course, goes along with all I have learned about the great love he had for her."

"It was a powerful love," said Don Miguel, smiling. "They made a wonderful couple. They loved each other more than they loved life itself."

"Tell me about Rosita," said Bartlett. "Was she really as beautiful as they say?"

The old man smiled again. "In all my life the only woman I ever saw who was more beautiful was Don Pablo's grandmother."

Don Pablo patted the old man's wrinkled hand. "You have always said that, Grandfather, and I believe it must be true. My grandmother was very beautiful, Mr. Bartlett. I never saw Rosita, but if she was anywhere near my grandmother in looks, she had to have been something to behold."

Bartlett saw the pained look come over Don Miguel's eyes. "I assume Mrs. Gonzales is no longer alive, Don Miguel."

The old man's lips quivered as he replied, "No, Mr. Bartlett. The cholera took her from me seven years ago."

"I'm very sorry, sir," Bartlett said. "Would you describe Rosita as she was when you last saw her, sir? I would like to know if I have it right in my book."

A faraway look came over the old man's eyes. After a long moment, he said, "Rosita was small. Maybe three inches over five feet. She had a face that was the envy of women and a magnetic attraction for men. Her skin was soft, rich, creamy. She had vibrant, flashing black eyes and long, ink black hair. When she moved, there was a grace about her that is hard to describe. It was, I think, a rhythm…yes, a very feminine rhythm that flowed out of her and left a distinct impression on everyone she knew. When Rosita would walk into a room, it seemed to come alive. She not only was beautiful on the outside, but on the inside as well. There was a warmth about her that made a person like her immediately. Even the young women who envied her for her beauty loved her. She was a remarkable young woman."

"Mm-hmm," said Bartlett. "I had some of the outward features, but you have added a new dimension for me. I'll have to restructure some of my descriptions of her. I appreciate this information."

"But remember, Mr. Bartlett," said Don Pablo, "my grandmother was even a more remarkable and beautiful woman than Rosita Murieta."

"I'll be sure to keep that in mind," said the reporter as he opened the small suitcase, which he had set on the seat beside him. Producing a notebook with scribblings on several pages, he turned to the first page and said, "Don Miguel, let me check some data with you that I jotted down while in your state of Sonora. Some of it was given to me by people who were not real sure they had all the facts. You are the only one who can confirm these things or correct them for me."

"I will do my best," said the old man.

There was a sudden interruption as the conductor's booming voice bellowed from just outside the window, "All abo-o-oard! All abo-o-oard!"

There were hasty good-byes said on the depot platform and the last passengers scrambled onto the train. Some of them made their way into the car where Allen Bartlett sat with his two new friends. When everyone was settled, there were a few seats vacant, including the one next to Bartlett.

The train's bell began to ring as the conductor repeated his call. The whistle hooted shrilly as the conductor stepped up between the last two passenger cars. He waved to the engineer and entered the rear car to begin punching tickets.

The big engine hissed a blast of steam, the whistle blew again, and the train lurched forward. The conductor's voice rang out, "Tickets please! Have your tickets ready! Tickets, please!"

Don Miguel Gonzales leaned forward and raised his voice. "We will take up our conversation as soon as things quiet down, Mr. Bartlett."

"Fine," said Bartlett. "I sure appreciate this. It's going to make my book a whole lot better. I think the fabulous mystery of the headless ghost haunting the hills and forests will make fascinating reading, but most of all, I'm interested in whether or not the head in the bottle is Joaquin Murieta's."

Don Miguel gave him a tight grin. "We will know the day after tomorrow, amigo."

"If it is," smiled Bartlett, "I can end my book on a positive note. I can say that Joaquin Murieta died as the California Rangers say he did. If it is not, then I can leave my readers with the strong assumption that Murieta pulled off one of the greatest schemes ever invented by a human mind. He outfoxed the California Rangers and escaped, letting them think the young Mexican they killed and beheaded was him. Instead of dying as a young man in a California canyon, he made his way back to Mexico and possibly even lives today as an old man in the high country of the Sierra Madre."

Giving the reporter another tight grin, Don Miguel Gonzales repeated, "We will know the day after tomorrow."

CHAPTER TWO

The San Francisco–bound train was some twenty minutes out of San Diego when the Pacific Ocean came into view on the left, reflecting the brilliant sunlight off its blue-green surface. Soft white foam lined the sandy beach where large waves washed up on the shore.

The passengers in car number eight had settled down and things were quiet. Thumbing pages in his notebook, Allen Bartlett said to Don Miguel Gonzales, "I visited the village of Alamos in Sonora when I was there. The padre in the old church was very kind and helpful. He showed me Joaquin Murieta's baptismal paper. It was dated February 11, 1830, which is the date you said you were born."

The old man closed his eyes and nodded silently.

Proceeding, Bartlett said, "The certificate identified the baby's parents as Joaquin and Rosalia Murieta."

Nodding again, Don Miguel said, "That is correct."

"There were some other papers filed with the baptismal certificate. They said that the baby's father was a laborer in a silver mining camp owned by Mayo Indians, which was located near Varoyeca, some fifteen miles south of Alamos."

"You are making me homesick, amigo. It has been so long since I left Sonora."

"I'm sorry, sir, I—"

"No, no," Don Miguel said with a wave of his hand, "I am not serious. It is true that the senior Joaquin Murieta worked for the Mayo Indians in the silver mine near Varoyeca. And his wife's name was Rosalia. Please proceed."

Nodding, Bartlett said, "The record at the church said Rosalia Murieta was a descendant of the Rubios family of Cadiz, Spain, but there was nothing said about her husband's ancestry. Later I asked some of the villagers about it, and they took me to an old Mayo Indian who had been a foreman at the mine when Señor Murieta worked there. He told me that Joaquin's father was also a Mayo Indian. Because he had married outside the tribe, he could not have any part of ownership in the mine, but they allowed him to work there."

"That is correct," agreed Don Miguel.

Rubbing the back of his neck, the reporter said, "I was amazed at how light-skinned the Mayos are."

"Yes," said the old man. "It was my friend Joaquin's mixture of Spanish and Indian blood that formed within him the romantic aspirations of the Spanish and the fighting skill and courage of the Indian. It was also that mixture, I believe, that made him so extremely handsome. His facial features seemed to be sculptured carefully by the hand of God. He had a square jutting jaw that bespoke the courage and determination that was built into his character. He was a born leader."

Bartlett scribbled some notes on a clean sheet, then said, "You brought up earlier that Joaquin was a conquistador. It is my understanding that he was trained in guerilla warfare before he was even in his teens."

"Yes. All the boys of Sonora were trained as conquistadores, starting at ten years of age. That is, if they qualified. Many, of course, did not. As you know, the state of Sonora was in a civil war with the leaders of Mehico at that time. The Mayo and Yaqui Indians, who worked the mines of Sonora, and the Mehican people who worked for them revolted against the heavy taxes leveled on the mines by the Congress in Mehico City. The revolt had begun in 1825."

"I remember reading that."

"Mr. Bartlett, there was very heavy fighting in that war. There was much bloodshed as the Sonoran conquistadores carried on guerilla warfare until Mehico's invasion by the United States army in 1846. At sixteen years of age, Joaquin Murieta distinguished himself in battle. He displayed unusual courage in the face of death and received a commendation for it three times by the conquistador leaders. He was a crack shot with both rifle and pistol."

"You weren't too bad with the weapons, yourself, Grandfather," said Don Pablo. "Didn't you also receive commendations?"

"Only one," replied Don Miguel, his face tinting. "I was not the fighter nor the leader that Joaquin was."

"Maybe you are being too modest," suggested Don Pablo.

"Maybe you are being too prejudiced toward me because my blood flows in your veins, Don Pablo," retorted the old man.

Don Pablo smiled. "Never."

Looking back at the reporter, Don Miguel said, "To proceed, Mr. Bartlett, Joaquin was also quite deadly in hand-to-hand combat with a knife, a machete, or his bare hands."

"I assume you saw him in action."

"I could tell you many stories," he said. "Joaquin was an inspiration to all of us…even the much older conquistadores. Young as he was, he became a leader. I have seen him kill many a man who was bigger and more experienced in battle than himself. One time we were fighting in a thick forest. I had been slightly wounded and was lying on the ground, bleeding. Joaquin happened to see me go down. Just as he started to come to me, three soldiers of the Mehican army bolted toward him from behind some heavy brush."

"Joaquin's rifle was already lying on the ground, empty. He had been using his revolver, and was down to one bullet. When the three soldiers charged toward him, he killed one with his last bullet, then pulled his knife and threw it, striking another one in the heart. The third man was big and husky, outweighing Joaquin by probably seventy or eighty pounds. Throwing down his weapon, he swore at Joaquin, saying he would kill the boy conquistador with his bare hands.

"Joaquin was very fast and agile. He dodged the man's big hands and kicked him in the groin. When the soldier doubled over in pain, Joaquin jabbed two stiff thumbs in the man's eyes, blinding him. He then chopped him in the throat with the blade of his hand. The big man went to his knees, gagging, with blood spurting from his eye sockets. Joaquin seized his huge head with his hands and twisted it violently. It snapped his spine, killing him."

Bartlett shook his head in wonderment. "And he was only a boy."

"Yes. At that time, he had just turned sixteen. He was a savage fighter, and as I said a moment ago, he became a leader among the conquistadores. This is why when trouble came from the gringos in the Mother Lode country of California, it was the young, tough, and resourceful Joaquin Murieta who led them in fighting back."

Bartlett was making notes. Without looking up, he said, "I knew about Joaquin's leadership ability, Don Miguel, and have covered the fact in my book. I just hadn't realized he was that great a fighter. I will make this clear before the book goes to my publisher." Then lifting his head and looking at the old man, he added, "I can see why the Mexicans of California still speak of him in reverent tones today as El Patrio."

"Yes," said Don Miguel. "Joaquin is the Patriot—the great liberator of California's Mehican population. As you will know, he fought hard to keep the gringos from taking land and property that his people owned in the gold country of northern California." He paused momentarily, then asked, "Did you learn that Joaquin was also an excellent horseman?"

"Yes, sir. I had known this before I went to Mexico. The people of Sonora, California, told me about it. They said Joaquin had made his living when first arriving in California by breaking horses to the saddle."

"Let me tell you, amigo, Joaquin was indeed a sight to behold when he swung into the saddle of an unbroken horse. Every time, the animals seemed to sense who was boss immediately. It never took him long to break them."

As the afternoon hours slowly passed, the three men discussed Joaquin Murieta's few years of banditry in the San Joaquin Valley of California—how he had led his people to fight back against the Anglos who did all they could to run the Mexicans out of the state. The conversation eventually turned to the revenge Murieta exacted on the men who raped and killed Rosita, and on those who hanged his brother, Carlos. By the time this was done, the name of Joaquin Murieta had planted fear in the hearts of Anglos all over the valley.

Don Pablo said to the old man, "Grandfather, do you know how many men Joaquin killed personally in his brief campaign as El Patrio?"

"I have no idea," answered Don Miguel. "I have never even heard an estimate. I have a feeling, though, that our amigo can tell you."

Turning his dark eyes on the blond man, Don Pablo asked, "Do you know?"

Allen Bartlett replied, "More than you would guess, Don Pablo. You've heard of William Bonney?"

"You mean Billy the Kid?"

"Mm-hmm. In 1881 when Bonney was killed at the age of twenty-one by Sheriff Pat Garrett, a writer for the *California Police Gazette* wrote an article comparing Billy with Joaquin Murieta."

"Really?"

"Mm-hmm. I suppose he made the comparison because they were both considered gunmen, and they both died in their twenties. At least this writer figured Joaquin was the man killed and beheaded by the California Rangers."

"How many men had Billy the Kid killed?"

"One for each year of his life," responded Bartlett. "Twenty-one."

"Some killer, eh?"

"Yes, but Billy was an amateur compared to Murieta. The most conservative estimate of the number of men Murieta personally sent to their graves was three hundred."

"Three hundred!" said Don Pablo, looking at his grandfather, then back at the reporter. "You are not kidding me?"

"Nope. And remember…that's the most conservative figure."

Don Miguel scrubbed a blue-veined hand over his mouth and mustache. "This is easy to believe, Mr. Bartlett. As we discussed earlier, Joaquin only became violent when he was forced to do so. The outrage toward the senseless crimes against Rosita, Carlos, and Joaquin's people became a burning, driving force within him. I, of course, was not in California to see this, but I have seen Joaquin angry. I can imagine what all of this did to him. He, indeed, would become a killing machine."

As the coach rocked and swayed to the rhythm of clicking wheels on steel tracks, the three men discussed the story of Joaquin Murieta's supposed decease. For fifty-three years it had been said the Deputy Sheriff Harry Love and his California Rangers had pursued the bandit leader and seven of his men a distance of nearly five hundred miles, from San Jose to the mountains east of the town of San Juan Capistrano. One of the Rangers was Bill Byrnes, who had once been a close friend of Murieta's. The Rangers had been formed specifically for the purpose of hunting down Murieta. Byrnes had gone along especially for identification purposes. He was the only ranger who knew what Joaquin looked like and could point him out.

Reaching this point in the conversation, Don Miguel said, "I have only heard sketchy reports of what happened when they caught up with the group, Mr. Bartlett. I am sure you know more than I or my grandson do about it."

"Well," said Bartlett, adjusting his position on the seat, "there in Cantua Arroya Canyon, the Rangers came upon the gang at dawn as they were gathered around a campfire. Bill Byrnes suddenly pointed to one man and cried out that he was Joaquin Murieta. The young Mexican hopped on a horse and tried to escape, but was caught and gunned down by one of the Rangers.

"There was a large reward for Joaquin dead or alive by the California legislature and numerous communities from Sacramento to Los Angeles. Rather than pack the bandit leader's body nearly five hundred miles to collect the reward, the Rangers decided to just take the head. They decapitated the body, left it lying in the canyon, and put the head in a sack. Somewhere early on the return trip, they placed the head in a large glass bottle and submerged it in brine for permanent preservation. Like I told you, the head still looks good today."

"So how did they decide who owned the head?" asked Don Pablo.

"Once the Rangers had seen to it that the head was bottled, it was auctioned off. Some kind of carnival-type man offered the highest bid—thirty-five dollars. For years he carried the bottled head all over California, making people pay for a look at it. I understand he did quite well. California had lived in terror over Murieta and wanted to see his severed head. However, the bottling of the head backfired on the Rangers."

"In what way?" said the old man.

"Well, when the bottle was displayed in San Joaquin Valley, a great number of people who had known Murieta said the head was not his. When news of this reached Harry Love and his Rangers in Sacramento, there was a big stink. They insisted that the head was Joaquin's, and many others who had known El Patrio agreed with the Rangers. However, with a great number of people casting doubt about it, many Californians, including their political leaders, insisted that Love and the Rangers had concocted a hoax. They demanded that the reward money be returned."

"But what about Bill Byrnes?" asked Don Pablo. "Wasn't his word good enough?"

Bartlett scratched at his ear and grinned. "Well, here's where it really gets strange. People insisted that Byrnes go before the state legislature, who had paid the greatest part of the reward, and testify under oath that the man he had pointed out was indeed Joaquin Murieta. Byrnes, however, had completely disappeared. He was nowhere to be found. In fact, he was never seen again."

"These details are interesting," said Don Miguel. "I had not heard these things. I simply knew that there was controversy as to whether the head really was Joaquin's. I can now understand it all better. Do you have an opinion as to what happened to Byrnes?"

"Only conjecture. But those who knew Murieta and insisted it was not his head in the bottle said that Murieta and Byrnes had put together a scheme. Byrnes would join the Rangers and be there if and when they ever caught up with the gang. Byrnes would then identify the wrong man while Joaquin was already on his way to Mexico. They believed that during all the excitement that was going on in Sacramento over the returned head, Byrnes hightailed it for Mexico and joined Joaquin in the Sierra Madres where they would live happily ever after."

"Did Harry Love and the Rangers have to return the reward money?" asked Don Pablo.

"It came real close to that, but there was a sudden change among the people in San Joaquin Valley who were pushing for it."

"And that was?"

"That was when people began to report the appearances of the Ghost of Sonora riding through the valley on a black horse, wailing in the darkness that he was Joaquin Murieta and wanted his head back."

Don Pablo shook his head and laughed. "Well, Mr. Bartlett, the whole mystery will be settled on Thursday when my grandfather views the head in the bottle."

"That will make a lot of us happy," said Bartlett.

Don Miguel only smiled.

Running his gaze between the two of them, Bartlett asked, "Are you gentlemen aware that there is a town in California bearing Murieta's name?"

Both Mexicans shook their heads.

"Where is this town called Murieta?" asked the old man.

"It is some thirty miles due east of San Juan Capistrano, near Cantua Arroya Canyon. We will get a view of the mountains where the canyon lies as we draw near Los Angeles. I should point out, though, that there has long been a dispute here in California as to whether Joaquin's last name has one or two *r*s. They have put two *r*s in the name of the town, but it should really only have one. The baptismal certificate the padre showed me in Alamos was spelled with only one *r*. So that is the way I have spelled it in my book."

"The one *r* is correct," said Don Miguel. "I never saw it spelled the other way."

"Good."

The railroad track had carried the train inland a mile or so, and the ocean could no longer be seen. A small village was visible to the west, nestled among the green, tree-lined hills that blocked the Pacific from view. A sprawling cattle ranch lay to the east. The lush pastures were dotted with several hundred head.

"The Head in the Bottle, Mr. Bartlett," spoke up Don Pablo. "How long has it been on display at the Silver Slipper Saloon in San Francisco?"

"It's been there for eleven years. Ownership of the saloon has changed hands twice since then. The present owner told me he thought the carnival man had died about twelve years ago, and that the man who owned the Silver Slipper at the time was finally able to buy it from the family after several months of hassle."

"I see."

"Since the saloon has been in possession of the head," said Bartlett, "thousands of curious spectators have gone inside to look at it. The proprietor doesn't charge anything to view it, but he says he sells so many drinks to the spectators that the head is making him a great deal of money. As I think I mentioned, he has a Mexican trio sing 'The Ballad of Joaquin Murieta' periodically. And to make it even more interesting, after the ballad is sung, an old timer who had once been on a stagecoach that Joaquin stopped and robbed tells the story of El Patrio's life and of his controversial death."

Don Pablo's brow furrowed. "Since the old timer saw Joaquin, Mr. Bartlett, can't he say whether the head is his or not?"

Bartlett laughed. "Every time he tells the story, somebody asks him that. I've been there and heard them do it."

"Well, what does he say?" asked Don Miguel, showing keen interest.

"He always gives the same answer. With a twinkle in his eye, he'll say, 'Nope, I can't positively say that the head in that there bottle was once on the shoulders of Joaquin Murieta, because durin' the holdup I wasn't lookin' at his face. I was lookin' at the black muzzle of his gun!'"

The two Mexican men laughed heartily.

Don Pablo laid a hand on the old man's shoulder. "Well, Grandfather, it looks like you are the only one who can settle the controversy."

Don Miguel eyed his grandson tenderly and smiled.

"I'll tell you what, Don Miguel," said Bartlett, "there's a lot of excitement in the Bay Area about your coming. Everybody there knows that in spite of all the disputation, skepticism, argument, and mystery over the Head in the Bottle, you are going to settle it once and for all on April 19."

"Will I be taken to the saloon to view the bottle?" asked the wrinkled oldster.

"No," replied Bartlett. "They had a write-up in the *Times*, giving details on the order of the day. From the moment they received your reply, armed guards have been in the saloon twenty-four hours a day to keep anything from happening to the bottle. At ten o'clock on Thursday morning, the bottle will be picked up at the Silver Slipper by a police wagon and transported to the ballroom of the Barbary Coast Hotel under heavy guard."

Don Miguel's bushy gray eyebrows arched. "Hmm. People are actually that interested in knowing about the head? They will go to that much trouble?"

"Yes, sir! I told you there's a lot of excitement about your coming. The paper said that officials of the Historical Society estimate there will be a huge crowd at the hotel. Probably five or six thousand people. Of course, most of them will be on the outside. The ballroom will only hold about a thousand. Those will be members of the Society from all over the country."

"This is exciting!" said Don Pablo.

"I know there'll be news people present from all over California," said Bartlett. "No doubt there'll be some from other states."

The old man tilted his head and jutted his jaw, nodding slowly. It was evident that he was impressed.

"At precisely ten-thirty, Don Miguel, you will view the bottle in front of that crowd. Whatever your verdict when you look at the face in the bottle, the occasion will be a milestone for the California Historical Society, and a day never to be forgotten."

As the train rolled northward up the Pacific Coast, the ocean came into view and disappeared repeatedly. Allen Bartlett looked at the elderly gentleman and said, "I will never be able to thank you enough for allowing me to have this interview with you, Don Miguel. I...I need to ask one more thing of you."

"If it is possible, consider it done, amigo." Don Miguel smiled.

The reporter cleared his throat nervously. "Well, sir, since we will not arrive in San Francisco until late in the afternoon tomorrow, I was wondering if you would mind reading the manuscript of 'Ghost of Sonora.' It would mean an awful lot to me if you would."

Don Miguel Gonzales smiled warmly. "I would be honored to read it, Mr. Bartlett."

"Wonderful!" The blond man reached into his suitcase. Producing three large envelopes that contained the manuscript, he laid them on the seat and opened the one on top.

Don Miguel had reached into his coat pocket for his reading glasses, and was cleaning them with a handkerchief as Bartlett said, "It's only a little over four hundred pages, sir. I had it put in type where I work. The lines are double-spaced, so it really isn't as large a manuscript as it might look."

"That is no problem, son," responded the old man softly. "I may have to read it in shifts. These eyes aren't what they used to be. They tire more easily these days."

"I understand, sir," said Bartlett. "Take your time...and as you read it, I would like for you to point out any discrepancies in the story."

"All right," replied Don Miguel, placing the glasses on his nose and hooking them behind his ears. Making himself comfortable on the seat, he began to read. The words before his eyes immediately secured his rapt attention:

In the shadowed and veiled history of the West there rides a mysterious horseman, who like the rider made famous by Washington Irving, has no head. He is the Ghost of Sonora. In life his name was Joaquin Murieta. Was he man or myth? Was he the "Napoleon of Banditry" as the California Rangers have charged, or was he El Patrio, the great liberator of the Mexicans of California? For your decision, here is his story…

CHAPTER THREE

I t was mid-September, 1848. In the lush and beautiful Sonoran valley of Real de Bayareca in northwestern Mexico, some two hundred people, dressed in typical bright-colored clothing, were gathered at the base of a grassy hill, enjoying a fandango. The sun shone brilliantly in a crystal clear sky, but its heat was countered by a cool breeze that came off the lofty peaks to the west.

The Mexican band comprised of guitars, trumpets, tambourines, and castanets was playing lilting music, and dozens of happy couples were dancing on the thick grass. Many of those not dancing were standing in a circle around the band and dancers, clapping their hands to the rhythm of the music. Others were standing around in small groups observing the gaiety or engrossed in light conversation. Still others were gathered near a wagon where tables had been set up for food and drink. Children ran about, laughing gleefully.

At the top of the grassy hill—unnoticed by the crowd—four Mexican men, dirty, unshaven, and wearing huge floppy sombreros were hunkered down, observing the activity below. All four were in their twenties, and along with foul body odor, had the smell of trouble about them.

Pancho Boroz, Luis Montoya, and Enrico Apodaca were huddled close to one another while their leader, Santiago Mendez, knelt on one knee a few feet away. Mendez was much bigger and stronger than the other three and had a mean expression that never left his eyes, even when he smiled, which was not too often. He was a cross-grained hombre with a hard, arrogant way about him, one seemingly born to be a troublemaker. Each man in the quartet wore a holstered sidearm and a large knife in a sheath and carried long-necked whiskey bottles.

Noticing that Mendez's eyes were fixed on the spot where the couples were dancing, Luis Montoya said, "Santiago, are we going to join the festivities?"

Mendez thumbed the sombrero to the back of his greasy head,

glanced at Montoya and replied, "Si." Taking a long pull from his bottle, he belched. "I have been watching a certain señorita. She is very beautiful."

"I see several like that," said Pancho Boroz. "I have been watching them all!"

The others chortled.

"How can you pick out one among so many beautiful ones, Santiago?" asked Enrico Apodaca.

"You are half-blind, perhaps," snorted the big man. "Take a look at the one who dances with the hombre dressed in black. They are now right in front of the band."

The eyes of Mendez's friends soon found the captivating young woman, whose long black hair reached midway down her back. A white carnation was pinned on the left side of her head. She smiled as her handsome partner wheeled her about on the grass, exposing a perfect set of white teeth, surrounded by luscious red lips. Her facial features were exquisitely beautiful under smooth, creamy skin.

The enchanting señorita was dressed quite modestly in a white high-necked peasant blouse with elbow-length puff sleeves and a red ankle-length skirt. When she whirled about, the full skirt lifted, displaying perfectly shaped calves and ankles. Her figure was a medallion of spirited, vital beauty.

Taking a swig from his bottle, Luis Montoya smacked his lips. "Aha! Now I see what you are talking about, Santiago!"

"Si!" Pancho Boroz took the bottle from his lips. "She is indeed more beautiful than the others!"

Enrico Apodaca said, "Si! She is a sight for very sore eyes!"

Santiago Mendez took another drink, sleeved saliva and whiskey from his thick lips, and declared, "I want her. It is time I get married, anyhow. The beautiful señorita will become my bride!"

"But what about the hombre who dances with her, Santiago?" asked Pancho. "By the look in his eyes, he adores her. Maybe they are engaged."

Hunching his thick, wide shoulders, Mendez said, "So? It wouldn't be the first engagement to be broken up because the bride-to-be found a better man!"

"But maybe she is satisfied with him and would not want you, Santiago." Boroz laughed.

"Hah!" Mendez's eyes were watering from the effects of the whiskey. "He is tall and handsome, maybe even muscular. But Santiago Mendez is taller, handsomer, and much more muscular! When she sees me, she will forget about him."

Enrico rubbed his chin thoughtfully. "I do not know, Santiago. Maybe it is best we not go down there. We will be very much outnumbered."

"Bah!" roared the big Mexican. "Take another look, Enrico. Not one man wears a gun. We are armed. They are not. If they give us a problem, we will put our guns on them while we back away. I will take my bride with me!"

While the music continued, several gaily dressed men were gathered around a balding, silver-haired man who wore expensive clothing and chewed on an unlit cigar. Standing a few feet from the group, two Mexican men looked on. One said to the other, "I am glad I stayed over one more day in my visit with you and Consuela, Rimando. To see such happy people is of great joy to me."

Smiling warmly, the other one replied, "Ah, *muy bueno*, Pasquale! I am very glad you stayed for this, too."

Eyeing the cluster of men who surrounded the wealthy-looking man, Pasquale asked, "Who is the center of attention over there?"

"That is Don Jose Gonzales," replied Rimando. "He is the richest man in all of Sonora."

"Oh?"

"Mm-hmm. He owns a gigantic ranch a few miles south of here in this same Real de Bayareca Valley. He has some five thousand thoroughbred horses and fifty thousand head of the best beef cattle. He sells his beef all over Mehico, even in the southern part of the United States and Territories. There are many cattle drives from his ranch every year."

"Hmm. He must be very rich."

"That he is. You should see his ranch house. It is huge and seems to spread everywhere. It has fourteen bedrooms."

Pasquale's eyebrows raised. "Fourteen bedrooms! Does he have a large family?"

"No. The house was built so huge only to display Don Jose's

riches. He is very proud of his wealth and wants everyone in Sonora to be impressed by it. The servants' quarters on his ranch would make the average citizen of Sonora envious."

"Is he generous with his money? I mean, does he give some of it to help better the community and aid the poor?"

"Hardly. He is very stingy, except when it comes to himself or his family. His wife died about a year ago. He spent a fortune on the coffin alone. Had it made special of cherry and lined with silver. He had a mausoleum built for her at the cemetery that had to have cost more money than you and I will make combined in our lifetimes."

Pasquale shook his head in disbelief.

"Don Jose is known for spending vast amounts of money on unnecessary things," continued Rimando, "just because they suit his fancy. What Don Jose wants, he has the money to buy…and Don Jose buys everything he wants."

"Must be nice," remarked Pasquale.

"I don't really think so," Rimando countered. "He is not a happy man, in spite of his riches. In fact, I think he is a very miserable man."

Don Jose Gonzales's conversation with his circle of admirers finally lost its luster, and soon the men scattered to find a dance partner or join another group for idle talk. Left alone, the wealthy rancher chewed on the unlit cigar in his mouth and turned toward the spot where the dancers skipped and turned about to the lively music.

Quickly Don Jose's attention was drawn to the beautiful young woman who danced with the stalwart-looking man in black. Her beauty and grace enraptured him. The wealthy man never mingled with the lower-classed people in the valley's town and villages. Most of the people in the crowd were strangers to him. He recognized a few faces, but could not recall their names. As he studied the young couple, the señorita was totally unknown to him, but the face of the handsome young man was vaguely familiar.

Don Jose worked at trying to figure out the identity of the young man while admiring the black-haired beauty. At one point, his attention was drawn to his eighteen-year-old son, Don Miguel, who was dancing with Maria Cortez, whom Don Miguel was planning to marry.

The rancher was glad for his son. Maria was very beautiful and came from a well-to-do family in the valley. While he pondered Don Miguel's future, Don Jose let his attention move back to the fascinating young woman. His eyes were fixed on her as the couple floated over the ground in graceful movement.

Suddenly Don Jose remembered that the young man was a friend of Don Miguel's. He had even been at the Gonzales ranch on occasion. But what was his name? It would not come to the rancher's mind.

The music stopped to the applause of the crowd, and the leader of the band announced that there would be a half-hour recess. The crowd quickly migrated to the eating area for food and wine.

Seeing his son and Maria walking past him, Don Jose motioned for Don Miguel to come to him. The young couple quickly drew up, holding hands and smiling. Maria kissed the older man's cheek and he patted her shoulder.

Still smiling, Don Miguel looked at his father. "There is something I can do for you, Father?"

"Si," replied Don Jose. "I am trying to think of your friend's name. That one over there."

Don Miguel followed his father's pointed finger. "Oh! That is Joaquin Murieta. You remember him. He has been to the ranch on several occasions. We were in the same class together in school. Don't you remember? Joaquin is my best friend."

Don Miguel hoped the incident would serve to stab the heart of his father, who had paid little attention to him all of his growing-up years. Don Jose had never cared about his son's interests or his friends.

"Oh, of course," nodded the older man, taking the dead cigar from his mouth. "I do remember him now. Joaquin Murieta. He is the young man who was decorated three times by the commander of the conquistadores for showing himself to be an expert fighter and so brave in the civil war."

Don Miguel had never been congratulated by his father for the decoration he had received during the war. He doubted if the old man even remembered it. But because of the love he had for his friend Joaquin Murieta, he felt no jealousy that his father recalled Joaquin's decorations. "That is correct, Father," he said. "Joaquin is a very rugged and brilliant fighter."

Inching up to the question he really wanted to ask, Don Jose stuck the soggy cigar back in his mouth. "What does your friend Joaquin Murieta do for a living?"

"He breaks horses to the saddle, Father. Joaquin is better at it than any of the men who break horses for us. Ranchers all over Sonora, and even in some other states, hire him. He has a certain touch with horses that is rare in a man."

"A man?" Don Jose chuckled. "He cannot be any older than you. He will not be a man until he turns twenty-one. What about Joaquin's family? Where do they live, and what does his father do?"

"They lived in Alamos when Joaquin was born," Don Miguel said, "but they moved to Arizpe when he was seven years old. They still live there. Señor Murieta is employed at the Mayo silver mine near Varoyeca."

"Mmm," said the rancher. "Mere peasants. I did not realize that your best friend was a peasant."

Don Miguel felt his blood heat up. He fought to control his temper. He despised his father's attitude toward poor people, but knew it was best to keep his anger inside.

Maria looked at him. She squeezed his hand, giving him strength to contain himself.

At this point, Don Jose came down to the root of his questioning. Gesturing toward Joaquin Murieta and his companion, he said, "That lovely young señorita with your friend, Don Miguel. Who is she?"

"Her name is Rosita Carmel Feliz," responded Don Miguel. "Joaquin and Rosita are engaged. They are to marry next spring."

The elder Gonzales, his gaze fixed on Rosita, said, "I suppose she is from a peasant family, too."

"She is."

"What is her father's name, and where do they live?"

Don Miguel had puzzlement showing in his eyes. "The Feliz family lives near Arizpe. Rosita's father's name is Ramon Feliz. He also works for the Mayo Indians at the silver mine near Varoyeca. Pardon me, Father, but why all these questions?"

"Just curious," replied the man.

Don Miguel glanced at Maria, then studied his father for a moment. "Father, you are very lonesome since Mother died. There are some widowed señoras around here who would love to dance with the handsome Don Jose Gonzales. Why don't you join in the fun?"

The rancher took the cigar from his mouth and waved his son off. "No, thank you. Dancing holds no interest for me anymore. You and Maria should get something to eat and drink before the music starts again. You two go have a good time. I will be fine."

As Don Miguel and Maria started toward the food area, Don Jose called, "One other question, son."

The young couple halted. "Yes?"

"Does Rosita Carmel Feliz attend mass at the church in Arizpe?"

"Regularly." Turning away with a quizzical look on his face, Don Miguel led Maria to the food.

Joaquin Murieta and Rosita Feliz were standing beside the table when Don Miguel and Maria Cortez drew up. Don Miguel saw that Joaquin was in conversation with a mutual friend, Chico Herrera, so he did not interrupt. Maria smiled at Rosita and they exchanged a few words.

While Don Miguel and Maria placed food on their plates, Chico Herrera said, "Joaquin, I was told yesterday about the big black outlaw you broke to the saddle at the Valdez ranch last week. Some tough horse, eh?"

Joaquin, who stood taller than most Mexican men, looked down at his friend and smiled. "You have that right, Chico. He was the toughest outlaw I have ever broken. Took about three times as long to bring him into submission. He almost threw me twice."

"Maybe one of these days you will meet your match," said Herrera.

Joaquin punched him lightly on the shoulder. "Never! The horse has not been born that can throw me!"

Herrera laughed again. "Well, I will say this: if there ever is one born that can throw you, it will be a black one. By the way, what is it about black horses that so interests you?"

"It is hard to explain," replied Joaquin. "There is just something about horses that color that captivate me. They just seem to have more spirit."

Chico looked his friend up and down. Joaquin wore black trousers, black boots, and a ruffled, long-sleeved black shirt with white piping across the back and on the two squared pockets. The shirt was open at the neck, exposing a black neckerchief. "Come to think of it, Joaquin, you seem to go for black clothing too."

"I feel best in black, but I seldom wear all black as I am today."

Chico was about to make another comment when the band began to tune up again. Don Miguel Gonzales stepped up and said, "Time for more dancing, Joaquin."

"I am for that!" the young man said, taking Rosita by the hand. "Come on, my darling, let's go."

Soon the music was in full swing and the dancing area was crowded with participants. Don Jose Gonzales stood alone, watching the fun. Moments later, he caught sight of four dirty, unshaven young Mexicans elbowing their way through the crowd toward the spot where the couples were dancing. Each one carried a half-empty whiskey bottle. There was a look of devilment in their watery eyes. People in the crowd eyed them with contempt when they smelled their foul bodies and saw that they were armed.

Don Jose hastened to a group of middle-aged men. "I think those despicable-looking toughs are here to cause trouble."

The men agreed. Together they walked toward the spot at the edge of the dance area where the troublemakers had stopped. The men who were dancing had not yet noticed them.

Santiago Mendez tipped his bottle up and took a long drink, then pointed at Rosita Feliz, who was facing him while dancing with Joaquin Murieta, and made a ribald remark about her to his friends. They laughed wickedly and downed some more whiskey. When Mendez made a second remark, Julio Vendanna, one of the middle-aged men, stepped up to him. "I do not know who you fellows are, but no one invited you here. We do not allow the kind of language at our gatherings that you are using. You will have to clean up your mouth or leave."

Big Santiago stared brassily at Vendanna with bloodshot eyes. "Is that so? And just who is going to make us leave?"

Vendanna's face reddened. Looking the big man square in the eye, he rasped, "We have men here who were in the civil war. They will show you off this property if you force them to."

Luis Montoya laughed. "We have weapons, big mouth! Where are yours?"

At that instant, Chico Herrera and another of Joaquin's friends,

Mando Ruiz, drew up. Herrera looked at Mendez. "I think you should know that the señorita you just spoke about belongs to Joaquin Murieta, a fighting conquistador!"

Mendez gave a belly laugh. "Hah! I can handle any big shot conquistador! I am going to take the beautiful señorita for myself!"

Mando Ruiz, who was five inches shorter than Mendez, looked up at him. "I am warning you, señor, it is best that you take your filthy friends and leave while you can. If you irritate Joaquin Murieta, you will be very sorry."

The Mexican bristled. "I do what I want and nobody gets in my way, little man! Understand?"

Mendez's booming voice reached the dancers and the band this time. The band stopped playing and the dancers stood still, looking toward the troublemakers.

Joaquin and Rosita were just a few steps away from Mendez and his crew. Mendez set his eyes on Rosita and said, "Hey, honey, why don't you let go of pretty boy there and come with a real man?"

It was Joaquin's turn to bristle. Blood pumped into his cheeks. He struggled with his temper. He had seen enough violence during the civil war to do him a lifetime. He would do his best to avoid it. Rosita knew how he felt. Grasping his arm, she felt his muscles tighten.

Mendez showed filthy yellow teeth in a lurid grin. "Come on, honey. You'll like me when you get to know me."

A crimson flush showed under Rosita's creamy skin. The high spirit in her welled up. "I would not go with you if you were the last man on earth! Take your vermin friends and vamoose before you make Joaquin angry!"

A male voice from the crowd cried, "Better listen to her, señor. Believe me, you do not want to tangle with Joaquin Murieta."

The swarthy Mexican laughed and spit in the grass, looking in the direction of the voice. His voice ran an arrogant note upward as he bawled, "Who is this pretty boy, Joaquin Murieta? Hah! I am the great Santiago Mendez, toughest fighter in Mehico!"

Every eye in the crowd was on Murieta as he pulled loose from Rosita's grasp and moved calmly toward the huge man. Halting only inches from him, Joaquin felt Rosita brush up behind him. "We are not here for fighting, Señor Mendez. You have come to the wrong place. We are having a good time with our fandango. You are interfering with our good time. I am asking you politely to take your three cohorts and find another place to cause trouble."

The liquor in Mendez kept him from using good sense. Although he did not reveal it, he had heard of Joaquin Murieta and of his fighting prowess. Rolling his massive shoulders, he grinned evilly. "All right, we will go." Then in a sudden move, he reached around Murieta and seized Rosita's arm. "But this one goes with me!"

Shafts of fiery rage flared up in Joaquin, showing in his black, piercing eyes. This dirty scum would dare touch his Rosita! Moving with the swiftness of a cougar, Joaquin grasped the bulky wrist of the hand that held Rosita and pressed savagely at the base of the hand. Mendez howled in agony and let go of Rosita.

Boroz, Apodaca, and Montoya exchanged glances, wondering what they should do. They had weapons, but they were grossly outnumbered. They had depended on their champion to lead them, but now he was in trouble.

Still gripping the wrist, Joaquin told Rosita to step away. When she did, he let go of Mendez. The huge man cursed and braced himself to throw a punch. A rock-hard fist lashed out like a bolt of lightning and caught him flush on the jaw. Mendez went down hard, sprawling on the grass and shaking his head.

Chico Herrera saw Enrico Apodaca tense up and go for his revolver with his free hand. Acting quickly, Herrera grabbed the whiskey bottle from the other hand and slammed him on the side of the head, breaking the bottle. Apodaca dropped like a pole-axed steer.

While the stunned crowd looked on, Murieta stood over Mendez, waiting for him to get up.

Quickly, Pancho Boroz swore, dropped his whiskey bottle, and clawed for his gun. Mando Ruiz whipped Boroz's knife from his other hip and rammed it into the gun arm. While Boroz was screaming and the gun was being snatched from his hand, Don Miguel Gonzales made a dive for Luis Montoya, who already had his gun out.

Grasping the gun hand with both hands, Don Miguel struggled with Montoya. They fought for possession of the weapon, but it did not fire because the hammer had not been cocked. The crowd stepped back as Don Miguel and Montoya stumbled about in the struggle. When Don Miguel saw the opportunity, he drove a knee into the man's groin. Montoya grunted and weakened. Don Miguel jerked the gun from his hand and cracked him hard on the temple with it. Montoya went down unconscious, and Maria Cortez was instantly at Don Miguel's side, clinging to him and trembling.

While men in the crowd were disarming Mendez's three friends, the huge Mexican struggled to his feet, swearing profusely at Joaquin Murieta.

Fire was blazing from Joaquin's eyes. Rosita stood with some of the young women, studying Joaquin's face. She knew it was too late to keep him from going after Mendez.

Murieta stood three paces from the man, fists clenched and ready. He could feel the heat rise in him like a boil, contempt bubbling to the surface in an uncontrollable rage. "You filthy swine! You dared to put your mangy hands on my woman!"

Mendez took a deep breath, shook himself like a wild beast about to charge, and bolted toward the smaller man with a wild roar. He swung a powerful right. Murieta met him halfway and lashed out with his own right. His punch was faster and it caught the big man flush on the mouth, splitting both lips. Mendez's huge fist missed its mark, and he took a backward step, shaking his head and spitting blood. Digging his heels into the grass, he rushed in again, pumping both fists.

Joaquin ducked, avoiding the intended blows, but before he could land another of his own, Mendez caught him under the arms in a bear hug, lifted him high, and slammed him hard to the ground.

The crowd looked on, wide-eyed. Rosita's hand went to her mouth.

Murieta rolled over with the speed of a cat, gasping for breath, and saw the big man's driving right boot as Mendez aimed for his ribs. Joaquin moved quickly and the boot swung past him. Joaquin scrambled to his feet and lunged with his head down, butting Mendez in the chest. The huge Mexican released a pained grunt and stumbled back three steps. Murieta knew he had hurt him, so he lunged again, harder, and butted his chest once more.

This time, Mendez was better prepared. He was unable to avoid the collision, but backtracked only one step as the breath gushed from his lungs. He jerked up a stiff thumb, going for Joaquin's eye. Murieta rolled his head out of the way and swung a hissing left that cut only air, but followed with a driving right that smashed Santiago's nose, starting a shower of blood.

While Joaquin was bracing himself for another attack, Mendez wiped a hand across his bleeding nose and mouth. When he saw the bright crimson of his own blood, he charged the smaller man, catching him with a powerful blow to the head. His skull thundering with pain and dizziness, Joaquin staggered, but did not go down. The bloody-faced man came at him again, murder in his eyes.

Rosita was biting on a forefinger and making a fist with the other hand, digging her fingernails into the palm. Joaquin's friends—Don Miguel Gonzales, Chico Herrera, and Mando Ruiz—stood by Mendez's two unconscious cohorts, who were beginning to come to. Pancho Boroz sat next to them on the ground, gripping his bleeding arm.

A Mexican man from a nearby village eyed the battle between Joaquin Murieta and Santiago Mendez and said to Don Miguel Gonzales, "I am afraid the man is going to hurt Joaquin. Should we move in and break it up?"

Don Miguel shook his head. "No! Joaquin would not want us to do that. Do not worry, amigo. I have seen Joaquin fight bigger and better men. Mendez is not going to hurt him. Mark my word. Joaquin will beat him."

As Mendez was charging at him again, Joaquin saw the murderous look in his eyes. Thinking fast, he made a dive for the ground, rolled hard into his legs, and knocked him down. When Mendez hit the sod, his revolver slid from its holster. Unaware of it, he rose to his feet, but just as he was straightening up, Murieta slammed his nose. Blood sprayed in every direction. Joaquin cracked him on the mouth again.

Sucking for air, Joaquin clenched his fists hard and went after his man again, swinging in red hot fury. Both hands were going with every ounce of power they could muster. Spitting blood and swearing, Mendez met him. The two men slugged each other repeatedly. Mendez was bigger and his punches packed terrific power, but Murieta was faster and was getting in more blows. It was dog-eat-dog, and the two battled until the breath gasped in their lungs and whistled through their teeth. With each breath, Mendez sprayed more blood. Joaquin's clothing was soaked with it.

Mendez could not believe the stamina the smaller man was displaying. Any man that size he had fought before had only lasted a minute or two. Murieta's invincibility was making the huge man more angry. His own strength was waning. He must finish Murieta off quickly. Taking a deep breath, he went after Joaquin with grim determination.

Murieta popped him twice more, dug a hard fist into his midsection, and backed away, dodging a swinging blow. Santiago faltered only momentarily, then charged in. Joaquin peppered him with swift rights and lefts, stemming the tide of Mendez's bulk with sheer grit.

Mendez missed a right, took another jab on the mouth, then gritting his teeth, he dashed in and slid his right arm around Murieta's neck. Grabbing his wrist with his left hand, he threw his feet in the air and sat down hard, trying to break Joaquin's neck. But the experienced conquistador knew all the tricks. As Santiago's feet flew up, Joaquin threw his weight against the man's chest and fell on top of Mendez, unhurt. Mendez's attempt to kill him angered Joaquin the more. He rammed a thumb back over his shoulder, jabbing him in the right eye.

Mendez howled and released the hold. Joaquin rolled to his knees and stood up, breathing hard. The Mexican's face was a mass of blood as he clambered to his feet, rubbing his injured eye. Swearing, he slapped leather and found his revolver missing. His hand went to his other hip and yanked the ten-inch knife from its scabbard. There was a moan among the crowd.

Wheezing and spraying blood, Mendez blinked his bloody eye. "Now you die, Murieta!"

As the huge man charged, Joaquin called on his conquistador training to save his life. He let Mendez get close enough to swing the deadly blade, then dodged it. While his weary opponent was off balance, Joaquin reached out, seized the knife arm with both hands, and pivoted his body. Instantly he was behind Mendez with the arm twisted against the big man's back. He gave it a harsh shove, tearing ligaments. Mendez screamed and let go of the knife. Still holding the arm with one hand, Joaquin caught the knife in midair.

Joaquin Murieta's wrath was blazing hot. The big Mexican not only had put his filthy hands on Rosita, but he had tried to kill him. Gripping the knife handle with the taste of revenge bitter in his mouth, he swung it back and aimed the blade for the big man's side.

Suddenly there was a scream. Rosita was beside him. "No, Joaquin! No! Do not kill him!"

Joaquin checked himself and looked at her.

Rosita was shaking her head. "No! Please do not kill him!"

Pulling his lips in a thin line, Joaquin nodded and said softly, "All right, my darling Rosita. I will let him live, but if he ever comes near you again, there will be no sparing him." Handing Rosita the knife, he rammed Mendez's arm upward. The ligaments cracked and popped loudly. Santiago Mendez screamed, turned pale, and passed out, falling to the ground in a heap.

Ignoring the blood on Joaquin's shirt and trousers, Rosita threw the knife down and rushed into his arms. A cheer went up from the crowd. Holding Rosita tight, Joaquin said, "I love you more than life itself, Rosita. You belong to me. That is all that matters in this world—that you belong to me. If any man ever dares touch you, I will kill him!"

Pushing back in order to look him in the eye, Rosita said with a tremor in her voice, "Joaquin, I have never seen you so angry!"

"He should not have put his dirty hands on you."

"But to kill him! Would you really have killed him? You told me when you returned from the civil war that you never wanted to take another life again."

"Under normal circumstances, I do not. But for a man to even make a move toward you, I will make him pay with his life. You are mine and only mine." Mendez's three friends were now on their feet. Joaquin said harshly, "Pick up your hero and get out of here!"

Pancho Boroz gripped his bleeding wound. "You did not have to break Santiago's arm!"

Joaquin's voice jumped at Boroz. "I did not break his arm! I only dislocated his shoulder. Get out of my sight before I decide to do worse to all of you."

The crowd pressed close and observed impassively as Enrico Apodaca and Luis Montoya picked up Santiago Mendez and stumbled toward their horses, which were clustered at the foot of the grassy hill beyond the spot where the band had been playing. Pancho Boroz followed, still clutching his wounded, bleeding arm.

When the troublemakers had passed from sight with the unconscious Santiago Mendez draped over his saddle, the crowd cheered Joaquin Murieta and his friends for the way they had handled the young toughs. Moments later the music started up and dancers were grabbing their partners. Joaquin and Rosita were still clinging to each other. Don Miguel stepped up. "Come on, you two," he said cheerfully, "the fight is over. Let us not allow it to ruin the fandango! Let us dance!"

As Don Miguel and Maria walked away, Joaquin looked at himself, then at Rosita. "Maybe I should go home and clean up."

Pointing to the blood she had gotten on her blouse and skirt, she said, "Seems I am almost as much a mess as you are! But it would take too long for us to go home and change. No one will care if we are bloody, especially since the blood is not yours." Tugging on his hand, she said, "Come on, darling, we came here to dance!"

Moments later Joaquin was whirling the woman he loved across the grass, and the trouble was soon forgotten.

When the last dance of the fandango was finished, the sun was setting on the western horizon. Don Miguel Gonzales, his arm around Maria Cortez, approached Joaquin and Rosita. "How about you two tying your horses to the back of my buggy and coming to the ranch for a while? Maria is coming along."

Joaquin smiled. "I really appreciate the invitation, Don Miguel, but I promised Rosita's parents I would have her home before dark. If I am to keep the promise, we must head for Arizpe immediately."

Don Miguel laughed and cuffed his friend on the chin playfully. "You may have promised her parents like you say, Joaquin, but I think it would be the same if it was midafternoon. I think you two just want to be alone together."

Joaquin, who was taller and more muscular than his friend, exposed an even set of snow-white teeth. "You know what, Maria? I think your man Don Miguel is not as dumb as he looks!"

Maria giggled.

Rosita put her hands on her hips and said in a mock-scolding manner, "Joaquin! You should not speak that way about your best friend!"

Don Miguel threw his head back and laughed. "Ah, Rosita, that is nothing. You should hear the way he talks about me when you are not around!"

The two couples had a good laugh together. Rosita and Maria agreed that the four of them would sit together at mass on Sunday as Maria was helped into the buggy by Don Miguel.

As Don Miguel and Maria drove away, Joaquin and Rosita turned toward the spot where their horses were tied to a clump of bushes. Holding on to Joaquin's hand, Rosita said, "Maria lamented to me today that we cannot have a double wedding."

Joaquin nodded. "Yes. Don Miguel has said the same thing to me several times. But such a thing is impossible. Don Jose will spend much money on his son's wedding. He would not want peasants like you and me being married at the same time and place." Folding her in his arms, he said, "But Rosita, my precious, you and I will be just as married though our wedding will cost only a few pesos."

Two carriages passed by with people calling and waving at the young couple. Joaquin and Rosita waved back and smiled. The crowd was slowly dwindling as those on horseback and others in carriages, buggies, and wagons were pulling out.

Rosita afforded the man she loved a sweet smile. Moving closer in his arms, she said, "Yes, my love. We will be just as married as Don Miguel and Maria, but a thousand times happier because I love you so much."

Joaquin squeezed her tight. "I agree we will be a thousand times happier, my sweet, but it will really be because *I* love *you* so much!"

Rosita laughed as Joaquin glanced around to see if any of the stragglers were looking their way. Satisfied that they were unobserved, he kissed Rosita long and tenderly.

They were not aware that Don Jose Gonzales had boarded his surrey and was casting a hard glance at the scene.

CHAPTER FOUR

At high noon on Sunday, the grassy meadows around Arizpe basked in the warm sun that shone out of a cloudless sky. Wildflowers swayed with the breeze as grasshoppers arched above them, their wings rattling. Hungry sparrows and buntings swooped down from the trees to intercept the insects in midair.

The bell in the tower of St. Felipe's was ringing as the worshipers emerged from the small, weather-beaten adobe building at Arizpe's south end. Several young couples stood around the front of the church, talking and laughing. Included among them were Don Miguel Gonzales, Maria Cortez, Joaquin Murieta, and Rosita Carmel Feliz.

At the door Padre Adamo Mendosa was greeting his parishioners as they came out. Mild shock showed on the middle-aged priest's features when he recognized the face of Don Jose Gonzales. Extending a friendly hand behind a wide smile, he said, "Don Jose! I am so glad to see you! Where were you sitting? I didn't notice you during the service."

The rancher shook Mendosa's hand and replied nervously, "I...I was back in the corner. It...uh...is rather dark in that area. I...uh...I was a little late getting here."

"Of course," said the priest. "My, my, Don Jose. How long is it since you have been to church? Other than for your wife's funeral, I mean."

Don Jose's face tinted. "Well, I...uh...I think it has been about...uh...about—"

"Twelve years?" said Mendosa.

"Your memory is no doubt better than mine, Padre. I...uh...really need to be coming to the services. I will try to be more faithful from now on."

"That I would love to see."

The rancher donned his hat and turned away, moving in a casual manner toward the group of young couples. He eased up beside his son, so as to be facing Rosita Feliz. When Don Miguel noticed his father, his head bobbed with surprise. "Father! Where did you come from? I mean…were you in the service?"

"Yes," replied the silver-haired man. "I was a little late getting here, so I sat in the back. It is somewhat dark where I was sitting."

"Did Padre Mendosa see you?"

"Why…uh…yes. I just shook hands with him."

"Good! He asks about you almost every week. I am sure he was glad to see you here."

"He seemed to be," said Don Jose, letting his eyes drift to the face of Joaquin Murieta. "Joaquin Murieta! You probably did not notice me, but I was at the fandango the other day. How are you?"

Joaquin had noticed Don Jose at the fandango, all right, but had not approached him because whenever he had visited the ranch, Don Jose had not been particularly friendly. Extending his hand, he shook Don Jose's. "I am fine, Señor Gonzales."

Still smiling as their hands parted, Don Jose said, "I want to say that I have never seen such fighting ability, young man. You really gave that ruffian what he needed. You learned to fight while in the conquistadores, I will wager."

"Yes, sir. The same place where Don Miguel learned to fight. If you think I am good, you should see him!"

Ignoring the statement, Don Jose set his eyes on the beautiful Rosita. She felt uncomfortable as he admired her elegantly sculptured features and the creamy complexion of her skin. "Ah, my lovely señorita," he said, doing a slight bow, "it has not been my pleasure to meet you. Joaquin, my boy, please introduce me to her."

Joaquin said, "Don Jose Gonzales, this is Rosita Carmel Feliz, to whom I am engaged."

Smiling, though the older man left her off balance, Rosita offered him her hand.

Taking the tiny feminine hand in his, Don Jose said, "Your beauty is enough to take a man's breath. It is refreshing like the sun's rays dancing on the surface of a mountain lake. It is fresh and stimulating like the rainbow of many colors after a spring shower. I cannot recall when I have ever seen such loveliness packaged in one captivating young woman."

Don Jose's flowery words and the extended holding of Rosita's hand had her visibly uncomfortable. Joaquin was irritated, but because the old man was Don Miguel's father, he made no move. Rosita pulled her hand loose and forced a smile. "I am glad to meet you, Señor Gonzales."

Don Miguel and Maria exchanged glances.

At that instant Rosita's parents emerged from the church and moved toward their daughter. The awkward moment passed as Ramon and Dolores Feliz drew up. Don Miguel quickly seized the opportunity to introduce her parents to his father.

Don Jose was quite warm toward the Felizes, telling them what a lovely daughter they had. Not aware of what had just taken place, Ramon and Dolores were charmed by the man's kind words and forceful personality.

Other family members gathered at the spot. Reyes Feliz, Rosita's older brother, came first and was introduced to Don Jose. Reyes was tall for a Mexican and quite slender. He had a thick mop of black hair and a thin mustache like Joaquin's. His face was built on angular planes with a jutting chin.

Next came Joaquin's parents and his two older brothers, Claudio, who had just turned twenty-three, and Antonio, who was twenty-one. They, also, were introduced to the rancher. Joaquin Murieta Sr. pointed out to Don Jose that they had another son, Carlos, who now lived in California. Carlos was the oldest at twenty-five.

That afternoon Joaquin and Rosita walked from the Murieta home after a delicious dinner and stood on the bank of the Sonora River, which flowed southward on the east side of Arizpe. Under the shade of an old cottonwood tree, they kissed several times, then Rosita sat down facing the river and leaned back against the cottonwood. Joaquin stretched out on the grass and laid his head in her lap. "My precious Rosita, you are beautiful from any angle!"

Rosita's face flushed. She broke into a smile and said, "As long as it is you who thinks so, it is all right."

Joaquin was silent for a moment. "Don Jose really made you uncomfortable, didn't he?"

"Very."

"He almost made me mad," Joaquin said. "He had no business

going on with all those fancy words and holding your hand all that time too. If he had not been Don Miguel's father—"

"I am so glad you did not show anger, darling," she said. "I will admit he had me quite nervous, but if you had done something, it would have hurt your relationship with Don Miguel. Besides, I am sure the old man meant nothing wrong. He is no doubt very lonely since his wife died. His loneliness probably just got the best of him, and for some reason he decided to warm up to me."

"You are probably right," said Joaquin. "After all, Don Jose is old enough to be your grandfather. Certainly he meant nothing by his strange behavior."

As the day grew older, Joaquin and Rosita exchanged words of love and adoration and made plans for their upcoming wedding and dreamed together of the future. They would one day have their own ranch. Joaquin was doing quite well as a broncobuster and was able to put away a sizeable amount of money each week. Within four or five years, they would be ranchers themselves.

Joaquin laughed. "Why, if Don Jose Gonzales doesn't watch out, I will give him some real competition at being the richest rancher in Sonora!"

Rosita leaned over and kissed him. "Do not laugh, my love. I have the utmost confidence in my future husband. I believe with all my heart that one day the name of Joaquin Murieta will be much more famous than that of Don Jose Gonzales."

The next day, Don Jose Gonzales had one of the servants hitch a horse to his favorite buggy and drive it up to the house. He climbed into the buggy and drove off the ranch, heading east. An hour later the buggy rolled into Arizpe and turned south.

Padre Adamo Mendosa was in front of the church building, doing some yard work. He looked up and smiled as Don Jose drew the buggy to a stop at the edge of the yard. Laying down the tool in his hand, Mendosa moved to the buggy as Don Jose alighted. "Good afternoon, Don Jose."

The rancher shook his hand and returned the greeting, then showed interest in the work Mendosa was doing in the flower garden. Mendosa led him to the spot and explained that he was planting some flowers. There would still be time before the cold weather came for them to take root. While they chatted, Mendosa told the rancher again how happy he was to see him at mass Sunday. Don Jose assured him he would be there more often in the future.

After a few minutes, Mendosa looked the rancher in the eye. "I do not think you drove all the way over here to make small talk, Don Jose. Is there something I can do for you?"

Don Jose lifted his expensive gray flat-crowned hat and scratched at his thinning hair. "Yes, there is, Padre. Actually, I need to know how to find the Ramon Feliz home."

"Oh," said Mendosa. "It is quite easy to find. Just go through Arizpe here on the main street, heading north. The Feliz house is a little over a mile north of town. You can't miss it. The house has a small room built on to it on the south side and is painted all white. There is a rusty old wagon in the front yard. You will see that Dolores has filled the wagon bed with dirt and made a flowerbed out of it. The place is on the right side of the road as you head north."

The rancher thanked him and began to return to his buggy.

Mendosa called after him, "Oh, Don Jose."

Turning around, Gonzales said, "Yes?"

"I assume you want to see Ramon. He is not home this time of day. He works at the silver mine over by Varoyeca."

Walking slowly back toward the priest, Don Jose said, "I only want to see the house today, Padre. I am interested in how Ramon keeps his property. If I am satisfied with how it looks, I am going to offer him a job in my ranch."

"Oh, that would be wonderful!" exclaimed Mendosa. "I am sure you would pay him better than he is making at the mine. They are quite poor. It would be wonderful if Ramon could do better financially."

Smiling broadly, Gonzales said, "Believe me, Padre, if I hire Ramon, he will make more money than he has ever made in his life."

"That is very generous of you," responded Mendosa.

"Tell you what, Padre," said the rancher, "if everything works out as I have planned, I will be coming to you one day soon on a very important matter."

Mendosa smiled, waved, and walked back to his flower garden, believing that the stingy rancher was finally loosening up. No doubt he had some kind of plan whereby he would make a large donation to the church. It certainly could use a new paint job…and some new pews.

Gonzales drove his buggy out of town and soon spotted the Feliz place. Holding the horse to a slow walk, he drove by, scrutinizing the house and two small outbuildings. He had lied to the priest. His interest was not in how Ramon Feliz kept his place, but rather, he wanted to see just how poor the Feliz family might be. The barn and toolshed had been painted recently. The small adobe house was clean, and the yard was neat, but it was definitely the home of a poor man.

Wheeling the buggy about, Don Jose passed the place slowly once more and smiled to himself. His money had always bought him anything he wanted. This time it would buy him a young and beautiful wife.

That evening, Ramon Feliz rode his horse into the yard after a hard day's work. Thin wisps of smoke trailed skyward from the small chimney at the back of the house. Dolores had supper cooking, and he was famished. Whatever she was having would be all right with him—just so he could sit down to the table and take his fill.

Dismounting at the corral, he led the horse through the gate and into the barn. Noting that Reyes's horse was already eating at the feed trough, he unsaddled his own animal and let it join the other for its meal. He scooped additional oats from a nearby grain barrel and dumped it into the trough to make sure there was enough for both horses.

When Ramon entered the kitchen, the sweet aroma of hot tamales met his nostrils. Dolores moved from the stove and smiled. "There is my hard-working man."

"Your hungry hard-working man," he said, folding her into his arms and kissing her cheek. "Those tamales sure smell good!"

"Get your hands washed and we'll be ready to sit down," Dolores said.

Ramon lifted a steaming teakettle from the stove and poured the hot water into a basin on a small table nearby. Adding some cool water from a pitcher on the table, he washed his hands and face, ridding them of dust from the silver mine. While drying his hands, he let his eyes roam across the room to his wife. Dolores was now forty-four, but looked five years younger. She had kept herself trim and was always clean, neat, and well-groomed. Ramon knew his daughter was beautiful, but she still had to go a ways before she would have the full loveliness of her mother.

At that moment, Rosita entered the room from the front part of the house, carrying a mop and bucket. There was a tiny wisp of black hair dangling over her forehead. "Hello, Papa," she said, giving him a warm smile. "Work hard today?"

"Just like usual," Ramon replied, returning the smile.

"Yes!" came the voice of Reyes. "Just like usual, Papa took his usual nap at the bottom of the mine!"

Laughing, Ramon wadded up the towel in his hands and threw it at his son. Reyes caught it in midair, laughed, and threw it back.

"All right, you two," scolded Dolores, "stop playing in the kitchen, or you will go to bed without your supper!"

"Well, Papa started it," said Reyes. "He threw the towel at me."

"No, you started it," spoke up Rosita. "You made fun of Papa, saying he took his usual nap in the mine!"

"I just spoke the truth."

Rosita loved her brother deeply and enjoyed giving him a hard time. "If you pick on Papa anymore, you can mop your own room from now on!"

"Oh, he wouldn't like that," said Ramon. "It would be too much like work!"

"Isn't that the truth?" said Rosita.

"Oh, you think so?" Reyes said, reaching out and messing up Rosita's hair.

She was about to retaliate when a loud knock was heard at the front door.

Reyes said, "I'll see who it is."

The sun had already set, but there was enough light in the sky to show Reyes a short, stocky Mexican on the porch. A white-stockinged bay with silver-studded bridle and saddle stood in the yard.

"May I help you?" Reyes said.

"I am Alfredo Romero. I have been sent here by Señor Don Jose Gonzales to speak to Señor Ramon Feliz. Is he at home?"

"Yes," nodded Reyes. "Please come in."

Romero removed his hat and stepped in. Ramon had heard his words and entered the parlor with a smile. Dolores and Rosita peered at Romero from the kitchen door.

"I am Ramon Feliz, Señor Romero. Did I hear correctly? You have been sent here by Don Jose Gonzales to speak to me?"

"Si," said Romero, shaking Ramon's hand. "I have been authorized by my boss to invite you and your family to dinner at his ranch house tomorrow evening at this time."

Dolores and Rosita silently exchanged glances, eyebrows raised. Reyes's mouth fell open.

Ramon blinked. "I do not understand. We only met him yesterday. Why…why would a man of Don Jose Gonzales's standing want to host a poor mine worker and his family for dinner?"

Romero hunched his shoulders. "Please, Señor Feliz, Don Jose never explains anything to me. I was given orders to come here and voice the invitation for him. He wants you and your family to come to the ranch for dinner. This is all I know. I am to return with your answer immediately. You…you will not turn him down?"

"Oh no!" exclaimed Ramon, looking at Reyes, then turning to eye his wife and daughter. "My family will be delighted to accept Don Jose's invitation. I am—we are just a bit overwhelmed. A thing like this could only happen once in a poor family's lifetime. You tell your boss we will be there. You say about this time. What time exactly should we arrive at the ranch?"

"Pardon me, Señor Feliz. I will be here with a surrey to pick you up at…shall we say, six o'clock?"

Ramon was both stunned and pleased. "You mean we even have our transportation provided?"

"Oh yes! When Don Jose Gonzales plays host to special guests, he does it first class." Turning toward the door, Romero said, "I will be here at six o'clock sharp tomorrow evening."

Ramon assured him they would be ready and told him to thank Don Jose for the invitation. When Alfredo Romero had ridden out of sight, Ramon closed the door, leaned against it and looked at his family, who stood facing him. Shaking his head, he palmed sweat from his brow. "I do not know why we have been chosen for this honor, but we are certainly going to enjoy it!"

At seven o'clock the next evening, the Feliz family rode with Alfredo Romero as he turned off the road and guided the surrey through the impressive archway that allowed access onto the Gonzales ranch. The entire spread was enclosed with a split-rail fence.

The surrey followed a winding road among tall timber and rich, grassy open fields that were heavily dotted with cattle. At that time of day, the mountains in the distance were deep purple. A small stream wound its way through the ranch, and in the last rays of sunset, looked like a golden ribbon. About a mile from where they had turned in at the gate, the surrey topped a gentle rise and from its high point, they could see the long sweep of the lush valley below. Nestled in a thick grove of cottonwood trees was the huge ranch house, flanked by several small buildings. Beyond them were a long bunkhouse and a pole corral that included two barns. All the buildings were constructed of large logs cut from timber on the property.

As they drew near the house, Rosita said, "Mama, how would you like to have to clean a house that size?"

Dolores let her eyes take it all in and touched fingers to her cheek. "It would take me a week just to sweep the floors!"

Alfredo Romero laughed and said, "We have six servants who care for the house, ladies. With that many people working together, it does not take so long to clean it."

The surrey rolled to a halt in front of the wide porch that made the one-story structure even more impressive. It had a double railing that ran along its outer perimeter and was decorated with several pieces of wooden furniture.

One of the wide double doors came open and Don Jose moved out onto the porch, followed by Don Miguel. Father and son stepped up and welcomed the Felizes to the ranch, and the family was escorted inside. They were all eyes as Don Jose guided them from the vestibule past the huge parlor and into the dining room. Reyes was impressed at the size of the fireplace in the parlor. There were tapestries on the walls, polished hardwood floors, and bold, inordinate furnishings, all of which gave it a definite air of luxury.

Standing near the rear door of the dining room—which led into the kitchen—was Gonzales's Chinese servant, Li Ho, who was clad in typical Oriental attire.

The Feliz women especially noted the lavish manner in which the table was set. There was food in abundance, including beef prepared in three ways. Wine and water glasses had been filled, and coffee cups stood empty, waiting to be filled with fresh brew.

"Li Ho," said Don Jose with a note of authority in his voice, "we are ready to dine. If you will seat the ladies, the gentlemen will then be seated, and we will begin."

Li Ho bowed and hurriedly seated Dolores Feliz on one side of the table, then seated Rosita on the other. Ramon took his place beside his wife and Reyes sat next to Rosita. Don Jose sat down at the head of the table and Don Miguel at the other end.

Hot coffee was poured by Li Ho, and the meal began. Don Miguel spoke to Rosita about her upcoming marriage to Joaquin Murieta while Don Jose asked Reyes what he did for a living. Reyes, who had just turned twenty, explained that he had been trained by Joaquin Murieta to break broncos and now was finding jobs quite easily throughout the valley. Since Joaquin was in such demand, many of the ranchers were hiring Reyes to break their horses in his place.

After several minutes had passed, Ramon Feliz looked at the rancher. "Señor Gonzales, pardon me, but I must ask you something."

Sipping from his wine glass, Don Jose swallowed, and set the glass down. "Of course. What is it?"

Ramon cleared his throat. "I very much appreciate your kindness to my family and myself, but it is a bit out of the ordinary for a man of your means to—well, to bring peasants into his house for a meal. May I be so bold as to ask to what we owe this kind gesture?"

Don Jose was finding it difficult to keep his eyes off the beautiful Rosita. Allowing himself only brief glances, he took a quick one, then set his gaze on her father. "Sometimes in a man's life, he meets people who just strike him in a very pleasant way. This is what happened to me when we met on Sunday. I told myself that you are very special people, and I wanted to get to know you."

Don Miguel could not believe what he was hearing. He had never known his father to have any desire whatsoever to rub elbows with poor people. When he had inquired as to why Don Jose was having them for dinner, the old man had brushed him off without a real answer. He had decided that no doubt the reason would come out while the Feliz family was at the ranch. If this was going to be Don Jose's only explanation, there was still a mystery about it.

Ramon flicked a glance at each of his family, and pressed Gonzales further by asking, "Pardon me again, Señor Gonzales, but what makes us very special people in your eyes?"

Before he realized it, Don Jose was looking at Rosita. His gaze clung to hers, then he caught himself and looked away. Though Rosita's eyes showed only curiosity, just to have them set upon him made his heart drum his ribs. "Sometimes words fail a man, Ramon. This is where I find myself at this moment. It is just that certain people have a…a…quality. Yes, that is the word. Upon meeting the Felizes, I found a certain quality. Should I say a quality of humble sincerity and wholesomeness that is rare in most people." Glancing once more at Rosita, then at Dolores, he added, "Of course, not to mention the exquisite beauty of these two lovely ladies."

The latter statement brought light laughter around the table. The only person who didn't laugh was Rosita. Though she forced a smile, she was struggling with strange feelings within. Every time Don Jose looked at her, she thought of the way he had held her hand too long and spoke flowery words to her. He was looking at her too much, and it made her nervous. Rosita and Joaquin had agreed that Don Jose was just a lonely old man and had excused him of his foolish actions on that basis. Rosita wondered now if there was not more to it.

Ramon was still a bit confused, but the explanation seemed sufficient and he dropped it there.

Don Miguel, who knew his father quite well, was certain there was more to all of this than had been expressed. He pondered on it silently.

When the meal was over, Don Jose gave the Feliz family a tour of the huge house. When they entered the man's den at the rear of the building, Ramon whispered to Dolores that their whole house would fit in the den with some room to spare.

When the entire house had been seen, Don Jose had Li Ho fire up four lanterns. Don Jose, Don Miguel, Ramon, and Reyes each carried a lantern as Don Jose led them on a tour of the yard and buildings. They did not enter the bunkhouse where the ranch hands were settling down for the night, but Don Jose did take them into one of the smaller houses where the servants lived. The one he showed them was unoccupied, and the rancher made sure his guests understood that no one was living in the house at the time. It pleased Don Jose when he heard Ramon remark that even the servants' houses were almost twice as large as their own.

When the tour was over, the Feliz family was taken back into the ranch house, where they were seated in the parlor and each given a glass of wine. Don Jose found all kinds of things to talk about while stealing furtive glances at Rosita.

After a while, Dolores called her husband's attention to the fact that it was getting late. It was almost bedtime and they needed to be getting home.

Don Jose commanded Li Ho to go to the bunkhouse and tell Alberto that it was time to take the guests home. Moments later, the surrey was ready and the group moved out onto the wide, sweeping porch. Don Jose thanked the Felizes for coming, saying that it had been a very enjoyable evening. He then approached Dolores, took her hand, bowed, and kissed it. "Señora Dolores Feliz, it has been a pleasure to have you in my home."

Dolores smiled and replied, "The pleasure has been mine, Señor Don Jose. Thank you for inviting us."

The rancher then turned toward Rosita, unaware that she was tensing up inside. Rosita felt a cold chill slither down her spine as Don Jose took her hand and kissed it. She was relieved when he let go immediately and spoke only briefly, thanking her for coming. She forced a few words of appreciation for the enjoyable evening and moved aside so Gonzales could shake hands with her brother and father.

As they rode away in the surrey, Rosita kept her thoughts to herself. Her parents talked all the way home about the wonder and beauty of the ranch, and of Don Jose's kindness. Reyes commented periodically, but Rosita had little to say. Feeling a degree of disgust for the old man, she put her mind on the man she loved. Tomorrow night she was scheduled to have dinner with Joaquin at the little cafe in Arizpe.

CHAPTER FIVE

As Don Jose Gonzales and his son bid good-bye to the Feliz family and entered the house, Don Miguel eyed him suspiciously. "Father, you have something up your sleeve, as they say in the United States. What is it?"

The older Gonzales ran splayed fingers through his thinning hair. "You ask too many questions."

Don Miguel held his father's gaze. "It has something to do with Rosita, doesn't it?"

Don Jose's face reddened. Tiny sparks flashed in his eyes. "I said you ask too many questions!" He turned and headed down the hall toward his den. Calling over his shoulder, he said, "When Alfredo returns, tell him I want to see him."

"I won't be up that late, Father," replied Don Miguel. "I am to be at the Valdez ranch early in the morning, remember?"

Don Jose recalled that he had ordered his son to attend a horse auction at the second largest ranch in the Sonora Valley. Silas Valdez had imported some new Arabian horses and had a stallion he was going to put on the block. The stud sounded like just what Don Jose was looking for, and Don Miguel was to take a look at him and purchase him if he was as good as they had been led to believe. There was never any problem of getting anything he wanted. Don Jose's representative could outbid anyone in Mexico.

Rubbing his chin, Gonzales said, "I forgot about that. All right. You go on to bed. I will watch for Alfredo myself."

"Can't you just talk to him in the morning?"

"The business I have for him will demand his attention first thing in the morning. I want him to have my orders tonight."

Don Miguel nodded silently, wheeled, and headed down another hallway, which led to his bedroom.

An hour later, Don Miguel lay wide awake in his bed, the darkness surrounding him. His window was open and he could hear the soft night wind toying with the curtains and the sound of countless crickets outside, giving their nightly concert.

Gonzales was troubled. His father was acting very strange. It was totally out of character for Don Jose to have any desire to be around poor people. And there was the obvious interest in Rosita. Nearly every time Don Miguel had observed his father from the opposite end of the table during the meal, the old man was looking at her. It was not a grandfatherly look of admiration for young beauty, but a hungry look…as if he desired her for himself.

Rolling his head on the pillow, Don Miguel said audibly, "No. It cannot be. I have to be mistaken." Then he thought of the way Don Jose had conducted himself toward Rosita in front of the church on Sunday. "No. It just cannot be."

The eastern horizon was blushing pink above the surrounding hills as Ramon Feliz trotted his horse up to the hitch rail next to the office shack at the Varoyeca mine. He greeted fellow workers who were standing nearby and dismounted. A twelve-year-old Mexican boy approached him. "Buenas dias, Señor Ramon."

Wrapping the reins around the rail, Ramon replied, "The same to you, Manuel. I will not be coming up for lunch today, so you be sure to water him at noon too, all right?"

"Si. I will take good care of him. You want I should go ahead and take off the saddle?"

"Might as well. He'll be more comfortable."

Leaving his horse to the care of the boy, Ramon took his lunch sack from a saddlebag and joined his friends. There was an eager look on all of their faces. One of them spoke up quickly, "Tell us, Ramon! How was your visit with the big-shot rancher?"

"Was the food good?" asked another.

Chuckling, Ramon said, "Indeed the food was good, and the visit was wonderful. Don Jose treated us like kings."

One of the mine workers raised his eyebrows. "Oh, so already it is Don Jose and no longer Señor Don Jose!"

"Well," said Ramon, waggling his head and crossing his fore-finger over his middle finger. "Don Jose and I are just like this."

Impressed, the Mexicans hooted and whistled. "So why did Don Jose have you and your family come to the ranch, Ramon? You said you would tell us this morning."

"I asked him why," responded Feliz, "and he said it was just because we are very special people and he wanted to get to know us."

Laughing, another said, "Well, all of us can understand about your beautiful wife and daughter being special, Ramon, but as ugly as you and Reyes are, it is a wonder Don Jose did not just invite the women!"

There was a round of hoarse laughter, then the dark-skinned men saw Arello Simone, the Mayo Indian foreman, emerge from the office shack and head toward them.

"Time to go to work," said Ramon Feliz.

The sun was just peeking over the eastern hills when Arello Simone returned to the surface after accompanying his men into the depths of the silver mine. He noted that young Manuel Ortego was currying one of the miner's horses. Just as Simone reached the door of the office shack, he saw a lone rider coming in from the south. Simone waited for the rider to draw near, then moved toward him. Reining in, the Mexican said, "Good morning, Señor. My name is Alfredo Romero. I am from the ranch of Don Jose Gonzales. I am here to see one of your workers, Ramon Feliz."

"I am sorry," replied Simone, "but Ramon has already gone down into the mine for the day. He will not surface until four o'clock this afternoon."

Dismounting to the squeak of saddle leather, Alfredo said, "It is very important that I see him immediately. I am sorry that I did not arrive before he went down. I had no way of knowing exactly what time the miners started to work."

"It would have been best if you had seen him at home," said the foreman.

Shaking his head, Alfredo replied, "Oh no. My boss did not want me to go to his home. He told me to see Ramon here at the mine."

"If you want to come back at four o'clock, you can see him then," said Simone, turning toward the office.

"But Señor, please," said Romero. "I told you it is very important that I see Ramon immediately."

The foreman halted, his tawny face tinting slightly with irritation. "Ramon is being paid to work. If he surfaces and takes time to talk to you, I will have to cut his pay for today."

"Please. You do not understand. My boss is a man who is used to getting what he wants. I dare not return to the ranch without delivering my message to Ramon Feliz."

"Just give me the message and I will pass it on to Ramon this afternoon," Simone said stubbornly.

"I cannot do that," replied the stocky Mexican. "My orders are to deliver the message only to Ramon. I can tell you this much: my boss wants to see Ramon, and though I do not know exactly what it is about, I can assure you that it is for Ramon's good. Believe me, for this he will not mind losing some wages."

The foreman pondered the situation. "All right. I will bring Ramon up." Turning toward the boy, who was still currying horses, he called, "Manuel! Go down into the mine and tell Ramon Feliz that there is a man to see him. It is very important. He must come at once."

Simone then excused himself and entered the office, closing the door. Alfredo expressed his thanks just before the door was shut.

Ten minutes later, Ramon and Manuel appeared together at the mouth of the mine. When Ramon saw the face of Alfredo Romero, he smiled broadly and waved. Manuel hurried back to the horses, and Ramon drew up, saying, "Good morning, Alfredo. The boy said you wanted to see me."

"Si. I have been sent by Don Jose to give you a message, my friend."

The look on Alfredo's face told Ramon that whatever he was about to hear, it was good. His heart picked up pace as he asked, "What is the message?"

"I am to tell you that Don Jose wants you to come to the ranch as soon as possible. I do not know what it is, but I am instructed to say that he has a very interesting proposition for you. I had to tell your foreman that Don Jose wants to see you, but other than that, you are to tell no one that you are coming to the ranch…not even your wife or children."

A bit stunned, Ramon said, "This must be something big."

"I am in the dark on it, Ramon. But Don Jose did say that it could mean a great deal of money for you."

Ramon's heart pounded with elation. For a moment he could

only hear the loud roar of the blood coursing through his ears. "I will ask Arello if I can go right now!"

Ramon hurried to the door of the office shack and knocked. Within seconds it came open, revealing the somber face of Arello.

"Arello," said Ramon, "I need to have some time off. As my friend Alfredo Romero told you, Don Jose Gonzales wants to see me. It is of utmost importance. May I go now and return as soon as possible?"

Simone stepped outside without answering and looked toward the rising sun. "It is important that we get as much silver ore out of the mine today as we can. If you go now, I will have to retain the entire day's wages. However, if you return to work right now and stay in the mine until noon, I will only take half a day's wages from your pay."

Looking over his shoulder at Alfredo, Ramon said, "Do you think it would be all right with Don Jose if I arrive at the ranch about one o'clock?"

Realizing that Ramon was under pressure from the foreman, Alfredo nodded. "I am sure it would be all right. Just as long as he sees you today."

Turning back to Simone, Ramon said, "I will get right back to work and surface at noon. Thank you for understanding."

"I do not really understand," Simone replied blandly, "but if it is that important, I am glad to do what I can."

Don Jose Gonzales was just finishing a late lunch in his kitchen when the door swung open and Li Ho appeared. "Ramon Feliz is here, Mr. Gonzales. He is waiting in the vestibule. Shall I seat him and tell him you will be out when you are finished eating?"

Gonzales swallowed the food that was in his mouth, picked up a coffee cup, and took three quick swallows. "No. I will see him now."

Brushing past Li Ho, who held the kitchen door open, Don Jose hurried along the hallway and smiled when he saw Ramon. Extending his hand, he said, "Ramon! Alfredo told me you would be here just about now. I am so glad to see you."

Holding his battered and dirty hat in his hands, Ramon met the rancher's grip. "I am sorry I could not get here this morning, Don Jose, but—"

"Alfredo explained about what the foreman said," cut in Don Jose. "It is no problem. I just wanted to see you as soon as possible."

Looking down at his soiled clothing, Ramon apologized again. "Please excuse my work clothes, Don Jose. Alfredo said I was not to even tell my family that I was coming to see you, so I could not go home and change without having to explain what I was doing."

The rancher put an arm around him. "I have seen dirty work clothes before, my friend. You did right by coming as you are. Let's go back to my den."

Ramon's imagination was running wild. Why the secrecy? What could this wealthy man possibly want with a peasant such as Ramon Feliz? In what way could something between them put money in Ramon's hands?

Halting at the door of the den, Don Jose gestured for his guest to enter, then followed close behind him. Pointing to a plush chair in front of the huge polished oak desk, the rancher said, "Sit right here, Ramon. Make yourself comfortable."

Ramon was concerned that he might soil the chair, but since Don Jose was not bothered by it, he obeyed and sat down. He had never felt such comfort. He watched as the man went to a cabinet behind the desk and produced a fancy glass decanter and two small glasses. Setting them down on the desk, he smiled. "Brandy, Ramon?"

Ramon had never even tasted brandy. He had promised Dolores that he would never be a drinker. However, the strange and wondrous occasion certainly allowed him to take just a small amount. Holding up his thumb and forefinger separated by less than an inch, he said, "Just a little, please."

Thinking Ramon was just being conservative for his host's sake, Don Jose poured the glass nearly full and handed it to him. Ramon responded with a weak smile and took a sip. The sting on his tongue made his eyes water. He lowered his eyes so the rancher would not think he had never experienced brandy before.

Don Jose poured himself a generous amount, then while remaining on his feet behind the desk, he raised his glass. "To our future relationship, my friend."

Mystified at the kind of treatment he was getting, Ramon lifted his glass, nodded with a smile, and took another sip. He could not imagine what kind of relationship he and the rancher could have together.

Don Jose downed a healthy amount, then sat down in his elegant desk chair and took the lid off a humidor. Extending it toward his guest, he said, "Cigar?"

Ramon Feliz had never smoked a cigar and didn't like the smell of them, but was fearful of insulting his host by refusing. Pulling one from the humidor, he smiled his thanks.

Don Jose took one for himself, returned the lid to its place, and bit the end off the cigar. Ramon clumsily followed suit, and the rancher fired a match. When both cigars were lit, Don Jose eased back in his chair, blew smoke toward the ceiling, and asked, "How's the cigar, Ramon?"

The mine laborer was feeling a bit uncomfortable, but drew a mouthful of smoke and released it. "Uh...just fine. Just fine." In spite of his discomfort, Ramon was delighted with the situation. Alfredo Romero had already let him know that Don Jose's mysterious proposition was going to bring him a great deal of money. That prospect in itself was intriguing, but to make it more pleasant, Ramon had never been treated so well in all his forty-six years of life.

"So how long have you worked in the Varoyeca mine?" asked Don Jose, not quite ready to broach the subject that was foremost in his mind.

"Twenty-four years. Since right after Dolores and I were married."

"Ah yes. Dolores. Lovely woman, Ramon. You are to be congratulated. She is really lovely."

Ramon had not placed the cigar in his mouth a second time. Ashes were building on its tip, but he was paying it no mind as he held it between his fingers. He was waiting for the man to come out with why he had wanted to see him.

"And your children, Ramon," Don Jose went on. "Fine young daughter and son."

"Yes. They are wonderful children."

"Reyes. Good-looking young man. Seems to be very intelligent and aggressive."

"Yes. Very. A man doesn't make it in the horse-breaking business without both of those qualities, along with some physical strength and courage."

"I will agree to that."

"I will have two young men like that in my family soon," said Ramon proudly. "Rosita is going to marry Joaquin Murieta next April. As you know, Joaquin is the one who taught Reyes how to break horses. Good boy, Joaquin. He is very strong, intelligent, and courageous. I will be so happy to have him as my son-in-law."

Don Jose felt his stomach turn sour, but ignoring Joaquin Murieta as a subject, said, "Your Rosita is the flower of this valley, Ramon. She is the most beautiful young woman I have ever seen."

Ramon Feliz nodded his head exuberantly. "That she is, Don Jose. That she is."

The rancher was quiet for a moment. He puffed on his cigar and blew a cloud of smoke. "Twenty-four years in the mine, eh?"

"Yes."

"Have the Mayos paid you well?"

"I get by."

"But have they paid you well enough to provide nice things for your family? Comfortable home? Plenty to eat and plenty to wear?"

Ramon squirmed on the overstuffed chair and cleared his throat. "A man does not work for someone else as a mine laborer and have what you call plenty, Don Jose. Like I said, I get by. Our home is small. Nothing fancy. Our horses are not the kind of stock you have here on your ranch. We have enough clothing to cover our bodies, but nothing like the quality you can afford. Dolores is a wonder with food. She can make a little go a long way. We have always done all right. Never did our children go to bed hungry."

Don Jose stuck the cigar between his teeth and blinked at the smoke that drifted into his eyes. "I have seen your home, Ramon."

"Oh?"

"I took the liberty of driving by it a couple of days ago. House is quite small. Clean, but small. Buildings are also small. You have obviously worked at keeping them in good repair."

"Yes." Ramon wondered where all this was leading.

Don Jose fitted the cigar in a groove in the ashtray on his desk. "You are no doubt wondering why I have asked you to come here today and why I wanted to talk to you without your family knowing about it."

His heart throbbing in anticipation of what was about to come, Ramon Feliz adjusted himself in the big chair. "Yes. I have indeed been wondering."

"Do you like being poor?"

Ramon's cigar, gathering yet more ashes on its tip, was sending tiny tendrils of smoke toward the ceiling. He studied Gonzales's features. "I suppose no poor man likes his plight in life, Don Jose. Does my poverty have something to do with why I am sitting here at this moment?"

"Yes, it does. I have a proposition for you. If you are compliable to it, you and your wife will never want for anything the rest of your lives."

Ramon swallowed hard. Butterflies seemed to come alive in his stomach and flit about. Certainly Don Jose Gonzales was in a position to do anything for a poor man he wanted to in order to remove all his wants for the remainder of his days on earth. Whatever it was that he must do to gain such favor, he would do—anything reasonable, of course. Don Jose would not want him to do anything unlawful or immoral.

At that moment there was a knock at the door. "Yes?" Gonzales called.

The knob turned and the door came open a few inches. The voice of Li Ho said, "Mr. Gonzales, Don Miguel has returned with the Arabian stallion that you sent him to purchase. He has purchased a beautiful mare, also. He wants to know if you would like to see them before he takes them to the barn."

The rancher's horses were his pride and joy, even above his fine breed of cattle. Don Miguel knew this and was merely following the pattern he had known all of his life. His father would always drop what he was doing to look at a new horse. This would be especially true with the stud that Don Miguel had been sent to buy if it was suitable to his father's tastes.

Don Jose stood up. "I will be right out, Li Ho."

"I will tell him." Li Ho closed the door.

Don Jose picked up the cigar from the ashtray and ground the fire from it. "Will you please excuse me, my friend? I sent my son to do a buying job for me, and I must see how he has done."

"Of course," said Ramon, rising to his feet. When he did, the cigar in his hand sprayed ashes on his pants, the chair, and the floor. He started to apologize, but Don Jose told him not to worry. He would send Li Ho in to clean up the ashes, and he would be back in a few minutes.

As soon as Don Jose disappeared through the door, Ramon took the opportunity to extinguish his cigar in the ashtray. The foul odor of the cigar was giving him a queasy stomach.

Only a few seconds had passed after the rancher left the room when Li Ho entered with a broom and dustpan. The mess was quickly cleaned up, and the Chinaman was gone.

Ramon Feliz was strung tight. What was Don Jose going to propose?

Slowly he moved about the room, eyeing the expensive paintings on the walls. Coveting the bear rug on the floor and the garish decor around him, he mentally embraced the thought of having this kind of wealth for himself. It was a pleasant contemplation. Whatever the rancher had in mind, if the results of his complying with the man's proposition would make him even reasonably comfortable financially and allow him to provide a higher standard of living for his family, it would be the most wonderful thing that could ever happen.

A tiny tingle slithered down his spine. There was no way he was going to turn Don Jose down, no matter what he wanted. His pulse throbbed. In a little while he would ride home and announce to his family that things were going to be a whole lot better from now on. For once in their lives, they were going to be better than dirt poor.

Nervously, Ramon flitted about the room. He checked the hundreds of books that lined the shelves of one entire wall. There were volumes in both English and Spanish. Like so many of the Spanish-speaking people of Sonora, Don Jose had put forth the effort to learn English. For anyone who dealt with the Americanos who often crossed the border and came into Sonora, knowing English was both mandatory and profitable. Much of Don Jose's cattle business was done with Americanos. Ramon wondered how many of the books the man had actually read.

After some twenty minutes had passed, Don Jose appeared,

closed the door behind him, and returned to his chair behind the desk while his guest once again took his seat. Taking his same position, leaning on his elbows, Gonzales smiled at Ramon. "All right. Now, where were we?"

"The…uh…proposition," said Ramon, the tingle touching his spine again.

"Oh yes." There was a pause. "Before I tell you what I have in mind, let me explain to you what I am offering. I wanted to lay it before you, and let you respond to it. Then you can tell your wife. If both of you agree to my proposition, you will immediately be given a hundred thousand pesos."

Ramon's mouth went dry. He could not believe what he was hearing. In two lifetimes in the silver mine, he would never earn that much money. A hot blanket of excitement seemed to descend over his flesh, burning through and heating up his blood.

Don Jose read the obvious reaction in the mineworker. "Does this seem preposterous to you?"

Working his jaw, Ramon finally freed his tongue. "It does, Don Jose. It is like I am dreaming. What…what must I do to come by this large amount of money?"

"Let me tell you more before I answer that question."

Ramon nodded.

"Last evening I showed you the unoccupied servants' house."

"Yes."

"Did you like it?"

"Oh, it is beautiful! And so big!"

"Did Dolores like it?"

"Very much. She spoke of it several times on the way home."

Looking pleased, the rancher said, "Good. How would you like to live in it for the rest of your lives?"

Ramon's excitement increased. "Why, I would love it! So would Dolores." Ramon's eyes danced with glee. "Are you offering me a job as one of your servants?"

"Not as a servant, exactly. Your position would be a little higher. You would be in charge of the grounds around the house and buildings. It would be light work for the most part, and anytime you needed help, you would call on the servants. If it involved more than they could handle, you would let me know, and I would obtain help from among the ranch hands. How does this sound?"

Blinking in disbelief, Ramon replied, "It is very much like a dream, Don Jose."

Pleased that it was going so good, the rancher went on. "Now, when I say for the rest of your life, I mean it. If you go along with my proposition, I will set it up with Don Miguel to keep you on as groundskeeper as long as you live. If you should die before Dolores does, she will be provided for, even with you gone."

Shaking his head, Ramon said, "I cannot believe this is happening."

"There is more. You will be given a salary comparable to what I pay my ranch foreman, and you will receive a generous supply of beef each week."

Ramon felt the raw quiver of exhilaration run through his body. "It sounds too good to be true, Don Jose!"

"Believe me, it is true."

Ramon wiped a shaky palm over his face and his voice trembled. "What is your proposition?"

Don Jose Gonzales laid his dark gaze on Ramon Feliz. "I want the hand of your daughter Rosita in marriage."

The words hit Ramon like a battering ram. His face drained of color as if all the blood had left his body. He was searching for his voice when Gonzales said, "Well?"

"B-but, D-Don Jose, Rosita's m-mother and I h-have already given our consent f-for her to marry Joaquin Murieta. His p-parents are in agreement, and we have already set the date for the wedding. There is no way I can—"

"Of course you can!" said Gonzales. "Do not tell me there is no way you can change it. You are Rosita's father. You have the right to change your mind."

Like cold molasses, a sinking sensation began to settle over Ramon Feliz. His dream of a better life was flying away like a frightened bird from a beast of prey. "I cannot do this thing, Don Jose. I am sorry, but—"

Anger flared in the rancher. "You are not sorry, or you would do it!"

Wringing his hands, Ramon said, "Even if I would say it was all right, Dolores would never stand for it."

"I believe you are wrong! When Dolores learns of my offer, and that the two of you will never be poor again, she will agree!"

Ramon rose out of the chair and began to pace back and forth in front of the desk. His voice showed strain as he said, "But even if Dolores would agree to it, Rosita never would. She is deeply in love with Joaquin."

"This is Mehico, Ramon," countered Don Jose, "not the United States. Our children do what their parents tell them to do. Marriages here are arranged by the parents every day, and the children obediently marry whom the parents have picked for them."

Ramon walked to a window and stared through it. His mind was a maelstrom of perplexity. He had come so close to being comfortable for the remainder of his life, and disappointment was a merciless claw in his innermost being. Not wanting to look at Gonzales, but desiring to speak his mind, he continued to stare out the window. "I very much appreciate your offer, Don Jose, but…but you are a man in your sixties. Rosita is seventeen. Joaquin is eighteen. They—"

"To be precise, Ramon," said Gonzales, walking up behind him, "I am sixty-six years of age. How many years do I have left? Fifteen if my health holds good? Maybe twenty if God is willing? Rosita will still be a young woman when I pass on. She will inherit the greater part of my wealth. She will be rich from the time she marries me and all the rest of her life. Would you deny her this? What will she have with this broncobuster Murieta?"

Ramon Feliz turned around. He looked at Don Jose, then at the floor, scrubbing a shaky hand over his face.

Don Jose smiled to himself. By the look in Ramon's eyes, he knew the peasant was going to give in. "Do you really want Rosita to go through life married to Murieta? He no doubt will do better than you have financially—unless he gets injured by some wild mustang—but I can give her luxury. As my wife, she will never know a need. She will be rich. Think about it!"

Ramon stared at the floor.

"And what about Dolores?" pressed Gonzales. "Doesn't she deserve something better than she has? Wouldn't it be wonderful if she had that nice big house to live in? And all its comforts? And plenty of money? And security if you should die before she does?

What will she have if you continue to work at the mine? Are you putting any money away for her?"

Ramon moved his head back and forth slowly. He raised his head and looked Don Jose in the eyes. "No, I am not. I do not earn enough money to do that."

"What if you should be injured in the mine and no longer be able to work there? That could happen, could it not?"

"Yes."

"Will the Mayos continue to pay you when you cannot produce for them?"

"You know the answer to that," Ramon said dully.

"Listen, my good friend. I will give you a guarantee that you will have the house to live in and enough money to live on if you should become unable to carry on your job here. What else can I do to convince you to give me Rosita for my wife?"

The poor man bit down on his lower lip. "Nothing, Don Jose. I will do it. Let me go home and talk to Dolores. Once I can persuade her that this is the thing to do, we will bring Rosita here to the ranch, and you can make your marriage proposal to her in the presence of her parents. We will not tell her why we are bringing her here. It will be best if she hears it from you first. As her father, I will then back you in the proposal."

Smiling broadly, Don Jose laid a hand on Ramon's shoulder. "I like that idea, my friend! Certainly when Rosita sees all that can be hers and what she is doing for her parents' future, she will not wish to resist her father's change of mind. I know she will desire to become my wife. As well as being beautiful, it is evident that she is a very intelligent young woman."

Ramon's thoughts ran to Joaquin Murieta. The young man was a fighter. He also loved Rosita very much. He would not take this sitting down.

"I see worry in your eyes, Ramon. What is it?"

Feliz took a deep breath and let it out slowly through his nose. "There will be trouble. Real trouble."

"Murieta?"

"Yes."

A vague expression of amusement tilted the corners of the rich man's mouth. "I will give the young man five thousand pesos and one of my thoroughbred Arabian horses. Every man has his price, they say. Certainly, being a poor man and an avid horseman, this will be enough to send him away happy and contented."

"Maybe so," said Ramon. "As you say, every man has his price."

You did, thought Don Jose. *Why not Murieta?*

Ramon Feliz bid Don Jose Gonzales adios on the porch of the huge house and swung into the saddle, unaware that Don Miguel was watching from the corral. With the promise of great financial gain warming his blood, he trotted the horse over the rolling hills toward the gate.

CHAPTER SIX

Y ou did what!" said Dolores Feliz, face livid with anger. "You told that—that old man he could have our daughter for his bride?"

"But, Dolores," said Ramon Feliz, rising to his feet at the kitchen table where he and his wife were sitting, "listen to me. I—"

"I am listening to you!" She jumped up and looked him straight in the eyes. "I am listening to you! And I do not like what I am hearing! This is my husband talking? The father of Reyes and Rosita Feliz? You speak like a madman!"

"But darling, please," pled Ramon, "you must think it over before you make a hasty decision."

Deep lines suddenly curved down from Dolores's lip corners into a set chin. The cast of her jaw was unrelenting. "Ramon, you fool! You cannot do this! You have already promised Rosita to Joaquin!"

Ramon took a step toward her, reaching out his hand. "Dolores, you do not have to yell at me."

"Get away from me!" she screamed, backing away until she bumped into the cupboard. "Don't you touch me! You deserve to be yelled at! Joaquin and Rosita are young and in love. You would destroy their lives just to make us comfortable? Where is your sense of right and wrong? I want no part of it! None! Do you hear me? How—" She choked on her words. "How can you ask Rosita to give up the man she loves to marry that disgusting old man?"

"But darling," said Ramon, moving closer to her. "Rosita will—"

"I said get away from me!" she hissed, her features deep red and hard as granite.

Ramon lifted open palms toward her. "All right. All right. I will not touch you. But darling—"

"Don't you 'darling' me, you selfish beast!"

Ramon wiped a palm over his sweaty brow. Keeping his voice low, he said, "Will you just listen to me?"

Dolores did not answer. She only glared at him with eyes of distrust.

"Rosita will forget Joaquin when she becomes the wife of Sonora's richest man. Do you not see? She would never have much with Joaquin. Broncobusters make better money than mine workers, I will admit, but not enough to really give their wives and families what they need."

Dolores gripped the edge of the counter with both hands until her knuckles turned white. "You are forgetting that Joaquin has plans to one day be a rancher."

"He will never be rich like Don Jose, if he ever makes it at all!"

"You don't know that!"

"You are kidding yourself, Dolores. Joaquin will never be anything but a broncobuster. That is, unless he gets injured by some wild mustang. Then what? How will he provide for Rosita, then? She could be in the utmost poverty. But think of this…when Don Jose dies in a few years, our Rosita will own the ranch, all the cattle, and all the blooded horses. She will be filthy rich! And besides, I will never have to work in that dirty old mine again. And we will have a beautiful house on the ranch. And…and you can finally wear nice clothes like I have always wanted to buy you. And—"

"I do not want that old man's charity!" yelled Dolores. "And for your information, Ramon Feliz, my daughter is not for sale! You are the sorriest excuse for a father I have ever seen! I would never have dreamed you could stoop so low!"

Dolores's harsh words triggered Ramon's temper. Face flushed, he lunged at her, seized her by an arm, and swung her around, slamming her down on a chair beside the table. The look in his eyes frightened her. She sat still as he continued to grip her arm. "I am the head of this house, woman! We do what I say around here! I came home to tell you of our good fortune, and you do nothing but scream and yell at me."

"You are hurting my arm," she said through gritted teeth.

Releasing his grip, Ramon stood over her and said, "I am going to keep my word to Don Jose. I am going to give him Rosita for his wife. It is best for all concerned…especially Rosita."

Dolores's fear was overridden by her anger. Eyeing her husband with cold malice, her voice bitter, she snarled, "You can do it, Ramon, and there is nothing I can do to stop you. But you will do it against my will!"

At that instant, Reyes came through the door. "What is going on here?"

Surprised to see his son home so early, Ramon muttered, "Nothing is going on here."

"Nothing?" Reyes blurted incredulously. "I could hear you two yelling at each other before I even turned into the yard."

His temper still hot, Ramon rasped, "What are you doing home so early?"

"I ran out of broncos to break at the Cordova ranch, so I came on home. What is the matter with you, Papa? You act like I have committed some kind of crime by coming home early. Is this argument going on because Rosita is away with Joaquin and I am not supposed to be home?" Moving up close, Reyes asked, "Has this kind of thing been happening often? I have never known my parents to show each other anything but love and kindness."

"No, son," replied Dolores, "this kind of thing has not been happening often. It has never happened before."

Running his gaze between them, Reyes asked, "Well, what is there to fight about?"

Dolores set her hard eyes on Ramon. "Well, why don't you confess to your son what you have done?"

Reyes' face showed puzzlement as he looked down at his father, who was five inches shorter than himself.

Ramon met his gaze, telling himself that Reyes would understand and be glad that the family would no longer be poor. "Sit down, son, and I will explain it to you."

Dolores sat with arms folded over her breast and looked on as the two men sat down across the table from each other. Reyes eyed his father guardedly, not knowing what to expect.

Clearing his throat, the elder Feliz said, "It is true, is it not, that we have always been poor? I worked hard to provide for this family as you and your sister were growing up, but—"

"You have done well, Father," said Reyes. "We have never gone hungry or without food and shelter."

"True, but still we have needed things that my low wages could not provide. I have always wanted to give my family a better house, better clothing, and things to make life more comfortable."

"I appreciate that, Ramon," said Dolores, "but the children and

I never complained about our lot."

"I know," replied Ramon, "but that did not keep me from wanting to give you something better."

"This is admirable, Father," said Reyes, "but what does our being poor have to do with what you are supposed to confess to me?"

Ramon Feliz cleared his throat again. "Don Jose Gonzales has made me an offer, son. An offer that will make us a well-to-do family and provide your sister with greater riches now and for the rest of her life."

Reyes studied his father's face for a moment. "My first inclination when you use the word 'offer' is to assume that Don Jose has offered you a job. But the pay would certainly not be enough to make the family well-to-do, and a job for you would have no bearing on Rosita's becoming even richer. So what is this offer which has caused you and Mama to fight?"

Dolores was glaring at her husband with burning eyes. He could feel the heat of them as he looked squarely at Reyes. "Don Jose has asked me for Rosita's hand in marriage, and I have agreed to it."

Reyes looked like he had been hit in the face with a leather strap. "You what?"

"Now wait a minute!" said Ramon defensively. "Let me tell you what Don Jose is offering."

A profound red heat took over Reyes's brain and showed in the color of his face. "This is preposterous! I do not believe my ears! Papa, you cannot do this! Rosita—"

"Let me tell you what is in the offer before you show your anger to me!" shouted Ramon, cutting across his son's words.

"I don't need to hear it!" Reyes lashed back. "You have no right to do this to my sister!"

"Reyes," said Dolores, forcing her voice to remain calm, "let him tell you the whole thing. He is going to do it, no matter what we say, so you just may as well hear it."

Ramon gave his wife a smoky glance, then turned to Reyes and began explaining Gonzales's offer in detail. When he had laid it all out, he closed off by saying, "So you see, when Don Jose dies, Don Miguel will inherit some of the riches because he is his son, but as his wife, Rosita will get the ranch and everything that is on it, plus more money than she can count in a year."

"And you and Mama will be set for life," Reyes said.

Thinking he was pulling Reyes to his side of the issue, Ramon smiled. "Yes! And don't think that we will forget you. Our riches will be your riches."

Lips barely apart, Reyes said levelly, "I don't want any part of such riches. You are not the father I have known all these years. You have changed into a greedy and coldhearted monster. You don't really care about Rosita's happiness. It is your own you are thinking about!"

Eyes bulging with rage, Ramon spat, "Don't you talk to your father like that! I do care about Rosita's happiness! She will have all the money she could ever need for the rest of her life."

Reyes shoved his chair back and stood up. "Money cannot buy happiness, Ramon Feliz! You are not considering Rosita's feelings at all. She is in love with Joaquin, and she should not be forced to marry a man she does not love—especially a man who is old enough to be her grandfather."

Ramon leaped to his feet, his features hard and rough as rimrock. "I have promised Rosita to Don Jose, and I am going to stand by my promise! Neither you nor your mother can stop me!" Breathing heavily, he looked at Dolores, who was weeping, then set his hot gaze on Reyes. "One day you will see the wisdom in my deed. Then you will crawl to me on your knees and beg my forgiveness!"

"I will do that the day the Texans give the Alamo back to Mehico!" said Reyes and stormed out the door.

The young man headed for the barn. He heard his father standing on the porch behind him. Ramon shouted, "Where are you going?"

Ignoring him, Reyes entered the barn and slipped the bridle on his horse. Ramon was still standing on the porch as Reyes draped the horse's back with a saddle blanket, then put the saddle in place and cinched it tight. He led the animal out of the barn. Looking toward the house, he saw that Ramon had vacated the porch and was nowhere in sight.

Reyes led the horse through the corral gate, closed it, and swung into the saddle. Nudging the animal forward, he headed for the road. As he neared the house, he heard his mother wail something he could not distinguish and suddenly Ramon burst through the back door, carrying his .41 caliber revolver. Face black with fury, he stepped off the porch, cocked the gun, and aimed it at Reyes. Dolores stood in the door, begging him to put down the gun.

Reyes drew rein as the black bore of the weapon lined on his chest. Ramon stepped close, holding the gun steady with both hands. "I asked you where you are going."

"You already know," Reyes retorted coldly.

"You are not going to be the one to tell your sister about this!"

"She has a right to know before she hears you tell her she is being sold for money!"

"You make it sound so cheap!"

"It is!"

Shaking the gun in a threatening manner, Ramon commanded, "Get off the horse! I will tell Rosita about it in my own way when she comes home."

"I don't like your way. I am going to warn her so she will know what is coming and have time to think about it."

"You will not get to the road. I will shoot you out of the saddle!"

Still at the door, Dolores screamed, "Ramon! Don't do it! Reyes, stay here! He will kill you!"

"She is right!" hissed Ramon. "I will kill you!"

Reyes looked down with cold eyes. "Does all that Gonzales money mean that much to you, Ramon Feliz?"

The anger Ramon was feeling now had his hands shaking. Keeping the muzzle lined on his son's chest, he replied, "I have been poor all my life. This is the one and only chance I have to change that. If you go and inform your sister about this, she will listen to you and make this thing more difficult. If I can talk to her first and explain it to her, she will see the wisdom of it and go along with it. Now get down off the horse."

"I am going to the Cristobal ranch to tell my sister what you have done. If you want to stop me, you will have to shoot me in the back." With that, Reyes put the horse into a trot and headed for the road.

He did not look back. He could hear his mother wailing and half expected a bullet to center his shoulder blades, but kept the horse moving at a steady pace. He still did not look back when he reached the road. Turning left on the road, he gouged the animal's sides, putting it into a full gallop.

At the Cristobal ranch, which was some ten miles west of Arizpe, Rosita Carmel Feliz was perched on the top pole of the corral fence, cheering Joaquin Murieta as he straddled a large gray roan. The horse bawled and snorted furiously as it bounded from fence to fence, doing its best to throw the unwanted weight from its back.

Several *vaqueros* stood at the fence waving their hats while whooping Joaquin. The pounding hooves of the horse lifted dust in the corral, adding to the excitement of the moment. Joaquin had few wild horses that fought him as long as the roan was doing.

While the action continued and Joaquin showed his stubbornness by staying on the bucking bronco's back, Rosita caught movement in her peripheral vision near the ranch house and turned around to get a good look. Instantly she recognized her brother on horseback and she knew Reyes had no doubt finished his day early. Often when this happened he would ride to wherever Joaquin was working just so he could watch him.

Rosita smiled and waved. Reyes waved back. She observed Joaquin and the gray roan in a battle of animal-against-man until her brother drew up and dismounted. Setting adoring eyes on him, she called above the sound of pounding hooves and shouting *vaqueros*, "Hello, big brother! Get off work early?"

"Yes."

"Must be wonderful to be so good at your job that you run out of horses to break before quitting time," she said in a joking manner. "Joaquin's got him a real fighter at the moment."

Looking past her, Reyes observed Murieta's hat fly off as the gray roan came down from a high jump and hit the ground solidly. "Looks like it."

Rosita knew her brother well. There was something in his dark eyes that conveyed a message. "Reyes, what is wrong?"

Knowing he could hide it no longer, the Mexican pulled his lips into a thin line. "Rosita, come aside from the noise and I will explain."

Wearing a western-style hat, white frilly blouse, split riding skirt, and feminine riding boots, Rosita let Reyes help her off the pole fence to the ground, then followed him till the noise was not a factor. "What is it?"

A solemn look etched itself on his handsome features. "I have something to tell you, Rosita, but I cannot tell you here. There is trouble at home."

Fear showed in her eyes. "Has something happened to Mama? Papa?"

"No, nothing like that, but it is very important that we talk. You must come home with me right now. I will explain the whole matter as we ride."

Looking over her shoulder toward the corral, Rosita said, "I must tell Joaquin that I am going. He should be getting control of this situation shortly. Can we wait a few more minutes?"

"Of course," he replied, taking her hand and walking her back in the direction of the corral.

They stood together and observed the gray roan slowly give up the fight. Reyes felt a warmth in his heart toward Joaquin. Rosita hadn't even married him yet, but there was already a brotherly relationship between them. Standing there beside her and watching Joaquin ride, he was more determined than ever to keep his father from going through with this selfish deed.

Within five minutes, Murieta was guiding the roan around the corral as if the animal had been a cow pony all of its adult life. The *vaqueros* cheered and applauded.

Spotting Rosita and Reyes standing together, Joaquin rode up to the fence. "Hello, Reyes. Too bad you were not here earlier. I would have let you break this one!"

Throwing palms up, Reyes replied, "Oh no! He is too wild for me. I am not in your league yet, Joaquin."

"Darling," spoke up Rosita, "I have to go home with Reyes right now. There is a problem."

Cocking his head, Joaquin asked, "Something serious?"

"Serious, but not life-threatening," Reyes told him.

"Your parents?" queried Joaquin. "Is someone ill?"

"No. Just an urgent family matter."

Joaquin looked at Reyes, then Rosita. "Do you want me to

come along? I have another bronco to break, but it could wait until morning."

Answering for his sister, Reyes said, "It is a very personal family matter, Joaquin. It is best that Rosita and I go alone."

Murieta swung from the saddle, handed the reins to a nearby vaquero, and climbed over the fence. Setting feet on the ground, he folded beautiful Rosita in his arms. "All right. If that is the way it must be." He kissed her on the forehead and the tip of her nose. "If there is anything I can do to help, all you have to do is whistle."

"Thank you," she said, giving him a warm smile. "At this point, I do not yet know what the problem is. Reyes is going to explain it while we ride."

Looking at Reyes, Joaquin said, "Rosita and I have plans to eat supper together at the Arizpe Café tonight. Shall I still plan on it?"

"It might be best that we contact you first," said Reyes. "This situation might take a little while to resolve."

Rosita eyed her brother quizzically.

"Whatever you say," said Joaquin. "You know where to find me."

Rosita rose up on her tiptoes and kissed his cheek. "I will see you later."

Brother and sister walked to their horses, mounted, and rode eastward, waving back at Joaquin Murieta. At first, Reyes led in a gallop, then when they were a half-mile from the ranch buildings, he slowed his horse to a walk, not wanting to have to talk to Rosita above the sound of pounding hooves.

"My imagination is going wild, Reyes. Please. What is wrong?"

Reyes's face was pallid as he brought up the name of Don Jose Gonzales and slowly explained the offer the rancher had made to their father. When the words sank in, there was both shock and anger stabbing through Rosita like bolts of lightning.

Yanking back on the reins, she stopped her horse. "But Papa cannot do this! It is wrong! All wrong!"

"I know," said Reyes. "I have told him so. So has Mama. She is totally against it."

"Not as much as I am!" hissed Rosita, jerking her horse's head around.

"What are you doing?"

"I am going back to tell Joaquin," came her quick reply. "He is involved in this. He has a right to know about it."

"Wait a minute!" said Reyes, pulling up beside her and laying a steady hand on her shoulder. "This thing will only cause real trouble between Joaquin and Papa. Joaquin will never need to know about it."

"What do you mean?"

"Papa was real angry at me, but you are a female. You are Papa's daughter. Maybe—well, at least there is a chance that Papa will change his mind about this horrible situation when he sees that you are going to refuse to go along with such a preposterous scheme. It is worth trying before we actually involve Joaquin."

Rosita thought about it, all the while fuming with anger. After a long moment, she looked at her brother and took a deep breath. "All right. As you say, it is worth trying. Let's go home."

Putting their mounts to a full gallop, they sped across the rolling hills. A quarter hour later, they turned their panting horses into the yard and dismounted at the back porch.

When they stepped into the kitchen, both parents were seated at the table. Rosita took one look at her mother's swollen eyes and the gray pallor of her face, then looked down at her father. Ramon stared up at her, his dark eyes steely.

Reyes looked around for the revolver, but it was nowhere in sight. His father no doubt had put it back in the drawer of a small cupboard that stood near the pantry. Reyes had not told Rosita of their father threatening him with the gun.

Rosita expected her father to speak to her, but instead, he ran his steely gaze to Reyes and ground out the words. "You've told her all about it, haven't you?"

"I told you I would."

"I should have pulled the trigger," came Ramon's cold words.

Rosita had moved to her mother and was holding her head close to her breast. She noticed the family Bible lying on the table. Dolores's face was pinched in mental anguish. Looking at her father, then her brother, Rosita said, "What is Papa talking about?"

Dolores spoke up. "Your father took his gun out of the drawer, cocked it, and pointed it at your brother just before Reyes came to tell you about this insane arrangement of his. He threatened to shoot him out of the saddle and kill him if he rode away."

Rosita stared at her father in a swell of disbelief and horror. "You—you would aim a gun at your own son and threaten to kill him?"

"Well, I didn't kill him, did I?"

"Papa!" gasped Rosita. "What has come over you? I have never seen you like this in all my life!"

"The devil has a hold on him," said Dolores. "He is filled with such a passion for money that he is willing to sacrifice his own daughter for it! I was just showing him that God's Holy Book says the love of money is the root of all evil."

"Bah!" said Ramon. "You have it all wrong, Mama! It is Rosita's future that I am thinking of!"

"And I say you lie!" countered Dolores, fearing her husband less with Reyes present.

Ramon pointed a stiff finger across the table at his wife. "You watch your mouth, woman!"

"Well," Dolores said, "if it is as you say, that it is Rosita's future you are concerned about, why not let her tell you what she thinks about this hellish pact you have made with the devil Don Jose Gonzales?"

"I will tell you what I think," spoke up Rosita, her black eyes flashing. "I think it stinks! No amount of money in the world could make me marry that evil old man, Papa! Do you hear me? He is evil! Joaquin and I have talked about the way he held my hand and flattered me at the church on Sunday. I also found him staring hungrily at me when we ate supper at his house last night. He is evil, I tell you!"

"Now, you listen to me, Rosita," said Ramon. "I am your fath—"

"You listen to me!" snapped Rosita, her words hissing like flying bullets. "I am in love with Joaquin, and you have already promised me to him! If it is as you say, that it is my future you are concerned about, then this discussion is over. I would rather live a normal life with the man I love, and have some financial struggle, than to live with your devil friend and be rich. Do you understand? So this discussion is over."

Ramon jumped to his feet, his face livid with rage. "It is not over, Rosita! I am your father, and I have a right to change my mind. I was mistaken to promise you to that broncobuster Murieta! He will never make you a good living. I want you to have money."

"I don't want money, Papa!" Rosita half-screamed. "All I want is to marry Joaquin and bear his children. If you push this any further, you are admitting that it is yourself you are thinking about and not me!"

"All right!" said Ramon. "So I am also thinking of your mother and me! Maybe we deserve some easier living!"

"Speak for yourself, Ramon," said Dolores. "I am not asking for any more than we have had. I am perfectly happy."

Ramon bit his tongue to keep from an outburst that would indeed prove that he wanted to quit working in the silver mine and live in luxury on the Gonzales ranch with only light chores to do. "Rosita, you owe it to your parents to make things easier for us. I am commanding you to marry Don Jose!"

Rosita bristled. Her teeth showed in an angry grimace as she said heatedly, "You cannot make me marry him, Papa! I flat refuse! Do you hear me? I will not marry that evil old man!"

Reyes, who had held his peace for several minutes, joined the argument, taking his sister's part. It became more and more heated as Ramon reminded the family that in Mexico the father had all authority. He was demanding that Rosita marry Don Jose Gonzales and there was to be no resistance on her part. This served to make the argument hotter.

CHAPTER SEVEN

At the Gonzales ranch, young Don Miguel watched Ramon Feliz mount up and ride across the hills, heading for the gate. Don Jose stood on the porch of the ranch house and kept his eyes on Feliz until horse and rider passed from view.

As Don Jose turned to enter the house, he saw his son looking at him from where he stood at the corral. Smiling, he motioned for Don Miguel to come to him.

A cold sensation settled in Don Miguel's stomach as he strode toward the house. He figured he was about to learn what his father's strange behavior toward Rosita Feliz was all about. He feared that he already knew. If it was what he was thinking, Don Jose would have to talk to Rosita's father to accomplish it. Ramon had just been at the house.

As Gonzales approached the porch, Don Jose pulled a cigar from inside his coat and stuck it in his mouth. Grinning and speaking around it, he said, "Well, my boy, how would you like to hear some good news?"

"About what?" asked Don Miguel, playing dumb.

"You asked me about something I had up my sleeve concerning Rosita Feliz, didn't you?"

Don Miguel's cold stomach grew colder. "Yes."

"Well, beautiful Rosita is about to become your stepmother! Ramon was just here and promised her hand to me in marriage. What do you think of that?"

"You want my honest opinion?" Nausea was being added to the iciness in Don Miguel's stomach.

"Of course. She is the most beautiful creature that ever graced this earth, and you know it." Don Jose struck a match and put it to the cigar. While he puffed it into life, his son stared at him. Looking at the younger man through a cloud of blue smoke, he said, "Well? Let's hear your honest opinion."

"It is absurd."

"Absurd?" Don Jose's eyes narrowed. "How many men my age have the opportunity to marry someone as young as she? And how many men any age get to marry a woman so exquisitely enchanting?"

"Father," Don Miguel said in a tone of disgust, "you are sixty-six years old! Rosita is only seventeen! Such a marriage would be nothing but miserable, even if there was no Joaquin Murieta to take into consideration. And besides that, even if she were not engaged to Joaquin, she would never marry you!"

Don Jose regarded his son with a hard glare. He jerked the cigar from his mouth and let the full blast of his temper thunder out. "That's what you think, young man. Rosita will marry me!"

"If you think your money will buy Rosita away from Joaquin, you are sadly mistaken, Father."

"You are forgetting something, Don Miguel," clipped the old man, ramming the cigar back between his teeth. "This is Mehico. Rosita is bound by Mehican tradition. She will obey her father and marry whom he tells her."

"Father, you do not know what you are doing. You saw Joaquin Murieta in action at the fandango. When he is angry, he is like a maddened bull! This thing will set him off. You are asking for real trouble. Joaquin loves Rosita very much. You are going to have a fight on your hands like you have never seen!"

With a wave of his hand, Don Jose retorted blandly, "There are men on this ranch who can handle the likes of him."

Don Miguel wiped a hand across his mouth and mustache and tilted his head downward. "You do not know the foolishness of that statement, Father. Joaquin could take on five of your men at one time and break all of their necks."

Don Jose shrugged his shoulders. "Then I will send twenty men to handle him. But I think you are wrong, my boy. I seriously doubt that there is going to be any trouble from your friend Murieta."

"And you base that assumption on—?"

"Every man has his price. I think I can guess Murieta's. He is poor, right?"

"Compared to us, yes."

"He also loves horses, doesn't he?"

"Very much."

"Well, then, as a gesture of good faith I will give your friend Joaquin Murieta five thousand pesos and one of my best Arabian stallions." He chuckled. "You watch. When he hears of this, he will forget his infatuation for Rosita and find himself another woman."

"Father, you have misjudged my friend Joaquin. I can guarantee you that he will not give Rosita up for any price. He will die first."

Don Jose's black eyes seemed to turn into hard bits of marble. A cruel sneer curled his mouth. "Then that is what he will have to do. I am in love with Rosita too. I want her, Don Miguel. And you know I always get what I want."

Don Miguel said no more. Pivoting, he left his father standing on the porch and walked toward the barn. When he heard the front door of the ranch house slam shut, he broke into a run. Dashing into the barn, he saddled his horse and rode across the lush green hills toward the gate.

Less than a half-hour later, he skidded his panting, lathered horse to a halt at the rear of the Murieta house in Arizpe, where he found Joaquin Sr. and his other two sons working on a wagon.

The three men looked up with surprise at Don Miguel's sudden entrance into the yard. Sliding from the saddle, Don Miguel asked, "Is Joaquin home yet?"

"No, he isn't," replied the father. "He will probably be here within the next hour or so. Is something wrong? You seem in a big hurry."

"I need to see him immediately," responded young Gonzales. "It is very important."

"He is at the Cristobal ranch all this week," volunteered Claudio Murieta. "If you head that direction, you will probably meet him on his way home."

"Thank you," said Don Miguel, swinging back into the saddle. "I will do just that."

Antonio stepped up close. "Is there trouble of some kind?"

The horse beneath Don Miguel Gonzales was Arabian and high spirited. It was eager to run again. Holding the reins tight as the animal pranced about, he replied, "Yes, there is trouble, Antonio, but the first person to know about it has to be Joaquin. If he wants his family to know about it, he can tell you." With that, he let the horse have its head and galloped away.

At the Cristobal ranch, Joaquin Murieta was kneeling at a large water trough outside the corral, washing the dust from his face and hair as Don Miguel came galloping in. Rising to his feet and shaking water from his wavy, coal black hair, Joaquin smoothed his hair down and dropped his wide-brimmed hat on his head. Instantly he saw the look of concern in Don Miguel's eyes.

Don Miguel slid groundward. "Joaquin, there is a serious problem."

The *vaqueros* had vacated the corral area, and Joaquin was alone. With a tone of contempt for his father's foolishness, Don Miguel told Joaquin the arrangement that had been made between Don Jose Gonzales and Ramon Feliz.

As the words came out in rapid speed, Joaquin listened, staring incredulously at his friend. Don Miguel told him of his father's plan to offer him five thousand pesos and an Arabian stallion in return for quietly backing away and letting him marry Rosita as arranged by her father.

By this time, wrath was tearing at Joaquin's handsome face. His voice was stern and uncompromising. "I will never let this happen! Ramon promised her to me and she is going to be my wife!"

Worry etched itself clearly on Don Miguel's swarthy features. "Joaquin," he said shakily, "I am your friend, and I have come to tell you of this wicked thing because I wanted you to know about it as soon as possible. I knew you would be angry, and I cannot blame you in the least. I told my father that you would fight him, and that he was asking for real trouble. I…I can only ask that you not harm him in any way in this battle. He is wrong—dead wrong—but he is still my father."

Joaquin's mind flashed to Don Jose's subtle improprieties toward Rosita, and their discussion about it. What they had tried to excuse as the old man's loneliness was actually covetousness and lust. Though his blood was running hot toward the vile man, he laid a hand on his friend's shoulder. "I understand your feelings, Don Miguel. You and I are very close. If it was any other man who had done this thing, he would suffer serious consequences…but because of our relationship I will not raise a hand against your father. But I will do what I have to to keep this diabolic arrangement from being fulfilled."

"I cannot blame you for this at all," replied Don Miguel, "but when you show resistance, my father will send men to kill you. He has already made that threat, should you try to stand in the way."

Joaquin thought about it for a moment. "If your father did that, my natural reaction would be to kill those men, then go after the man who sent them. I have been involved in more than enough violence already in my life, but I know myself well enough to tell you that if I stayed here, I would shed blood. So…I have no choice. I must take Rosita and leave Sonora."

Face pinched in anguish, Don Miguel said, "No, Joaquin. Sonora is your home. It is not right that you—"

Young Gonzales' words were cut off by the thunder of hooves as Claudio and Antonio Murieta came riding in and drew rein. Dismounting in a cloud of dust, they moved to their brother, concern showing on their faces. "Don Miguel told us there is some kind of trouble," said Claudio. "We decided to come because you might need us."

"There is fire in your eyes, Joaquin," said Antonio. "What is the trouble?"

Breathing heavily with anger, Joaquin told the story to his brothers. Claudio and Antonio were visibly upset about the situation. They grew more agitated when they learned that Joaquin was planning to take Rosita and leave Sonora.

"No," said Claudio with a brittle snap. "This is wrong! We must stand against Don Jose and fight him!"

"That's right," agreed Antonio. "I realize Don Jose is Don Miguel's father, but he is wrong in what he is doing. He must be stopped!"

"This will only cause bloodshed, my brothers," said Joaquin. "I have promised Don Miguel I will not harm his father." He paused a moment, then added, "Possibly if we go to the source of this problem, we can solve it without a bloody fight and without Rosita and me having to leave Sonora."

"But Don Jose is the source of the problem, Joaquin," said Claudio.

"Not really," countered Joaquin. "If Ramon will withdraw his promise to Don Jose like he has withdrawn it to me, there is no more problem. Don Jose has great respect for the customs of our country. Without her father's consent, he would never take Rosita for his wife."

"That is, as long as Ramon is alive," said Don Miguel. "The way my father is acting, I do not think he would stop at anything to marry Rosita."

"You mean your father would actually put Ramon to death?" asked Joaquin.

"I would not put such a thing past him," replied Don Miguel.

"Well, I guess we will have to take this bull by one horn at a time," said Joaquin. "First, I will go and try to reason with Rosita's father. If I can get him to withdraw his promise to Don Jose, we will then deal with Don Jose before he tries to kill Ramon. If, however, Ramon refuses, I cannot fight him, either. No matter how wrong he is to do what he has done, he is still Rosita's father. I cannot in good conscience bring myself to fight him. I will just take Rosita and leave."

"And what about Don Jose, Joaquin?" asked Claudio. "He just might come after you with a vengeance no matter which way this goes with Ramon. What then?"

Joaquin rubbed the back of his neck. "Then I will definitely have to take Rosita and go."

"Where to?" asked Antonio.

"California," came the quick answer.

"California? You mean because Carlos is there?"

"That is part of the reason. Certainly I would like to see our brother again. But as all of us know, gold has just been discovered in northern California. Maybe I will just go and claim my share of it."

The three men rode with Joaquin as he whipped his horse into a gallop and went to Arizpe. When they dismounted in front of the Feliz house, they could hear loud voices coming from inside. The loudest was that of Rosita Feliz.

Looking at the others, Joaquin said, "It sounds as if my Rosita is putting up some very stiff resistance."

"That is for sure," said Claudio. "From what we just heard, she is telling her father off in no uncertain terms!"

As they walked toward the open front door, Don Miguel said, "I think I hear Señora Feliz weeping."

"And it sounds like Reyes is trying to get in some words on Rosita's behalf," spoke up Antonio.

Just as they stepped up on the porch, they heard Ramon swear at Rosita, and she began sobbing. Joaquin had planned to knock, but the sound of Rosita's piteous sobs was enough to draw him through the door in one quick thrust. His brothers and Don Miguel were on his heels.

All eyes inside the house swerved to Joaquin as he burst into the parlor. When Rosita saw him, she sobbed his name and threw herself into his arms.

"Nobody invited you in here!" said Ramon. "Get out!"

"The only way I get out is to take Rosita with me!" Joaquin held her tight. "Señor Feliz, I have always respected you as an honest, hard-working man, a man of your word. What is this I hear that you have gone back on your word in regard to Rosita and me? In the presence of my parents, you promised me her hand in marriage. She and I are in love and want a life together. Do you not care about her happiness?"

Ramon eyed him with sharp hostility. "Her happiness is exactly what I am thinking of! When she marries Don Jose, she will be rich for the rest of her life." Shifting his hard gaze to young Gonzales, he said, "Isn't that so, Don Miguel? I assume you know that I have changed my mind about Rosita marrying this broncobuster and have promised her to your father."

Don Miguel thumbed his hat to the back of his head. "It is true that if Rosita married my father, she would be rich for the rest of her life, Ramon, but somehow I have a hard time thinking of a girl a year younger than me as my mother. And it is also difficult to see why you would want a man twenty years your senior as a son-in-law."

"It doesn't matter about sensible things, Don Miguel," said Reyes. "All my father can see is pesos. Lots and lots of pesos."

"Not for myself, Don Miguel," said Ramon. "It is for my daughter's happiness."

Dolores started to say something, but Rosita beat her to it. "Papa, I have told you repeatedly for the last two hours that money does not buy happiness! If I cannot be married to Joaquin, I do not want to live!" Drawing a deep, shuddering breath, she bared her teeth. "And I promise you, Papa, that if you make me marry that disgusting old man, I will kill myself! Then what will happen to your house on the Gonzales ranch? Do you think Don Jose will let you live there and keep all of those sugarcoated promises he made to you? Hah! With me dead, you and Mama would be thrown off the ranch and left with nothing!"

Joaquin squeezed Rosita tight. "You are not going to marry Don Jose, darling. You are going to marry me." Setting his glittering black eyes on Ramon Feliz, he added, "And your father's greed is not going to keep us from being married."

Deep smoldering wrath burst into flame within Ramon Feliz. He could see the riches that would be his slipping through his fingers. Blind with rage and thinking of nothing but removing Joaquin Murieta from the picture, he left the chair where he sat, and pushing past Don Miguel, who stood near the door that led to the kitchen, he went to the small cupboard that stood near the pantry and jerked open the drawer.

In the parlor, Dolores heard the familiar sound of the drawer scraping and cried, "Stop him! He went in there to get his gun!"

Claudio Murieta bounded past Don Miguel and bolted toward Ramon, who was turning from the cupboard, gun in hand. Ramon sidestepped Claudio, cracked him on the head with the gun, and headed for the parlor. He took only two steps when Don Miguel closed in, smashed him with a rock-hard fist, and sent him to the floor, dazed and lying flat on his back. The rest of them came in as Don Miguel was taking the revolver from Ramon's curled fingers.

Joaquin, Rosita, and Antonio stepped around Ramon and dashed to Claudio, who was up on one knee, holding his hand to a cut on his temple. Rosita poured water from a bucket into a pan and reached into a drawer for a cloth as Joaquin hoisted his injured brother on to a chair at the table. Rosita immediately began pressing the wet cloth against the cut, saying it was not deep.

In the parlor, Dolores was kneeling beside her husband, who was rolling his head and moaning. There was blood at the corner of his mouth. Seconds later, he sat up, looking around. Eyeing Don Miguel, he growled, "You are not like your father, young man. He has good sense."

"Don Miguel showed good sense in knocking you down and

taking the gun away from you, Ramon," Dolores said pointedly. "You are the one not showing good sense!"

Ignoring her, Ramon scrambled to his feet and set his hot glare on Joaquin Murieta, who stood in the kitchen. Pointing an accusing finger at him, he spat blood and saliva as he said, "I'll kill you, Joaquin! I'll kill you! You are ruining my opportunity for riches!"

Reyes jumped in front of him. "That is exactly it, Papa! You are not thinking of Rosita's happiness in the least. You are only thinking of your own. You just said it, yourself!"

Wiping blood from his mouth with his sleeve, Ramon ignored his son. "If I do not kill you, Don Jose will!"

Dolores broke into sobs. In a fit of rage, Ramon wheeled and bolted outside, swearing at the top of his voice. Rosita put her arms around her mother and held her close. Above Dolores's weeping, Joaquin said, "Rosita, we must leave Mehico. I cannot bring myself to fight with your father, nor Don Miguel's father."

Rosita nodded silently, then led Dolores to a chair and sat her down, speaking soft words of comfort to her. When the sobbing eased, Joaquin knelt down and looked into Dolores's tear-stained face. "Mama Dolores, I am so sorry for what has happened."

"It is not your fault, Joaquin. You did nothing to bring this on. It is Ramon's fault. Somehow he has let the devil get control of him."

"I have no choice but to take Rosita and leave here."

Dolores sniffed. "I understand. It will be hard to see her go, but I agree it will be best. Where will you go?"

"California. As you know, my brother Carlos is there. I will find him. Maybe he can help me find a job. I might try some gold prospecting too."

"California is so far," Dolores said, her voice quaking.

"I know," nodded Joaquin, reaching up to take hold of Rosita's hand. Looking at the beautiful Rosita, he said to Dolores, "I will take care of her."

"I know you will. How soon will you leave?"

"It is best if we leave tonight." Flicking a glance at Don Miguel, Joaquin said, "This will give us a head start in case your father decides to send some of his men to kill me and bring Rosita back. He will not find out until some time tomorrow that we have gone. We can be many miles from here by then."

Don Miguel stepped close. "I hate to see the two of you go that distance alone, Joaquin. It will be dangerous."

Claudio and Antonio both agreed, saying Joaquin and Rosita should not go until they find other Mexicans making the trip. They would be much safer traveling with a group of people.

"If we wait till whenever that will be, I will have a confrontation with Don Jose," said Joaquin. "I cannot fight the father of my best friend."

"Joaquin, I will travel with you," spoke up Don Miguel. "Then if my father sends men to overtake you, I will be there to persuade them not to do it."

"No," said Joaquin. "They would not listen to you. It would only make matters worse between you and your father. I cannot let you do it. I will carry plenty of weapons and ammunition. Rosita and I will be fine."

Joaquin's brothers and Reyes Feliz volunteered to go along, but Joaquin knew if they did, they would lose their jobs. He assured them that he could take care of both Rosita and himself.

With that issue settled, Joaquin stood up and said to Rosita, "In order for us to properly travel to California together, we should be married before we leave."

A soft light came alive in Rosita's dark eyes. "I agree, darling. Do you suppose we can get Padre Mendosa to perform the ceremony on such short notice?"

"When we explain it, I am sure he will."

"This is the right thing to do," said Dolores. "I had such big plans for my little girl's wedding, but I would rather see it this way than to have violence between Joaquin and Don Jose."

"Well, we had best be getting ready," Rosita said. "I will pack a few articles of clothing. It will not take me long."

Moving close to the young couple, Don Miguel laid a hand on each of them. "You will need good horses for this trip. I have a couple of Arabian geldings that are hardy and reliable. I will give them to you as wedding presents."

Joaquin and Rosita thanked him sincerely. Don Miguel turned toward the door and said, "I will ride like the wind and bring them back. You must be on your way as soon as possible."

"Bring them to our house, Don Miguel," said Joaquin. "I will go right now and make arrangements with Padre Mendosa, then come and get Rosita. We will pack the horses at our house where my weapons are, then go to the church for the wedding. That way, as soon as the vows are said, we can mount up and ride. It is best that we put as much distance as possible between ourselves and the Gonzales ranch tonight."

Don Miguel dashed out the door, saying he would be back within an hour.

Mother and daughter embraced. Rosita whispered, "I am sorry that it has turned out this way, Mama."

"Me too, honey," said Dolores, "but it is out of our hands. You two are so right for each other. I know God will take care of you."

Claudio said, "Joaquin, Antonio and I will head for the house now and make up a travel pack for you. We will also break the news gently to our parents that you and Rosita are leaving tonight and that there will be a wedding first."

"All right," agreed Joaquin. "While Rosita is packing her things, I will go see Padre Mendosa."

"And I will stay here and handle Papa in case he comes back," said Reyes.

"That is a good idea," said Joaquin. "If he does and you have to tell him what we're doing, don't let him ride to the Gonzales ranch and tell Don Jose. Once we are married, things will be different, but the more time that passes before Don Jose learns of this, the better."

"I will do my best," nodded Reyes, "even if I have to hog-tie him."

Just after darkness had fallen that night, Joaquin Murieta and Rosita Carmel Feliz stood before the priest in the little adobe church building and took their vows. In attendance were Joaquin's parents and brothers, Dolores Feliz, Reyes Feliz, and Don Miguel Gonzales. Ramon Feliz had not returned to his house since storming away in a fit of anger.

The wedding ceremony had a gray pall over it because of the unpleasant circumstances, but the couple managed to show a degree of happiness when they were pronounced husband and wife. Their kiss was long and sweet. Congratulations were offered by those in attendance and many tears were shed. Joaquin told all of them that one day he and Rosita would return, at least for a visit, but they would have to wait until there was no danger of a bloody confrontation with Don Jose. Padre Mendosa bid the couple good-bye, saying he would pray for them.

Following the newlyweds outside to where the two Arabian geldings were tied at hitching posts, the well-wishers watched the groom lift his bride onto her new horse. She had dressed herself in a split skirt for comfortable riding.

Joaquin then strapped on a double-holstered gun belt and checked the loads in the two rifles that rode in boots on his saddle. Reyes Feliz stood beside his mother and put an arm around her shoulder as Joaquin and Rosita rode away and were quickly swallowed by the darkness. No one in the party moved until the sound of the pounding hoofbeats died out.

The two new mothers-in-law embraced and wept together for a few minutes, then everybody headed for home.

When Dolores Feliz and her son walked in their house, they found a grim-faced Ramon waiting. He was seated at the kitchen table, cracking his knuckles. "Where have you two been? Where is Rosita?"

Mother and son looked at each other, then Dolores said, "She is with Joaquin."

"Where did they go?"

"For a ride."

Ramon's features crimsoned by the light of the lantern that hung over the table. "For a ride where?"

Dolores sat down at the opposite end of the table wearily. "Newlyweds do not ordinarily tell anyone where they are going for their honeymoon."

Ramon jumped to his feet, anger pulsating in his face. "Honeymoon! Are you telling me they got married tonight?"

"That is correct. It is too late now for you and Don Jose to complete your little scheme."

Scowling, Ramon ran his gaze between mother and son. "I want to know where they went!"

Reyes said, "It doesn't make any difference where they went, Papa. Joaquin and Rosita are husband and wife now. You might as well simmer down and forget it. The Don Jose thing is over."

Ramon swore and banged his fist on the table. Dolores jumped and blinked at him. Shaking his shoulders and showing his teeth in an angry grimace, Ramon exploded, "I want to know where they went, do you hear me?"

Face pinched, Dolores looked at Reyes. With their eyes, they agreed to keep it their secret.

Ramon read it. His features truculent and purple, he turned toward the door, grumbling under his breath. He bowled his way out of the house with his wife and son looking on in disgust.

Stomping angrily to the barn, Ramon saddled his horse and galloped out of the yard. Guiding the animal by the dim light of the stars, he headed for the Gonzales ranch. Ramon had an idea where his daughter and Joaquin were going. Joaquin had a brother in California. The man would bet his last peso that was where they were headed. He would inform Don Jose of the situation. Don Jose would send some of his hard-bitten men to track the couple down. They would kill Joaquin and bring Rosita back.

Ramon smiled to himself as the night breeze brushed his face. With Joaquin dead, Rosita would come to her senses and see the wisdom of her father's agreement with Don Jose. She would marry the wealthy rancher and Ramon Feliz's dream of financial security would be realized.

CHAPTER EIGHT

The newlyweds picked their way steadily through the dark night, taking a road that would lead them out of the Real de Bayareca and eventually to the rugged Camino del Diablo, the dangerous and bleak trail that ran across western Mexico just south of the Arizona border. At the extreme southeast corner of California, they would pick up another trail that would lead them northward to Los Angeles, the "city of angels."

About three o'clock, a slender moon put in an appearance. Its added light in the star-studded sky helped them to see well enough to pick up their pace. As they rode, Joaquin said, "Don Jose will find out sometime today what has happened. I do not think any of those who know we are headed for California will tell him. Certainly Don Miguel will not."

"How long do you think it will take Don Jose to figure it out for himself?"

"Not too long. He is plenty smart. If he doesn't already know it, he will probe until he learns that I have a brother in California. That will be his clue. But…if it takes him a day or two to figure it out, we will be far enough ahead of his pack of wolves to keep them from catching up to us."

"I hope so," said Rosita with feeling. "I don't want you to have to fight them. I hope your days of violence are over forever."

"I would love to know they were," Joaquin replied. "I don't want to have to fight anybody again. More than anything, I don't want to ever have to take a human life again."

"I am so glad you feel that way, darling. But I know you, and I know how hard you fight to protect me. I love you for that…but I am praying that such a moment will never come."

Climbing out of the Real de Bayareca, they soon found the Camino del Diablo. When they reached the crest of a long, steep slope, they reined in and gave the horses a chance to blow. Looking down over the great sweeping valley they had always called home,

Joaquin Murieta and his new wife felt a touch of sadness. The deep shadows in the valley cast by the dim light of a partial moon and millions of twinkling stars seemed to beckon them back.

"It is hard to leave here, darling," said Rosita.

"Yes. But to avoid bloodshed, we have no choice. One day we will be able to return and see our loved ones."

"Only when Don Jose is dead, I am afraid."

"I am sorry, my sweet. I know it is difficult for you to leave your mother and Reyes."

"Yes. And…and if Papa was the man he used to be, it would be difficult to leave him too. I still love him, Joaquin."

"Of course you do. Maybe some day the two of you can be reconciled."

"I will pray to that end."

Joaquin clucked to his horse and put him in motion. "We had best keep moving."

The westward trail was an arduous one, leading the travelers up and down steep slopes amid tall timber and huge rock formations. The air in the high altitude was cold, and they had to stop long enough to pull jackets from their packs. After putting them on, they embraced, enjoyed a long, lingering kiss, then mounted once again and pushed on.

It was almost dawn when Joaquin sensed that his bride was growing weary, and in spite of her wool jacket, she was chilled. Halting at the pinnacle of a rocky peak, he said, "I think we should rest for a while. You are tired and cold. I will build a fire. You can sit by it and get warm while you are resting. We will cook breakfast, and fill our stomachs for the long day ahead."

"Do we really have that much time?"

"We have to rest periodically, or we will run out of strength to keep going. The horses need to rest too."

"But if Don Jose sends his men, we will not be moving away from them."

"They will not even begin to come after us until much later today," he assured her. "We will have a good head start."

Halfway down the slope, they came upon a level spot that was secluded by heavy brush. Rosita sat on a fallen tree with her back to a huge boulder while Joaquin gathered wood and built a fire. When the flames roared and gave off sufficient heat, Rosita moved close, opened her jacket, and let the welcome heat drive away her chill.

"I need to gather some more wood. You get nice and warm, and I will be back in a few minutes."

Dawn was a gray hint over the peaks to the east as Joaquin's search for short lengths of wood took him out of the clearing and into the dense timber. As he carried an armload back to the fire, Joaquin Murieta's sixth sense came alive within him. Somehow he knew they were not alone. Dropping the wood on the fire, he bent close to Rosita. "I think we have company."

"What do you mean? Did you see something? Hear something?"

"No. It is just my instincts. I can feel a presence. I am going to circle the area and check it out. Do not worry. You will never be out of my sight."

Moving back into the shadows of the forest, Joaquin flattened himself against a tree and listened. Only seconds later, he heard the distinct shuffle of boots on the soft ground. He looked in the direction of the sound and saw four figures moving stealthily toward the clearing. Keeping Rosita in view, Joaquin shifted positions in order to follow the movements of the men. He was sure they had stashed their horses some distance away so they would not alert the travelers by the noises of their animals.

As the shadowed figures moved toward the spot where Rosita sat by the fire, Joaquin knew they were Don Jose's men. Somehow Don Jose had learned about their departure shortly after they left and had figured out the direction of their flight. He would let them get within the firelight before making his move.

At the fire, Rosita Murieta peered into the darkness about her, spooked by Joaquin's uncanny senses. Her head bobbed sharply when she beheld the four dusky figures emerge from the surrounding darkness and move toward her, guns drawn.

"You will stay right there and be very quiet!" hissed the one in the lead. "Where is Joaquin?"

Instantly Rosita knew these were Don Jose's men. How had they learned of their leaving, and how had they caught up to them so quickly? A sharp pang of fear stabbed Rosita's heart. Where was Joaquin? Why had he allowed them to get so close to her?

"I asked you where your husband is, Rosita!"

From his place in the deep shadows, Joaquin recognized the leader as Rubin Montalban. He had seen him and the others many times while visiting Don Miguel at the Gonzales ranch. Though the other three faces were familiar, he did not know their names. As Montalban spoke sharply to Rosita while looking around the area, Joaquin raised his gun and took careful aim.

Standing over Rosita at the fire, Montalban growled, "You might as well tell us where he is, Rosita. We are taking you back to marry Don Jose. The quicker we get this over with, the better it will be for all of us."

Suddenly a shot roared from the gloom and the gun flew out of Montalban's hand. The impact of the bullet on the heavy metal sent slivers of pain up the Mexican's arm.

Quickly the other three brought their revolvers around and fired into the surrounding darkness at the sound of Joaquin's gun. Another shot blossomed from the wall of darkness and one of the Mexicans went down, dropping his weapon and clutching his shoulder.

Rubin Montalban dived for his revolver and picked it up as the other two were blazing away in the direction of the second shot. Montalban took one look at the weapon by the firelight and realized that the impact of the bullet had damaged the cylinder. The gun was ruined. It would never fire again. Turning angry eyes toward the two men still on their feet, he shouted, "Kill him, you fools! Kill him!"

"We cannot see him!" snapped back one of them. "He keeps moving!"

"He is like a ghost! We do not know where he will be next!"

Abruptly, from a spot halfway around the circle of light, Joaquin appeared with two smoking revolvers. "All right, you two! Drop your guns!"

The two Mexicans threw their guns down as if they had suddenly turned red-hot.

As he moved in on them, Joaquin saw the wounded man on the ground make a grab for the gun he had dropped. Joaquin's left-hand revolver roared, hitting the man's gun and sending it scooting away out of reach.

Rosita dashed to Joaquin and stood by him, folding the jacket tightly around her.

"It is all right, my sweet," Joaquin said. "Rubin, you had better see to your wounded compadre, there."

The bleeding Mexican struggled to his feet, holding his shoulder. "It is not bad, Rubin. Just nicked me enough to make me drop my gun."

Black eyes flashing, Rosita said, "You only received a nick because my husband intended it that way. He can shoot the wing off a fly at fifty paces. You had best be thankful he did not kill you."

"How did you learn of our leaving so soon?" Joaquin said to Montalban.

"Rosita's father arrived home after the wedding. Neither Dolores nor Reyes would tell him where you had gone. He only knew that you had gotten married and left. He remembered that your brother lives in California, so Don Jose sent us after you."

"Sent you to kill me and bring Rosita back, right?"

"Right."

"Well, you failed, Rubin. I could shoot all four of you down where you stand, but I have no desire to kill you. However, no one is going to take my Rosita from me. Not you. Not anyone who looks like you. I am going to allow you to go to your horses and ride back to Don Jose. You tell him if he sends you or anyone else, I will not be so lenient next time. I will kill whoever it is."

Fear showed on all four faces. Montalban swallowed hard. "Joaquin, we cannot go back without her. Don Jose will have us shot."

"Then go somewhere else," said Murieta tartly. "But do it now. Get on your horses and ride."

The one with the bleeding shoulder looked at Joaquin with wide eyes. "Without our guns?"

Murieta looked at him as if he had not heard him correctly. "You are joking, aren't you?"

"Of course not. Certainly you aren't going to make us ride these mountains unarmed!"

Joaquin shook his head. "If I let you have your guns, you would just sneak up on me and shoot me in the back. Do you really think I am dumb enough to let you do that? I said get on your horses and ride. Do not let me see your ugly faces again. Next time I will lose my temper."

"Joaquin," argued Rubin Montalban, "there are brigands on this trail and wild animals. If either would decide to attack us, we would not have a chance."

"What kind of chance were you going to give me, Rubin?" asked Joaquin. "You followed us with the full intention of killing me. You just admitted that. Were you going to give me some kind of sporting chance?"

Montalban did not answer.

"Joaquin," said Rosita, "what if they have more guns in their saddlebags or carry rifles in their saddle boots? They will still follow us and shoot you in the back."

"They don't."

"How can you be sure?"

"Two reasons, my sweet. One: I know *vaqueros*. They never carry rifles, and they always carry only one sidearm. Two: if they had more guns, they would not be so afraid as you see them."

"Maybe it is an act, just so you will think they do not have more guns."

Joaquin smiled. "No. These hombres are too stupid to do that."

"Stupid!" said Montalban. "Why do you say we are stupid?"

"You came in here knowing I had to be somewhere in the vicinity, yet you let me get the drop on you. Like I said, you are stupid."

One of the others spoke to their leader. "Rubin, you must persuade him to let us have our guns. Swear to him that we will not follow and try to shoot him in the back."

The fear Montalban was feeling showed in his dark eyes as he looked at Joaquin. "Please, Joaquin. You must give us back our guns." Remembering, then, that his own was out of commission, he changed it to, "I mean, give them back their guns!"

"Swear to him!" the same man urged.

Raising his right hand, Rubin said, "Joaquin, I swear to you on the grave of my dead mother—if you will give them their guns, we will not follow you. Have mercy! It is extremely dangerous for us to be riding in this rugged country without weapons."

"If you do not do as I tell you immediately, I will take your horses and you will be walking in this rugged country without weapons!"

Glumly, Rubin Montalban looked at his companions. "It is of

no use. Let us go."

Heads low and shoulders slumped, the four Mexicans left the clearing and disappeared in the forest. Joaquin said to Rosita, "I wonder if they will have the courage to return to Don Jose without you."

"I doubt it. They will probably stay far away from the valley at least until they hear that Don Jose is dead."

Joaquin quickly reloaded both revolvers, slipped them into their holsters, then took his bride in his arms and kissed her. "Some way to spend a honeymoon."

Reaching up and stroking his face tenderly, Rosita said, "I would rather spend this kind of honeymoon with you than the horrible nightmare I would have had with that old man."

Joaquin kissed her again. "We will have our breakfast, then I want you to lie down and get a couple of hours' sleep. Since we have taken care of Don Jose's henchmen, we do not have to hurry anymore."

The Murietas ate breakfast together with Joaquin keeping wary eyes and ears for anything unusual around them. Though he had sent the four Mexicans away, he still was not sure they had seen the last of them. And even if they had, there were still the brigands and wild animals as Rubin had said.

While Joaquin kept watch, Rosita took a three-hour nap. Seeing that she was refreshed, Joaquin helped her into the saddle and they continued their journey.

For the next two days, they moved slowly through the rough, broken mountain country, stopping periodically to rest and fill their canteens. The going was rough as they rode down into rocky arroyos, crossed long stretches of hard-topped mesa, and threaded through heavy timber on steep mountainsides. On the third day, they dropped down out of the mountains onto parched desert land.

The temperature was much hotter on the desert, and they were on foot at times, wading through ankle-deep sand while leading the horses. Powdery dust rose in their faces and heat waves shimmered before their eyes in the distance. Around them grew creosote bush and cactus, along with long-stemmed ocotillo. From time to time, small desert creatures skittered about them, leaving fresh tracks in the wind-blown sand.

At one point, when they had led the horses through a mile-wide sea of sand, they stopped and took long drinks of their canteens. Rosita wiped the back of her hand across her mouth and running her gaze about them, said, "I can see why they named this trail the Camino del Diablo. Only the devil would be comfortable here."

Joaquin agreed as he hoisted his wife into her saddle. They rode for several more hours, and as the sun was setting directly ahead of them, Rosita saw the uneven rooftops of a town nestled in a low spot. "Darling! Look! A town!"

"Mm-hmm. This is the first of several towns we will pass through on our journey. It is called Carmel."

"Carmel! Do you suppose they named it after me? My middle name, I mean?"

Joaquin laughed. "Of course they did! Maybe someday they will name a town in California after you."

"Oh no. I have a feeling that my husband will become famous in California. It is for him they will name a town!"

Joaquin laughed again. It felt good to laugh. It was even more wonderful to hear his Rosita laugh once more. The anguish and misery Rosita's father and Don Jose had caused in Sonora would soon be forgotten as they ventured into California and a new life.

Carmel was a small town with a tumbledown stable, food store, dry good store, café, and saloon. The stable and the two stores stood directly across the town's unnamed main street from the café and saloon. Dark-skinned people along the street gave them friendly looks as they rode in. Scattered about in no particular order on both sides of the street were adobe houses and rickety frame huts.

The lowering sun was casting long shadows over Carmel as Joaquin said, "Let's eat first, then maybe we can find somewhere to sleep tonight. There doesn't seem to be a hotel."

Rosita agreed. They hauled up in front of the cafe and stiffly left their saddles. A mule and two horses were tied close by. The café door stood open. Joaquin allowed his bride to enter ahead of him. There was a grizzled old Mexican with a ratty beard at the first table, and two young men were giving their order to a potbellied waiter with a stained shirt and apron at a table against the far wall. Joaquin decided that the mule outside belonged to the old codger.

Guiding Rosita toward a table in the middle of the room,

Joaquin saw the waiter move toward the kitchen.

"Joaquin Murieta! What are you doing here?"

Joaquin looked toward the table and saw two friendly faces. Hermano Perez and Angelo Danero rose to their feet, smiling. It was then that Rosita recognized them too. Both men had worked as *vaqueros* on a ranch at the south edge of Real de Bayareca where Joaquin was often hired to break mustangs. Rosita had been with him on a few occasions. Both men smiled and greeted Rosita, then shook hands with their old friend. Joaquin informed them that he and Rosita had just been married and were on their way to California to begin a new life. Perez and Danero congratulated them, asking where in California they were headed. Joaquin explained that his brother Carlos was last known to be living in Los Angeles. Once they found Carlos, they would decide what to do next. He added that they might even go north to the goldfields and try some prospecting.

The faces of the two men lighted up when Joaquin mentioned the goldfields. They informed him that they were going there to try their luck, also.

Deciding they should sit together for the meal, the Murietas joined Perez and Danero, then called the waiter and gave their order. When the meal came and they began to eat, Angelo Danero said around a mouthful of food, "Joaquin, I am surprised that you and Rosita are making this trip alone."

Not wanting to divulge the problem that had caused them to marry ahead of schedule, Joaquin said, "We did not realize the trail was considered so dangerous until someone along the way brought it up. So far, we have encountered no vicious animals or brigands."

"That is good," said Perez, "but there is still a long way to go. Are you starting out again in the morning?"

"Yes."

"Then why don't you travel with us the rest of the way?" said Perez. "We have to pass close to Los Angeles on our way north."

The newlyweds looked at each other and smiled. "We would like that, my friends," said Joaquin.

"We will like it even better," put in Angelo, "for two reasons: One is because we will feel safer with a fighter like you along, Joaquin, and the other is because this traveling party sure will be prettied up with Rosita in it!"

"She's a lot prettier than Joaquin, that's for sure!" said Perez.

Everyone had a good laugh, then Angelo asked where the Murietas were going to stay for the night. When Joaquin said they were going to try to get a room, and if that did not work, they would camp at the edge of town, Perez and Danero asked them to camp with them. They had set up a tent on the west edge of town near a small creek. Joaquin and Rosita could sleep in the tent and the two men would sleep in bedrolls on the creek bank. The Murietas took them up on it.

The next morning after breakfast beside the creek, Joaquin told his friends that he needed to go back into town and pick up a couple of items at the store. Rosita would go with him and they would be back shortly. Perez and Danero said they would roll up the tent and prepare to leave, so that when the Murietas returned, they could hit the trail.

Five minutes later, Joaquin and his bride dismounted in front of the store and went inside. They were unaware of the lone rider who hauled up at the saloon across the street and observed them with cold, malicious eyes.

Pancho Boroz left his saddle and dashed into the saloon. He quickly made his way to a table at the rear of the building. "Santiago!" he said, approaching the table. "You will never believe who I just saw go into the store across the street!"

Santiago Mendez was in conversation with his other two cohorts, Enrico Apodaca and Luis Montoya. Each man was nursing a shot glass with a half-empty whiskey bottle in the center of the table. Mendez's right arm rode in a sling. Looking up at Boroz, the huge Mexican said, "If I will not believe it, Pancho, why bother to tell me?"

"It is only a figure of speech, Santiago. What I mean is that you have talked about one day going back to Sonora to kill the man who dislocated your shoulder. Now you will not have to make the trip. He is right here in town."

Mendez stiffened, adjusting the sling. "Joaquin Murieta is here in Carmel?"

"In the store across the street," Pancho said. "And he has his beautiful woman with him."

The big man divided a glance between his three friends, then set his gaze on the door. "You are sure it was Murieta you saw, Pancho?"

"Positive. And I certainly would not mistake that gorgeous female for another. It is them, all right."

Mendez slid his chair back and stomped across the floor to a dirty, fly-specked window that revealed a portion of the street. The others gathered close, trying to get a view.

Santiago let his gaze skip along the horses that were tied to the hitch rail in front of the store. "Which horses are theirs, Pancho?"

"The two sturdy-looking ones closest to the door," replied Boroz, rubbing the wound he had sustained in his arm at the fandango.

"Hmm," grunted Mendez. "Expensive horseflesh. I wonder what they are doing here."

"From the looks of those bedrolls and food packs," said Enrico Apodaca, "I would say they are traveling somewhere. Probably just passing through."

Santiago cast a furtive look over his shoulder at the bartender behind the bar. He was in conversation with the saloon's only other customer and was paying no attention to Mendez and his friends. "We will follow them. When the time is right, Murieta dies! I will take his woman."

At that moment Joaquin and Rosita emerged from the store. Joaquin stuffed something in the food pack and helped Rosita into the saddle. "It is them, all right." Mendez showed his yellow teeth in a wicked grin.

They waited until the couple was trotting up the street, then stepped outside and went to their horses. As they mounted up, Mendez said, "This time Santiago wins the fight."

"But your arm," said Luis Montoya, "you cannot fight him."

"I did not mean a fight in that sense," replied Mendez. "I simply mean that I will find a way to kill him. I will know how to do it when the right moment arrives. With just the two of them, it will be easy."

Following from a distance, the four dirty men kept Joaquin and Rosita in sight. They drew rein when the couple pulled off the road and met up with two men. When the Murietas rode away in the company of the two men, Pancho Boroz cursed. "Now it will not be so easy."

"Do not fret, Pancho," said Mendez. "If we handle it correctly, Joaquin Murieta will still be at our mercy. He will die and the beautiful woman will be mine."

"Santiago, we must be very careful," warned Luis Montoya. "We had heard of Murieta's resourcefulness and fighting ability before we met up with him at the fandango. He is very tough and very smart."

Mendez looked at his arm in the sling. "I know about that, Luis." Turning around in the saddle, he patted the handle of a large machete that stuck out of the saddlebag. "I have an idea that may just put that tough hombre in a position so I can torture him good before he dies."

"You are planning to somehow get the drop on him, tie him up, and hack him to pieces with the machete?" asked Apodaca.

"Something like that." Mendez grinned. "They have to camp somewhere tonight, and we have plenty of time on our hands. So we will follow them and wait until everything is just right. Come on, they are getting too far ahead of us."

The sun's last rays were dying out on the western horizon as the Murietas and their friends made camp in a shallow arroyo, surrounded by a virtual forest of mesquite trees, plus catclaw, ocotillo, and rabbitbrush. Since the air was quite warm, the tent was ruled out for sleeping. As a safety measure, they would keep a fire going all night and sleep in their bedrolls within its circle of light.

Rosita cooked supper over the campfire while the men fed and watered the horses. They ate the meal by twilight, and soon darkness settled over the desert.

Fresh wood caused the fire to crackle and pop between them as Joaquin and Rosita sat on the ground facing Perez and Danero. They talked optimistically of their future in California for a while, then decided to turn in.

While the others were preparing to bed down, Angelo Danero volunteered to go into the thick stand of mesquite and gather more dead wood for the fire. He would be responsible for keeping the fire going all night.

Joaquin and Rosita lay in separate bedrolls side by side and held hands till they both fell asleep.

From time to time during the night, Angelo awakened and tossed additional wood on the fire. It was almost dawn when he woke up and realized the wood was about gone. Quietly, he slipped from his bedroll and headed into the surrounding mesquite to gather more wood. They would need it for cooking breakfast.

As dawn brightened the eastern sky, Hermano Perez opened his eyes and noticed that the fire had gone out. Only a few wisps of smoke rose from the black heap of ashes. He could hear the Murietas breathing evenly, which told him they were still asleep. Just as he saw that Angelo's bedroll was empty, movement caught his eye at the edge of the arroyo. Two men were coming at him, guns drawn.

Perez's hand went down under his blanket for the revolver that lay next to him inside the bedroll, but his hand froze as one of the men bellowed, "Don't do it, Señor! Get both hands in the air, or I will kill you!"

Joaquin stirred, opened his eyes, and blinked sleepily as he beheld the two familiar Mexicans that stood over Hermano, who was raising his empty hands. Rosita moaned and came awake just as Pancho Boroz lined his gun on Joaquin. "Do not move, Murieta!"

Enrico Apodaca kept his weapon trained on Perez, who was in a sitting position with both hands raised over his head.

Rosita fixed her sleepy gaze on both men and quickly recognized them as the troublemakers at the fandango. Joaquin lay flat on his back, feeling the lumps that pressed both thighs under the blanket. He had left his double-holstered gun belt in one of his saddlebags and placed both revolvers inside the bedroll. He was thinking about what to do when he heard Santiago Mendez's bull-like voice roar at him from the edge of the mesquite forest, "Before you try anything foolish, Murieta, it is best that you look over here!"

Joaquin's head came around quickly. He heard Rosita gasp as he focused on the scene. Next to Mendez, Luis Montoya stood over Angelo Danero, who was bent low on his knees with his hands bound behind his back and a gag in his mouth. His hat lay nearby. Montoya held a large machete with both hands. It was poised directly above Angelo's neck. One swift swing downward and Angelo's head would be severed from his body.

Mendez said, "It is my turn this time, Murieta! Now throw that gun out that I know is under the blanket and stand up with your hands held high! Make a false move and your friend loses his head!"

"Joaquin," said Rosita, a quiver in her voice.

"Stay where you are, darling," he whispered. "Keep lying flat."

Acting as if the blanket was entangling him some, Joaquin slipped one of the revolvers under his belt at the small of his back. Gripping the other one, he shed the blanket, stood up, and tossed the gun at the feet of Pancho Boroz. Then he slowly raised his hands above his head.

"Now, Murieta," said Mendez in an authoritative tone, "I am going to get even with you for the beating you gave me and what you did to my shoulder. I will then leave your dead, tortured body to the wild animals and take your woman for myself."

Rosita gasped again.

Joaquin noted that Mendez held no weapon. He needed some kind of distraction, anything that would give him two seconds to draw the gun from behind his back, cock it, and fire it at the man who held the machete. Once Luis Montoya was taken care of, the others would be next.

Santiago Mendez provided the distraction that was needed when he laughed. "Well, now that we have Joaquin Murieta disarmed, let's begin the fun! Luis, cut the man's head off!"

Rosita let out a fearful squeal as the eyes of Boroz and Apodaca swerved toward Angelo Danero to watch him be beheaded. In that brief opportune space of time, Joaquin's hand flashed behind his back and came around with the gun blazing. The first slug tore a hole through Luis Montoya's head, killing him instantly. The machete dropped harmlessly to the ground. Before the inexperienced Boroz and Apodaca could react, the former conquistador dropped them with bullets through their hearts.

With his right arm in the sling, a surprised Santiago Mendez was reaching across his body for the revolver on his right hip. Just as he closed his fingers on the butt and started to draw it, Joaquin fired two bullets into his chest, exploding his heart.

As the morning breeze carried the gun smoke away, Rosita rushed to her man, flinging her arms around him. Hermano Perez hurried to Angelo Danero and untied him.

An hour later, the Murietas and their friends rode away from the arroyo, leaving the bodies of the four Mexicans to the buzzards and the wild animals.

Perez and Danero spoke with amazement of Joaquin's adept handling of his gun, thanking him sincerely for saving their lives.

Rosita looked at her husband. "I am sorry that you had to take human life once more, Joaquin, but you had no choice. I pray it will never have to be again."

Joaquin's facial features were hard as he said through his teeth, "They had it coming. What a horrible thing to cut a man's head off!"

CHAPTER NINE

Marshal Colby Cullins kissed his wife, Beth, thanking her for the good breakfast, and strapped on his .44 caliber revolver. Taking his hat from the rack by the door, he stepped outside into the cool autumn air.

There was a serious look on his heavily lined face as he walked the wide streets of San Jacinto toward the town's main thoroughfare. It was early and few people were stirring about.

Turning his gaze to the east, he saw the sun's golden tide of light spilling down the misty slopes of the Little San Bernardino Mountains, giving its Midas touch to the valley. He looked at the thin fog that lay in patches along the way, born of cool, moist air descending on warm ground.

San Jacinto, inland from the Pacific some fifty miles and a distance of some seventy-five miles southeast of Los Angeles, had been his town for twenty years. For two decades he had been the lone lawman in San Jacinto and had brooded over it like a mother hen. *A lot they care,* he thought with a touch of bitterness. *It's been my town for all this time, and now they're talking about taking it away from me. Too old, am I? Horsefeathers! Ingrates, that's what they are.*

As he turned onto the main street, Cullins thought about the meeting he had had the day before with the town council. Gil Majors, the council chairman, was no spring chicken himself. He was a good ten years older than Cullins. Colby had reminded him of it too. All Majors did was say that he didn't pack a gun and wasn't responsible for protecting San Jacinto's citizens.

And then there was Alex Banes, San Jacinto's gunsmith. Alex would soon turn sixty. You'd think he'd have some understanding about putting on some years. Of course, owning his own business and working on guns and selling them was different than wearing one that you might have to use at any moment. At least Alex had worked up the gall to say such a thing to Colby in the meeting yesterday.

Then, of course, there were the other three councilmen, Sid Warren, Frank Jones, and Barry Frame. None of them had even seen forty-five yet. A lot they knew how he felt. Sure a lawman had to be alert. Sure he had to have fast reflexes and be tough as nails. Well, ol' Colby Cullins could lick many a man half his age, and when it came to handling his gun, he hadn't slowed a bit. At least not that he could tell.

Colby turned onto the main street and waved at a couple of old codgers who sat on a bench in front of the bank. They were always there when Colby walked to the office. He wondered if they didn't sometimes spend the night there.

The marshal's boots made a hollow sound as he moved along the boardwalk. None of the merchants were in their places of business yet, but this was normal. Cullins had made a practice—since he pinned on the badge twenty years ago—to be the first to turn a key in a lock in the town's business section. He took the responsibility of being San Jacinto's lawman very seriously. If there was trouble, he wanted to be readily available.

Reaching the office, he unlocked the door, pocketed the key, and stepped inside, leaving the door ajar. He took a large key ring from a peg next to a small table that held a pitcher and washbasin. Above the table was a mirror. Pausing to eye himself in the mirror, he removed his hat, smoothed down his thinning gray hair, and combed his bushy gray mustache with his fingertips. "I don't think you look so bad," he told his reflection. "Still pretty handsome and rugged-lookin'. Don't look old enough to retire, that's for sure."

Placing his hat on a wall peg, he opened the door to the cell area and moved into the dim hallway. He approached the first of two cells. Using the key on the big ring, he turned the lock, rattling it extra loud, and swung the door open. The jail's only occupant stirred on the bunk at the sound of the door and sat up, rubbing his eyes. He was a wrinkled old man with a few strands of white hair and no teeth.

"Okay, Harry," said the marshal, "your sentence is up. You can go now."

Scratching his ribs, the old man smacked his sunken lips. "Before breakfast, Colby? I oughtta at least get breakfast."

"It was one A.M. when I put you in here for being drunk and disorderly, Harry. One A.M. yesterday morning. Your sentence was twenty-four hours in jail. I wasn't about to get up in the middle of the night just to come over here and let you out. You cut into my sleep night before last. I wasn't about to let you do it to me two nights in a row. Your sentence was up over five hours ago. No free breakfast on the town this time."

As the town drunk shuffled his way out the office door onto the boardwalk, Colby Cullins sat down behind his desk and sighed. A calendar lay before him. Picking it up, he sighed again. "Well, today's Tuesday, October 17, 1848. Two days left to be fifty-four. What is it that makes fifty-five sound so old to some people? Old for a *lawman,* that is."

He thought back to yesterday's meeting with the council. They were going to think on it, then have their own private meeting about it on Friday. Colby would get the final word then. *Yeah,* he thought, *then they had the gall to ask if I'd stay until they could find a younger man—that is, if they decided for sure to ask for my resignation since I am turnin' fifty-five. That's gall, all right.*

Tossing the calendar aside, Cullins slumped in his swivel chair, propped his booted feet up on the desk, and laced his fingers behind his head. Staring at the ceiling, he brooded gloomily over the situation. Twenty years of faithful service…but what did anybody in this town care? Not a whit. He could fall dead where he sat, and nobody would miss him till they needed him. Well, *almost* nobody. He did have a few loyal friends. Gabby Smith would miss him. Ol' Gabby always came by the office at least once a day to chat for a while. He did, at least, until his arthritis started getting worse. Sometimes he'd miss a day.

And then, of course, there was Ben and Esther Tracy. Whenever they came to town for supplies, they'd always spend a few minutes with him. Then…yes, then there was Abner Coats over at the livery. He kept Colby's horse for free. Never would let him pay for the feed. Abner was a true friend.

Colby thought of a few others who might care if the council put him out to pasture. Strangely enough, they were all his age or older. The younger set seemed to take him for granted. They were plenty glad to have him around when trouble came, but other than that, they couldn't care less if he lived or died. Then a pleasant thought warmed his heart. *Tommy Watkins*. There was a young feller who cared about Colby Cullins.

Tommy was an orphan boy of thirteen, who lived in San Jacinto with Sadie Bender, his old maid aunt. Sadie appreciated Colby. She no doubt would care if his badge was taken from him. But Tommy…Tommy was a bright spot in Colby's life. Six months ago, he was working as a stable boy for Abner Coats. He was chasing a rat around inside the barn with a big stick. The rat darted into a stall where a horse was locked up. The horse got spooked and went wild, stomping and kicking for all it was worth. Tommy was caught in a corner of the stall and got his legs all smashed up before Abner could let the horse out and get to him.

The doctor put Tommy's legs in casts, but gave little hope that he would ever walk again. Well, the boy at least got to where he could stand on the legs, but he couldn't walk without crutches. Sadie didn't have the money to buy crutches, so Colby talked it over with Beth. They decided to rob their cookie jar savings and buy crutches for Tommy. It was Beth's idea to have Sadie and the boy over for supper and present the crutches to him after his little belly was full. Colby had gone to Sadie's humble little shack and carried Tommy to the Cullins house for the occasion.

The marshal smiled to himself as he recalled the moment that he went to the closet and brought out the crutches. He never saw such a happy little feller in all of his life. Ever since that day, Colby and the boy had been fast friends. Tommy hadn't missed a day since then. Every morning between ten and eleven o'clock, Tommy's bright face would appear at the door. Colby looked at the old clock on the wall. His young friend would be by in about three hours or so.

The marshal's thoughts returned to the sore point at hand. He had evil thoughts about the five councilmen. There was a time when the leaders of San Jacinto were plenty glad to have Colby Cullins wearing the badge in their town. Like the time those wild, drunken cowboys from the Bar-J ranch came in whooping it up and shooting like maniacs. It was Cullins who went out there on the street with his sawed-off shotgun and faced them down. Nobody even offered to help. He handled it all by himself. Jailed the whole bunch and made their boss come into town and see to it that their fine was paid, and that they paid for all damages to personal property.

They have short memories, those high and mighty councilmen. Don't seem to remember occasions like that. There have been plenty of times when troublemakers came to town and more than met their match in the tough marshal of San Jacinto. Yeah. How about that day not so long ago when those three outlaws rode in, expecting to clean out the San Jacinto Bank. Little did they know that Colby Cullins would be in there making a deposit when they came through the door, waving their guns and shouting that they were holding up the bank. A few bullet holes had to be plugged up in the walls and the teller's cages, but they carried two of the robbers out to the cemetery and buried them, and the third at this minute was sitting in a cell at the prison up by Chino.

Colby wondered if the people of San Jacinto realized that many an outlaw steered around this town because of the reputation of their marshal. *Hmpf,* he thought, *things'll warm up around here when they bring in some snotty-nosed, inexperienced kid and pin the badge on him! Soon's word spreads that I'm out and he's in, this town'll be run over with no-goods. Then they'll be sorry. They'll wish they had ol' Colby back.*

The aging marshal's soliloquy was interrupted by activity on the street as the town sprang to life. Merchants were opening their shops and traffic stirred dust along the main thoroughfare. It wasn't long till Gabby Smith put in his welcome appearance. Colby heated up the stove and made coffee. The two old friends chatted for quite a while, with Colby bemoaning his unfair situation and Gabby agreeing with him wholeheartedly that the men of the town council were muttonheads.

Smith finally lifted his arthritis-stricken body from the chair where he had been sitting and hobbled out the door. This left Cullins alone to think on his plight, and Colby took up with it immediately. He recalled—for his own benefit—many other occasions when he saved life and property in his town. The longer he thought on it, the worse he felt toward the men of the council, who would ponder his fate for a few days, then let him know what they had decided.

The lawman's meandering thoughts came to a sudden halt as the familiar sound of crutches tapping on the boardwalk met his ears. Rising from the swivel chair, his heart quickened pace as he strode to the door. He got there just as young Tommy Watkins drew up. When the boy saw him, he smiled warmly and said in a cheerful tone, "Good morning, Colby!"

"Good mornin' to you, pal!" Cullins responded. "C'mon in here and sit a spell."

Tommy Watkins had sand-colored hair and a face dotted with freckles. As they sat down to talk, Colby noticed that Tommy's hair was starting to cover the tops of his ears and was getting long enough in the back to touch his shirt collar. "Looks like it's about time for my favorite boy to get his hair cut."

Tommy's face tinted. Shaking his head, he said, "I can't let you pay for any more haircuts, Colby. Aunt Sadie said she'd cut it whenever she can find time."

"Yeah, but you don't want her to cut it, do you?"

"No. I hate it when she puts that bowl on my head and cuts around it. Makes me look real dumb. But it costs too much money at the barbershop, and—"

"We'll hear no more talk like that," said the marshal, standing up. "Beth and I are very happy to have a boy to spend our riches on. C'mon. Let's take you to the shop and get you fixed up. Who knows? Maybe today some pretty girl will show up in town, just lookin' for a handsome, well-groomed boyfriend. We wouldn't want her to overlook you, would we?"

Marshal Colby Cullins and Tommy Watkins moved down the street together, not unnoticed by the people on the streets. Everyone knew the close friendship that had developed between the two. Tommy was getting good on the crutches. He was now able to keep up with the marshal when they walked together.

Cullins paid the barber for Tommy's haircut and left the boy in the chair, telling him to come back to the office when he was through.

Moments later, Cullins found himself at his desk, doing some paperwork he had been putting off for several days. He hated paperwork.

Over half an hour had passed when Cullins heard coarse laughter on the street, followed by loud voices. Just as he was rising from the chair to investigate, Ned Matterly, owner of the clothing store next door to the marshal's office, stuck his head in. "Colby, we got trouble out here! Young hoodlums are giving Tommy Watkins a hard time."

Hearing that, Cullins doubled his speed and bolted out the door. In the direction of the barbershop, he saw a small crowd—mostly women—clustered on the boardwalk, looking on as three young men were off their horses, taunting young Tommy about being a cripple. The marshal was nearly halfway between his office and the spot where Tommy stood when one of the three whipped out his gun and began shooting at the boy's feet. "Let's see you dance on those crutches, crip!"

Shot after shot raised dust as Cullins ran hard toward the scene. The instant he barged in, shouting for the shooting to stop, the young hoodlum turned toward him, holding his smoking revolver ready for another shot and regarded Cullins with a sneer.

The citizens of San Jacinto who were looking on, thought of what the men on the town council had been saying. Colby Cullins was getting too old to do his job. They observed as the marshal moved to within six feet of the hoodlum and said in an authoritative tone, "Put that gun away, sonny!"

Colby's weapon was still in its holster. The other two no-goods were wearing guns, but had not drawn them. They were standing a few paces away, next to their horses.

While the marshal was waiting for the youth to obey his command, he looked at Tommy. "Are you all right?"

Tommy nodded wordlessly, biting his lips.

Turning back to the youth—who was no more than twenty years old—Colby saw that he was still holding the gun. There was a defiant look on his face.

"I told you to put the gun away, kid," said Cullins. "We don't allow this kind of stuff in our town. You'd better be mighty glad you didn't hit this boy, I'll tell you that much. Now you three put your posteriors on those saddles and ride out of here."

One of the others spoke up. "C'mon, Wiley. We've had our fun. Let's go."

"You just hold on, Mort," responded Wiley, waving off his friend with his free hand. "I'll handle Grandpa."

"Let him alone, Mort," said the other one. "He's gotta put this lawman down so's he can brag about it to his pa."

"That's right, Harold," said Wiley. "Pa ain't gonna chide me no more about bein' afraid of lawmen." Then to Cullins he said, "I'm not too sure I have to do what you say, Grandpa."

His first use of the word *Grandpa* put a spark of anger in Colby's gut. The second time, it burst into flame. Taking another step toward Wiley while the gathering crowd looked on wide-eyed, he held out an open palm and snapped, "Give me the gun, kid!"

Feeling safe with his own weapon already in his hand and the marshal's still in its holster, Wiley lined the muzzle on Cullins' chest. His eyes dilated as he eared back the hammer. The dry, clicking sound echoed off the sides of the buildings.

San Jacinto's citizens stood in fearful silence.

Colby Cullins' features were like granite. There was gravel in his voice as he wiggled the fingers of the extended hand. "Give me the gun."

Waggling his head in a cocky manner, Wiley grinned. "Well, Grandpa lawman, why don't you just see if you can take it away from me?"

The one called Mort interjected a shaky, "Wiley, you're gonna get yourself in real trouble. Let's go."

"Shut up, Mort!" said Wiley, without taking his eyes off Cullins.

Holding his voice level, Colby said, "Your pal is tryin' to give you some sound advice, kid. You are threatening an officer of the law with a deadly weapon. All of these people are witnesses. If I arrest you for this, you'll stand trial before the circuit judge. I guarantee you, he'll put you behind bars for at least five years. I'm gonna give you a chance to quit playin' the fool. Just give me the gun and ride outta here."

Wiley laughed. "Ride outta here without my gun? No way, old-timer. How's about if I put a slug in you and ride away with my gun still in my hand?"

"Try it, son, and you'll be sorry. I'll not only take the gun away from you, but I'll give your head a good clout when I do it. Give me the gun."

Wiley's eyes were crowded with the obvious desire to defy the man who wore the badge. "Seems to me, old man, you're not thinkin' too good. It's *me* holdin' a gun on *you*. So I'm tellin' you to give me your gun."

Without wavering, Cullins said, "I warned you!" Even as he spoke, he lunged for Wiley. The hammer of Wiley's gun snapped on a spent shell, giving off a hollow sound. There was a unified gasp among the crowd. Cullins seized the gun and yanked it out of the young hoodlum's hand. He brought the butt of the gun down on Wiley's temple with purposeful force.

Wiley went down hard, blood spurting from the side of his head. He lay motionless.

Turning toward the crowd, Cullins addressed a knot of men and said, "Somebody fetch Doc Smithers. He'll have to stitch up that gash. Tell him to come to the jail. This young smart aleck is gonna learn a lesson. He's under arrest. When Judge Harrison rides in here next week on his circuit, Wiley Whatzizname is standin' trial for attemptin' to shoot and kill an officer of the law."

At that instant, Wiley's two friends mounted their horses. The one called Harold set hard eyes on Cullins. "You just made a big mistake, Marshal. Wiley's last name is Candler. That name mean anything to you?"

The name Wade Candler was quickly whispered among the crowd. Everybody west of the Missouri knew that Wade Candler was an outlaw killer. He had put many a man six feet under—including a few lawmen who decided they could arrest him.

Running his gaze over the crowd, Harold held his mount in check. "That's right, Marshal. Wiley is Wade Candler's son. Now, if I were you, I'd get Wiley sewed up and let him come with us. We're supposed to meet up with his pa a few miles north of Los Angeles in a couple of days. If you let Wiley go, maybe he can cool Wade down so's he don't come down here lookin' for you."

Colby Cullins narrowed his eyes and set his jaw. His words came out like sharp bits of cold steel. "Wiley Candler just tried to kill me, son. Like I said, he's under arrest, even though he doesn't know it. He will go to trial for it. And that's that."

Harold turned his horse so as to face northward. Mort followed suit.

Regarding the aging lawman over his shoulder, Harold said levelly, "I hope you know how to pray, Marshal. You're gonna need it."

With that, Wiley Candler's friends galloped out of San Jacinto. While one man headed for the doctor's office, Colby Cullins directed two others to pick up the unconscious youth and carry him to the jail.

Gil Majors, the chairman of the town council, stepped up to Cullins. "That was a fool thing to do, Colby. You acted like a greenhorn."

"What are you talkin' about?" Colby asked, looking him square in the eye. "The kid put his gun on me and pulled the trigger when I came at him. You know there's a law in California about that kind of thing. I'd be doin' him no favor by letting him get away with it. And if you're worried about his pa—"

"That's not what I'm talking about, Colby," said Majors. "When I said you acted like a greenhorn, I was talking about the way you moved right at the muzzle of his cocked gun. If there'd been a live cartridge in that cylinder, you'd be dead right now."

"That's just the point, Gil. I knew there wasn't a live cartridge in the gun."

"How'd you know that?"

"I'm an experienced lawman. The young greenhorn that you hire if you decide to take my job from me would never have thought to count the shots Wiley fired when he was tryin' to make Tommy dance. There ain't no such thing as a seven-shot six-shooter!"

"Oh," Majors grunted. "I…uh…I guess that was good thinking, Colby. But—"

"But what?"

"Well, you handled the kid quite well. But at your age, what are you gonna do when his pa shows up?"

Cullins eyed the man coldly. "I'll handle Wade Candler…and my age has nothin' to do with it."

As Colby followed the men who carried the unconscious Wiley Candler toward the marshal's office and jail, the townspeople began immediately discussing how long it might take Wade Candler to get to San Jacinto, and what he would do to get his son out of jail. Everybody knew that Candler had a few toughs who rode with him.

An hour later, Colby stood at the office door and listened as the doctor explained young Candler's condition. It took fourteen stitches to close up the gash, and the power of the blow had given him a severe concussion. When the doctor commented that it was not necessary that Cullins hit the kid so hard, Colby said flatly, "I warned him that if he didn't give me the gun, I'd clout him a good one."

As he passed through the door, Smithers mumbled, "Well, let no one say you don't keep your word."

Colby turned and winked at Tommy Watkins, who was sitting in the chair that faced the marshal's desk. Standing over him, he said, "You're sure you're all right, Tommy?"

"Yes, sir." The boy smiled. "Those bullets came close, but none of them touched me."

"Okay. Well, I guess I'd better go check on my prisoner. You want to go with me?"

"Sure."

Ten minutes later, as marshal and orphan were coming back into the office from the cellblock, Beth Cullins and Sadie Bender entered. Word had traveled to both women of the incident on the street. Sadie thanked Cullins for going to her nephew's rescue. She left, taking Tommy with her.

Beth closed the office door and wrapped her arms around her husband. She had heard how he rushed at Wiley Candler to take the gun away from him and how the hammer dropped, but fortunately it fell on a spent cartridge. She asked why he had made such a daring move, letting him know she disapproved of it. When he explained how he knew the gun would not fire, she felt better about it.

Still holding onto him, Beth looked up into his eyes. "Colby, this Wade Candler thing frightens me. You know he's a killer. When those boys tell him what you did to his son and he learns that you mean to see that he goes to prison, Candler is going to come here with blood in his eye. You know that, don't you?"

Colby nodded silently.

"Colby," she said, almost in tears, "you can't stand up to the likes of Candler and however many men he brings with him."

"I have to."

"You know you can't count on any of the men in this town to back you. You've seen that before."

He sighed. "Yeah, I know. But it's my job, honey. Maybe this is my way to show that bunch on the town council that I can still do it, even though I'm about to turn fifty-five."

Tears finally appeared in Beth's eyes. "No, honey. One man alone can't do it. They'll kill you. Let the councilmen have their ol' job. Let's you and me move away right now. It won't take us long to load the wagon. We can be gone within a couple of hours. Please."

Colby's head moved back and forth slowly. "Can't do it, Beth. I've never run from a fight in my life. I ain't about to start now. Young Candler broke the law and he's got to pay the consequences."

"But he won't pay the consequences if his father kills you and takes him out of the jail. So what's the use in putting your life on the line? I'm sure it's too late to just let the kid go. If you are going to live, we've got to get out of this town where Wade Candler can't find you."

Colby Cullins set his jaw and looked deep into her eyes. "Beth, darlin', even in the face of the fact that the council may give me my walkin' papers on Friday, I'm still bein' paid to wear this badge and carry the responsibility that goes with it. It just ain't in me to turn and run. Whatever Wade Candler brings to this town, I'll have to deal with it…in my own way."

"Even if it makes me a widow?"

Colby swallowed hard. "You knew I planned to be a lawman when you married me, Beth. It's the only thing I ever wanted to do. I have to ask you to understand. I'd rather be dead than have to live every day lookin' in the mirror and shavin' the face of a coward."

Beth was silent for a long moment. Then she sighed, stood on her tiptoes, and kissed his mouth. "I…I really wouldn't want you to be anything other than what you are, Colby. You are the finest man who ever drew breath on this earth. Far be it for me to try to change you. All right. You handle that bunch when they show up. I'll have supper ready that day at six o'clock, just like all the other days. And when you've done it, I've got a feeling there'll be five hotshots who'll beg you to stay on as marshal of San Jacinto."

CHAPTER TEN

On Tuesday, October 17, 1848, Joaquin and Rosita Murieta crossed the Mexico-California border just south of a small town known as Pilot Knob, California. They had parted company with Hermano Perez and Angelo Danero at a village some sixty miles south of the border. Hermano had taken ill and wanted to stay in his own country until he was feeling better and was able to travel. The Murietas had offered to stay until that time, but both men urged them to go on, since they did not know how long it would take Hermano to get well.

It had been a long stretch across the Mexican desert and the Murietas were running low on food. At Pilot Knob's only trading post, they replenished their supply and pushed northwestward along the foothills of the Chocolate Mountains. They camped that night in a shallow ravine beside a bubbling spring with the Chocolates towering above them.

Studying a crude map that someone had given him, Joaquin estimated that they were now just four days from Los Angeles. Realizing he was so near to Carlos, he had a hard time getting to sleep. The two brothers had always been very close.

At sunrise the next morning, they cut due west of the Chocolate Mountains and were soon moving along the southern tip of the Salton Sea. They were amazed to find seagulls so far inland, even though the Salton Sea was a large body of water. When they had passed the western edge of the sea, they angled northwest again, traveled till sundown, and camped with the Santa Rosa Mountains in view to the north.

The next day, Joaquin and Rosita rode along the western side of the Santa Rosas, talking eagerly of finding Carlos and making their fortune in California. By midafternoon, they left the Santa Rosas behind and angled a bit more to the northwest. The sun was lowering toward the earth when they spotted the uneven rooftops of a town. They drew rein, and Joaquin studied the map. "This has to be

San Jacinto, darling. Maybe they will have a hotel."

"That would be nice. After all these nights sleeping on the ground, a nice soft bed would sure feel good."

As they drew near the edge of San Jacinto, the sun was setting behind a bank of slender, long-fingered clouds, staining them a blood red. Joaquin noted the clouds and the way the sunset seemed to turn earth and sky the same color. He felt a coldness slide against his spine and a tiny stirring of his sixth sense, but said nothing to Rosita. Moving in a casual manner so she wouldn't notice, he touched the butts of both his revolvers.

There was a strange quietness as they entered the town, moving slowly past adobe houses and small frame huts. There was no one in sight in the yards or on the broad street. "Joaquin, where are the people?" Rosita said.

"Must be something going on in the center of town."

Seconds later, they drew near the business district and found men, women, and children bunched up in little groups, looking toward a graphic scene on the street in front of the marshal's office.

Five men were astride their horses and the man in the middle was in a shouting match with a lone silver-haired man who wore a badge and held a double-barreled twelve-gauge shotgun. Both hammers were cocked and the muzzles trained on the middle man. The lawman was standing on the boardwalk directly under a sign that read:

Marshal's Office and Jail
Colby Cullins, Town Marshal

Joaquin flicked a glance at his wife. "Looks like trouble. Let's see what we can find out."

Reining in close to a small group, Joaquin dismounted and approached a middle-aged man. The man turned to acknowledge his presence. "Howdy, stranger."

"Hello. What is going on?"

"Ever hear of Wade Candler?"

"No."

The man's eyebrows arched. "What part of the country you from?"

"I am from the state of Sonora, in Mehico. My wife and I crossed the border two days ago. We're headed for Los Angeles."

"Oh, that explains it. Wade Candler is one bad dude, Mr.—"

"Joaquin Murieta."

"Well, Mr. Murieta, Wade Candler is an outlaw and a cold-blooded killer. He's the one on the middle horse who's hollering at our marshal."

"What is the problem?"

"Well, on Tuesday, Marshal Cullins was forced to arrest Candler's son, who rode in here with a couple of his friends and started trouble. When Cullins told them to get out of town, young Candler pulled a gun on him. The marshal took the gun away from him and whacked him on the head with it. Bloodied him up pretty bad. He arrested the kid for putting the gun on him and is holding him in the jail until the circuit judge comes through so's he can be tried and sentenced to prison."

"I see. And it seems that Wade Candler wants his son released, from the way it sounds."

"Yep. And ol' Colby is as stubborn as a Missouri mule. As you can tell, he ain't givin' in to Candler and his cronies."

Joaquin ran his gaze to Cullins, looking for someone who might be standing with him. Noting the absence of any help from men in the town, he said to the man, "Why aren't some of the men up there beside the marshal?"

The man cleared his throat nervously. "Well, you see…uh…we figure Colby gets paid for protecting this town. We don't. So…it's his problem."

Joaquin could not believe his ears. He had seen many such incidents in Mexico, but the townsmen would always rally to the defense of their constable if he needed them. Wiping a hand across his mouth, he said, "The way those men are shouting at each other, there is going to be gunplay."

"I'm sure of it."

"But the marshal is outnumbered five to one. Even if he gets two of them with the shotgun, the other three will kill him."

"Probably," said the man without emotion.

Face red with anger, Joaquin turned and walked back to Rosita, who sat on her horse a few feet away. As he walked, he pulled his guns, checking the loads.

Rosita's eyes were wide. "What are you going to do?"

"The marshal is facing those five outlaws alone, darling," he replied. "It seems gringo Americanos have a strange way of thinking. That man over there told me no one will help the marshal because they are not being paid to do it. Since he wears the badge, they consider it completely his problem. I cannot stand by and watch him get killed. I must help him."

"But it is too dangerous, Joaquin," said Rosita. "It will still be just two men against five. You won't stand a chance. I...I thought you wanted to stay away from violence."

"Maybe if I step in, there won't *be* any violence."

Rosita's eyes showed the fear that she felt. She was glad her husband was a brave man, and that he cared what happened to the lone lawman, but she wished the world was a place of peace. Nodding, she said weakly, "I understand. Please be careful."

Joaquin smiled up at her, patted her hand, and wheeled about. As he pushed his way through the crowd, he noted that none of the five outlaws had yet drawn his gun. Leaving his own in their holsters, he made his way closer to the center of attention.

Colby Cullins's features were hard and fixed as he listened to Wade Candler's harsh voice say, "He's only a kid, Cullins. Give him a break. Didn't you ever make a mistake when you were his age?"

"Not *that* kind!" snapped Cullins. "I never drew a gun on a lawman!"

Wade Candler was an ugly man of forty-five. He sat in the saddle, bent forward, his long face resembling that of a droopy vulture. His hair was the color of iron, and his eyes like discs of steel. His face was red with anger. "I came here to get Wiley out of your jail, Marshal! It can be the easy way or the hard way. It's up to you."

"There isn't any easy way and there isn't any hard way," said Cullins. "To put it as blunt as I know how, there isn't any way you're gettin' him out. He broke the law and he's gonna pay for it."

There was a glint in Candler's eyes as he growled, "You tin stars are really stupid, Cullins! You'll die just to prove a point! But when you're lyin' dead in the dust, what difference will it make? We'll take Wiley outta that cell when you're dead!"

"You'll have lots of fun tryin'. So happens I knew you were comin', and I hid the only key to that cell where nobody can find it. It'll take days to cut the bars so's that no-good kid can get out.

Besides, you won't be around to see it, either. You will notice that both of these barrels are aimed at your chest. You think you can survive two smokin' loads? I told you a few minutes ago, and I'm tellin' you now. Turn those critters around and ride outta here. Your scare tactics don't frighten me."

Candler looked around at his men and spit on the ground. "He's a fool, boys. Looks like he ain't gonna leave us no choice but to kill him."

Candler's men were hard and tough. They had the look of men who had faced death many times. However, they did not comment on Candler's words. They would let their leader make the first move.

Standing in the door of Alex Banes's gun shop, the five town councilmen looked on, worry showing in their faces.

"Colby's got more guts than I gave him credit for," Frank Jones said. "How many lawmen would stand up and face bloody outlaws the way he's doing?"

"Not many," responded Gil Majors in a whisper. "Not many."

"I think he handled that smart-mouth kid pretty good the other day," put in Sid Warren. "Maybe we've been a bit hasty thinking about putting him out to pasture."

"Yeah," said Majors. "I'm thinking maybe we have. I can't picture some young lawman who's still wet behind the ears doing what Colby's doing."

"We need the man watching over this town, gents," spoke up Barry Frame. "I say we're in an official meeting right now. My vote is to keep Colby on as marshal till he says it's time for him to step aside."

"Okay by me," said chairman Majors. "Everybody in agreement?"

It was unanimous.

Then Alex Banes said, "There's only one problem right now, gentlemen. I'm not too sure Colby's going to come out of this alive."

Nobody commented. They only looked silently at the scene in front of the marshal's office, knowing it could explode at any minute.

Wade Candler decided he had wasted enough time with the hicktown marshal. He would make one more threat. If it didn't work, Colby Cullins would have to die. Eyeing the crowd of onlookers, Candler couldn't see a man he thought would offer any resistance. In fact, some of the townsmen would probably even help them cut the bars on Wiley's cell, just to get the outlaws out of town as quickly as possible.

Candler jutted his jaw, showed his teeth in anger, and set determined eyes on the aging marshal. "Cullins, it's apparent you're facin' us all by yourself. I'm gonna give you one more chance. Ease those hammers down and lay the shotgun on the boardwalk. Go inside, open Wiley's cell, and bring him out. You haven't got a Chinaman's chance of comin' outta this alive if you don't. You're outnumbered five to one."

"Not anymore, he isn't!" came a sharp voice that startled the outlaw leader and his men. "It is five to *two* now!"

Joaquin Murieta had waited until just the right moment to detach himself from the crowd. As he spoke, he moved up beside the marshal, both guns drawn and cocked. Colby Cullins kept his gaze locked on the Candler bunch, but observed the dark-skinned man from the corner of his eye. He could make out the two guns that were leveled on the outlaws. The crowd looked on, stunned to see a perfect stranger involving himself in the situation.

"I don't know who you are, mister," said Cullins, "but you're sure 100 percent welcome!"

Wade Candler's jaw slacked as he beheld the determination on the face of the newcomer. With four barrels now pointed at him, he sagged in the saddle and whispered to his men, "Remember what we did that day in Fresno." Then in a loud voice, he said, "Okay, Cullins. We won't fight you. Just be fair to my boy, will you?"

"He'll get a fair trial."

"All right, boys. Let's go."

A sigh of relief swept over the crowd as the outlaws began turning their horses about.

From the side of his mouth, Colby said, "Watch 'em, stranger. I don't trust 'em."

Joaquin was about to reply that he did not trust them either, when suddenly all five outlaws whipped out their guns, twisted in their saddles, and opened fire. To their surprise, Cullins and Murieta had vacated the spot where they stood and returned fire instantly from ten feet to the side. Colby's shotgun unleashed in a double deep-throated roar, blowing two of the outlaws from their saddles.

The women screamed and men shouted as they scrambled to take cover.

Joaquin Murieta's gun spit fire rapidly, cutting the other three outlaws down. All five lay dead in the street as the evening breeze blew the smoke away.

Cautiously, the people crept back, eyeing the lifeless forms of Wade Candler and his cronies. Rosita Murieta dashed to her husband, throwing her arms around him.

Relieved that it was over, Marshal Colby Cullins looked around. "Everybody all right? Nobody got hit with a stray bullet, did they?"

"Everybody's all right, Colby!" shouted a man from the middle of the street. "Thanks to you and that handsome Mexican!"

The crowd pressed close, congratulating their marshal on a job well done and thanking the stranger for going to Cullins's aid. Some of the women spoke to Rosita, telling her what a brave man her husband was.

While the people were still pressed close around Cullins and the Murietas, the five councilmen threaded their way through the press and stood before them. Gil Majors shook the marshal's hand. "Colby, just before the shooting began, we had an official meeting. All five of us decided that we were foolish to even consider putting you out to pasture. This town needs you. We've decided that when it's time for you to retire, *you* will tell *us*. Is it a deal?"

"It's a deal," said Cullins, "but I think this stranger is due some thanks. If he hadn't sided with me I'd be dead, and you'd be lookin' for a new marshal."

"That's for sure." Gil Majors turned toward Joaquin, who stood nearby, talking to a couple of men.

Before Majors or the other councilmen could get to Murieta, Colby Cullins reached past them. "Young fellow, I want to thank you for pitchin' in and helpin' me! You saved my hide."

Joaquin showed him a mouthful of even white teeth. "You are welcome, Marshal. I saw that no one was going to help you, so I decided it had to be me."

At that moment, Beth Cullins rushed into her husband's arms and wept. She had known the standoff was taking place, but could not bring herself to come and watch it. Once she received word that Colby was unhurt, she had hurried to the scene.

Introductions were made as the councilmen spoke to Murieta, thanking him for what he had done and admitting that their marshal would have been killed if he had remained alone.

Joaquin set his eyes on the councilmen while Colby, Beth, and Rosita observed. "What is it with you gringo Americanos? I do not understand why Marshal Cullins was left alone to face those outlaws. I must have counted fifty men who are able-bodied. Are all of you cowards?"

Beth Cullins let go of her husband and folded her arms across her breast and said to the councilmen, "I want to hear the answer to this one."

The five men exchanged nervous glances, then lowered their heads. Gil Majors cleared his throat gingerly. "I'm afraid you hit the nail square on the head, Mr. Murieta. We've always taken the approach in San Jacinto that the man who wears the badge gets paid for facing the kind of situation you saw here today. I…I see, now, that we were wrong. We…we were taking the coward's way out, trying to put all the responsibility on our marshal. Again, I say we were wrong. Dead wrong. There are times when situations demand that he have help. Like the one that just happened."

"Now we're getting somewhere," said Beth.

Apologies were made to Colby Cullins by the councilmen, and speaking for all the able-bodied men in the town, Gil Majors told him he would never face such a circumstance alone again. They would have a meeting of all the men in San Jacinto and prepare themselves for these kind of occasions.

"This I am glad to hear," said Joaquin Murieta. "Bravo for all of you!"

The bodies of the outlaws were carried away and the crowd dispersed. After thanking Joaquin once more for helping their marshal, the councilmen excused themselves. The Cullinses and the Murietas were left alone.

Colby asked, "Where are you two headed?"

When Joaquin explained about their plan to look for Carlos Murieta in Los Angeles, Beth said, "Colby, why don't we have these young people stay at our house tonight? I'll fix them a meal they won't forget. They can get a good night's rest, and after a hearty breakfast in the morning, they can be on their way."

Colby agreed.

Joaquin looked at Rosita, then back at the couple. "This is very kind of you, but we would not want to be a bother."

Colby laid a hand on Joaquin's muscular shoulder. "My friend, after what you did for me today, you could never be a bother. Please let us show you a little appreciation for it. We would be honored to have you stay in our home. And let me tell you somethin'—my missus can cook! You're gonna enjoy supper and breakfast both."

As the Murietas led their horses and walked with the marshal and his wife toward their home, Joaquin looked over his shoulder toward the western horizon. Only a faint hint was left of the blood-red sunset. Again, his instincts had been correct. Blood was shed while the sun was going down.

When they entered the small parlor, Beth said, "Colby, what about Wiley Candler? I guess somebody should tell him that his father is dead. And did you forget about his supper?"

Colby snapped his fingers. "Ain't that the berries? I plumb forgot about that smart-mouthed kid. Aw, let him wait a while. I'll get his supper to him from the cafe like usual, a little later. Guess he can wait that long to find out about his pa."

When the delicious meal was finished and Joaquin was rubbing his full stomach, Beth smiled. "Now, I want everyone to sit still. I have a little surprise."

She disappeared into a walk-in pantry and soon emerged with a birthday cake bearing fifty-five lighted candles. "Happy birthday, sweetheart!"

"This is your birthday?" said Joaquin. "Well, happy birthday, Marshal!"

"Yes! Happy birthday!"

Colby looked across the table lit by the glow of the lanterns. "If it wasn't for you, Joaquin, this would have been my death day, too. How can I ever repay you?"

Joaquin smiled. "Repayment is not necessary, my good friend. Who knows? Maybe someday you will save my life!"

Shortly after sunrise the next morning, Joaquin and Rosita Murieta thanked the Cullinses for their kind hospitality and swung aboard their mounts. There were tears in Beth's eyes as she said, "Whenever you two make a trip home to Mexico, please stop and see us."

"We will most certainly do that, ma'am," said Joaquin.

Colby looked up at the young man who had saved his life. "Remember that you've always got a friend here, Joaquin. If there's ever anything I can do for you, just let me know."

"I will do it. Adios."

The Murietas arrived in Los Angeles late in the day on Friday, October 20. They were surprised to find the city with so large a population. Joaquin had thought that all he would have to do was ask a few people in order to locate Carlos. They took a hotel room and rested for the night.

The next day, Rosita stayed in the room while Joaquin went about the city in search of his brother. He returned late in the afternoon, dejected because he had found no one who knew Carlos.

Their money was running low, so Joaquin rode to some of the ranches in the San Fernando Valley and found work breaking horses. Getting the hotel room at a weekly rate was a help to their limited budget. Evening after evening, Joaquin moved about Los Angeles, trying to find some lead on Carlos. He tried restaurants, saloons, and everywhere else people gathered, but there was no trace of his brother. After three weeks, Joaquin told Rosita that Carlos must not have stayed in Los Angeles very long, because no one seemed to know him. There was no way to learn where he had gone. The two of them would stay in Los Angeles until they could save up some money, then they would go north to the goldfields.

On a bright morning a week later, Joaquin rode onto the Flying W Ranch in the San Fernando Valley. Several days earlier, rancher Ches Williams had hired him to break a dozen wild mustangs for him. Their agreement was that Joaquin would report for work at the Flying W as soon as he finished two other jobs he had already lined up.

Reining in at the bunkhouse, he dismounted and looked toward the door. Two cowboys came out, kidding each other about something, and stopped when they saw him. They eyed him reflectively, exchanged glances, then in unison said, "Good morning."

Joaquin noticed the curious way they looked at him, but only responded with the same words, then said, "I am looking for the foreman, Bob Tally."

"Oh, sure." One of the cowboys threw a thumb over his shoulder. "He's inside. First bunk on your left."

"Thank you."

The cowboys walked away. Joaquin stopped short when he heard one of them say, "For a second there, I thought it was Carlos, didn't you?"

"Sure did, but those Mexicans all sort of look alike. Have you ever noticed that?"

"Yeah," replied the other. "Only this guy *really* looks like Carlos. Enough to be his brother, that's for sure."

Joaquin was hurrying after them. "Wait a minute! I need to talk to you!"

The bowlegged pair stopped, turned around, and waited for him to catch up.

"Excuse me," said Joaquin, his heart pounding with excitement. "I could not help but hear what you were saying. This Carlos that you say looks like me—is his last name Murieta?"

"Yeah! And you two sure look alike!"

"That is because Carlos and I are brothers! My name is Joaquin Murieta."

"See? I told you he looks enough like Carlos to be his brother!" said one of them.

"My wife and I came to California from Mehico a month ago," said Joaquin. "We have been looking for Carlos. How is it that you know him?"

"He worked here on the ranch for several months."

"But he is gone?"

"Yeah. Quit about six weeks ago, I guess it was."

"Do you know where he went?"

Both men shook their heads. "Nope, but Bob Tally might know."

"Thank you both so much. I appreciate the information."

"You coming to work here?" asked one.

"Just for a couple of days," replied Joaquin. "I am here to break a dozen mustangs that were recently brought in from the range."

"Oh, sure. Bob told us someone had been hired to do it. Ain't none of us ranch hands wants that job."

Joaquin thanked them again and started for the bunkhouse. Upon reaching the door, he stepped inside and saw a tall, lanky man in his early fifties sitting at a small table. There was no one else in the building.

The tall man was writing on a piece of paper with the stub of a pencil. As Joaquin entered, he looked up and smiled. "Howdy. Somethin' I can do for you?"

"I am Joaquin Murieta, sir. Are you Bob Tally?"

"Sure am," said Tally, dropping the pencil and rising to his feet. He shook Joaquin's hand with a firm grip. "Been expectin' you. Are you ready to meet some real tough outlaws? These mustangs are really wild."

"Sure am." Joaquin noticed that Tally was now studying him carefully.

"You think I look like someone you know, right?" asked Joaquin.

"Yeah. Carlos Murieta. You two have to be brothers."

"We are. I have been looking for Carlos for a month. He was supposed to be living in Los Angeles. I just learned from a couple of your men that he worked here, but quit and left several weeks ago."

"Right."

"Do you know where he went?"

Tally rubbed his pointed chin and thought a moment. "Yeah. Yeah, he told me he was going up north to see if he could make a fortune diggin' gold."

"Did he say where up north?"

"Mm-hmm. I remember he said the town he was heading for has the same name as the state he was born in down in Mexico."

"Sonora?"

"That's it. Sonora."

"There is a town in California named Sonora?"

"Yes. It's not far from Placerville, I understand. Placerville's right on the edge of the Sierra Nevadas where the gold was discovered by a fella named John Marshall last summer. Are you going after Carlos?"

"Yes. Just as soon as I finish my job here on the Flying W. So all I have to do is follow the Sierra Nevadas north and I will come to

Placerville?"

"That's right. When you find that you are getting into the area, just ask where you might find Sonora. Folks up there will be able to tell you. From what Carlos told me, many of the people from your state have settled there. They established a town of their own and named it Sonora in memory of their old home in Mexico. I understand the Mexicans have set up their own claims and are doing well in pulling gold out of some very rich veins."

"Thank you for the information, Mr. Tally," said Murieta. "Now, let me at those mustangs. I must get them broken as fast as possible."

CHAPTER ELEVEN

Joaquin Murieta took his young bride and headed north. One day in early December, he and Rosita drew their horses to a halt at the crest of a grassy hill and looked at the town of Sonora below, surrounded by tall timber. Rosita took a deep breath, ran her gaze to the towering snowcapped Sierras to the east. "Oh, Joaquin! It is beautiful here! I know we are going to be very happy."

Nudging his horse close to hers, the handsome Spanish-Indian leaned from the saddle and kissed her tenderly. "I would be happy anywhere with you, my love, but such magnificent country around us makes it even better."

Moments later, they rode into the small town, admiring the log cabins that had been built by its citizens. Joaquin commented to Rosita that there was not one adobe house in sight.

"Are you going to build an adobe house, Joaquin?"

"No, ma'am. I think log cabins are just fine."

Mexicans on the street greeted the young couple with smiles and some even offered a friendly wave as they passed by. Both were looking for familiar faces. As they neared the center of town, where a few shops and stores had been built of logs, Rosita pointed toward the general store. "Joaquin! Look! It is Juanita Lucero!"

At the same time, Juanita spotted them and ran into the street, calling their names. Both dismounted and embraced her. Juanita was in her early twenties and had been a schoolmate of both of them.

"I think you two are married, no?" Juanita said.

"Yes," said Rosita.

Wiggling her eyebrows, Juanita said, "You are so lucky, Rosita. How many women get to marry so handsome a man?"

"You are so right." Rosita turned to warm her husband with a smile.

A bit embarrassed, Joaquin asked, "How is Tomas, Juanita?"

"He is fine. Will he be glad to see you!"

"Is he digging gold?"

"Yes…and doing quite well. We are very happy here. Have you come to dig gold?"

"Maybe. I will probably try to make a living breaking horses for a while. At least until we can get settled in. It sort of depends on what my brother Carlos is doing. Can you tell us how to find him?"

"I have no idea."

"You mean he is not here in Sonora?"

"No," she said, her voice growing weak. "Carlos was here, but he disappeared about a month ago."

"Disappeared?" echoed Joaquin. "What do you mean?"

"Well, Carlos came in here all excited about digging gold, and as I understand it, was working at staking his claim. Tomas and I had him in our home for meals a few times. It seemed that everything was going good for him—then one day he was gone."

Joaquin frowned. "Do you think he was a victim of foul play?"

The pretty Mexican woman shrugged her shoulders. "I…do not think so. At least there has never been any evidence of it. Tomas even went over to Stockton and talked with the sheriff about it. Sheriff Miller told him that he would let him know if anyone ever found a body or anything like that. We have never heard any more. Tomas also made a point to ask among the gold miners, but even though some of them knew Carlos, no one knew where he had gone."

"I will do some asking around of my own," Joaquin said. "Maybe there will be somebody who talked to him and knows where he went."

"Are there others here from home, Juanita?" asked Rosita.

"Oh yes," Juanita replied, then listed off the names of a dozen families from Sonora, Mexico, whom they knew. "It is wonderful what has happened to our Mehican people here. Half of the gold that is being taken out of the mountains is by our people. Some are even on the verge of actually being rich. They have bought up great parcels of land and are settling all over this area, planning to live out their lives here."

The Murietas were invited by Juanita to stay in their home until they could find living quarters. Tomas was indeed happy to see them and also welcomed them to stay in their home.

Joaquin spent the next three days looking up all the families from Sonora, Mexico, that Juanita had told him about. None of them knew where Carlos had gone. At the close of the third day, he told Rosita that he would try to break horses for a living until he was ready to attempt mining for gold. He would continue to ask people wherever he went in the area if they knew Carlos. There had to be somebody somewhere who knew where he had gone.

The next day, Joaquin rode his horse from ranch to ranch, offering his services as a broncobuster. Soon he was working steady and making a good living.

The Murietas wanted to live in Sonora, but since the town was so new, there were no houses available. Joaquin told Rosita he would build them a house in his spare time. It would take several months, but he would get it done as soon as possible. The Luceros assured them they were welcome to stay with them until the house was done. Tomas offered to help and told Joaquin he was sure there were other men who would pitch in.

The beautiful, spacious log house was finished in May 1849, and the couple moved in. Joaquin had bought ready-made furniture in Stockton, and Rosita loved it. It felt good to be in her own home.

Joaquin's reputation as a broncobuster spread to points far and wide. He was staying comfortably busy. Rosita, wanting to spend as much time with her husband as possible, often accompanied him to the ranches and cheered him as he rode the wild horses. It was still in the back of Joaquin's mind to someday turn to gold mining, but he enjoyed his work and was doing so well that he was satisfied for the time being to stay with breaking horses.

As the months passed, Joaquin continued to put out the word that he was looking for his brother. He would not give up hope that one day he would find him.

On a cool afternoon in October 1849, Joaquin rode a snorting, bucking horse in the corral of a small ranch a few miles south of Sonora. While the rancher and a couple of his cowhands looked on, they noticed two riders trotting toward them. Immediately they recognized Roy Thompson and his foreman, Roger Folger. Thompson was owner of the Box T, the area's largest and most successful ranch.

The ranchers and their men greeted each other, then Thompson glanced at the horse and rider battling it out inside the corral. "I was told that Joaquin Murieta was breaking a couple of horses for you today. That him?"

"Yep," replied rancher Mike Osteen. "He tamed a wild one this morning, and did such a good job, the horse is already gentle as a lamb."

Thompson was a big man in his early sixties. He had an ample belly and a nose that looked like it had been broken three or four times. Grinning, he tilted his hat to the back of his head. "Pretty good at what he does, I understand."

"I've never seen anyone like him."

"You won't mind if I talk to him when he's done here?"

"Of course not."

Nodding, the rancher turned his attention fully to the action inside the corral. He knew horses, and he knew men. This was a gallant horse. It was giving the fight everything it had. But the man in the saddle was quite determined to stay there.

As the rough ride continued, Thompson turned to his foreman. "This Mexican is exactly what I'm looking for."

Folger arched his eyebrows. "Mexican? That's the first time I've heard you use that term. You've always called 'em greasers before."

"Yeah, but a man who can ride like that deserves respect. He's a Mexican."

Soon Joaquin had the horse trotting around the corral, obeying his every signal. Osteen stood up on the bottom pole of the corral fence and applauded. "Good job, Joaquin! Good job!"

Murieta patted the animal's neck, then handed the reins to one of the cowboys and slid from the saddle. Climbing the fence and landing on the outside, he said, "Just let me know when you've got some more for me to break, Mr. Osteen."

"Sure will," replied Osteen, handing him a small leather pouch containing gold dust. Then gesturing toward the rancher, he said, "Joaquin, this big fella is Roy Thompson. He's owner of the Box T. He wants to talk to you."

"The Box T?" said Murieta. "I have ridden past your ranch many times, Mr. Thompson. I'm honored to meet you."

Thompson shook hands with Joaquin and introduced him to Folger. "You've been recommended to me by ranchers all over the valley, son. I guess you know my place is the biggest one around."

"Yes, sir. I know."

"Like to talk to you. Are you heading home now?"

"Yes, sir."

"How about we ride that direction together?"

"Certainly."

Bidding Osteen good-bye, the three men mounted up and headed toward Sonora with Joaquin riding in the middle. As they moved at a moderate trot, Thompson said, "Joaquin, are you aware that I not only run some forty thousand head of beef cattle, but I'm also in the horse business?"

"I have heard that, sir."

"For the last fifteen years, I've employed a man full-time just to break horses to the saddle for me. We bring in enough wild ones from the California ranges to keep one man quite busy. What I'm leading up to is this. The man I've had breaking broncs for me for the past four years tried to do a ride last week when he was half-drunk. Mustang threw him and killed him. I've heard so much about you that you were the first man to come to my mind for the job. How'd you like to come full time with me?"

Joaquin was a bit overwhelmed. "You mean work for you strictly? Not break broncs for anyone else?"

"Yep. Save you a lot of time. As you know, the Box T is only eleven miles southwest of Sonora. No trick at all to make that ride every morning and evening."

"Can't disagree with that."

"I'm not a skinflint, either, son," said Thompson. "How much you make a week breaking horses?"

"Well, that depends, sir. If the work is steady, I do pretty good."

"What do you call steady?"

"Eight hours a day, six days a week. I always take Sundays off to spend with my wife."

"I take it the work has been pretty steady."

"Yes, sir. Once in a while there'll be a day that's not full."

"So in a steady week, what's the pay?"

Joaquin thought on it a moment. "Runs about forty to fifty dollars a week, sir."

"Well," said Thompson, adjusting his large frame in the saddle, "that's pretty good wages for a fella your age. But I want you bad.

How about if I pay you a hundred and fifty dollars a week? You can have both Saturdays and Sundays off. You'll get all the beef you and your missus can eat, too."

Joaquin was stunned. He had never dreamed of making that much money, even digging gold. Most of the gold-digging Mexicans in Sonora were netting about a hundred dollars a week, working seven days. Smiling broadly, he extended his hand toward the rancher. "You've got yourself a new broncobuster, Mr. Thompson!"

"Good!" Thompson met his grip. "How soon can you start?"

Rubbing his chin, Joaquin said, "I want to be ethical with the ranchers who have already engaged me to break horses for them. You understand that."

"Of course. I wouldn't want you to be any other way."

"Well, if I work some extra long hours, I should be able to start working for you in two weeks. Is that all right?"

"I'd like to have you sooner," replied Thompson, "but I can live with that. You'll just have a big bunch of outlaws waiting to be broken when you start."

"I don't mind that, sir. I can handle it."

"That's the spirit!" Thompson laughed. "Okay, let's see…this is Friday. How about if you report to work two weeks from Monday?"

"Sounds good. Two weeks from Monday it is."

"Fine. You'll report for work at seven o'clock. I'm not always available, but you just see Roger and he'll get you started."

"All right, sir," said Joaquin, his heart pumping with joy.

"And by the way," added Thompson, "you can eat lunch every day with the rest of the ranch hands in the mess shack."

"Thank you, sir. Oh! One other thing…"

"Yes?"

"Sometimes my wife, Rosita, likes to ride to work with me and watch me in action. Will that be all right?"

"Certainly. If she's good-looking, you might have to watch some of the boys around her!"

"She is very good-looking, sir. I will keep a sharp eye on your boys!"

Rosita Murieta was thrilled with her husband's steady job at the Box T Ranch and sent him off to work on the first day with a hug and a kiss. She would wait until he had become accustomed to working there before she rode along to spend a day and watch him ride.

Arriving at the ranch just before seven o'clock, Joaquin was impressed at its size. Thompson could give Don Jose Gonzales a run for his money. The pastures were well stocked with horses and cattle. The two-story ranch house was literally a mansion and was constructed of thick Ponderosa pine logs. The barn was quite large and the other outbuildings were well built.

Just as he rode into the complex of log buildings, Joaquin spotted Roger Folger emerging from the L-shaped bunkhouse. The foreman spotted him and waited for him to ride up.

"Good morning, Joaquin," said Folger as the handsome man threw his leg over the saddle and touched ground.

"Good morning."

"Ready to go to work?"

"Sure am."

"Okay," said Folger, "excuse me a second." Turning back to the bunkhouse, he stuck his head in the door and gave someone an order to herd the first mustangs to be broken into the small holding area next to the corral where they would be ready for saddling.

At that moment, three lanky cowboys came from the direction of the mess shack, which was nearby. Folger stopped them and introduced them to Joaquin. They gave him a warm handshake and welcomed him to the Box T. One of them commented that he was glad it was Joaquin who had to break the wild horses and not him. His companions laughed, and one of them said, "Tim, the only way you could break a horse would be to show him your face! That mug of yours would stop a stampede of wild horses!"

Joaquin laughed with them. They walked away, wishing him luck with the mustangs. He was feeling good about working at the Box T. He told himself that if all the ranch hands were as friendly and jovial as those three, he was going to enjoy working there.

"Well, Mr. Broncobuster," said Folger, "we'd best get to the barn. I'll let you pick the saddle you want to use."

On the way to the barn, they encountered four more cowboys, who seemed as friendly and happy as the others. The big barn door was open, and when they stepped inside, the familiar odor of horse-flesh, old leather, hay, and dried-up manure met Joaquin's nostrils. His attention was drawn immediately to the hayloft overhead. Large clumps of hay were being pitched down into a feed trough at one end of the barn. Joaquin could tell that there were two men using pitchforks, but he could not see them.

There was an old wagon in one corner and a couple of harnesses hanging on the wall just inside the door. On the dirt floor beneath the harnesses were a couple of double-trees and a single-tree. On the opposite side of the barn was a string of horse stalls and sitting astride the partitions that separated the stalls were several saddles of different shapes and styles.

Gesturing toward the saddles, Folger said, "There they are, my friend. Choose the one you want, throw it on your shoulder, and we'll head for the corral."

As Murieta moved toward the saddles, he saw the two men who had been pitching hay descending from the hayloft on a sturdy-looking ladder. Long, shaggy blond hair dangled to their shoulders from under their wide-brimmed hats. When they reached the floor and turned toward him, Joaquin noted how much they looked alike in spite of the difference in their size. He was sure they were broth-ers.

The small one was about Joaquin's size and close to his age. The large one looked to be in his late twenties, and was without a doubt the biggest man Joaquin had ever seen. Reflecting on the size of Santiago Mendez, he decided that this man would dwarf Mendez. He was at least six and a half feet tall and no doubt would weigh close to three hundred pounds. He had massive muscular arms, thick sloping shoulders, a neck like an oak tree, and bulky thighs that pressed tight against his pant legs.

"Hey, fellas," said Roger Folger, "I want you to meet Joaquin Murieta. You will remember that Mr. Thompson told you he had hired a new man as Box T's broncobuster. Joaquin, this is Garth and Derk Lindgren. They are from Sweden."

Murieta did not see the friendliness in the Lindgren brothers like he had seen in the other ranch hands earlier. Neither man smiled. Attempting to make the best of it, Joaquin extended his hand toward the huge one first. Garth did not meet his hand. Towering over Murieta, he eyed him coldly and grunted in a heavy European accent, "Mr. Thompson didn't tell us he had hired a greaser."

Joaquin bristled at the use of the word and felt his blood heat up. Struggling with his temper, he said, "I am sorry you have a dislike for people from my country, Mr. Lindgren. Have some of my Mexican brothers done something bad to you?"

Garth turned his thick lips downward. "Naw, me and Derk, we just don't like greasers. They came here to California wanting to hog all the gold and buy up all the land."

Folger spoke up, a sharp edge in his voice, "Wait a minute, Garth. The Mexicans have as much right to dig for gold and own property here as anyone else. They're not hogging anything. Plenty of gringos are getting their share of gold and buying up their share of property. You need to change your thinking on this matter."

"We ain't never going to change our thinking about greasers," said Derk, turning up his nose at Joaquin.

Anger was crawling up Murieta's spine like a hot snake. He fought it, knowing that he was the new man at the Box T, and didn't want to get started off on the wrong foot. The Lindgren brothers, however, were making it difficult.

"Yeah!" said Garth. "I say they ought to be sent back to Mexico."

Indignation flushed Joaquin's face. He held his voice in control, but it quavered with fury as he said through his teeth, "If that is so, then the straw-haired Swedes ought to be sent back to Sweden."

A brassy grin curved Garth's lips and his pale blue eyes glinted. "Maybe you would like to be the one to deport us, little man."

"That's enough, Garth!" said Folger. "You two have work to do. Get to it!"

Garth gave Joaquin Murieta a wolfish glare, held it for a few seconds, then said, "Let's go, Derk."

When the Lindgren brothers were gone, Roger Folger said, "Joaquin, I apologize for this. I had no idea they felt that way toward Mexicans. I'm sure they'll get used to having you around and won't bother you."

"I hope that is true," replied Murieta. "Now, let me take a look at these saddles."

During the next couple of weeks, Joaquin only saw the Lindgren brothers a few times, and that from a distance. They did manage to give him a cold stare once, letting him know they still had an aversion to him working at the Box T. What he didn't know was that they were secretly planning to find some way to make him fight Garth. The huge Swede would cripple him so he could no longer break horses, if he could just get him into a fight.

After Joaquin had been employed at the ranch for three weeks, Rosita tagged along with him for the first time. Joaquin made a special point to introduce her to Roy Thompson, who was on his front porch when they rode in.

When Joaquin helped his beautiful wife from her saddle at the corral, the cowboys who were standing around whistled playfully. Unaware that the Lindgren brothers were looking on from the shadows of the barn, Joaquin laughed and gave a friendly warning to all the ranch hands to stay away from his wife.

Garth and Derk continued to watch as Joaquin introduced Rosita to the men at the corral. Soon the lovely young woman was perched on top of the corral fence, and her husband was aboard his first bucking horse of the day. Garth said to his brother, "I think we have been presented with a way to get Murieta to fight me."

"I don't know exactly what you're thinking, but it has to do with his wife, doesn't it?"

"Mm-hmm. We will have to wait for just the right time, but I am sure it will come. He will probably bring her here often, if I have it figured right. They seem to be very close, and she no doubt wants to be with him as much as possible. We will be patient, little brother, but soon that dirty greaser will be gone from the Box T."

During the next two weeks, the Lindgren brothers noted that Rosita Murieta came to the ranch with her husband twice a week. It was Tuesday of the following week that everything fell into place so they could put their plan into action.

They were inside the barn, observing Rosita on the corral fence, just as Joaquin finished breaking his last horse for the day. Joaquin climbed up on the fence, whispered something to her, then hopped down and helped her to the ground. They were close enough to the barn for Garth and Derk to hear Joaquin tell Rosita to head for the spot where their horses were tied, adding that he had to talk to Roger Folger for a few minutes. Rosita nodded and walked away.

Garth chuckled and said, "Okay, little brother. Now is the time. She has to walk right by the big door of the barn to get to the horses. You know what to do."

Derk snickered. "Yeah. Just don't be late doing your part. There is talk among the men that Murieta used to be a Mexican conquistador. I do not want to fight him for very long."

"Do not worry," said Garth. "I will be close by."

Rosita was humming a happy tune to herself as she rounded the corner of the barn and headed for the Arabian horses, which were tied to hitching posts in view of the big ranch house. Suddenly Derk Lindgren emerged from the shadows of the barn and planted himself in front of Rosita, grinning and looking at her wantonly.

Rosita saw immediately that he was up to no good. She veered to the side in an effort to avoid him. Quickly, he jumped in front of her, blocking her path once more. She attempted to go around him. Anticipating her move, he moved in front of her again.

Anger surfaced. Showing him the sharp hostility of her blazing black eyes, she snapped, "Get out of my way!"

"Aw, now, honey," said Derk, tilting his head and acting hurt, "I think you and I should get to know each other. My name's Derk. Couldn't we be friends?"

"No, we couldn't!" She started around him again.

Jumping in her path, he said, "You might as well face it, honey. It's destiny. You and me were meant for each other. How about a little kiss?"

Rosita's lips pulled back over her teeth in a grimace of fury. "Don't touch me, you dirty scum!" As she spoke, she dragged the back of a hand across her eyes as if to wipe away some sort of feral haze.

Derk reached out and seized her by the wrist. She screamed, and at the same instant, Joaquin came around the corner of the barn. "Hey!" He broke into a run.

Derk turned his head and saw the former conquistador coming at him like a maddened bull. The diversion of his attention eased his grip on Rosita and she jerked herself free. At the same instant,

Joaquin hit Derk with a body slam and they both landed hard in the dirt with the Swede's breath gushing from his lungs.

Joaquin, boiling with anger, flipped Derk facedown, sank steely fingers into his hair, and pounded his face savagely against the ground. Blood spurted from his nose and mouth.

Suddenly Joaquin heard a wild roar, almost like that of a huge bear. *"Murieta!"*

Joaquin looked up to see that Garth Lindgren had wrapped Rosita in his powerful arms and was holding his hand over her mouth. Rosita's eyes were bulging with fear.

"You want to see something!" the man said, taunting Murieta. In a quick, smooth move, he took his hand from Rosita's mouth and planted a kiss on her lips. Rosita made a gagging sound.

Dropping Derk's bloody face into the dirt, Joaquin sprang to his feet and stood spread-legged. The veins in his temple and neck stood out like swollen cords of rope. "Get your filthy hands off her!"

It had worked out exactly as the big Swede had planned it…except for his brother getting bloodied up so severely in such a short time. With a crooked grin curling his mouth, he let go of Rosita and gave her a rude shove away from him. She stumbled and almost fell.

Derk lay on the ground behind Murieta, spitting blood and cursing.

Garth extended both arms toward Joaquin and motioned at the angry husband. "You don't like what I did, little greaser? Come and get me!"

Joaquin Murieta flicked a glance at Rosita as she was backing away from what she knew was going to be the field of battle. She noticed several cowboys coming that way from the bunkhouse. She wiped a hand across her mouth and spit on the ground, as if to cleanse herself from the foul mouth that had touched her lips.

"Are you all right?" asked Joaquin.

Rosita spit a second time and nodded. "Yes, except for a putrid taste in my mouth." Worry then showed in her eyes as she said, "Joaquin, he is so…so big."

Turning blazing eyes back to Lindgren, who stood with his extended hands inviting combat, Joaquin said to Rosita, "When a man does what he just did to you, it doesn't matter how big he is."

CHAPTER TWELVE

Seven ranch hands arrived at the scene and drew up just as a furious Joaquin Murieta charged the hulking giant, fists ready.

Garth tried to dodge the first punch, but Joaquin was too fast and accurate. The blow struck the hollow of the jaw, and Lindgren's head snapped back. On the rebound, Murieta popped him with a stiff left jab, then followed quickly with a second smashing right to the jaw. The Swede staggered, blinked with surprise at Murieta's speed, then released a roar and closed in. A massive fist glanced off Joaquin's temple, but he felt its effect.

The smaller man pounded the Swede's nose, then caught a solid blow on his own jaw. He felt his feet leave the earth and the ground seemed to fly up and slam his back. The lowering sun was in Joaquin's eyes as he looked up to see a monstrous shadow descending over him like some gigantic prehistoric bird.

Joaquin rolled in time to escape the nearly three hundred pounds of determined man. Garth hit the ground with a heavy thump and his opponent leaped to his feet.

Murieta saw two of the ranch hands move close to Rosita and flank her while he waited for Garth to get up. He knew they were attempting to encourage her. Derk Lindgren had crawled next to a tree and was looking on while wiping blood from his face.

When Garth rose, Joaquin charged again. He drove four punches in succession to the man's face. Lindgren staggered, but came back strong. "I'm going to break you in half!"

The audience of cowboys stood spellbound. Rosita was biting her lower lip as one of the men next to her spoke soft words of reassurance.

Joaquin ducked a whistling fist and popped Garth's lips with a powerful blow. Both lips split and spurted blood. Another blow slammed his nose. In a rage, the huge Swede swung wildly as Joaquin was coming in again. Joaquin connected, but so did Garth. The fist chopped Murieta's jaw. Bright lights flashed in Joaquin's head as he went to the ground. It seemed for a few seconds that he was falling through a black, endless hole.

The sharp pain of a heavy boot in his ribs cleared Joaquin's brain, and he rolled aside to avoid being kicked again.

Rosita winced when she saw Lindgren's foot connect with her husband's rib cage. To the cowboys who flanked her, she said, "Can't you stop this before that monster kills Joaquin?"

"I don't think Joaquin would look favorably on us if we stopped it, ma'am," said Willie Marks, who stood on her left. "He's plenty mad at Garth, and it's my opinion that Joaquin is not going to let Garth kill him. You did say that Garth actually kissed you?"

"Yes," she replied, the thought sickening her.

Curly Bender said, "Your husband wants to punish Garth for what he did, ma'am. He's willing to take some punishment in order to do it. But I think Joaquin will come out the victor—from what I've seen thus far, that's my opinion."

Putting a shaky hand to her cheek, Rosita said, "I certainly hope you are right."

The two combatants were now winging at each other and circling. Slowly, they were edging closer to the barn. Murieta clobbered his opponent another time on the nose, which was flowing freely with blood. Garth shook his head, sleeved away some of the blood, and charged after him like a bull elephant. Joaquin leaped aside, evading him, and cracked him on the ear as he stumbled by.

Maddened by the smaller man's agility as he bumped into the wall of the barn, Garth whirled about and charged at Murieta again. Joaquin's wrath was still hot. He ducked two swinging fists and caught the giant with a savage uppercut. It popped Garth's head back, and Joaquin quickly drove a hard blow to his stomach. The Swede's midsection was solid. He bent forward from the blow, but pain shot all the way up Joaquin's arm to his shoulder.

Lindgren clipped him on the jaw, and Joaquin staggered in a circle, trying to stay on his feet. Garth rumbled after him, swinging wildly. Murieta took two steps backward to avoid the powerful fists and found his back against the barn wall. He saw a big fist zeroing in on his face and dodged it. The fist banged the hard wood of the wall. Lindgren howled and grabbed the fist with the other hand. The skin was torn and blood surfaced on the knuckles. His big face was now soaked with blood from his nose and lips.

Joaquin was setting himself to deliver another punch, but Garth surprised him by lashing out and landing a solid blow to his forehead. He was down again, but Garth was too busy inspecting his damaged hand to go after him. Joaquin rose to one knee, shaking his head. The Box T grounds seemed to whirl about him. As the whirling sensation began to subside, he caught a glimpse of Rosita's pale features. He could see the trepidation in her eyes.

The ground seemed to shake as the monster came at him again. Joaquin rose to his feet and backed up, still a bit dizzy from the last blow. Suddenly his back was against the barn wall again. The big bloody right fist was hissing toward his face. Instinct—born from so many fights in the past—caused Joaquin's head to jerk sideways. Lindgren's bruised fist cracked the wall again. He let out a painful yell. Snarling viciously, the man threw his weight against Murieta.

Joaquin found himself wrapped in a vise. His feet were off the ground. Garth apparently had broken his hand and could no longer use it as a fist. He had Joaquin in a deadly bear hug, gripping him under the arms.

Murieta felt the power of the Swede's arms forcing the breath from his lungs. His ribs were popping. Garth was behind him, his fetid breath filling one ear. Like a prairie fire in a high wind, Joaquin's fury grew. Gritting his teeth, he threw his hands back and jammed a thumb in each eye. Garth howled and tried to shake them loose, but Joaquin had a firm grip on the long, stringy hair with his fingers, and the thumbs stayed where he planted them.

Screaming wildly, the giant threw the smaller man ten feet through the air. Joaquin hit the dirt rolling, gasping for breath. Lindgren was holding his hands to his eyes, staggering around the doorway of the barn.

A slight dizziness claimed Murieta as he struggled to his feet, sucking for air. He turned and looked at Rosita, who stood forty feet away. Her beautiful face was screwed tight, and she was wringing her hands. The mental picture of Garth forcing his mouth on Rosita's lovely lips renewed his wrath. Thunderous fury raged within him, possessing him until everything blurred in his vision except Garth Lindgren.

Joaquin went after him like a ravening wolf. Crimson fluid was bubbling from Garth's nose and running from his mouth as he rubbed at his damaged eyes, trying to clear the haze that filmed them. Noticing that there was no one cheering the monster from the sidelines, Joaquin wondered if they cared what happened to him. Even Derk was strangely silent.

Murieta waited for Garth to stagger his direction, then planted his feet and sent his fist pistonlike to the Swede's jaw. Garth's head whipped to the side, spraying blood. He staggered again, blinking to focus with his eyes. One, two, three more hissing punches dumped the man on the ground. He was lying on his back, halfway through the open door of the barn.

"Come on, Garth!" said Murieta scornfully. "I'm not through with you!"

Lindgren rolled to his knees, shaking his enormous head. His shoulder-length hair hung over his face. Lifting a hand to spread the dirty, blood-soaked hair, he blinked and focused on a single-tree that was lying among other wagon parts next to the wall, just inside the barn door. Murieta was waiting outside, with the setting sun at his back.

Garth struggled to get up, feigning dizziness, and purposely stumbled toward it. Seizing the four-foot length of wood and metal with both hands, he charged into the orange sunlight, swinging it violently. Joaquin ducked and it cut air over his head.

The man gained his balance and swung again. The metal rings in the ends of the single-tree gave off a harsh sound. Joaquin spun around, placing his back to the open door of the barn. Garth chopped at his head. Again, the lithe Mexican ducked. The deadly single-tree slammed the doorjamb with a deafening bang, showering splinters in every direction.

Rosita let out a frightened whimper.

As the Swede righted himself, Joaquin sent another blow to his battered nose. Wildly, Lindgren charged. Their bodies thumped with the impact and they went down, Garth on top of Murieta.

Holding the single-tree with both hands, Garth jammed it horizontally downward at Joaquin's throat. Joaquin met it with both hands, pressing against the giant's weight and brawn. The piece of wagon equipment quivered between them. Lindgren grunted, doing all he could to force it downward and crush the smaller man's

Adam's apple. Murieta glared at him, teeth clenched, meeting him strength for strength.

The captivated cowboys stood in awe.

Rosita Murieta prayed.

At that moment, foreman Roger Folger appeared, with another ranch hand by his side. Fixing his gaze on the two combatants, Folger moved up beside one of the five men who stood shoulder-to-shoulder and asked what Lindgren and Murieta were fighting about. The cowboy shrugged and said, "I don't know. Marks and Bender are over there with Mrs. Murieta. They've been talking to her. They oughtta be able to tell you."

Leaving the other ranch hand with the group, Folger kept an eye on the fight and made his way toward Rosita and the two men who flanked her.

In a desperate effort to force the single-tree against Joaquin's throat, Garth moved his bulk forward to add weight. Murieta's senses told him the huge man had moved too far forward. He was overbalanced.

Suddenly Joaquin flung his knees upward, catching Lindgren on the rump. The man flipped over, head first. Whirling around, Murieta twisted the single-tree from the man's grasp. Now the lethal length of wood and metal was in the other combatant's hands.

Both men came to their feet. Lindgren was still having trouble seeing clearly, but he rushed at Murieta, attempting to overpower him with his weight and brute force before Murieta could bring the single-tree into play.

Joaquin, however, was fast. He swung the single-tree hard, aiming for the man's head. It connected with a loud crack, and Lindgren's head split open with the impact. He fell flat, but in desperation, rose up on one knee. Groaning, he shook his head, endeavoring to tear loose the cobwebs that clung to the walls of his brain.

Roger Folger had only begun to ask Rosita and the two cowboys what the fight was about when he heard the sound of the single-tree connecting with Lindgren's head. He spun around in time to see Garth go down, then lift himself to one knee.

At that moment, Derk was running toward Murieta, screaming obscenities at the top of his voice. Joaquin turned to meet him. Holding the single-tree with his left hand, he made a fist with his right, and met Derk with a stunning blow. Derk went down like a rotten tree in a high wind. He was out cold.

Murieta turned back to Garth, who was still glassy-eyed, on one knee. He gripped the single-tree with both hands. The onlookers saw that he was going to hit Garth again. This time, it would be a lethal blow.

Folger darted toward him, shouting, "Joaquin! Don't do it!"

Blind with fury, Murieta ignored him. He swung the heavy length of wood and iron behind him to gain all the force possible. Rosita's scream penetrated the flame in his mind. He checked his swing and turned to look at her. She was standing only inches from him.

"Don't do it, Joaquin!" she cried. "Don't kill him!"

The fire in the Mexican's sooty eyes began to assuage. He met her fearful gaze, then looked at Garth Lindgren, who was blinking against the pain in his wounded eyes and attempting to stand up. He lowered the single-tree and wiped blood from the corner of his mouth. "All right. If you are satisfied, this will go no further."

Laying a trembling hand on his arm, she said tightly, "What he did was wrong, Joaquin, but I don't want him killed. I don't want you to ever kill again."

Joaquin dropped the single-tree and took a few steps to a water trough beside the barn. Rosita walked with him. "Is your mouth cut bad?"

"No," he replied, kneeling at the trough. "One of his punches just mashed my teeth into the side of my mouth. It'll be all right."

As Joaquin buried his head in the cool water, Rosita noticed Roy Thompson riding in from the road with his wife on a horse beside him.

Thompson quickly noticed the group gathered at the barn and aimed that direction. Mrs. Thompson guided her mount to the porch of the house, dismounted, and headed for the door.

Roger Folger was in conversation with Garth Lindgren, who was now sitting on the ground beside his brother. Derk was lying on his back, hazy-eyed, and wondering where he was.

Thompson sized up the situation, drew up to his foreman, and looking toward Murieta, said, "Roger, I assume Garth and Derk were fighting with Joaquin. What happened?"

"Well, it's like this. Mrs. Murieta told Willie Marks and Curly Bender that Derk tried to corner her, asking her to kiss him. Joaquin came on the scene about that time and laid into Derk. While Joaquin was pounding Derk's face in the dirt, Garth grabbed Mrs. Murieta and kissed her."

Before he would let Garth say anything, Thompson called Joaquin and Rosita to him, asking to hear their version of the incident for himself. When they had given it, Thompson asked Garth, "Is this true?"

Garth flicked a glance at Derk, who was now sitting up and listening. "I suppose that is about the way it happened."

"You suppose?" snapped Thompson.

"Well, it was something like that."

There was anger in the rancher's voice as he said, "I don't know how it is in Sweden, Garth, but in this country you keep your hands off another man's wife."

The blood around Garth's mouth and nose was beginning to cake, but the gash on his head was flowing freely. He was holding a dirty bandanna against it. With effort, he rose to his feet. "Mr. Thompson, in Sweden we don't have greasers moving in and hogging our natural resources. All those Mexicans who have come here are taking gold out of the hills that could eventually be had by white folks. They are also buying up land that we could one day afford to buy. I hate greasers."

"So what has that got to do with you manhandling and kissing Mrs. Murieta?" pressed Thompson.

The man avoided Thompson's gaze by looking at the ground. His split lips were pressed tight.

"Garth, I asked you a question."

The Swede only stared at the ground.

When Garth didn't answer, Roger Folger said, "I think I have it figured out, boss."

"Tell me," said Thompson.

"The way Mrs. Murieta said Derk came onto her first, then Garth did what he did, I would say it was a setup to force Joaquin into fighting Garth."

The look that came over Garth's features was enough to prove that Folger had hit the nail on the head. Roy Thompson said,

"Looks like you bit off more than you could chew when you took on Joaquin, Garth. Are you ready to apologize to Mrs. Murieta and Joaquin?"

Garth Lindgren was a proud man. It went against his grain to make apologies. He also had heard Roy Thompson call Mexicans "dirty greasers," and speak of his distaste for them. But since it was known that Thompson deeply admired Joaquin's talent for breaking horses, Garth knew he must keep his mouth shut and make the apologies. He made the apology. Derk made his, also. Though Joaquin and Rosita were skeptical as to the sincerity of the apologies, they accepted them, and the incident was over.

As the months passed, there were no more encounters with the Lindgren brothers, who kept their distance from both Murietas. Joaquin thoroughly enjoyed his job and was happy with the money he was making. He and Rosita grew closer together and fell deeper in love every day. She was his inspiration when she often cheered him as he broke some of the toughest horses he had ever ridden in his life.

On Tuesday, May 7, 1850, Rosita was sitting on the corral fence watching her husband riding a particularly powerful and stubborn horse. It had rained the day before and the horse was kicking up mud instead of the usual dust. The California sun shone down from a clear sky.

Rosita was shouting encouragement to Joaquin when she noticed three men riding in from the west. Sunlight glinted from the badges worn by two of them. The third man was elderly and looked quite frail. There were no ranch hands around the corral at the moment.

The three riders saw Rosita and guided their mounts in her direction. As they drew up, the huskier lawman touched his hat. "Good morning, ma'am. I'm looking for the ranch foreman. Could you tell me where I might find him?"

Rosita looked toward the bunkhouse and was about to point it out as the likely spot, but at that moment, she saw the foreman coming that direction. Pointing with her chin, she said, "That is him heading this way right now."

Rosita glanced at Joaquin, who was still fighting to take control of the wild animal he was riding, then put her attention on the three men as they introduced themselves to Folger. The heavyset lawman was San Joaquin County Sheriff, Ed Miller. The smaller one was his deputy, Charlie Ivans. The thin, elderly man was introduced as Jacob Speltzer, owner of the general store in Stockton.

Listening close, Rosita learned that Speltzer had been robbed at his store on Saturday by a lone Mexican gunman. When he gave a description of the robber to the Stockton townspeople who had gathered around, one man spoke up and said there was a Mexican working at the Box T Ranch who fit the description perfectly. The man was a leather craftsman and saddle maker who had often delivered saddles, harnesses, bridles, and other leather goods to the Box T. As Sheriff Miller gave Folger the description, Rosita was stunned. The lawman was describing her husband. Her heart leaped in her breast when she heard Folger say, "The man you're describing, Sheriff, is our broncobuster, Joaquin Murieta. That's him on that bucking horse in the corral."

Hooking his thumbs in his belt under his paunch, Miller said, "I want to talk to Murieta as soon as he's done with that horse."

Rosita eased herself down from the fence, worry showing on her face. This had to be a case of mistaken identity. Joaquin had not been to Stockton in over a month, and besides, he would never rob anyone of anything. Remaining silent, she watched with trepidation as Joaquin finished his ride. As soon as he slid from the saddle, Roger Folger was there to tell him that Sheriff Miller wanted to see him.

When Joaquin came through the gate with Folger, Rosita moved alongside him, placing a hand in the crook of his arm. She noticed the look of puzzlement that was on her husband's face. Miller introduced himself and his companions to Murieta, then explained the situation.

Joaquin's mouth pulled tight at the implication. "Sheriff, this is all a mistake. I did not rob any store—in Stockton—or anywhere else."

Ignoring his flat denial, Miller turned to Jacob Speltzer. "Okay, Jake. Take a good look at him."

Curious ranch hands began gathering around as Speltzer reached inside his coat and produced a pair of wire-rimmed spectacles.

Placing them carefully on his nose and hooking them behind his ears, he set his gaze on the broncobuster. His wrinkled face tinted immediately. "Yep, Sheriff, that's him. That's the dirty greaser who robbed me on Saturday. Arrest him! I want my money back too!"

Stung by the accusation, Joaquin stiffened and let his anger show. Heat was creeping up his spine. "Sheriff, this man is mistaken! I am not the man who robbed him!"

Raising a hand, palm forward, Miller said, "Now, just cool down! If Mr. Speltzer says you're the man who stuck a gun in his face and took his money, I have no reason to doubt him."

"But he's mistaken!"

"Where were you at one-thirty last Saturday afternoon, then?" asked Miller.

Joaquin put a hand to his temple and looked at the ground. "Well, let me think a moment."

"I can tell you exactly where he was, Sheriff," said Rosita. "He was with me at Sparrow Creek, which is about five miles southwest of here."

"I know where it is, ma'am," Miller retorted. "I assume you are Mr. Murieta's girlfriend."

"I am his *wife!*" she said tartly. "We were on a picnic together."

"Mr. Thompson gives Joaquin Saturdays and Sundays off, Sheriff," interjected Folger.

"My wife is telling you the truth, Sheriff," said Joaquin. "We left our home in Sonora and rode to the creek over by Skyline Rock. We got there about noon and stayed till around three o'clock."

"Did anyone else see you?" asked Miller. "Someone who could verify your whereabouts at the time of the robbery?"

"Why do you need the word of someone else?" said Joaquin. "My wife is telling you the truth. Are you saying she is lying?"

"A wife cannot be a witness in her husband's defense in California, sir," said Miller. "Now, did anyone else see you?"

The Murietas looked at each other for a brief moment, then both shook their heads. "No," said Joaquin. "We didn't see anyone along the trail or at the creek."

The sheriff turned to Speltzer and asked, "Are you dead sure this is the man who robbed you?"

The old man fixed his eyes on Murieta once again and studied his features carefully. "Yes, sir! This is the man! I want him behind bars! I want my money too!"

"All right," said Miller, turning to Joaquin. "Murieta, I am arresting you for the robbery of the general store in Stockton on Saturday, May 4."

Rosita's fingernails were digging into her husband's arm as Joaquin bristled. "No! I did not do it! You cannot arrest me for something I did not do!"

"Sheriff, wait a minute," said Folger. "Let me get Mr. Thompson out here. He needs to be in on this."

While the foreman was hurrying to the big ranch house, cowboy Curly Bender detached himself from the group of onlookers and approached the sheriff. "Excuse me, Sheriff Miller," he said in a soft tone. "I have to tell you that I think this is definitely a case of mistaken identity. Joaquin has worked here long enough for us to get to know him. He is no thief or robber. He's a hard-working man. He does a job on this ranch that nobody else wants and he does it mighty good. There's just no way he could be the man who robbed Mr. Speltzer."

The group of ranch hands voiced their agreement in unison.

Miller eyed them carefully. "Tell you what, gentlemen. Half the men in California prisons once seemed to be good guys. You need to face the fact that men can fool you. I can testify to that as a lawman."

"Excuse me, Sheriff," spoke up Rosita, a tremor in her voice. "But is it not true in this country that the law has to prove a man's guilt?"

"Yes'm," replied Miller. "That'll be done in court. Your husband will get a fair trial."

"By that you mean Mr. Speltzer will point my husband out in front of a judge and jury as the man who robbed him, and the law will then have proven his guilt."

"That's about it, ma'am."

"Some law!" she snapped. "My husband is innocent, but because this man is mistaking him for someone else, my husband will go to prison!"

Joaquin was about to speak when Roger Folger arrived with Roy Thompson. The rancher was visibly upset. Miller explained the entire situation to him, saying Murieta had to be the man or Mr. Speltzer would not have pointed him out.

A flush spread on Roy Thompson's cheeks. Fixing Joaquin with a hot glare of disdain, he blurted angrily, "I give one of you dirty greasers a job, and you pull something like this! I'm paying you well, Murieta! Why did you have to rob Mr. Speltzer?"

Joaquin's blood was hot. "I did not do it!" There was a caustic edge in his voice that he made no attempt to soften. "Speltzer is either lying, or is gravely mistaken—I don't know which! But I am telling you, I didn't rob him! Rosita backs me in that fact, but nobody will believe her! This is an outright miscarriage of justice!"

Paying no heed to Joaquin's words, Miller commanded his deputy to place him in handcuffs. Charlie Ivans pulled the cuffs from his belt and stepped up to Joaquin, telling him to turn around and put his hands behind his back. When it appeared that Joaquin might try to fight his way out of the situation, Miller pulled his gun, cocked the hammer, and pointed it at him. "I don't like the look in your eye, greaser. You just stand still and let Charlie put the cuffs on you."

Rosita's temper was at the breaking point. Her entire body shuddered at the sound of the ratchets on the handcuffs as they closed over Joaquin's wrists. Stomping to Jacob Speltzer, she hissed through clenched teeth, "You dirty gringo liar! My husband did not rob you and you know it! Why don't you tell the truth? You need someone to blame, so it has to be my husband!"

Charlie Ivans hastened to Rosita and put his hands on her shoulders. "Lady, calm down. This kind of outburst won't help anything."

Joaquin saw red. "Get your hands off her!"

Ivans let go of Rosita and moved back toward Joaquin. "Keep your mouth shut, greaser, or I'll—"

Joaquin's foot lashed out and caught the deputy squarely in the groin. Ivans's face jerked out of shape, turned white, and he fell to his knees, groaning.

Before anyone could stop him, Joaquin kicked the deputy on the side of the head. Ivans fell over, unconscious.

Roy Thompson shouted for some of the ranch hands to jump Murieta and subdue him. When they tackled the broncobuster,

Rosita pounced on one of them, scratching his face severely. Roy Thompson swore and grabbed her. Before he got a good hold on her, she pivoted and clawed his cheeks. He let go immediately, placing his fingers to the burning claw marks. A cowboy named Hardy Simmons seized her, attempting to lock her arms next to her body, but she moved too quickly for him and got his left ear between her teeth.

Simmons howled and tried to pull her loose, but the more he pulled at her, the greater the pain. Sheriff Ed Miller ended it by drawing his gun and standing over the spot where four cowboys were holding Joaquin on the ground. Aiming the revolver at Joaquin's head, he shouted at Rosita, "Let go of the man's ear, or I'll shoot your husband!"

Rosita obeyed, spitting Simmons's blood from her mouth and wiping it from her face. The bleeding cowboy dashed to the bunkhouse to doctor his torn ear.

Cowboy Curly Bender had not helped to subdue Joaquin Murieta. As the ranch hands jerked Joaquin to his feet, Bender stepped up to the sheriff. "Pardon me, Sheriff Miller, but I'd like to ask you a question. Would you really have shot Joaquin in the head if the lady had not let go of Hardy's ear?"

"Don't bother the Sheriff, Curly," said Roy Thompson. The rancher then turned to Joaquin and Rosita, and said, "I am truly sorry I hired a greaser. I've learned my lesson. I'll never hire another."

"Come on," said Miller, taking Joaquin by the arm. "I've got a cell waiting for you in Stockton."

The Murietas rode their own horses as Miller and Ivans escorted them toward Stockton with Jacob Speltzer in the party. Rosita was told that she could go home to Sonora, but she insisted that she would stay with her husband. She would find a place to stay in Stockton while Joaquin was waiting for his trial so she could be near him. There was no discussion about what she would do when he was sent to prison.

Discouraged and angry, the Murietas were silent during the ride to Stockton. It was late afternoon when they pulled into town. Miller told Speltzer he would need to come with him to the office and sign a statement that Joaquin Murieta was indeed the man who had robbed him.

When they hauled up in front of the sheriff's office, a middle-aged lawman was sitting on a bench near the door with a young Mexican in handcuffs sitting beside him.

Miller recognized Harvey Smith, town marshal of nearby Farmington, California. Swinging from his saddle while the rest of his party was dismounting, he said, "Howdy, Harve. What have we here?"

"I heard about Jake Speltzer bein' robbed Saturday, Ed," said Smith. "This fella I've got cuffed here is Arturo Selica. He robbed a store in my town this mornin', but some of the townfolk were alert enough to catch him off guard. They captured him and disarmed him. I figured Mr. Selica may just be the dude who robbed Jake, though he denies it. Thought I'd bring him over here and let Jake take a look at him."

By this time, Joaquin and Rosita were on the boardwalk with Charlie Ivans and Jacob Speltzer. Miller immediately saw the strong resemblance between Arturo Selica and Joaquin Murieta. Ivans and the Murietas saw it too. Rosita smiled at her husband.

Already feeling embarrassed for the way Joaquin had been treated, Miller said, "Jake, put your glasses on and take a gander at this Mexican here on the bench. I think maybe there has been a case of mistaken identity."

Charlie Ivans lifted his hat, scratched his balding head, and avoided Rosita's scornful eyes.

Jacob Speltzer put on his spectacles and stepped close to Selica, who was jerked to his feet by Smith. Speltzer's mouth dropped open with a gasp.

"Well?" asked Miller.

The old man swallowed hard. "This is the man who robbed me, Sheriff."

"You're absolutely sure this time, Jake?" asked Miller.

"Absolutely," replied Speltzer, pointing to a scar on the Mexican's cheek. "I hadn't thought about the scar until I saw it again but I recollect it clearly." Then to Selica he said sternly, "I want my money back, you dirty robber!"

Selica would not meet the old man's hot glare. Guilt was written all over his face.

The next morning at the Box T, Roy Thompson stood on his front porch in the presence of the Murietas while Sheriff Ed Miller explained about Arturo Selica eventually breaking down the day before and admitting that it was he who had robbed Jake Speltzer. Joaquin and Rosita stood beside Miller, holding hands. They were certain that once the rancher heard the truth, Joaquin would be welcomed back to his job.

A few ranch hands passed by and looked on as Miller was telling the story.

"So," said the sheriff, finishing his explanation, "I'm sure you'll put Joaquin back on you payroll, Mr. Thompson. Right?"

Roy Thompson touched the scabbing claw marks on his face and scowled. "No!" he snapped. "I meant what I said yesterday. I've learned my lesson. I'll never hire another greaser."

It was Rosita's temper that exploded first. Lips splayed back over her teeth, she stepped close to the rancher, eyes flashing with fire. Her voice was filled with rising resentment. "How can you do this? Is it because I scratched you? That would not have happened if you had believed us in the first place!"

Exasperation showed on Thompson's face. "Now look, lady, I—"

"Joaquin was proven innocent, Mr. Thompson! You are being totally unfair!"

"I can hire and fire who I want, ma'am," he said, being careful not to overstep his bounds. He recalled what happened to the Lindgren brothers when they did. "I own this ranch, and—"

"If Sheriff Miller and Mr. Speltzer hadn't shown up here at all, Joaquin would still have his job. Right?"

Thompson looked at her blankly.

"Right?"

"I don't want to talk about it, ma'am," he replied tonelessly.

Joaquin had started to silence Rosita a moment before, but he let her squeeze the man further. It was enjoyable watching the little Mexican spitfire make him squirm.

"You don't want to talk about it because you are doing my husband wrong, and you know it! Tell me something, Mister Hotshot Rancher: is Joaquin the best broncobuster you ever saw, or have you seen better?"

Uncomfortable under the hot glare of Rosita Murieta, Thompson cleared his throat nervously. "He is the best I ever saw, ma'am, but like I said…I'm not hiring any more Mexicans."

Rosita opened her mouth to speak again when Joaquin touched her arm. "Darling, you have let off your steam at the man. I have stood here and let you do it so you would feel better. It is obvious that he has made up his mind. There is no use arguing with him."

Joaquin's words calmed Rosita and she turned toward the horses.

To Thompson, Joaquin said, "I was just beginning to think maybe you gringos were decent people, Mr. Thompson, but you have changed my mind."

As the Murietas were mounting up, the sheriff looked Thompson in the eye. "This is really not right, sir, and you know it."

The rancher met Miller's steady gaze for a few seconds, then turned and headed for the door of the house, muttering his hatred for Mexicans. He opened the door, passed through without looking back, and slammed it hard.

Miller swung slowly into his saddle. "I'm sorry it worked out this way, Joaquin. And I'm sorry for calling you a greaser. I can't blame you for feeling as you do about gringos."

"Apology accepted," said Murieta. "I really shouldn't feel bad toward all gringos. There are good ones and bad ones—just like there are good Mehicans and bad ones."

"Yes," said Rosita, "a bad Mehican named Arturo Selica just messed up our lives."

Trotting over the hills toward the ranch's main gate, Miller and the Murietas saw a rider angling toward them from a thick stand of pine trees, coming at a full gallop. As he came nearer, they recognized Curly Bender.

Drawing rein, Joaquin said to Rosita and the sheriff, "Speaking of good gringos, here comes one now."

Curly Bender skidded to a halt and said to Joaquin, "Glad I caught you. I couldn't let Mr. Thompson see me talking to you without getting fired, but I have good news for you."

Adjusting his position in the saddle, Joaquin said, "Well, I could use some of that kind for a change."

"I remember that you are interested in the whereabouts of your brother, Carlos."

"I sure am!" Joaquin's eyes lit up. "You have heard something of Carlos?"

"Yes. I have a Mexican friend named Rinco Alvarez who is working a mine a few miles from Sonora. Last night I went to visit him at his cabin. I was telling him about you and what had happened yesterday. When I said the name Murieta, he asked if you were related to a Carlos Murieta. I told him that you were brothers, and that you were trying to find him. Rinco told me that he and Carlos had become friends while Carlos was in Sonora, and that Carlos had gone to San Francisco."

"San Francisco?" said Joaquin. "Did he say why?"

"Rinco said that Carlos had run into some kind of trouble while trying to stake a claim so he could dig for gold. He got discouraged and took off for San Francisco. This is all Rinco knows."

Smiling warmly, Joaquin said, "Thank you, Curly. You have been very kind to both Rosita and me. We will not forget you."

As Bender rode back toward the thick stand of trees, Joaquin turned to Rosita. "Darling, we are going to San Francisco."

CHAPTER THIRTEEN

Joaquin and Rosita Murieta arrived in San Francisco early in the third week of May. They took a room in a hotel, and Joaquin immediately began a search for his brother.

The very next day, Joaquin happened upon an old friend from Sonora, Mexico, while searching for Carlos along a busy street. Manny Sepulveda was happy to see his old friend, and was even happier to hear that Joaquin had taken Rosita Carmel Feliz for his wife. Joaquin immediately asked if Manny had seen Carlos, and was thrilled to learn that the two of them had been together only a few days before.

"Manny, do you know where I can locate him?"

Sepulveda's features showed concern. "I think so. He is down on his luck, Joaquin. If something does not happen soon, I am afraid he will drink himself to death."

"Where can I find him?" asked Joaquin, worry penciling deep lines in his forehead.

"Do you know where the Barbary Coast is?"

"No, but I can find it."

"It is not far from here," Sepulveda told him. "I can give you directions. You will probably find Carlos at the Bull Moose Saloon. It was there that I ran into him last week. He is in bad shape emotionally."

Ready to head for the Barbary Coast immediately, Joaquin said, "Just tell me how to get there."

Manny gave him directions, then said, "Marlena will want to see you and Rosita, Joaquin. Let me tell you how to find our house. Please come and see us."

"We will do that," said Joaquin, shaking his hand. "If I find Carlos, we will come tonight."

Just over a half hour later, Joaquin Murieta entered the Bull Moose Saloon on San Francisco's Barbary Coast. The place was relatively dark. Having come in from brilliant sunshine, it took his eyes a moment to adjust. There were a few customers at tables, talking quietly. A lone man at the bar caught Joaquin's attention. It was his brother. Carlos was hunched over the bar, turning a glass of beer in his hands.

Moving across the room, Joaquin stepped up behind him. "Hello, brother."

Carlos's head came up and he spun around on the barstool. His bleary, bloodshot eyes widened as he focused on the face of his youngest brother. "Joaquin!" he gasped. "What are you doing here?"

"Looking for you."

Carlos slid off the stool, threw his arms around his brother, and broke into tears. As Joaquin held him tight, the bartender drew up behind the bar. "Anything wrong?"

"No," said Joaquin. "He is my brother. I have been looking for him for a long time."

"I understand," nodded the bartender. "Can I get you something to drink?"

"No, thank you. We'll be leaving in a moment."

The bartender shrugged and walked away.

Gripping Carlos's shoulders, Joaquin held him at arm's length. "I have much to tell you. Rosita and I are married and she is waiting at the Pacific Hotel for me to return…hopefully with you. Come on. Let's go."

As the Murieta brothers made their way along the street, Joaquin said, "It was Manny Sepulveda who told me where I might find you, Carlos. He said you're down on your luck. I want to hear about it."

"I will tell you, but first I want to hear about our family at home, about your wedding, and what has brought you and Rosita to California."

By the time they reached the hotel, Joaquin had filled Carlos in on everything that had happened in Mexico, including why he and Rosita married earlier than they had planned and why they had come to California. He brought him up to date with all the other news, explaining the recent events at the Box T Ranch and how he had learned that Carlos was in San Francisco.

They entered the Pacific Hotel just as the sun was going down over the ocean and walked to room number eight. Joaquin tapped on the door and listened as light footsteps approached from inside. When the door opened, Rosita set her dark eyes on Joaquin, then looked at his brother. "Carlos! He found you!"

Joaquin ushered the man through the door and closed it behind him as Rosita embraced her brother-in-law. Carlos's eyes were quite clear as he congratulated Rosita for marrying his brother, then embraced her again.

Joaquin immediately explained to Rosita about running into Manny Sepulveda, which resulted in his finding Carlos.

"Manny Sepulveda!" she said excitedly. "I remember that they were planning on going to San Francisco when they left our valley. How is Marlena?"

"She is fine. Manny gave me their address and asked that we come to see them. I told him we would come tonight if I found Carlos."

"Oh yes! It will be so good to see them. We will go after we have fed Carlos a good meal in the hotel dining room."

When they sat down to talk, it was apparent that Carlos was in a state of deep depression and anger over what had happened to him on the goldfields.

"What was it?" Joaquin asked.

"Crooked gringo. Man named Chester Handley."

"What did he do?" asked Rosita.

"Well, about seventeen months ago, I purchased some land from Handley in the foothills of the Sierras, just east of Placerville. There was no doubt it had gold in it. I bought mining tools and wood for a sluice box, and was ready to start digging for gold when two law officers came and told me I had to leave the property. I asked why, and they said I was trespassing. When I told them I had recently purchased the land, they informed me that the property still belonged to Mr. Handley."

"Didn't you have papers to prove that you had bought the property?" asked Joaquin.

Scratching his head, Carlos replied, "Well, this is where the whole thing went crazy. I had paid Mr. Handley in cash, using the last money I had, other than enough to buy the tools and supplies. Together we carried the sales papers to the land title office in Placerville and left them with the man in charge. He was to title the land in my name. When I took the law officers to the office, the other man was gone from the company and someone else was in charge."

"So what did he do?"

"He looked in the files and said all he could find were the papers that showed Chester Handley as owner of the property. When I told him about the sale, he said that with the coming of the gold rush, some land titles had been messed up. He suggested that my official sales documents had been lost, along with some others."

"But you didn't have a cash receipt?"

"No. The man asked me the same question. I explained that Mr. Handley seemed to be an honest man and since the papers were safe in the hands of the title company, I didn't demand a receipt. What a fool I was."

"Did you go to Handley and face him with it?" asked Rosita.

"Yes, and he flat denied that I had ever given him any money for the land. When I showed my Murieta temper, he told me to produce a receipt or leave. I had no choice but to leave."

Joaquin's own temper was hot by that time. "Tell you what, brother. We'll just go to Placerville and put some Murieta pressure on Mr. Chester Handley!"

Carlos's eyes dulled. "We can't, Joaquin."

"And just why not?"

"Because two weeks after I faced him with his dirty deal, he was thrown from a horse and killed. Broke his neck. Somebody else owns the property now."

"But this just isn't right," said Joaquin. "If there was some way you could prove you paid that crook for the property, the California authorities would force a proper settlement from his heirs. Do you know if he had any family?"

"Yes, he did comment on his family when we were having a friendly talk. He has a wife and three adult sons. They live somewhere in the Placerville area. Maybe right in the town."

"Were there any witnesses to the transaction?" Joaquin asked, rubbing his chin. "Someone who actually saw you pay Handley for the property?"

"Yes. A friend of mine. His name is Enrico Flores. He was with me at the time. He saw me pay Mr. Handley sixteen hundred dollars for the land."

"Where does Flores live?"

"In Placerville."

"There is still hope then, Carlos," said Joaquin. "We need to talk to an attorney here in San Francisco and tell him the story. Unless I am totally wrong about the law, the attorney will tell us that he can draw up an affidavit for your friend Enrico Flores to sign, stating that he personally witnessed the transaction. With that document in our hands, we will go to Placerville and have Flores sign it in front of an attorney there. The law will then force the Handley heirs to give you back the money. You can return to the goldfields and purchase another piece of land."

"It is worth a try, but I do not know an attorney here. I wouldn't know which one to pick."

"Maybe Manny could tell us about one," said Rosita.

The reunion between Manny and Marlena Sepulveda and the Murietas was a happy one. When the situation was explained to the Sepulvedas, Manny was able to tell them of a reliable attorney. Marlena invited them to come back the next evening for supper.

After spending an hour with the attorney the next day, the Murieta brothers found that Joaquin had indeed been correct. An affidavit was prepared by the attorney while they waited. Since Carlos was out of funds, Joaquin paid the attorney from his own dwindling resources. Carlos promised to pay his brother back once he was bringing in some money.

At the supper table that evening, Joaquin and Carlos explained that they would have to go to Placerville to claim the money Carlos had paid to Chester Handley. The Sepulvedas invited Rosita to stay with them until Joaquin could return for her. Rosita gladly accepted. The matter was settled, and the next morning Joaquin and Carlos rode away on the two Arabian horses.

At Placerville, the Murieta brothers learned that Enrico Flores had moved to the town of Murphy's Diggings, some forty-five miles south. Riding out immediately, they covered a little more than half the distance by dark. Entering a small village, they were able to find lodging with some Mexican people for the night.

The next day, they rode into Murphy's Diggings just before

noon. Gold had been discovered in all of the surrounding hills and the town was booming. As a result, Murphy's Diggings had become the focal point for gamblers, con men, merchants, would-be miners, and other types of people who had devised schemes to get rich in a hurry. Stores, shops, gambling halls, and saloons were being built at a furious pace along the town's main street.

The Murieta brothers only had to ask one man to learn that Enrico Flores was employed as a desk clerk at the California Hotel, the town's newest and fanciest. Joaquin commented on the great number of Monterey cypress trees that grew along the street as they dismounted and tied the Arabians at the hitchrail. He wondered if a forest had once stood there and many trees had been felled to carve out room for streets and buildings.

Elbowing their way through the throng that moved along the boardwalk, they entered the plush lobby of the hotel and were spotted immediately by Flores from behind the desk. "Carlos! I am glad to see you! Did nothing work out for you in San Francisco?"

"Not much," replied Carlos, reaching over the counter to shake Flores's hand. "I was able to find enough work to barely stay alive, that's about all."

Carlos introduced Joaquin to Flores, then between customers, explained why they had looked him up. Once he understood the situation, Flores said, "I know a good attorney in Vallecito."

"How far away is that?" asked Joaquin.

"Just four miles."

Enrico Flores looked at the large clock that hung in the lobby. "I get an hour for lunch beginning at twelve-thirty, Carlos. I know the attorney quite well. Since you and I are friends, he will probably not charge you anything to witness my signature on the affidavit. It is no problem if I miss lunch. We can ride there, get it taken care of, and return in time for me to be back at the desk, I am sure."

"Good!" exclaimed Carlos. "Can I get your horse for you?"

"Oh," said Flores, throwing his hands to his cheeks. "I forgot. I don't have a horse right now. Mine got sick and died, and I haven't bought a new one."

"Tell you what, Enrico," said Joaquin. "You can ride my horse. I will just wait here in the lobby until you get back."

"You will like both of Joaquin's horses, my friend. They are Arabians…all the way from Mehico."

Flores laughed. "Sounds good. I've never ridden a true Arabian horse."

Carlos and Joaquin Murieta had not noticed a group of some twenty half-drunken miners who were gathered across the street from the hotel when they rode up. The miners were standing around, passing four or five whiskey bottles among them when one named Ben Wiggins pointed out the two Mexicans who had just dismounted from the Arabian horses and were crossing the boardwalk toward the hotel.

The miners had a champion who led them. Bill Lang was a tall, muscular man with an unholy hatred for Mexicans and an insatiable desire for material gain. When Wiggins brought his attention to the two dark-skinned men and the beautiful animals they were leaving at the hitchrail, Lang grinned and took a long pull on the bottle in his hand. "Let's go take a look at them horses, fellas."

The twenty miners held up traffic while they crossed the street and collected at the hitchrail in front of the California Hotel. The Mexican riders had already passed into the lobby.

Handing the bottle to another miner, Lang looked the Arabian horses over. "Boys, take my word for it. You are lookin' at real horseflesh, here. These are thoroughbreds if ol' Bill Lang has ever seen thoroughbreds. Pure Arabian stock. Worth no less than four thousand dollars apiece—prob'ly closer to five thousand."

The miners knew their champion and they were aware of what was in his mind. Attempting to please him, one of them said, "Bill, these here Arabians look mighty familiar."

"I was thinkin' the same thing, Nick. These look exactly like the animals that were stolen from me last week." He belched. "In fact, I'm sure of it. These are my horses. Didn't I see a couple of grimy greasers ride up on 'em?"

"That's what I seen," spoke up one of them.

Several passersby paused to look and listen to the loud conversation of the miners. The others in Lang's group agreed that they had seen two Mexicans ride in on their leader's animals.

Knowing he had the attention of at least two dozen towns-people, Lang said, "Boys, what's the penalty for horse thievin' in these parts?"

"Hanging!"

"That right, folks?"

Only two men answered from the crowd, but both of them agreed emphatically that the only justice for a horse thief was the hangman's noose.

"Well, folks," said Lang, "I mean to get my horses back…and I'm thinkin' that the dirty greasers who stole 'em oughtta have to pay for their wicked deed!"

The miners shouted their agreement just as Enrico Flores and Carlos Murieta emerged from the hotel.

Unaware of what the miners were shouting about, Carlos led his friend to the hitchrail, pointing out Joaquin's Arabian. At that instant, Bill Lang stepped up. "Where are you two goin'?"

The rude approach irritated Carlos. "What business is it of yours?"

Viciousness was in Lang's voice as he said, "It's 100 percent my business if you're plannin' on ridin' *my* Arabians, greaser!"

"Pardon me?"

"You heard me!" said the tall man, his eyes mere slits. "These horses were stolen from my place last week."

Enrico Flores's brow furrowed. He looked at Carlos. "Can this be?"

"Of course not."

"You two know the penalty for stealin' horses?"

Carlos swallowed with difficulty. "These horses were not stolen, mister. They belong to my brother. He's right inside the ho—"

"Get a couple ropes, boys!" bellowed Bill Lang. "We'll teach these thievin' greasers a lesson!"

While two miners left the scene after ropes, the others began to make a circle around Enrico and Carlos. "Enrico, we'd best call for the town marshal."

"There is no town marshal," Flores said. "Murphy's Diggings has no law at all."

Bill Lang laughed hoarsely. "*We* are the law in this town, greaser! And we hang horse thieves!"

People on the street remained aloof as the two Mexicans were seized by rough hands and dragged to a large cypress a few yards up the street. They were not fond of Mexicans and they feared the miners. No one was about to lift a finger to save Flores and Murieta.

The two miners arrived with the ropes and began forming hangman's nooses. Enrico Flores cried, "This is not right! We did not steal those horses!"

"They belong to my brother in the hotel!" shouted Carlos. "Somebody go tell him what is happening!"

No one in the crowd moved.

When the ropes were tossed up over a sturdy limb fifteen feet off the ground, Carlos screamed at the top of his lungs, "Joaqui-i-i-n! Joaqui-i-i-n!"

In the hotel lobby, Joaquin Murieta was relaxed on an overstuffed sofa. He could hear the loud voices of the miners, but paid them no mind. He was used to the sounds in mining towns. He was resting with his head back and eyes closed when above the voices and noises of the street, he heard Carlos calling his name.

Jumping up from the sofa, he darted out the door and immediately saw a crowd gathered up the street at the foot of the tall cypress tree. Again he heard his brother calling him. He shoved his way through the crowd. He was stunned to see Carlos and Enrico in the hands of the miners, who had slipped nooses over their heads and were tightening them on their necks. Both men were terrified.

When Carlos saw his brother, he cried, "Joaquin! Help us! This big man says the Arabians are his; that we stole them!"

Joaquin demanded harshly, "Let them go! Those horses are not yours…and they did not steal them!"

"Get outta here, greaser!" roared Lang. "These *are* my horses, and these filthy thieves are the ones who stole 'em!"

Joaquin was unarmed and quite obviously outnumbered, but the situation was desperate. He lunged at Lang, swinging a haymaker. Fist met jaw, and Lang went down. Another miner jumped him, trying to wrestle him to the ground. Joaquin smashed his nose with an elbow, then chopped him savagely with two blows to the jaw.

Before the miner even hit the ground, there were four more on the angry Murieta. He flattened another one before two more jumped in and helped the others pin him to the ground. Carlos and Enrico looked on helplessly.

All eyes turned to Bill Lang, who was on his feet, wiping blood from the corner of his mouth. A look of baleful malevolence was in his narrowed eyes. "Nick," he said to one of the miners, "go get my bullwhip."

Strong hands held Joaquin down, with the left side of his head pressed against the ground. Trying to look up at Lang, he gasped, "Those horses are not yours and you know it! If you hang my brother and his friend, you are committing cold-blooded murder!"

A scowl of diabolical anger came over Bill Lang's ugly face. "It ain't murder when you hang horse thieves. It's justice! And you, greaser, are trying to interfere with justice. For this you will pay!" To the miners who were holding him down, he said, "Tie the dirty greaser to the tree!"

Joaquin squirmed and twisted to free himself, but to no avail. They ripped his shirt from his back and within a few minutes he was lashed to the tree with his bare back exposed.

The crowd looked on impassively as Bill Lang accepted the bull-whip from the man who had gone after it. In order to intimidate Murieta, he cracked the whip close to his ear without letting its tip touch flesh. Carlos and Enrico stood rigid beneath the overhanging limb, looking on in terror. The nooses were cinched tight around their throats and miners held the ends of the ropes, which were looped over the husky limb overhead.

Lang popped the whip close to Joaquin's head another time, then let its length lay partially coiled at his feet like a snake. "Greaser, you're gonna be sorry you interfered!" With that, he drew back his hand and laid the whip across Joaquin's back.

Gritting his teeth, Joaquin took the lash without jerking.

"Tough guy, eh? Well, let's see if this one will hurt a little more!"

The whip burned a furrow beside the bright-red welt that had already appeared on Joaquin's back. Biting hard, he still did not flinch. Cold sweat beaded on his brow. He was tied to the tree so that he had a full view of the two condemned men. Setting his pained eyes on Carlos, he started to speak, but the whip lashed him again, even harder.

Tears filled Carlos's eyes. "Stop!" he screamed. "Do not whip him any more!"

"Shut up, grease bucket!" roared Lang. "You'll get yours shortly!"

The crowd observed without emotion as the whip laid welt after welt on Joaquin Murieta's back, though they were amazed how he took it without flinching. Soon the welts became stripes and blood flowed. When Lang saw that his victim was about to pass out, the lashing stopped. Letting the whip drag sinuously on the ground behind him, Lang moved around to face Joaquin. "You are a tough little greaser. Never saw anybody take a whippin' like you did. 'Course, you will remember it for some time to come every time you move."

Joaquin's entire body pulsated with fiery pain and sweat soaked his face. His mouth was dry as a sand pit, and to make it worse, he was breathing hard. He turned languid eyes toward his brother and Enrico Flores. They both were looking on Joaquin with pity. Then their attention was drawn to Bill Lang, who stood before them and hissed through his teeth, "Now it is your turn, greasy thieves!" A wicked smile of satisfaction spread over his mouth as he said to the miners who held the ropes, "Hang 'em!"

Other miners joined in to help string up the Mexicans, whose hands were tied behind their backs. When the ropes came taut, both condemned men stood paralyzed in a swell of disbelief and terror. They managed to eject tiny whimpers as strong hands began to pull on the ropes, sliding them over the limb. As their feet left the ground, they gagged, squirmed, and kicked violently. Up and up they rose until their feet churned air ten feet off the ground.

Engulfed in a mixed paroxysm of grief and wrath, Joaquin Murieta released a wild, wordless wail as he watched Carlos and Enrico dangling like toys at the end of a string.

There were gasps in the crowd as two women fainted. Men carried them away while the rest of them looked on, mesmerized by the graphic scene.

The eyes of both victims bulged and stared out over swollen purple cheeks as they writhed in agony, gagging, kicking and twisting.

Joaquin forgot his burning back for the moment as he wailed again. As the slow deaths came on, Joaquin could no longer watch. Instead, he let his hate-filled eyes move from man to man amongst the twenty lynchers, memorizing their faces and particular characteristics. His greatest animosity was centered on Bill Lang, who seemed to be enjoying the hanging more than anyone else.

After several minutes, it was over. The bodies dangled lifelessly, swaying a little in the gentle afternoon breeze. Joaquin looked up at his dead brother. Carlos's eyes—like those of Enrico—were distended from their sockets, and had become lusterless and dry as stones.

There was a scraping ache in Joaquin's throat, a bulging pressure in his head, and a volcano of hatred in his heart toward the miners who had so brutally taken the lives of his brother and Enrico Flores. Blinking against the sweat that ran into his eyes, he looked at Bill Lang, who stood nearby. Lang was laughing and making a joke about the way the dead men's heads hung at an angle against the ropes.

Joaquin's strength had completely drained away, but he visualized Lang's throat in the grip of his own two hands. At that moment, nothing would have given him more pleasure than to strangle the life from the man. Yes, and when Lang was dead, Joaquin would enjoy bringing the same fate to the rest of the heartless killers. *Someday...* he thought. *Someday...*

Lang then turned to Murieta. "I hope you learned your lesson, greaser. Don't ever meddle with white men...especially when they are exactin' justice on stinkin' greaser horse thieves."

With that, the miner walked away, followed by the others. Joaquin clenched his teeth as he watched the miners lead the Arabian horses down the street. His blood boiled. The devilish miner would murder Carlos and Enrico, calling them horse thieves, just so he could steal the Arabian thoroughbreds for himself. In Joaquin's mind it was an even more horrendous crime because Lang was stealing the animals given so graciously to Rosita and himself as wedding presents by his best friend, Don Miguel Gonzales.

Looking around at the crowd, Joaquin hoped to see someone coming to release him from the tree. But they all turned and walked away, saying they hoped the news of this incident would spread far and wide. Maybe the greasers in California would get the message and go back to Mexico where they belonged.

Joaquin lifted his gaze to the hanged men above him. He wanted to weep for his brother, but no tears would come. He was so filled with hatred and the need for vengeance that no other emotion could crowd into his heart.

Running a dry tongue over equally dry lips, Joaquin leaned against the tree. His arms ached from being wrapped around the trunk; his wrists hurt from the ropes that bound them together; but more than these, his bleeding back felt like it was on fire. He could feel his heart throbbing in his chest as he wondered how he was going to get loose from the tree.

Still breathing raggedly, Joaquin wished for water to slake his burning thirst and thought of Rosita. He wished she were there to bathe his stripes and cover them with something that would ease the pain. On a second thought, he was glad she was not there. He would not want her to see him like this, and he would not want her to have experienced the awful hanging of Carlos and his friend.

Abruptly, Joaquin was aware of footsteps drawing near. He opened his eyes and beheld a tall, lanky gringo with a hunting knife in his hand. The man was in his late twenties: handsome, dark-haired, with a well-trimmed mustache, friendly pale blue eyes, and expensive clothes.

"Hold still," said the stranger in a soft voice, "and I'll cut you loose."

CHAPTER FOURTEEN

The stranger carefully cut the rope that bound Joaquin Murieta's wrists and eased him to the ground so that he lay belly down. Eyeing the bloody stripes on his back, he said, "You're going to need a doctor's attention. There's one just down the street. I'll be back."

"I have very little money in my pocket, sir. I doubt that there's enough to pay the doctor."

"I'll take care of it," came the reply. "The doctor is quite reasonable, anyhow."

Gritting his teeth in pain, Joaquin twisted his head, and looked up at him. "I don't know who you are, but I sure appreciate your help."

"Name's Bill Byrnes. I'm a professional gambler. I was in a poker game at the Golden Lantern Saloon when the ruckus started out here on the street. We had just finished a hand, so I excused myself and came out to see what was happening. I got here in time to see you being lashed to the tree." He looked up at the hanging bodies. "I take it these are your friends."

"The one closest to you is my brother."

"I'm sorry," said Byrnes. "If I had felt there was anything I could do to stop it, I would have tried, but one man against all those miners wouldn't have a chance. They'd have killed me too."

"I understand."

"I had to wait till Lang and his pals were clear out of town before I could even cut you down. If they'd seen me move in to help you, they'd have beaten me or worse."

"Lang?" said Joaquin, the name bitter on his tongue. "So that's the big ugly one's name."

"Yes. Bill Lang. Meaner'n a teased snake, as you found out. I hate it that he and I have the same first name."

While the man was letting the name Bill Lang sink into the reserves of his memory, Byrnes asked, "What's your name, my friend?"

"Joaquin Murieta."

"Well, Joaquin, you just lie there and try to relax. I'll be back in a few minutes with the doctor."

A few townspeople had collected along the street, observing while Bill Byrnes cut Murieta loose, but no one offered assistance. As the gambler hastened away, Joaquin lifted his head slightly and looked at them. When they felt the pressure of his eyes on them, they mumbled and left. Joaquin felt a growing disgust toward gringos. Had he, Carlos, and Enrico not been Mexicans, none of this would have happened.

Moments later, Byrnes returned with a middle-aged man whom he introduced as Dr. Miles Lawson. When the doctor knelt beside Joaquin and examined the damage done by the bullwhip, he said to Byrnes, "We have to get him to the office where I can work on him."

"We'll have to carry him, Doc," said the gambler. "That's going to hurt him. Since my hotel room is a lot closer, why don't we just take him over there?"

Ten minutes later, Joaquin Murieta was lying down on the bed in Bill Byrnes's room. While the doctor prepared to work on him, Byrnes asked, "How did this whole thing get started, Joaquin?"

"I'm not really sure," came the reply.

Murieta gave a brief explanation as to why he and Carlos had come to Murphy's Diggings, then told how he stayed in the hotel lobby, thinking that Carlos and Enrico were riding to Vallecito.

As Dr. Lawson began painstakingly washing the bloody stripes, Joaquin gritted his teeth and told of how he heard Carlos calling his name from the street, and what he found when he arrived at the scene under the cypress tree.

When Byrnes heard of Lang's accusing the two Mexicans of stealing the Arabians, his comment was, "Sounds like Lang. He's the greediest man I know, and he'll stop at nothing to get his hands on anything of value."

"Yes. Even murder."

"It isn't the first time he's murdered for material gain," put in Lawson as he began applying salve to the lacerations. "He's already killed several Mexicans and taken their gold claims."

"What about the Calaveras County sheriff?" asked Joaquin. "Won't he do something about Lang?"

"He would if he could get proof on him," said Lawson, "but people in these parts are scared spitless of him and his bunch. Nobody will tell what they know for fear they'll end up dead too. Lang hates your kind, Mr. Murieta, and aims to do his part to rid California of every one of you."

"That's right," said Byrnes. "And until the law can catch Lang red-handed, he'll go on killing Mexicans almost at will."

Joaquin said no more, but his mind was churning. He gritted his teeth once more while the stinging salve bit into the open wounds, and even broke into a cold sweat, but not once did he flinch.

"You're a tough bird," commented Lawson. "Seldom do I find a man who can feel the kind of pain you're feeling, yet not really show it."

"It is my conquistador training, doctor. We were taught that though the body experience pain, we are not to allow the mind to give into it."

"Ah, so that's it," nodded the doctor. "I've heard about the conquistadors. Rough and tough bunch, I understand."

"I guess you could say that. You have to be a little rough and tough to be accepted by the conquistadors, then they make you a lot rougher and a lot tougher."

Lawson said no more until he finished applying the salve, then told Joaquin his back would need cleaning and more salve applied everyday for ten days. By that time, he should be able to wear a shirt again and slowly start getting back to his normal life.

Byrnes paid Lawson, then asked him to come to the hotel every day, saying he was paying for a room in the hotel for Joaquin until he was well enough to leave Murphy's Diggings. Joaquin protested, saying Byrnes should not foot the bill for his medical attention, nor for his room, but the gambler quieted him by saying if Joaquin would feel better about it, he could pay him back someday.

When the doctor was gone, Joaquin worked himself to a sitting position on the edge of the bed. "Bill, my friend, I must ask a very big favor from you."

"Sure."

"My brother's body still hangs from the tree. I need to get it down, along with Enrico's body, and have them buried."

"Of course," said Byrnes. "I'll hire a couple of men around town to dig the graves. There's a small cemetery just outside of town. They can be buried there."

"Is there a priest or a preacher in Murphy's Diggings? I hate to have them buried without some sort of service."

Shaking his head, Byrnes said, "Nobody like that anywhere near here that I know of."

"All right," said Joaquin solemnly. "I will just have to have a service for Carlos in my heart. I suppose you should let the owner of the hotel know about Enrico, too."

"He probably already knows by now, but I'll see about it while I'm at the desk getting a room for you. In the meantime, you ought to lie back down and rest."

"I will pay you back just as soon as I can for all this is costing you, my friend."

"Fine." The gambler picked up his hat. "Just don't worry about it, okay?"

A slight frown furrowed Murieta's brow. "I hope I won't insult you by asking this, Bill, but why are you doing this for me? Until a little while ago, we had never met."

Byrnes walked to the door, took hold of the knob, then turned and replied, "Let's just say that there have been times when I've been down on my luck and someone has helped me. I know what it's like to be in your place."

Joaquin showed him a broad smile. "You're all right for a gringo." Then his features hardened as he added, "But there are some gringos who need to pay for what they did to my brother. Twenty of them, in fact. And since there is no law to make them pay, I will do it myself."

"You will only get yourself killed if you try it, Joaquin. There's no way you can take on twenty hard-nosed men like Lang and his bunch. I don't mean to sound indifferent about your brother's death, but the best thing you can do is to forget it. Your getting killed sure won't bring Carlos back."

"They've got my horses, too. I would sure like to get *them* back."

"It'll mean taking on all twenty of them. Best leave it alone." With that Byrnes left, closing the door behind him.

Rolling belly down on the bed, Joaquin struggled with the

hatred he was feeling toward Bill Lang and his men. They murdered Carlos and Enrico, took the Arabian horses, and just walked away. Pondering on it for a while, he was sure he could conceive a plan to kill every one of the lynchers one at a time. He would save Bill Lang until last. Make him sweat it out.

While thoughts about the lynchers raced through his mind, suddenly Joaquin thought of Rosita. She was so dead-set against violence and he had told her he would refrain from killing ever again. She believed him. If he went after Lang and his bunch and did kill them one by one, it would make her very unhappy and lower him in her eyes. Slowly he weighed it out. Rosita's love and respect meant more to him than getting revenge on Carlos's killers. And besides, if he should fail in his plan to kill them one by one—and get himself killed in the process—he would go to his grave and leave Rosita behind. More than anything, Joaquin wanted to live out his life with the most wonderful person he had ever met. Nothing was worth risking that.

The next day, Joaquin obtained paper and pencil and wrote a letter to Rosita. In the letter, he explained about Carlos's death, giving every detail. He then told her of the beating he had taken with the bullwhip and of Bill Byrnes coming to his rescue. He explained further about the time it would take him to recover, and how his newfound gringo friend was paying the bills, adding that as soon as possible Byrnes would be paid back.

On the seventh day since Carlos's hanging, Joaquin was sitting at the open window of his hotel room, observing the activity on the street. There was heavy traffic at the assayer's office a few doors away, across the dusty thoroughfare. There was no doubt that the miners were doing well.

Dr. Miles Lawson paid his daily visit, caring for Joaquin's wounds and saying that he was healing nicely. His patient told him that there was less pain every day and that he was enjoying more freedom of movement.

Lawson had been gone about an hour when there was a tap at the door. Joaquin raised his voice and bid him enter. Byrnes came bearing the gift of a new shirt, saying that in a few more days Joaquin would be able to wear it.

Joaquin thanked him, expressing once again his appreciation for all that Byrnes had done. He rose from his chair and looked through the window toward the assayer's office. "Bill, I've been thinking."

"And I know who you've been thinking about. Your beautiful Rosita. It won't be long now and you can go to her."

Laughing, Joaquin said, "I will not deny that I've been thinking about my Rosita, but lately, along with some definite plans."

"Oh? What kind of plans?"

"Well, I've been sitting here every day watching those miners come and go from the assayer's office. I have decided to take up gold mining. Rosita deserves the best, and I can better provide for her by mining gold than by breaking horses."

"Sounds like a good idea," said Byrnes, "but have you considered the fact that it takes money to stake a claim?"

"Uh…yes. That's the one problem I will have to work out."

"You have a rich uncle?"

"No."

"How about a friend who just cleaned up good in a poker game?"

"Bill, I'm glad you did well in your poker game, but you have already put out a lot of money on me. I can't let you do it."

"How about if we make it a partnership? I'll pay for staking the claim. Then when you start pulling gold out of the ground, I'll take half of the profit until I've made my stake money back. Now what would you say to a deal like that?"

Joaquin stared at him in absolute awe. "You would really do this for Rosita and me?"

"Sure."

Joaquin shook his hand, and they established the agreement between them.

"I want to write Rosita another letter and tell her about this," Joaquin said. "Will you mail it for me?"

"Of course. You write it, and I'll be back to get it a little later."

Alone once again, Joaquin hastily penciled a letter to his wife, informing her that they were going into the gold mining business and explaining the financial arrangements he had made with Bill Byrnes.

On the tenth day since his beating with the bullwhip, Joaquin was told by Dr. Lawson that he was healed up enough to wear his shirt, and within another five days, could travel to San Francisco. Bill Byrnes came by the hotel room just as Lawson was getting ready to leave. Byrnes paid the doctor the final bill and was delighted to hear of Joaquin's condition. When Lawson was gone, Joaquin thanked his friend once again for his kindness.

Smiling broadly, Byrnes told Joaquin he was welcome. Then he said, "I've got some good news."

"Yes?"

"About an hour ago, while I was in a card game at the Golden Lantern, a miner friend of mine told me about a claim that is available."

"What does he mean, 'available'?"

"Well, it's a claim that has been worked some by an elderly miner. The old fella died day before yesterday. He was a widower and all alone, so there's no heir to the claim. Now that California is a state, the law says in such a case the state owns the claim. We can buy it at a very low price if we take advantage of it right away. What do you say?"

"It has been paying off well?"

"Quite well."

"Where is it?"

"Just outside of Saw Mill Flat. You know where that is?"

"Yes. It is about six miles straight north of Sonora, right on the east edge of New Melones Lake. This is good. Rosita and I can still keep our house in Sonora. I can ride to the claim to work every day."

"Oh! I almost forgot. The claim has a small two-room cabin too. My friend says it's practically new and in good shape. You mentioned how Rosita liked to be with you at times when you were breaking horses. This way, if she wants to accompany you from time to time when you're working the claim, the two of you could stay in the cabin and not have to go back to Sonora for the night."

"Sounds too good to be true," said Joaquin, shaking his head. "But since it's available, let's go over there and take a look at it."

Finding the claim and cabin to be ideal, the new partners purchased it with Bill Byrnes's money. Since the cabin was only three miles from Murphy's Diggings, Byrnes said he would stay there and watch over the claim until Joaquin could go to San Francisco and bring Rosita. Claim jumpers were common and the place would need to be watched. By Byrnes being seen around the cabin early mornings and at night, it would keep the jumpers from trying to move in. Byrnes could stay in Murphy's Diggings during the daytime to keep up his gambling.

With additional money loaned to him by his friend, Joaquin bought a horse and rode to San Francisco. Byrnes also provided him with the funds to buy a horse for Rosita so they could make the return trip together.

On August 4, 1850, Joaquin and Rosita arrived in Sonora. The next day, he took her—along with Bill Byrnes—to the claim at the Saw Mill Flat. She immediately fell in love with the little cabin and was thrilled with the claim. She expressed her appreciation to Bill Byrnes for all he had done by giving him a sisterly hug.

With the help of Bill Byrnes's miner friend, Joaquin quickly learned how to extract the gold ore from the earth and wash it in the sluice box. Soon he was working on his own. Rosita stayed at the cabin every day for the first week, even helping her husband at the sluice box. They had done so well by the end of the week that they were able to pay Bill Byrnes half of what they owed him. Rosita spent most of her time at the claim site the next ten days, and with her help, Joaquin was able to pay Byrnes in full.

To celebrate their debt being paid, the Murietas took Byrnes to supper at Sonora's fanciest café. That night, as Joaquin and Rosita were preparing to retire for the night, she wrapped her arms around him and kissed him sweetly. "Darling, we haven't talked about it very much, but I want to tell you that I am proud of you."

"We haven't talked about what very much?" he asked, holding her tight. "And for what are you proud of me?"

"I am referring to Bill Lang and those awful miners who hanged Carlos and put those scars on your back."

"Oh." Joaquin had thought much about the miners, but had said nothing to her.

"I am so proud," said Rosita, "because you have not decided to go after them. You have not stained your hands with their blood. You told me you were through with violence in your life and you meant it. Thank you."

Joaquin kissed her again. "I want no more to shed blood, my sweet. Though I wish Lang and his friends were all dead, I will not pursue them to bring it about. We are very happy now and doing well. We will just enjoy each other."

As the days came and went, Joaquin worked hard at mining gold. More and more, Rosita was spending her time at the claim site, or at least nearby in the cabin. She loved being near the man she had married. From time to time, Bill Byrnes came by the cabin in the early evenings to visit and also to partake of Rosita's good cooking. They had let it be known that he was always welcome.

One evening, after a particularly good meal, Byrnes leaned back in his chair and patted his full belly. "Joaquin, my friend, you are a very fortunate man."

"That I am," said Murieta, "but to what particular category are you referring?"

"The wife-mate category."

Rosita, who was seated across the table from the gambler, blushed.

"I will agree 1000 percent to that. Rosita is the most beautiful and wonderful wife any man ever had."

"And she can cook," said Byrnes.

"Yes, and if I do not be careful, Rosita's good cooking will make me fat."

Bill Byrnes laughed. "I'm sure that's true." Then his features took on a serious mien. "It is more than Rosita's good looks, wonderful personality, and excellent cooking for which I say you are fortunate, my friend. I have observed the deep love that you two have for each other. I envy you, Joaquin. It must be truly wonderful to have a woman love you like she does."

"That it is," agreed Joaquin, taking Rosita's hand in his own.

"I hope someday to find a woman who will love me like that."

Rosita smiled and reached across the table with her free hand to pat Bill's arm. "I am sure that someday that very woman will walk into your life, Bill. You are a kind and generous man. You will make some woman a good husband."

"Well, when I find her, I hope she and I will be as happy together as you two are."

"If she is the right one, you will be," Joaquin assured him.

As the weeks passed, Rosita stayed at the claim site and did light work alongside her husband. From time to time they stopped to embrace and kiss in spite of the dust and dirt on their clothes and faces. In the evenings they took walks in the woods together finding their love rooting deeper and growing stronger.

Joaquin had his moments when he relived the hanging of Carlos and Enrico and the horrible whipping he had taken, but he kept it to himself. He did not want Rosita to know that he was still nursing the desire to punish them for what they had done.

One particular day, while the two of them worked side by side at the sluice box, Joaquin had Lang and the other nineteen miners on his mind. A vitriolic hatred was burning deep inside him. He envisioned himself wringing the life from every one of them, and beating Bill Lang to death with his own bullwhip.

"You're awfully quiet today, my love," Rosita said, breaking into his thoughts.

Joaquin stopped what he was doing. "Am I? I'm sorry."

"What are you thinking about? Some other woman?"

Joaquin took her in his arms, bent his head low, and looked into her eyes. Their lips were nearly touching as he said, "There is only one woman I think about, beautiful Rosita. And you know who it is."

She smiled. "I know. I just wanted to hear you say it."

They enjoyed a long, lingering kiss, then went back to work.

That night in the bedroom of the small cabin, Joaquin lay awake long after Rosita's soft, even breathing told him she was asleep. Once again, his mind went back to that horrible day. He could hear Carlos calling his name and see himself running up the street to the cypress tree. He recalled the awful shock of finding his brother and Enrico Flores standing there with the ropes draped over the tree limb and the nooses around their necks. Like it was happening all over again, he felt the strong hands of the miners lashing him to the trunk of the tree. Then came the burning, biting tip of the bullwhip tearing at his back.

It was a cool night and the bedroom windows were open, allowing the breeze to flow freely through the room. But the hatred Joaquin Murieta was feeling radiated heat. Sweat beaded on his brow and gathered at the back of his neck, slithering down between his shoulders.

Slipping quietly from the bed, he moved into the cabin's larger room, opened the door, and stepped out onto the small porch. The night breeze touched the sweat on his face and cooled him. He could hear an owl hooting somewhere in the forest and see the treetops swaying against the star-studded sky. *How long will this hatred so grip me? I must suppress this powerful need to have revenge on Lang and his cohorts for what they did. I must do it for Rosita's sake. I must.*

Getting a grip on himself, Joaquin returned to the bedroom and slipped carefully under the covers. Rosita was still sleeping soundly. Forcing his thoughts away from Carlos and his horrible death, Joaquin finally grew sleepy and soon drifted into slumber…

Suddenly he was in the lobby of the California Hotel in Murphy's Diggings. Carlos's terrified voice was calling his name. His feet were instantly pounding the soft dirt of the street and he was drawing near the spot under the cypress tree where a crowd was gathering.

Then he saw them: Carlos and Enrico, eyes wild with terror, held in the grip of the miners. Nooses were cinched around their necks, with the ropes flung up over the lowest limb. For some reason Joaquin knew the big man with the ugly face was in charge of the hanging. Quickly, he knocked the man down and turned to fight off the others. Strong hands were gripping him…forcing him to the ground. He was struggling…struggling…

"Joaquin! Wake up!"

Abruptly the struggling stopped and Joaquin opened his eyes. He could feel Rosita's hands gripping his shoulders and could make out her concerned features in the darkness of the bedroom. Sweat bathed his face.

"You were having a bad dream, darling," Rosita said softly. "Are you all right?"

Joaquin sat up and wiped sweat with a forearm. "Yes. I'm all right."

"What were you dreaming about?"

"I…I don't remember," he lied. "It's over, now. You get back to sleep."

Joaquin lay back on his pillow as Rosita crawled under the covers beside him. He kissed her, then turned on his side. She scooted up close and began to rub his back. As her tender fingers found the ridges of the scars from the bullwhip, she said, "Joaquin?"

"Uh-huh?"

"You were dreaming about Carlos and how you got these scars, weren't you?"

After a lengthy silence, he replied, "Go to sleep, darling."

"You didn't answer my question."

Another long pause. "We'll talk about it in the morning."

Sitting up, Rosita said, "We will talk about it right now."

Joaquin rolled over and focused on the outline of her head and shoulders in the gloom of the night.

"Darling, you must get this thing out of your system."

"I know. I know. It's eating at my innermost being like a wild thing. Those men got away with murdering my brother, Rosita. They should have to pay for what they did."

"You lust for vengeance, don't you?"

After a brief silence, he replied, "Yes. Yes, I do. I'd like to—"

"Joaquin, do you know what God's book says?"

"About what?"

"Vengeance."

"No."

"It says vengeance belongs to the Lord. He will repay the wrong-doers. You must let Him take care of Bill Lang and his wicked friends."

Joaquin reached out and stroked her smooth cheek. "My wife speaks with much wisdom. I will do as you say. I will leave the vengeance for Carlos's death in the hands of the Lord."

"That is the right attitude, my darling. I am so glad you will let God handle it."

Leaning over, she kissed him, then lay once again under the covers. Soon Rosita was sound asleep. Joaquin lay awake with hatred toward the heartless miners burning fresh and hot within him. He told himself he would like to help the Lord out in exacting vengeance on the dirty killers, but because of Rosita, he would resist the temptation.

CHAPTER FIFTEEN

As the weeks passed, Joaquin and Rosita Murieta worked side by side, producing gold ore from their claim and selling it to the assayer in Saw Mill Flats. They were doing so well that they decided come spring, they would pay one of their Mexican neighbors to watch over their property so they could make a trip to southern California and visit their friends, Colby and Beth Cullins. It would be good for them to take a break from their labors and spend some time with the Cullinses.

Rosita expressed her wish that they could go back home to Mexico and visit their families, but in the same breath, she remarked that as long as Don Jose Gonzales was alive, it would mean only trouble for them to return.

The claim just to the north of them belonged to a lone Mexican man named Franco Rodriquez. They decided to ask Franco if he would mind watching the place for them when they made their trip. The two claims were only fifty yards apart. Franco lived in a tent, since he didn't have a cabin. They would invite him to stay in the cabin while they were gone. If Franco could not help them, they would ask their neighbors to the south, Andino and Margarita Cabrera. The Cabreras were quite friendly toward the Murietas, and their cabins were only some seventy yards apart.

It was the first week in October when Joaquin finished a day's work and, leaving Rosita to fix supper, walked to the Rodriquez claim. Upon approaching the tent, he found Franco washing a battered, bleeding face.

Franco, a man in his early sixties, looked up through puffy, swollen eyes. "Hello, Joaquin."

"Franco, what happened?"

"Gringos," came the bitter reply. "I was in town selling my ore this afternoon. Three of them jumped me as I was heading home. Dragged me into the woods and beat me till I was almost unconscious. They said I should leave California and go back to Mehico."

"Dirty swine!" exclaimed Joaquin. "Tomorrow you and I will go into town. You will point them out to me. I will make them sorry for what they did to you."

"No, Joaquin. It is no good, my staying here. I have done well with my claim. I will take my money and go back to Mehico. Maybe you should consider doing the same thing. You have a young and beautiful wife. I have heard many gringos in Saw Mill Flats speak of her in wicked ways. I think some of them would even kill you to get their hands on her."

Joaquin's breathing was harsh. "Just let them try it."

"You and Rosita have done well with your claim, Joaquin. To avoid bloodshed, why don't you sell out and go back to Mehico with me?"

"The only place we would want to go if we returned to Mehico would be Sonora, Franco, but there are reasons you do not know about that would keep us from returning there."

"I see. Then at least keep a close watch on Rosita."

"I will do that."

Franco Rodriquez was gone in two days. A week after that, Joaquin and Rosita heard in town that Franco had sold his claim to five gringos, who would be moving onto the property the next day.

While working alone at his sluice box the next morning, Joaquin observed five big, burly gringos ride in and set up a large tent where Franco's small one had stood. Deciding to make an attempt at being friendly with them, Joaquin laid down his tools and walked toward them.

George Hadley, the biggest and burliest of the five men, was their leader. While the others were carrying supplies into the big tent, he was busy doing some repair work on the sluice box.

Bob Dix, Harry Worth, Myron Ackerly, and Clarence Keaton, like their leader, were dirty, long-haired, full-bearded, and hard-drinking men. One glance at the bunch would tell a person that they could get mean...real mean. Harry Worth wore a gold earring in his left ear, pirate-style. He had the meanest look of the five.

It was Worth who first noticed the dark-skinned man heading toward the campsite in the shadows of the towering pines. Setting the picks and shovels down, he said to the others, "Boys, we got company."

While the others turned and followed Worth's pointed finger, George Hadley looked up from the sluice box and swore. "It's a slimy greaser. Must own the claim on that side of us."

Bob Dix had a tobacco cud in his mouth. Spitting a brown stream, he said, "Wonder what he wants."

"He wants to get his greasy hide hung on a tree if he messes with us," remarked Clarence Keaton.

Even as Keaton spoke, the quintet fixed their eyes on the approaching Mexican and knotted close together.

Joaquin picked up on their hard-bitten demeanor the moment he saw them collecting together and eyeing him with disdain. He knew before he spoke that they were not going to be friendly, but since he had come this far, he would at least make an attempt to let them know he wanted to get along with them.

Joaquin smiled. "Good morning, gentlemen. My name is—"

Harry Worth guffawed. "Gentlemen!" said. "Did you hear that, fellas? The greaser called us gentlemen! We ain't never been called by that fancy name before!"

The others laughed.

"My name is Joaquin Murieta. I am your nearest neighbor to the south. I understand you are the ones who bought this claim from Franco Rodriquez."

"Yeah." George Hadley stepped closer to Murieta. "That's one way to get rid of stinkin' greasers—buy 'em out."

"There are other ways, too," spoke up Myron Ackerly.

Joaquin realized immediately what he was up against. Keeping a control on his temper and holding his voice steady, he said, "I am sorry you men feel that way about Mexicans. We mean no harm, and we have as much right to stake claims as you gringos. I came over here to welcome you and to show myself friendly. Why is it you feel this way about Mexicans?"

"Well, for starters," said Hadley, "all of us are veterans of the recent Mexican-American War. You heard of that?"

"Of course."

"Well, ain't that enough to make us hate your innards?" snapped Hadley.

"We had our reasons for fighting, the same as you," said Joaquin, "but I do not hate Americanos."

"Well, we hate you, greaser," said Bob Dix. "Best thing for you to do is head back to Mexico."

"Like I said, we have as much right here as you do. We are staying."

"Well, while you're stayin'," said Hadley, "you just stay off of our property. Because if you show up over here again—"

Hadley's words were cut off by what he saw standing at the edge of the trees near the Murieta cabin. Rosita, curious about her husband's visit to their new neighbors, was fully visible in the bright morning sunlight. Her long black hair lay in lovely swirls on her shoulders and the skirt and blouse she wore did not hide her gracious figure.

Noting Hadley's stare, Joaquin turned to look behind him. When he saw Rosita, he wished she had not made herself known. He did not blame her, for she was only interested in her husband's approach to their new neighbors.

"Now there's the type of greaser I like, George!" said Clarence Keaton.

Hadley smiled, showing a mouthful of crooked, yellow teeth. "Mm-mmm! Tell you what, Murieta, next time you're feelin' neighborly, you stay home and send the little señorita!"

"Señora," corrected Joaquin. "She is my wife."

"Well, send her anyhow," chortled Harry Worth.

Disgusted with the situation, Joaquin turned and walked toward Rosita, his temper aflame.

"What happened?" she asked. "I could not hear what they were saying."

"It was best that you couldn't," said Joaquin, taking her by the arm and escorting her away from the miners' view. Laying hands on both of her shoulders, he looked her square in the eye. "Do not ever make a move in their direction, darling. They are wicked, vile men. If I am not here and you ever see them coming this way, get in the cabin and lock the door. Understand?"

"Yes. I understand."

Later that afternoon, Rosita was working the sluice box with her husband when she happened to glance in the direction of the gringo miners. Three of them had halted in their work, and were staring at her.

Joaquin noticed her spin around quickly and put her back to them. Shooting a glance in their direction, he saw them grinning at him. "You must ignore them, darling. Do not even look that way."

Her hands trembled. "They are indeed vile men, Joaquin. I wish they had not come here. I can feel it in my bones. There is going to be trouble…real trouble."

Taking both of her hands in his, Joaquin asked, "Do you want to leave?"

"No. It is not right that such evil men should drive us away from our own property and the good living we are making."

"Then we must be very cautious," Joaquin told her. "Do as I say, and do not look in their direction any more."

"I won't. But why do they have to look at me like that?"

Folding her in his arms, Joaquin attempted to soothe her. "Everywhere we go, I see men looking at you. They have never seen such exquisite beauty before."

"Joaquin Murieta, you are a flatterer."

"No flatterer," he countered, brushing back a lock of hair that had fallen over her forehead. "I speak the truth. You are the most beautiful woman that ever walked this earth. I cannot blame men for admiring you and I cannot blame them for envying me."

"But those men are not merely admiring me. There is wickedness in their eyes."

"I know. This is why you must not look their way anymore, and as I said, if I am not here and you should see them heading this way, you get inside the cabin and lock the door. I brought my guns from the house a couple of weeks ago. They are in the cupboard next to the stove."

"Yes, I saw them. But I don't want to use them and I don't want you to use them, either."

"I understand. But if you do have to use them, do not hesitate."

The Murietas returned to their work, sorry that Franco Rodriquez had sold his claim to George Hadley and his vile friends.

Four days later, Rosita was washing breakfast dishes in the cabin when Joaquin slipped up behind her, and raising her long hair, kissed the back of her neck. Though her hands were wet, she pivoted and wrapped her arms around him. They kissed soundly, then she said, "My darling, you are such a romantic man. I hope you will always be this way."

"Never fear." He kissed the end of her nose. "With the beautiful Rosita Carmel Feliz Murieta as my wife, I could never be anything but romantic."

"But what about when I am old and gray and wrinkled?"

"Time can never take away your beauty in my eyes. As long as there is life in Joaquin Murieta, he will be romantic toward his lovely Rosita."

They kissed again, and Joaquin stepped outside. He moved off the porch and headed toward the sluice box. He was surprised to see Myron Ackerly and Clarence Keaton picking up tiny bits of gold from the bottom of the box. Anger flared within him, but he held it in check as he approached them. "What are you doing?"

Ackerly regarded him phlegmatically. "Seein' if your gold is any better than ours."

"Pardon me, but what you are doing is known as trespassing. You must not touch my gold or my sluice box."

Keaton drew himself up to full height, which was about two inches taller than Joaquin. "Tell you what, grease ball. You Mexes have no right at all to these claims. Best thing for you to do is take your gorgeous wife and hightail it back to the old country."

Squaring his jaw, Murieta parried, "You need to do a little studying, mister. If you do, you will learn that there were Mehicans digging gold out of these particular hills almost two years before one gringo set foot in here. Don't tell me what my rights are. We Mehicans have been kind enough to let gringos buy our claims at times. You are the latecomers, not us. Do not tell me that my wife and I should go back to Mehico. We are staying right here, and we are going to work our claim until it runs out."

Murieta's direct words stirred the poison of Keaton's hatred for Mexicans. Squaring his shoulders, he eyed the smaller man heatedly. "You're a troublemaker, Murieta! Just like all greasers!" Doubling up a fist, he gusted, "Why, I oughtta—"

"Throw it, and I'll break your arm!" warned Joaquin, fire building in his black eyes.

Ackerly touched his friend's shoulder. "C'mon, Clarence. We'll deal with this greaser later."

As the two miners walked away, Joaquin said loudly, "I have tried to be peaceful with you! Stay off my property and there will be no trouble!"

Rosita came out the door when the miners were back on their own land and joined him at the sluice box. He explained what had happened.

That evening, Bill Byrnes dropped by for supper and was welcomed by the Murietas. During the meal, Joaquin told his friend what had been happening with the five gringos and of the incident that morning at the sluice box.

Byrnes listened intently. "It's too bad there have to be people like them in the world, Joaquin, but I guess we're stuck with them."

Joaquin grinned. "If all gringos were like you, my friend, the world would be a much better place."

Byrnes chuckled and adjusted his position on the chair. "Well, Joaquin, I have my faults too. One of them is that I love your wife's cooking." He lifted an empty plate and looked at Rosita. "Could I have some more of those delicious tortillas, please?"

While Rosita was dishing up a fresh supply of tortillas at the stove, Bill said to Joaquin, "I totally sympathize with you in this gringo problem, but I suggest that you try to remain cool. Any trouble with them could lead to violence. With Rosita here at the cabin, she might get hurt."

"Maybe I should leave her at the house in Sonora."

"You will not," came Rosita's level reply as she turned from the stove and set a steaming plate in front of Byrnes. "My place is here with you, Joaquin."

"Just be careful, won't you?" Bill said to both of them.

Late the next afternoon, the Murietas returned to the claim site after selling a load of gold. As they hauled up to the cabin and dismounted, Joaquin heard digging sounds coming from the notch in the hill above the sluice box where he had been taking out the ore.

Looking at Rosita over his horse's back, he said in a low tone, "You go in the cabin and lock the door. I think I know what is going on."

Fear pinched Rosita's lovely features. "Joaquin, you should not go up there alone. Why don't you go get Andino Cabrera and some of our other Mehican neighbors to side with you first?"

"Maybe I should just go in the cabin and strap on my guns," he replied with heat in his voice.

"No! Please! It will only lead to bloodshed! Just get some of the neighbors."

"Even that could lead to violence," Joaquin said, turning and walking away. Over his shoulder, he called, "Get in the cabin and lock the door."

Climbing the hill, Joaquin struggled with the anger that was building up inside him. The gringos were doing everything they could to get him riled—and it was working. When he topped the hill and looked down into the wide hole where he had been digging his gold, he found Clarence Keaton and Harry Worth. Keaton was using a pick, and Worth was using a shovel to load ore in Joaquin's wheelbarrow. Both men stopped what they were doing when Joaquin appeared.

Joaquin maintained control of himself and said in a suppressed voice, "Aren't you gringos a bit confused? Your claim is over that way. You are digging on my property."

The miners looked at each other. "Well, whattya know, Harry," said Keaton, "we done strayed too far from our claim and didn't even know it!"

Worth laughed heartily. Joaquin noticed the earring swinging loosely with his head movements. He had a strong urge to grab it and tear it loose from the ear.

As his laughter subsided, Worth said, "I'm not sure about that, ol' buddy! This sure looks like our claim! I think it is our claim! Greasers don't have rights to no claims around here. It has to be ours!"

Murieta's face was a grim mask. "I do not want trouble from you men, but you are making it difficult for me. You are using my tools and stealing my gold. I want you off this property this instant, and I want you to stay off."

Clarence Keaton dropped Joaquin's pick and edged up close to him. "If you don't want trouble, greaser, pack up and head for Mexico."

"That is not going to happen," Murieta replied in a flat, emotionless tone. "Now get off my property."

Again, Keaton doubled up his fist, and again Joaquin warned, "Throw it, and I'll break your arm."

There was a dry rustle in the Mexican's voice. It carried a foreboding hint that he could back up his threat. Though Keaton was a larger man than Murieta, the gringo miner felt a touch of fear that one-on-one, the dark-eyed man might do him some damage. Keaton was not positive Harry Worth would back him if he lit into Murieta. Opening the fist, he chuckled hollowly. "Let's go, Harry. We told this greaser to pack up and git. If he doesn't do it, we ain't to blame for what might happen."

Joaquin descended the hill behind them and stood in front of the cabin eyeing them until they were on their own property. Not once did they look back. Turning toward the porch, he saw Rosita looking at him through the window. Forcing a grin, he said, "It's all right, darling. They'll leave us alone now. I'm going to work."

That evening, Rosita set a hot meal in front of her husband and sat down at the table. "Joaquin, I am so proud of you. Once again those beasts tried to provoke you to violence, but you stayed cool."

Joaquin was about to say if they provoked him again he doubted that he could refrain from violence when there were heavy footsteps on the porch, followed quickly with the door bursting open. Suddenly five big men were filing through the door, their faces fixed with determination to do evil.

Joaquin heard Rosita cry out in fear as he sprang from his chair and sent a smashing fist to the face of Harry Worth, who was first through the door. Worth's head snapped back, and he flopped to the floor, dazed.

Thinking fast, Joaquin grabbed the chair he had been sitting in and used it to smash the face of Clarence Keaton. The man groaned and fell on top of Worth. The other three bowled after Joaquin and smothered him with punches. Though he got in some good blows, they soon had him on the floor, kicking him savagely. Joaquin cried, "Rosita! Run!"

But Rosita was lunging for a butcher knife that lay on the kitchen counter. Just as she turned around with the long-bladed knife in her hand, Bob Dix grasped her wrist and twisted it hard until she dropped it.

Joaquin had kicked George Hadley in the groin, and Hadley

was bent over in agony. Myron Ackerly kicked Joaquin in the head with all his might, sending him rolling. Harry Worth was up and pounced on Joaquin, pounding him with his fists.

When the butcher knife slipped from her fingers, Rosita clawed at Dix's face, raking her fingernails across his eyes. He swore and blindly hit Rosita with his fist, sending her reeling into the table. She bounced off the table and crumpled to the floor, her eyes glazed.

Joaquin, bleeding from the nose, slipped past one of Ackerly's hissing boots and grabbed the leg. He had Ackerly down when both Harry Worth and George Hadley converged on him, using kitchen chairs to pound him into unconsciousness.

Joaquin Murieta was first aware that he was still in the world when the black vortex that had swallowed him seemed to be twirling him upward, and he could hear Bill Byrnes's voice calling his name. Opening one eye, he could see Byrnes standing over him, holding a burning lantern. The coppery taste of blood was in his mouth and his head was throbbing with pain.

Suddenly it all came back. The last thing Joaquin remembered was seeing Rosita ricochet off the table, and at the same time, feeling his hands gripping the leg of one of the miners as the man fell.

The lantern was now on the table and Byrnes was helping him to his feet. "Rosita," he whispered. "Bill, where's Rosita?"

"I don't know," said Byrnes. "I just got here and found you on the floor."

Joaquin wondered why he could only open his left eye. Raising a shaky palm and rubbing his right eye, he could tell it was caked with blood. Clawing at the dried blood, he was quickly able to get the eye open.

"Looks like a real brawl happened here. Was it those gringo miners you told me about?"

"Yes," answered Joaquin, a bit unsteady on his feet. "They—Rosita! I must find Rosita!"

Shaking his head to clear the cobwebs that seemed to stick to his brain, Joaquin picked up the lantern and headed for the bedroom. Byrnes followed slowly, afraid of what Joaquin might find.

When Joaquin reached the bedroom door, he held the lantern

high, then stopped abruptly. What he saw caught his breath short. Stepping back toward the approaching Byrnes, he gasped, "Wait a minute, Bill. Don't go in there."

"Rosita?"

"Yes. Don't come in until I call you."

The gambler headed back to the kitchen cupboard, intending to light another lantern.

Stepping into the bedroom, Joaquin Murieta felt like he was in a nightmare, as if what he was seeing was not real. His heart thundered in his breast as he took in the scene before him and made his way to the bed. His hands trembled as he set the lantern on the nightstand. Rosita was spread-eagled on the bed with her wrists and ankles tied to the bedposts. Her body was smeared with blood and her face was battered and swollen beyond recognition. The bedding beneath her was pooled with blood. He could see that she was hemorrhaging severely.

Grabbing a blanket from a dresser drawer, Joaquin covered Rosita and called for Byrnes.

When the gambler entered the room carrying another lantern, he took one look at the semiconscious woman and gasped.

"Bill," Joaquin said shakily, "you must ride fast and bring Dr. Lawson."

"I'm on my way." Byrnes dashed into the larger room. He set the lantern on the table, went through the door and into the saddle, and galloped away in the darkness.

In his haste, Byrnes had not seen the small group of Mexican neighbors who were headed for the Murieta cabin. Andino and Margarita Cabrera had heard the ruckus earlier and hastened to gather more neighbors to help them investigate.

Standing outside the cabin, they crowded close to the front porch and strained to see through the open door. "Should we go in?" asked one of the men.

"I don't know," said Andino. "That man who rode away is Joaquin's good friend, Bill Byrnes. By his haste, I would say that someone is hurt. He may be going for a doctor."

Hesitant to interfere and yet wondering if they could help, the Mexicans discussed what to do. They were unaware that Clarence Keaton and Harry Worth were standing nearby in the shadows.

Inside the cabin, Joaquin Murieta was struggling between two emotions: fear for Rosita's life and wrath toward the five gringos. Feeling numb all over, he cut the cords that held Rosita's wrists and ankles to the bedposts, then knelt down beside the bed. His own pain was forgotten. "Darling, it is Joaquin. Can you hear me?"

Rosita moaned and rolled her head.

"Can you hear me?"

Turning her face toward the voice, Rosita slowly opened her expressionless eyes and worked her broken jaw. "Joaquin…they…they…"

"Do not try to talk," said Joaquin. "Save your strength. I just wanted to tell you that Bill was here, and he has gone to Murphy's Diggings for Dr. Lawson. It won't take very long. I will get a cloth and some water and wash your face."

Lifting a listless hand, Rosita focused on his blood-caked features. "Joaquin…"

"Don't try to talk, darling."

"Joaquin," she said weakly, "I…I…love…you."

His heart pounding, Joaquin said, "I love you, too, Rosita."

A smile graced Rosita's puffy lips. She sighed deeply and closed her eyes. Her body trembled slightly, and Rosita Murieta stopped breathing.

By this time, Andino Cabrera and another neighbor named Pablo Vargas were standing at the bedroom door. Undetected by Joaquin, they observed the horrible moment when he watched his beloved Rosita die. Throwing his arms around her neck, he sobbed, "Rosita! My darling, Rosita! Come back to me! Come back to me!"

In respect to Joaquin's sudden anguish, the Mexicans retreated to the porch where several others had gathered. Above the sobs that came from within the house, Andino said to the group, "Rosita has just died. She had been beaten on the face something terrible. There was blood on the bed, and we saw cords lying on the floor. I think she had been tied to the bedposts and raped."

Margarita's voice quivered as she said, "Those five gringos who bought Franco's claim…I know they were giving Joaquin trouble. Rosita told me that they looked at her with wanton eyes. They are the ones who did this!"

"They must be punished!" said Pablo Vargas.

The rest of the group agreed.

In the shadows several yards away, Harry Worth said, "Clarence, we'd better tell George about this. We gotta hightail it outta here!"

At the big tent, George Hadley and the others were stunned to learn that Rosita had died. They were aware that frontier justice would overlook their beating of Joaquin Murieta, but such a brutal crime that resulted in Rosita's death would not be overlooked. Hastily they gathered their things, folded up the tent, and left under cover of darkness.

The Mexicans on the porch of the cabin waited in numb silence as they heard Joaquin weeping in the bedroom. Soon Bill Byrnes returned without Dr. Lawson, who was delivering a baby somewhere in the Sierras and no one knew when he might be back to Murphy's Diggings. The Mexicans informed him that Rosita had died.

Saddened and feeling sick at heart, Byrnes quietly entered the house. Joaquin's weeping had quieted some, but he could still be heard as Byrnes headed for the bedroom. Pausing at the bedroom door, he found Joaquin sitting on the bed holding Rosita's blanket-covered body in his arms, cradling her like a mother would hold a baby.

Sensing his presence, Joaquin looked up at his friend with swollen, bloodshot eyes. His face was as expressionless as a mask. As he held the lifeless form in his arms, he could feel the heat rising within him like a boil. He had never known such anger. Hatred was bubbling to the surface in intractable rage. Barely moving his lips, he said, "Rosita told me that vengeance belongs to the Lord, Bill. Not this time. This time vengeance belongs to Joaquin Murieta. I am going to kill every one of them."

At the moment, Bill Byrnes had nothing to say.

The next day, Joaquin buried Rosita in the cemetery at Sonora. Bill Byrnes stood with him, along with many Mexican friends and neighbors. When the Mexicans had spoken their condolences and were gone, Joaquin stood over the grave, his face like granite. Byrnes laid a gentle hand on his shoulder and said, "Joaquin, you mustn't take the law into your own hands. Let's go to Placerville and report this to Sheriff Ward Steffen. Let him handle it."

Murieta's black eyes showed little pinpoints of fire. "No, my friend. I will handle it myself. The men who did this are gringos.

Sheriff Steffen is a gringo. He will do nothing. I could rally my Mexican friends and go after Rosita's killers. They would help me to execute what is known as frontier justice, but this is for me to handle. Rosita was my wife. Vengeance belongs to Joaquin Murieta."

Not wanting Joaquin to entangle himself in deep trouble, Byrnes said, "Look, my friend, let's at least talk to Steffen and try to get him to go after those killers. How about it? Please."

Because of his love for Bill Byrnes, Joaquin gave in. They made the ride to Placerville and talked to the Calaveras County Sheriff Ward Steffen. Steffen listened as Joaquin told him the story, adding that the five miners had vacated their claim the same night they raped Rosita.

The sheriff showed instantly that he was not interested in trying to bring in the miners. He used the excuse that he only had one deputy and couldn't afford to be away from the office as long as it might take to hunt the killers down.

Outside the sheriff's office, Murieta and Byrnes mounted their horses. With a disgusted look on his face, Joaquin asked, "Are you satisfied now?"

Brow furrowed, Bill said, "Joaquin, I can understand your desire to bring justice on those dirty rats, but if you kill them, it will only lead to more trouble for you."

"What do I care about trouble? My Rosita has been taken from me. What do I care about anything? Except to send her killers to burn in hell!"

Knowing further words were useless, Bill Byrnes clucked to his horse and headed out of Placerville with Joaquin riding silently beside him.

CHAPTER SIXTEEN

On October 23, 1850, George Hadley and his four friends were camped on the bank of the Stanislaus River near Columbia, California. As the sun was setting behind a thick bank of clouds, staining the western sky a blood red, Rosita Murieta's killers were currying their horses and cleaning their saddles with saddle soap. They were unaware that a pair of black, smoldering eyes was watching from the deep shadows of the woods nearby.

When darkness began to fall, Harry Worth built a fire and began cooking supper. The dancing flames reflected from the golden earring in his left ear.

During supper, the five miners were laughing and joking. One of them mentioned Rosita Murieta's name and joked about how she fought them when they tied her wrists and ankles to the bedposts. Another one said something in a low tone and there was a round of ribald laughter.

They sat around the fire for another hour, then George Hadley stood up, scratched his ribs, and yawned. "I don't know about you guys, but I'm turnin' in."

The others agreed that it was time to hit the bedrolls. Harry Worth commented that since it was his turn to wash dishes as well as cook, he would do his job, then hit the sack.

At dawn, Clarence Keaton awakened and threw back the covers of his bedroll. It was his turn to build the fire and cook breakfast. Sitting up, he rubbed sleep from his eyes and flicked a quick glance around at the others. No one else was stirring. Keaton yawned and reached for his boots, which lay within arm's reach. While he was pulling the boots on, Harry Worth's bedroll caught his attention. He had not noticed it a moment ago, but the roll was flat. Harry was not in it. Deciding Harry must be taking care of early morning necessities somewhere nearby, he stood up and yawned again.

He started to turn toward the spot where he would build the fire when something strange caught his eye. At first he thought the subdued light of dawn was playing tricks on his eyes, but stepping close to Worth's bedroll, he froze in his tracks, mouth gaping. "Ge-e-e-orge!" he screamed. He repeated it until George Hadley was awake and scrambling out of his bedroll.

Hadley and the others got up and stood beside Keaton, whose bulging eyes were transfixed on a bloody object laying on top of Worth's covers. Hadley gasped and swore. Harry Worth's bloody left ear was on the blankets, the golden earring still in its lobe.

The stunned miners were sleepily trying to reason out what had happened when Myron Ackerly drew a ragged breath and pointed to the edge of the forest some eighty feet away.

All eyes swung to the spot. Harry Worth's body was hanging by the ankles from a large tree limb. His throat had been cut and his right ear had been stuffed in his mouth.

Panic washed over the four miners like a wave of icy water.

Keaton turned to Hadley and gasped, "George! You don't think it's—"

His own blood chilled, Hadley stuttered, "M-Murieta?"

"Yeah!"

Though in shock, Bob Dix argued, "Naw, it couldn't be. Why, that greaser—"

"George!" said Myron Ackerly, pointing to the spot where Harry Worth's body hung.

At that instant, Joaquin Murieta materialized from the deep shadows of the forest, dressed totally in black. He held a cocked revolver in each hand. As he walked slowly toward them, the dark muzzles stared at the frightened miners like two menacing eyes of death.

Faces pallid with fear, the four men threw up their hands.

"M-Murieta," stuttered George Hadley, "d-don't kill us! P-please! Have m-mercy!"

Beneath the brim of his black, low-crowned hat, Murieta's ebony eyes were like the dead of winter. "Like the mercy you showed my Rosita?"

Cold tremors were running the length of Myron Ackerly's body. His face was an alabaster mask of terror. Falling to his knees, he interlaced his fingers in a pleading fashion and sobbed, "Please, Murieta! I'm sorry for what I did to your wife…really sorry! Please don't kill me! I mean it! I'm sorry! Really sorry!"

"Not as sorry as you are going to be when you get to hell."

One of the revolvers roared.

By October 31, Joaquin Murieta had sold his gold mining claim to another Mexican and had gone into a partnership with Bill Byrnes. Together they had purchased the Sluice Box Saloon in Murphy's Diggings. Joaquin kept his house in Sonora and rode the short distance to Murphy's Diggings every day. Byrnes watched over the bar and gambling tables and Murieta handled the business end.

At first, some of the saloon women tried to warm up to Joaquin, but he was chained to Rosita's memory and quickly brushed them off. Many a night, he lay in bed and cried out in the dark for his beloved wife. Sometimes he had nightmares, reliving the awful night of her death. The only consolation was that the men who had ravished Rosita had paid for it with their lives.

Late in the afternoon on November 8, Bill Byrnes was leaning against the bar in the Sluice Box Saloon, chatting with a couple of customers. There was activity at a few of the gaming tables.

As Byrnes was listening to one of the men tell about a new vein of gold that had been found near Placerville, he noticed a tall, slender man in his midtwenties pass through the batwings. He wore a heavy gun on his hip and a badge on his chest and was obviously looking for someone.

Excusing himself, Byrnes left the men at the bar and approached the lawman. "May I help you?"

"Yes. I'm looking for Joaquin Murieta. I understand he works here."

"He's half-owner," replied Byrnes, noting that Deputy Sheriff, Calaveras County, was engraved on his badge. "I can get him for you. I see that you're Sheriff Steffen's deputy. What's your name?"

"Clay Towner," said the deputy, extending his hand.

Meeting it with a firm grip, Byrnes said, "I'm Bill Byrnes, the other half of the ownership."

"Glad to meet you."

"Is there some kind of problem, Deputy?"

"Might be," responded Towner, hitching up his gun belt. "I'll know more when I talk to Murieta."

"He's in the back office," said Byrnes, turning away. "I'll go get him."

"Better yet," spoke up Towner, stepping up beside him, "why don't I just talk to him back there?"

With the deputy on his heels, Byrnes tapped on the office door and pushed it open. Joaquin was at the desk, with papers spread before him and a pencil in his hand. He looked up as the two men entered and noted the badge on the stranger's shirt.

"Joaquin," said Bill, "this is Deputy Sheriff Clay Towner from over at Placerville. He says he needs to talk to you."

Rising, Murieta asked, "What do you need to talk to me about?"

"Maybe you'd rather this would be private," said Towner, flicking a glance at Byrnes.

"No need," said the dark-skinned man. "Bill and I are partners. We have no secrets."

Towner shrugged his shoulders. "Okay. Mind if we sit down?"

Joaquin gestured toward a chair that sat next to the wall. Towner slid it close to the desk and sat down. Byrnes pulled one from the opposite wall and sat. Joaquin set his dark gaze on Towner and said, "Now what can I do for you, Deputy?"

"Just answer a few questions."

"All right."

"On October 20, you reported to Sheriff Steffen that five gringo miners had raped your wife and that she had died as a result of it. You gave their names as George Hadley, Harry Worth, Bob Dix, Clarence Keaton, and Myron Ackerly."

"Yes," said Joaquin. "My friend Bill was with me when I made the report."

"I was out of town that day," Towner said casually, "so I missed you."

Joaquin nodded silently.

"I want to advise you that I just came from Saw Mill Flats and talked to your neighbors about this."

"Yes?"

"Now, I would like to hear your version of what happened between you and the five miners and what they did to you and your wife."

Joaquin's blood heated up as he told the deputy about the miners moving next to his claim and how things developed from that point. He gave the details of how they had burst into the cabin, pummeled him into unconsciousness, and beat and molested Rosita. When he finished by saying that Hadley and his cohorts had packed up and disappeared the same night Rosita was molested, he asked, "Why are you so interested in all of this, Deputy? Your boss showed little concern at all."

Leaning forward in the chair and looking Joaquin in the eye, Towner said, "Couple of weeks ago—October 24 to be exact—some prospectors found those five miners dead on the bank of the Stanislaus River over by Columbia. Four of them had been shot to death, and one had his throat cut. All of them had been mutilated."

"Mutilated?" interjected Byrnes, eyes wide.

"Yes. Each man had his ears cut off." Looking at Joaquin, Towner asked, "What about it, Murieta?"

Joaquin stiffened in his chair. "What do you mean, 'what about it?' Do you expect me to break down and cry because those filthy beasts who raped and killed my wife got themselves shot and mutilated?"

"That wasn't what I'm—"

"They probably did the same thing to some other Mehican's wife and her husband did what I should have done: put together a citizens' posse and executed some frontier justice!"

Bill Byrnes was studying Joaquin as he spoke the harsh words. His friend's facial features and flashing eyes betrayed nothing.

Towner sucked in a deep breath and looked hard at Joaquin. "So you're telling me you know nothing about these men being killed."

"Nothing," Murieta said flatly.

Something in the lawman's inner being told him that Murieta was lying, but without a shred of evidence as to his guilt, there was no way he could arrest him. "Okay, Mr. Murieta. That's all I wanted to ask you. Thanks for your time."

When the deputy was gone, Bill Byrnes lifted himself from the chair and gave Joaquin an I-know-you-did-it look, but did not put it in words. "Well, I'll get back to our paying customers."

Joaquin smiled. "And I will get back to this paperwork so we can keep accommodating our paying customers."

Byrnes was back in less than five minutes, tapping on the door. As it came open, Joaquin looked up and said, "Yes, my friend?"

Grinning, Bill said, "You've got company."

"Don't tell me that wet-nosed deputy is back."

"Nope. These are relatives of yours—all the way from Sonora, Mexico!"

"What?" he gasped, rising from the chair.

At that moment, Claudio Murieta and Reyes Feliz appeared, pushing past Byrnes, smiling broadly.

"Claudio! Reyes!" exclaimed Joaquin. "What are you doing here?"

"We have come to live in California and get rich like you!" said Claudio as he embraced his brother.

After Reyes had embraced his brother-in-law, Bill said, "Joaquin, these fellas and I have already introduced ourselves. I'll…uh…leave you to catch up on family matters."

Byrnes walked away, leaving the door open. Joaquin hugged both men again. "How did you find me?"

"It took a little effort," replied Claudio, "but once we found your house in Sonora, a teenage boy told us you are half-owner of this place. So…here we are!"

"We expected to find Rosita at the house, Joaquin," said Reyes, "but no one answered the door. The teenage boy seemed very shy. He would not comment on where she might be. How is she? Is there a little Murieta on the way, yet?"

Firing his own question rapidly behind Reyes's, Claudio asked, "Have you found Carlos yet?"

Both men saw Joaquin's countenance sag. His eyes dulled as he said grimly, "Both of you better sit down."

Slowly and methodically, Joaquin told his brother and brother-in-law of Rosita's horrid death. When Reyes and Claudio had wept and finally gained control of their emotions, Joaquin followed the sad news with the story of Carlos's death. There were more tears.

Reyes said bitterly, "Joaquin, we must find those dirty gringos and bring them to justice."

Joaquin stepped to the door and looked down the hallway toward the front of the building. Seeing no one, he turned back and said, "I have already done that." He then proceeded to tell them of how he executed Rosita's killers on the bank of the Stanislaus River, then told them of Deputy Clay Towner's visit a short time ago.

"I'm glad you took care of them, Joaquin," Reyes said. "From what you tell us, the gringo laws in this state would never have done it."

"I am glad, too," said Claudio. "But Joaquin, what about those twenty dirty skunks who murdered Carlos? We should band some of our people together, track them down, and execute them."

Joaquin explained that he did not go after the men who had hanged Carlos because of what it would have done to Rosita, reminding Reyes and Claudio how she felt about violence. If he had tracked them down and killed them it would have hurt her deeply and he would have lowered himself in her eyes. His love for Rosita was greater than his need for vengeance over Carlos's death.

Claudio's dark eyes narrowed and vexation lay tightly across his face. "Rosita is gone now, Joaquin. Carlos's murderers are still running free. Are you going to just forget about them?"

Joaquin sighed. "Claudio, by now those men could be anywhere. They could have scattered twenty different directions."

"But they need to pay for what they did."

Joaquin put an arm around his brother's shoulder. "Believe me, Claudio, I would love to see them die for killing Carlos, but trying to track them down would be a waste of good time. I will tell you this, though. I still remember every one of their faces. I promise you, if I ever see one of them, he is a dead man."

Claudio Murieta nodded and wiped a tear from his cheek. "You are right. It would be impossible to find those killers now. But I believe you. If you ever see one of them, you will make him pay."

"You can bet your last peso on it."

Reyes and Claudio moved into Joaquin's house with him and set about to find a claim nearby to purchase. Within a week, such a claim was found, and they began digging for gold.

At dusk on November 22, Joaquin had just ridden up to his house in Sonora and was about to put his bay gelding in the small corral when Reyes and Claudio came riding in after a hard day's work at their claim. They were talking to each other, and Joaquin could tell by the sound of their voices that they were upset.

Opening the corral gate and leading the bay into the corral,

Joaquin looked over his shoulder and said, "Hey, boys, what are you so angry about?"

Both men rode through the gate and reined in. As he was sliding from his saddle, Claudio said, "More crimes against our people, that's all. I think it's time we form a vigilante band and start hanging some dirty gringos!"

"What happened?" Joaquin loosened the cinch strap under his horse's belly.

"Do you know where Camp Connell is?" Claudio asked him.

"Yes. It's in the Sierra Nevada foothills a few miles north of Murphy's Diggings. Why?"

"Well, when Reyes and I were just coming into Sonora, we met Tomas and Juanita Lucero on the street. Tomas told us that yesterday a bunch of gringo miners hanged six Mehican miners who had refused to leave the territory. Hanged them right outside of Camp Connell, and the gringo lawmen will do nothing about it!"

"Yes, it seems these same gringos have hanged other Mehicans in these parts, too," said Reyes. "Their leader is some dirty snake called Bill Lang."

Joaquin was lifting the saddle from his horse's back when the name Bill Lang hit his ears like a sledgehammer. His heart lurched. Pivoting with the saddle in his hands, he thundered, "Bill Lang!"

Both men stared at him. Joaquin's face was a sudden mask of fury. His widened eyes seemed as they would burst from their sockets. A large purple vein throbbed in his temple. One side of his mouth drew back in a grimace of rage.

"That name means something to you, Joaquin," said Reyes. "What is it?"

The hatred pulsating in Joaquin Murieta was almost a tangible thing as he said hotly, "Bill Lang and his bunch are the ones who hanged Carlos! It was Lang who put the scars on my back! I guess I had never mentioned his name to you."

"Apparently not to Tomas, either," said Claudio, "or he would have known to come and tell you."

"I only vaguely remember talking to the Luceros about it. I must have neglected to mention Lang's name." Carrying the saddle toward the barn he said, "Tomorrow I am going to Camp Connell."

Both men followed, telling Joaquin they were going with him.

Hanging the saddle on a wall peg, Joaquin told Reyes and Claudio that they must stay and work their claim. He would handle Lang and his cohorts by himself. The tone of Joaquin's voice was enough to keep the two men from arguing with him. They had no choice but to let him take care of Carlos's killers alone.

At nine o'clock the next morning Joaquin was emerging from his office at the saloon, placing his black flat-crowned hat on his head as Bill Byrnes was coming down the hall toward him.

"Good morning, partner," said Byrnes, noticing the foul look on Murieta's countenance. "Everything all right?"

Pausing, Joaquin said, "I wasn't sure what time you might be coming in, so I left a note for you on my desk. I came in at three o'clock this morning and got all my paperwork caught up. As the note will tell you, I may be gone a few days."

Eyebrows arched, Byrnes echoed, "A few days? Where are you going?"

"Personal business, Bill. I can't tell you."

Joaquin had not noticed the newspaper Byrnes had under his arm. Unfolding it and extending it toward him, Bill said, "Before you go, you better look at this."

Joaquin took the paper and unfolded it, exposing the front page. His lips pulled tight as he read the bold, glaring headlines:

FOREIGN MINERS TAX PASSED
BY CALIFORNIA LEGISLATURE

Joaquin Murieta did not have to read the article to know what had happened. Anglo mining companies had been putting pressure on the lawmakers in Sacramento to levy a burdensome tax on all Mexican miners that would force them out of business. His anger kindled, he wadded up the paper. "We were here before the greedy gringos were! What right have they to do this?"

"They outnumber you, my friend. They have no right to do what they are doing, but they have the power to make it law, and to make it stick."

"This tax will not put all of my people out of business," Joaquin said, sneering. "Many Mehicans have done well. They have enough money to pay the taxes."

Byrnes nodded. "The Sacramento politicians are aware of this possibility. They have other plans in the making. They're going to give this new law a little time. If they don't see all the Mexican claims crumbling, they'll pass another law. I've already read about it. They're going to call it the Greaser Act. When it passes, no Mexican will be allowed to own property in California. That will definitely put them out of business. All their land will be taken from them, including their homes and mines."

Murieta banged a fist into a palm. "They cannot do this! It is not American!"

Byrnes reminded his partner that California had become a state earlier that very year. The state was sovereign and could do what it pleased.

"Then I will have to give up my half of the Sluice Box," said Joaquin acidly.

"Not on your life. If the law is passed, you will give up your half of this place only on paper. You will still be my partner, and you will still take half of the profits. I'll pay you rent secretly on what would be your half of the building."

The fire left Joaquin's eyes. A slight smile tugged at the corners of his mouth. Laying a hand on Bill's shoulder, he said with feeling, "You are truly my friend. Your loyalty means more to me than I could ever tell you."

Byrnes made a fist and playfully clipped Joaquin's angular chin. "Hey, pal, when a man's a true friend, his loyalty never alters."

"Thank you. That road runs both ways, you know. I will see you in a few days."

Boiling inside over the new law and what the avaricious gringo lawmakers were doing to his people, Joaquin swung into the saddle and headed for Sonora. He was especially angry over what the new law would do to Claudio and Reyes. They had come all the way from Mexico to make a decent life for themselves, and now they would be unfairly taxed out of business.

Arriving at his house in Sonora, Joaquin dashed inside and returned moments later, carrying a strange bundle. Tying it behind his saddle, he rode fast to Saw Mill Flats. There he rode up to Andino Cabrera's claim and led his bay horse inside the barn, closing the door behind him.

Andino and Margarita were at their sluice box a few yards from the cabin. They saw Joaquin ride in, and staying busy, watched him emerge moments later. Joaquin was dressed totally in black, including the double-holstered gun belt. The coal black horse he led from the corral had a black saddle and bridle to match. As he closed the corral gate and mounted up, he waved to the couple.

The Cabreras waved back and watched the man in black ride away. When horse and rider had disappeared in the deep shadows of the tall pines, Andino said, "It seems Joaquin has found some more gringos who are in need of punishing, Margarita."

"God bless him." She smiled.

It was dark when Joaquin Murieta arrived at Camp Connell. The full moon was silver against the deep blackness of the night. Leaving his black gelding in the thick forest that surrounded the small town, he moved stealthily along the main street, keeping to the shadows. As he crept unnoticed along the street, his eyes were studying the horses that were tethered at the hitching posts. Nearing a saloon, he could hear the laughter that was coming from inside. Light from the windows showed him one of the Arabians in front of the place.

Bitterness made its claw scratches at the corners of his mouth when he saw it was the one that had belonged to Rosita. His blood heated up, racing through his system and swelling his desire to destroy. Getting a grip on it, he told himself he must be patient.

Shrouded in the deep shadows across the street, he waited. Sooner or later the Arabian's rider would emerge from the saloon. When he did…

In the next hour, several patrons came and went from the saloon. Each time someone came out, Joaquin stiffened and watched to see if one of them would mount Rosita's horse.

Nearly two hours had passed when three miners came out, laughing and making cracks about the painted-up women inside the place. There was enough light to expose their features. Two of them were not familiar to Murieta, but the sight of the third face made his blood run hotter. It was one of the twenty faces he had kept engraved in his memory.

Joaquin's heart quickened pace when the familiar miner stepped in the stirrup and settled on the back of Rosita's Arabian. The other two mounted up and aimed their horses eastward. The one on the

Arabian pointed its nose to the west.

"Good to see you again, Wes," said one of the other two. "It's been a long time."

"Sure has," spoke up the other one. "When I get back to Missouri, I'll tell Ma Coggins I saw her little boy."

"You do that." The man on the Arabian laughed.

With that they parted company, riding opposite directions.

CHAPTER SEVENTEEN

Miner Wesley Coggins rode the Arabian westward out of Camp Connell at a leisurely pace. Lifting his gaze upward beyond the towering pines, he smiled at the moon. Life had been good to him. Since hooking up with Bill Lang, he had made himself more than thirty thousand dollars in the goldfields. Some of it had been stolen and some of it earned.

Earlier in the evening Coggins was with some of the miners from Lang's camp, enjoying a good time at the saloon. What a surprise to see Zeke Bassler and Willie Stark come ambling through the door. Coggins had worked with them back in the 1840s at the grain mills in St. Joseph, Missouri, which was his boyhood home.

Coggins had called Bassler and Stark to his table, and after shaking hands with them, had introduced them to his miner friends. When it was time for the group to head back to the claim site, Coggins told them he wanted to stay a little longer and chew the fat with his old pals. What a joy it had been to tell Brassler and Stark how much money he had made since hooking up with Lang. The Mexican situation had come up in the conversation, and Coggins lost no time in letting his friends know how much he hated greasers.

Glancing at the moon as he rode toward the camp, he realized he had shorted himself on sleep by staying longer with his friends, but that was all right. It had been good to spend some time with them—especially since he could brag a bit.

The moon was casting weird shadows in the forest as Coggins weaved his way among the trees. In the bleak stillness of the night, a solitary owl hooted somewhere overhead.

Abruptly there was a muffled sound of hooves on a bed of pine needles and before he could tell which direction the sound was coming from, a rider on a black horse materialized from the shadows directly in front of him. The suddenness of it and the sight of the rider clothed in black caused him to gasp as he quickly drew rein. The obscure moonlight amid the deep shadows restricted his vision, but before he tried to focus on the rider's face, he was aware of silver light glinting from twin revolvers that were trained on his chest.

His heart thudded wildly as he drew a sharp breath. "Wh-what d-do you want?"

The mysterious rider nudged his black mount closer while using one of the gun muzzles to tip his hat back so as to expose his face. "Revenge."

Coggins's whole body shook. The shadowed moonlight cast a pearl gray luminescence on the features of the rider, giving him a cadaverous look. "R-revenge. F-for what?"

"You helped hang my brother and his friend at Murphy's Diggings on May 26. Remember?"

"Well, I d-don't know. I—"

"You stood by and laughed while your big ugly leader, Bill Lang, nearly beat me to death."

"M-mister, y-you've got the w-wrong man," lied Coggins.

"Shut up! Don't lie to me! That horse you're sitting on belonged to my wife! You stole it!"

"No! I…bought the horse from Bill Lang, but I didn't have anyth—"

"Shut up! Stop your lying! I memorized every one of your faces that day. You were one of them!"

The terrified miner's eyes bulged. Licking his lips nervously, he said, "L-listen, mister, I r-really didn't want any part of it. I was just—"

"Get off that horse!" Murieta said.

Frightened out of his wits, and clearly recognizing the rider as the Mexican Bill Lang bullwhipped at Murphy's Diggings, Coggins threw his leg over the saddle horn and slid to the ground. Quivering in the dappled moonlight, he squeaked, "Wh-what are you gonna do?"

Looking down at him with stern eyes and leveling both muzzles on his chest, Murieta said, "I am going to ask you a question, and I want the truth. Is Bill Lang at the camp where you are going?"

Coggins cleared his throat shakily. "Well, it's Lang's camp, but he ain't there right now. He's off somewhere doin' some business. I don't even know what it is. He's supposed to be back in a day or two."

Lifting one gun and lining it on the miner's sweaty face, Murieta snapped, "If you're lying to me—"

"No! I ain't lyin'. Bill ain't there. I swear it!"

"All right. Another question…"

"Y-yeah?"

"How many men who were in on hanging my brother and his friend are still with Lang?"

Wiping a nervous palm over his face, the frightened miner said, "Well…let me think a minute. Uh…well…uh…there'd still be…uh…ten, includin' myself."

"Where are the other nine?"

"They've…uh…scattered and are workin' their own mines in other goldfields along the foothills of the Sierras."

"I am surprised the whole bunch hasn't scattered," mused Joaquin, "especially your ugly leader."

"Not Bill," said Coggins. "He ain't scared of nobody. And we that stayed with him ain't either, as long as he's with us."

"Mm-hmm. I noticed that."

"Huh?"

"He isn't with you right now, and you look plenty scared."

Coggins did not comment.

"How far is it to the camp from here?"

Using his chin as a pointer, Coggins replied, "It's just over that next hill—about a quarter-mile."

"Well, I'm about to break a promise," said Joaquin.

"Huh?"

"I promised another one of my brothers that the first man I saw who had been in the bunch that hanged Carlos, I'd kill him on the spot. But I am not going to kill you at the moment. I need you to carry a message for me."

The miner's knees buckled and he sighed with relief.

"I have a message for Bill Lang," said Murieta.

"Yes, sir?"

"You tell him that I am going to kill the other nineteen men who helped hang my brother, then I am going to kill him. Got that?"

Mouth dry, Coggins said, "Yes, sir."

"Now take the reins of my wife's horse and lead it toward the camp. I am going to follow. When we get to within fifty yards of the camp, I want you to stop. Understand?"

"Yes, sir."

On shaky legs, Wesley Coggins looped the reins over the head of the Arabian and continued westward, leading the horse. Seconds later they moved out of the shadows into a spot of bright moonlight. Noting the stock of a rifle protruding out of Coggins's saddle boot, Joaquin asked, "What kind of rifle is that?"

"Henry," the miner said over his shoulder.

"Looks like a big gun."

"Yes, sir. It's a buffalo gun. Fifty caliber."

"There are no buffalo around here. Why such a big gun?"

"Somebody gave it to me. It's a good conversation piece, and I figure it's good protection. Would-be troublemakers will leave a man alone when he's got a gun that big. Blow a fella's head off from a hundred yards away."

When they were still in the woods but some fifty yards from the mining camp, Murieta dismounted, tied Wesley Coggins to a tree, and gagged him with his own bandanna. He then produced a long-bladed hunting knife from a saddlebag. When Coggins saw the deadly weapon in Murieta's hand, his eyes bulged and a nasal whine emerged from him. The volume of the whine increased as the Mexican sliced off both of his ears and stuffed them in his shirt pocket. Blood flowed freely down both sides of the miner's head.

Mounting the Arabian and leading the other horse, Joaquin drew close to Coggins, who was whining shrilly against the gag. "Now scream. Scream loud so the men in the camp will come and find you before you bleed to death. Be sure to give Lang my message." Yanking the bandanna from Coggins's mouth, Joaquin Murieta rode away in the night with the man's screams echoing through the dense forest.

At sunup, Murieta rode into Andino Cabrera's corral aboard the Arabian, leading the black gelding. Andino came quickly from the house to greet him. He rejoiced when Joaquin told him what he had done to Wesley Coggins, and was glad to know that Joaquin had at least been able to get one of the Arabian horses back.

Joaquin told him his plans to exact justice on every man who had hanged Carlos Murieta and Enrico Flores and told Andino to spread the word amongst the Mexican people. He wanted them to know that from now on, the gringos who mistreated Mexicans and passed laws against them were going to suffer at the hands of Joaquin Murieta. After he had executed Bill Lang and his gang of killers, he was going to launch a crusade in behalf of the Mexicans in San Joaquin Valley and make the gringos sorry they had dared to rise up against them.

After a hearty breakfast with the Cabreras, Joaquin rode away on the black horse with the buffalo gun in the saddle boot.

Andino immediately rode into Saw Mill Flats and told everyone of Joaquin Murieta's intention to execute every man who helped hang his brother, and of his pending crusade. There was rejoicing among the Mexicans, and before sundown the word had been spread to every Mexican mining camp in the area and to every town—including Murphy's Diggings. When the message came to the ears of Bill Byrnes, he understood then what Joaquin's "personal business" was. He wondered if he would ever see his partner again.

That night under a moonlit sky, miner Derek Smith was riding eastward toward Bill Lang's camp through the dense forest. Smith had been in the group that hanged Carlos Murieta and Enrico Flores and was one of the men who had lashed Joaquin Murieta to the tree in preparation for the bullwhipping.

Riding his own horse, Smith was leading the Arabian gelding that had belonged to Murieta. Suddenly a lariat came hissing out of the shadows, dropped over Smith's upper body, and cinched tight. One quick jerk yanked him from the saddle and he hit the ground hard. His hat flew off and landed several feet away. Before he could collect himself and pull his gun, it was in the hand of the man who stood over him in the moonlight, dressed in black. The two horses immediately came to a halt.

Looking up at the dark form that stood over him, Smith said, "I ain't got no money, mister!"

"I'm not after your money," the man said coldly, looking down at his face, which was fully exposed in the silver spray of light.

"Wh-what do you want?"

"At first, all I wanted was my Arabian gelding that that dirty rat Bill Lang stole from me. But now that I see who you are, I want revenge."

Smith's blood ran cold. He knew who the man in black was. "P-please, mister. D-don't kill me! I'm sorry for what I did, but you have to understand. I had to do it, or Bill would've worked me over with that bullwhip."

"You lie! I well remember the way you laughed while you were tying me to the tree."

Smith swallowed hard. "P-lease! I'm sorry! Don't k-kill me!"

"What are you doing leading the Arabian? Where have you been with it?"

Wanting to get up but afraid to move, Smith replied, "Bill had let his brother Jack use it to ride to a new claim site that Jack's working over by Mokelumne Hill, a few miles west of here. He sent me over there yesterday morning to get the Arabian and bring him back. I stayed over and helped Jack set up his sluice box."

"This Jack is Bill Lang's brother, eh?"

"Uh-huh."

"Was Jack with the rest of you the day you hanged my brother and his friend?"

Smith did not answer.

Cocking Smith's gun and aiming it between his eyes, Murieta hissed, "I asked you a question! Was Jack Lang part of the hanging party that day?"

"Y-yes! But please don't tell him I told you! He'll kill me!"

"He will never get the chance."

Midmorning the next day, Wesley Coggins was sitting on a wooden crate in the Lang camp, near the dwindling fire that had been used to cook breakfast earlier. He had been treated by a doctor in the nearby town of Dorrington. His head was wrapped in a large bandage and his face was quite pale.

Coggins was watching some of the miners as they carried the body of Derek Smith into the camp. His horse had come in riderless at sunup and the miners went into the forest in search of Smith. As they lay the body down a few feet from him, Coggins saw that both of Smith's ears had been cut off and stuffed in his shirt pockets. He had been stabbed through the heart.

At the same time, Bill Lang came riding in from his business trip. He glanced at Coggins's bandaged head, then set his gaze on the body of Derek Smith. He asked what was going on. A miner named Emmett Bondy said, "It's that greaser you bullwhipped at Murphy's Diggings, boss. He jumped Wes night before last when he was ridin' in from Camp Connell. Gave him a message to give to you, then cut his ears off."

Lang's face went purple. Swearing profusely, he turned to Coggins. "How do you know it was that particular greaser?"

"Because he told me that's who he was," replied Coggins. "Said we hanged his brother and stole his two Arabians. It was him, all right."

"What was his message for me?"

"He said to tell you that he was gonna kill every one of the men who helped hang his brother, and then he'd kill you last."

"Looks like he's off to a good start," spoke up Jim Wheeler, who had led Derek Smith's horse in. "He killed Derek sometime last night and took the other Arabian. You remember that Derek was bringing the animal back to you."

"You're sure it was this same greaser who killed Derek?"

"Positive. Take a look. He cut Derek's ears off, just like he did Wes's."

"Yeah?" said Lang, looking at Coggins. "Well, if he's gonna kill all of us, why did he let you live?"

"So I could bring you his message."

"Then he's plannin' on killin' you yet, right?"

"I...I suppose so," shuddered Coggins.

Bill Lang went into a tirade, pacing back and forth between Wesley Coggins and the mutilated body of Derek Smith, yelling that no dirty greaser was going to intimidate him. Some thirty miners were standing around, taking it all in. Nine of them were those who had helped hang Carlos Murieta and Enrico Flores.

While Lang was pacing and cursing in anger, his diatribe against the hated Mexican was cut short by the deep-throated roar of a large, high-caliber rifle. The slug tore through Wesley Coggins's head, sending him reeling off the wooden crate.

Lang froze in his tracks, swinging his head in the direction of the shot, which had come out of the nearby woods. The miners began scattering for cover. Jim Wheeler whipped out the revolver on his hip and made a dive for a large fallen tree that lay near the campfire. The big buffalo gun boomed from the forest again, and Wheeler was dead with a fifty-caliber bullet through his heart before he hit the ground.

When no more shots came, Bill Lang shouted for his men to grab their guns and go after the sniper. Cautiously, they spread out and made their search, but to no avail. The rifleman had disappeared. When they returned to the center of camp, Lang gave orders for Smith, Coggins, and Wheeler to be buried.

While the graves were being dug, Bill Lang paced back and forth at the center of the camp, trying to decide what to do. He knew there were sixteen men left—besides himself—who were targets of the Mexican. Seven were still with him. Among the nine who were in other areas of the goldfields was his brother, Jack. Something had to be done to stop the man from further carrying out his threat.

After the three men were buried, Lang called the seven miners together while the rest of them patrolled the perimeter of the claim site to be sure the killer did not sneak up on them again. Sitting the seven men down close to the pile of ashes where the fire had been, he stood before them. "Fellas, we're gonna have to stick close together till this maniac can be stopped. Anybody know his name?"

There was no response for a few seconds, then Emmett Bondy said, "When his brother hollered for him that day at the tree, he called out the name *Joaquin*. I don't think we ever heard his last name."

Lang spat. "Well, this *Joaquin* whatsizname is bent on carryin' out his own style of execution, but we're not gonna let him drive us from our claim. We'll let a few of the other guys keep watch at all times while the rest of us keep diggin' and sluicin'. In the meantime, we need to get Sheriff Ward Steffen in here so's we can inform him of what's goin' on. He'll have to put a posse together and hunt that rabid greaser down. Then we gotta warn as many of the other nine as we can so's they can protect themselves."

"We don't know where most of 'em are, Bill," spoke up a miner named Walt DeFoe. "In fact, I guess the only one where we really know his whereabouts is your brother, Jack."

Lang lifted his hat and scratched his head. "Yeah, I guess you're right. Well, we sure gotta warn Jack. I need a man to ride over to

Mokelumne Hill right away and let him know about this."

When there were no volunteers, Lang showed his temper. "What we got here, a bunch of cowards? Either I get a volunteer, or I volunteer somebody."

The miners wanted to tell Lang to go himself, but to do so would rile him. This would bring out the bullwhip…or worse. The men who worked for Bill Lang made very good money. It was the money that kept them there, in spite of his vile temper and brutal ways. Doing his bidding was part of the deal.

A miner named Bart Meakins stood up. "I'll go, Bill."

"Now we're gettin' somewhere," said Lang. "Okay, Bart, you're excused. Make it fast and get right back here."

While Meakins was galloping away, Lang said to the others, "Now, I need a man to ride to Placerville and bring the sheriff."

"Would you care if two of us go, Bill?" asked Nick Roma. "It's a lot farther to Placerville than to Mokelumne Hill. Be safer with two ridin' that far together. Who knows? Maybe that snake-eyed greaser is just waitin' to follow somebody outta this camp and hit 'em on the trail. He'd be less apt to take on two men."

Nodding, Lang said, "Sure. Pick your man and go."

Before Roma could say a word, Walt DeFoe volunteered to go with him. While they were heading for their horses, Lang said to the rest of them, "Okay, guys, we got work to do. Let's dig gold and get richer."

Less than an hour later, the miners who had not been part of the group that had hanged Carlos Murieta and Enrico Flores approached Bill Lang at the sluice box. They had discussed the situation among themselves and decided the money they were making was not worth the risk of getting killed. They had helped Lang and the others hang those Mexicans on the outskirts of Camp Connell on November 21. Maybe this blood-hungry Mexican might start killing the gringo hangmen for that incident too.

They had the courage to march up to Lang and tell him they were leaving. There was nothing he or the others could do about it. When they walked away after giving their immediate resignations, Lang swore at them vehemently, calling them every name he could think of, including yellow-bellied cowards and deserters.

For the rest of the day, Bill Lang and his remaining men dug gold and worked their sluice box, nervously watching over their shoulders. The sniper did not return. At sundown, they assembled at the center of the camp and decided who would build the fire and cook the meal. Leaving the men to that task, Bill Lang headed for his small cabin at the edge of the clearing. His men were sleeping in tents, but he allowed himself the luxury of the cabin.

Still cursing the deserters under his breath, he stepped up on the porch, turned the doorknob, and pushed on the door to open it. For some reason, it seemed to resist his hand as if it had become very heavy. Putting a bit more muscle to it, he shoved on it. It swung open, but it did not open all the way. Something was obstructing its normal swing. Squeezing past it and moving inside, he looked behind the door and gasped at the sight that met his eyes. Bart Meakins was hanging on the coat hook on the backside of the door. The hook had been rammed through his neck at the base of his skull. There was a bullet hole centered in his forehead and his sightless eyes stared vacantly into space. His ears had been sheared off and were stuffed in his mouth.

Bile rose up in Bill Lang's throat. His face lost color as he dashed out the door and forced his legs to carry him toward the cluster of men at the center of the camp. Almost staggering as he drew up, he choked out the words, "Bart...Bart..."

"What's the matter, boss? What about Bart?"

Pointing toward the cabin, Lang said weakly, "He's...he's dead. Hangin' on the back of my cabin door."

Suddenly all eyes swerved to the edge of the forest close to the cabin as a lone horse came in at a trot, bearing a body draped over its back.

Emmett Bondy hurried to catch the reins and saw that the dead man was Jack Lang. His ears had been sliced off. Stopping the horse, Bondy turned to Lang. "It's your brother. He's dead."

Bill Lang bent over to examine the face of the earless victim and let out a wild, wordless wail. The miners were abruptly on the verge of panic as they drew their guns and let their eyes search the edge of the trees all around them. One of them said shakily, "This...this ain't makin' sense. We're dealin' with some kind of supernatural phantom here. This guy seems to know everything that's goin' on!"

When they took Jack Lang's body from his horse, they found his ears in one shirt pocket and a note in the other. The folded slip of paper had Sheriff Ward Steffen's name on the outside. Deciding they should read its contents, it was handed to their leader. Bill Lang opened it with trembling fingers and read it silently.

"What's it say?" one of the miner's asked.

Lang wiped the back of a hand over his mouth. "It says:

Sheriff Steffen,

The unfair tax that has been levied on my people has made me very angry. When I am through with my present task, I am going to organize a revolt that will make your dirty California lawmakers wish they had left the Mexicans alone. Blood is going to be shed. Let me warn you also. If the California legislature passes the Greaser Act, there will be RIVERS of blood!

It's signed, Joaquin Murieta!"

"So that's his last name," said Emmett Bondy. "Murieta."

"You guys know what his 'present task' is, don't you?" said one of them. "It's to kill every one of us!"

The frightened miners armed themselves heavily and ate supper while scouring the woods around them with fear-filled eyes. As soon as they had finished eating, they hastily buried Jack Lang and Bart Meakins in a single shallow grave, laying one body on top of the other. After that, they crowded themselves inside Bill Lang's small cabin for the night. None of them slept. They were eager for Nick Roma and Walt DeFoe to return with the sheriff.

Staying in a close knot, the miners emerged from the cabin at sunup and ate breakfast at the campfire. They decided not to work the mine that day. They would wait for Roma and DeFoe to arrive with the sheriff. One of them fearfully suggested that maybe Roma and DeFoe were already dead. Maybe they had not made it to Placerville. Bill Lang countered the idea by saying Murieta would not stop his two messengers. He knew they were going for Steffen. By leaving the note for Steffen in Jack's pocket, he expected Bill to give it to him when he arrived with Roma and DeFoe.

The words were hardly out of Lang's mouth when three riders trotted in from the woods. Roma and DeFoe had indeed returned with the sheriff.

Bill Lang poured out his woes to Steffen, telling him of Derek Smith, Wesley Coggins, Bart Meakins, Jim Wheeler, and his brother Jack being murdered. The sheriff informed Lang and the others that four miners had been found dead in the thickets some twelve or thirteen miles north. Each one of them had been relieved of his ears. When Steffen reeled off their names, Lang and his frightened men knew that the four men had been a part of the lynching party at Murphy's Diggings. Joaquin Murieta was carrying out his promise.

The sheriff told Lang that he was aware of the Murphy's Diggings lynching before Roma and DeFoe had arrived at his office. No charges would be pressed because of the sheriff's hatred for dirty greasers. Steffen went on to say that in the past few days Joaquin Murieta's name had become a household word among the Mexicans in the valley and he was fast becoming a hero to them.

It was then that Lang remembered the note. Fishing it from his shirt pocket, he gave it to Steffen, saying it looked like the state had a hot potato on their hands.

Steffen read it and swore. He was fully aware that with his hero status Joaquin Murieta could marshal an army of Mexicans and produce his rivers of blood. Folding the note and placing it in his pocket, he said, "I'll have to get this message to Sacramento."

"Those politicians ain't gonna do nothin', Sheriff," said Lang. "They're safe from Murieta. So he's *your* problem. What are you gonna do about him? He's gonna kill the rest of us if you don't stop him."

"I'll try to find men in the valley towns who will be deputized," said Steffen. "We've got to band together and find this lunatic before he finishes his present task and passes on to the next one."

"What should we do, Sheriff?" asked one. "Try to hide somewhere till he's caught?"

"Won't do any good," said Lang. "He found Jack, and he found those four guys the sheriff just told us about. Best thing for us to do is fortify ourselves right here and wait till he's caught."

Steffen agreed and mounted up, saying he was going to Murphy's Diggings to talk to Bill Byrnes. Since Byrnes and Murieta were partners and good friends, maybe Byrnes would have some idea where the black-hearted killer was hiding. After all, Byrnes was an upstanding citizen. Certainly he would not withhold information that could lead to Murieta's capture.

Eleven nerve-racking days passed. Lang and his six remaining men lived like prisoners at the camp site, staying inside the cabin most of the time. They were afraid to work in the mine and at the sluice box for fear that Joaquin Murieta would sneak up on them. But with all their fears and watchful care, there had been no sign of him.

The miners spoke often of Sheriff Ward Steffen, wondering if Murieta had not shown up because the sheriff and his posse had captured or killed him. They figured if that was the case, however, Steffen would come and advise them immediately. Since the sheriff had not shown up, they had to assume that Murieta was still at large, which meant they were in danger every minute.

Miner Oscar Oleson had suggested that the reason they were being left alone for the time being was because Murieta was tracking down the rest of the men who were part of the lynching party. The others agreed, but took little comfort in the possibility. The phantomlike killer could show up again at any time.

On the twelfth day, Sheriff Ward Steffen rode into the camp with a sixteen-man posse. He brought bad news. Joaquin Murieta was still on the loose and the earless bodies of four more miners had been found. One had been killed near Stockton, another on the banks of the Merced River, and a third was found dead in the woods just south of Placerville. The fourth had been tracked down and murdered as far south as Aurora, Nevada. Lang and his men knew that the mysterious man in black had now whittled down the original lynching party to seven men—themselves.

Steffen rubbed the back of his neck. "I don't understand it. I know that greasers all over the state are now hailing Murieta as their hero, but I still can't figure out his uncanny intelligence system. As speedily as he found and killed those last four men, it is evident that he had no trouble whatsoever locating them."

Alf Landon, another of Lang's remaining six, said with a tremor in his voice, "I don't know about the rest of you, but I'm leavin'! I should've took off while Murieta was trackin' down those other guys."

"Runnin' would be stupid, Alf," Bill Lang said. "Murieta found all the others. He'll find you too. Take off and you'll be all alone. The only way the seven of us are gonna come out of this situation alive is to stay right here and fortress ourselves up good until Sheriff Steffen and these men can capture Murieta."

Steffen agreed that Lang was right, saying there was strength in numbers. The safest thing to do was to stay together.

"I take it you weren't able to learn anything from Bill Byrnes, Sheriff," Lang said.

"Nothing," replied Steffen. "Byrnes said he hadn't seen hide nor hair of his Mexican pal since the day he left the office saying he'd only be gone a few days."

Assuring the miners he would advise them when Joaquin Murieta was apprehended, Steffen rode away with his posse. The frightened miners went to work on Lang's cabin, making it more secure. They agreed that no man would venture out of sight of the cabin. When they needed to go to the outhouse—which was some thirty yards to the rear of the cabin—they would go no less than two at a time.

Pressing home the importance of their sticking together, Bill Lang told them, "The life of each one of us is in the hands of the others. We must be alert at all times and never be without our guns."

"Don't worry, boss," said Nick Roma, "even when I eat, I'll do it with one hand. The other one will be holding my cocked revolver."

CHAPTER EIGHTEEN

T wo days after Sheriff Ward Steffen and his posse had been at the Lang camp, dawn came to the San Joaquin Valley with a gray eastern sky.

Emmett Bondy and Alf Landon stepped out of the cabin together, yawning and rubbing their eyes. Revolvers in hand, they moved off the porch, rounded the corner of the cabin, and headed toward the outhouse. Fear showed on their faces as they cautiously studied the shadows in the forest around them. Their feet moved hurriedly over the snapping twigs and crackling leaves, crunching them into the yielding ground. They were in a hurry to take care of their business at the outhouse and get back to the cabin.

Inside the cabin, Walt DeFoe and Nick Roma began preparing breakfast on the little woodstove. Bill Lang was up, washing his face in a basin. Oscar Oleson and Ben Wiggins were still on the floor in their bedrolls.

Roma was about to make coffee and found that the water bucket was all but empty. Seeing that DeFoe was occupied with bacon and flapjacks, he said, "Bill, we need water. Will you walk with me to the creek?"

Picking up a dirty towel and dabbing at his face, Lang replied, "Get one of those sleeping beauties on the floor to go with you."

Roma was irritated that Lang never took his turn at anything, but he dared not voice it. He moved to Oleson and Wiggins. "Hey! Oscar! Ben! I need one of you guys to go with me to the creek!"

When neither stirred, he jostled Wiggins with the toe of his boot. "Hey! Ben! Get up!"

Wiggins turned over, mumbling a swear word, and lay still.

When he did the same thing to Oleson and got the identical reaction, Bill Lang said stiffly, "Aw, Nick, you'll be all right. Run on out there and get the water."

Roma's eyes took on a harried expression. "Sure, run on out there and let Murieta kill you, Nick," he said in a mocking tone. "I thought we had an agreement. Nobody'd leave the cabin alone. There'd always be at least two at a time."

Dark shadows of weariness surrounded Bill Lang's eyes. "In the time you've wasted trying to get somebody to go with you, you could've already been out there and back. Go on and get the water!"

The tone of Lang's voice told Roma he had best do as he was told. An icy trickle of fear slithered down his spine as he picked up his revolver, grabbed the bucket, and moved outside. Walking guardedly toward the creek, he kept a sharp eye all around him. The creek was some forty-five yards from the cabin, the last twenty yards being beyond the edge of the clearing. When he reached the deep shadows of the trees, it seemed he could feel the presence of Joaquin Murieta, eyeing him like a ferocious beast of prey. The sensation was so real, he could almost feel the phantomlike fingers of Murieta clawing at the back of his neck.

He broke into a run. When he reached the creek bank and knelt down to dip the bucket in the water, he was breathing so hard, his lungs hurt with every pull of air. His haste caused him to drop the bucket in the stream. When he made a quick lunge to grab it, he went off balance and fell in. The creek was only two feet deep, but he stumbled as he tried to get up, and dropped the revolver. The bucket was being carried away with the current. Leaving the gun for the moment, he jumped up, waded fast, and seized the bucket. Turning around midstream, he headed back for the gun. Just as he was reaching into the water for it, a cold voice from the shadows said, "Leave it there. You won't need it."

The sun was lancing its yellow rays through the cabin windows as Oscar Oleson and Ben Wiggins slipped out of their bedrolls with the aroma of hot food tantalizing their nostrils. Bill Lang was at a window, looking in the direction of the creek and swearing at Nick Roma for taking so long to come back with the water. He wanted his morning coffee.

Walt DeFoe turned from the steaming skillets on the stove. "Nick's not the only one takin' his time, Bill. What about those slowpokes at the outhouse? I need to go out there myself."

"So do the rest of us," said Lang. "But no sense more'n two goin' at a time. You're right, though. Those guys have been out there long enough. Go outside and holler at 'em." Snickering, he added, "Maybe they fell in!"

Oleson and Wiggins laughed at Lang's humor as Walt DeFoe opened the cabin door. DeFoe sucked in a quick, sharp breath, staring at the water bucket that was sitting on the porch right in front of the door.

The three men in the cabin looked his way. "What's the matter?" said Lang.

"He's back!" squeaked DeFoe, his voice quavering.

No one had to ask who DeFoe was talking about. All three rushed up beside him and looked into the bucket that Nick Roma had carried to the creek. The pail was wet and laying on the bottom were two bloody ears.

Ben Wiggins gasped. "He got Nick!"

Bill Lang swore, trying to cover his own inward fear. Showing only anger, he pulled his gun from its holster, cocked the hammer, and growled. "This thing has gone on long enough. Grab your guns. That dirty greaser is out there in the woods. There are still six of us left. There's only one of him. Let's get the guys at the outhouse and go after him!"

Oleson, Wiggins, and DeFoe followed their leader out the door, guns drawn and hammers eared back. Running their eyes in every direction, the four of them hurried toward the outhouse. As they drew near, they could see the door was standing ajar. Lang was the first to reach it. When he swung the door fully open, he froze, eyes bulging. The others crowded close and had the same reaction. Lined neatly across the edge of the seat were four bloody ears.

"He got Alf and Emmett too!" Wiggins said.

"What do you suppose he did with the bodies?" asked Oleson.

Wiping a shaking palm over his eyes, Bill Lang stepped in, saying, "I think I know."

Peering through the two holes in the plank, he could see the crumpled corpses of Bondy and Landon at the bottom of the hole. Their shirts were smeared with blood and their revolvers lay on top of them.

Joining Lang to look, the others were horrified.

Lang's voice was tight as he said, "That dirty greaser stabbed 'em both to death."

"How'd he get 'em down there?" asked DeFoe.

"Plank ain't nailed down," replied Lang. "Just fits tight on the frame."

"Oh."

"What I want to know," put in Ben Wiggins, "is how one man could stab two to death before at least one of 'em could fight back."

"Especially without us hearin' a sound," interjected Oleson.

"It's weird," said DeFoe. "I tell you, the guy ain't human. It's like…like he's got some kind of spooky powers we don't know nothin' about."

"Maybe he ain't doin' it alone," suggested Oleson. "Maybe he's got an accomplice."

"No," said Lang. "Every report we've heard when he's been seen, he's been alone. This is Murieta's own personal revenge. There ain't no accomplices. He's human, all right…but he's also a well-oiled killing machine."

Walt DeFoe was shaking like a leaf in a cold autumn wind. His face screwed up and tears bubbled in his eyes. "I wish we hadn't hung Murieta's brother! If we hadn't done that and you hadn't bull-whipped him, Bill, none of this would be happenin'!"

"Shut up!" rasped Lang. "No sense cryin' over spilt milk! What's done is done! Now we gotta make the best of it."

DeFoe quickly stifled his weeping, wiping away the tears that had touched his cheeks.

"What are we gonna do with the bodies?" Wiggins asked Lang.

The big man eyed him blandly. "You want to dig 'em outta there?"

"Nope."

"Then they stay where they are."

Ben Wiggins backed out and holding his gun ready, scoured the surrounding area with fearful eyes. "C'mon, fellas," he said with a dry throat. "Let's get back inside the cabin."

The frightened miners rushed back into the small log structure and bolted the door. They knew Nick Roma's body was out there on the creek bank, but as far as they were concerned, it could stay there. Gripping their guns, they paced the floor, looking periodically out the windows. Panic was running through them like a cold river. They could hardly think for the icy fear that held them in its grip. Though now they felt little hunger, they forced themselves to eat the breakfast that was on the stove. They ate it dry, for no one wanted to go to the creek for water.

Four days passed.

Not one of the survivors inside the cabin had a moment's peace. The deadly man in black was playing cat-and-mouse with them. Sooner or later, somebody had to leave the cabin for water, if for nothing else.

By the fifth day, their food supply was almost gone. At sundown, Bill Lang was stretched out on his cot while the others were sitting on the floor with their backs to the wall. Oscar Oleson was sucking on a button, trying to work up some saliva in his mouth. Speaking around the button, he said, "I can't stand this any longer. I'm gettin' outta here as soon as it's totally dark. Ain't much moon right now. This is the best time to go."

"That's right," agreed Ben Wiggins. "I'm goin' with you. Murieta may have supernatural powers, but maybe one of 'em ain't seein' in the dark. I can't stand bein' cooped up in here no longer."

Walt DeFoe wanted to go too, but kept silent. He waited to see Lang's reaction to the decision Wiggins and Oleson had just made.

Lang sat up, set his booted feet on the floor, and eyed the two men with disdain. "Fools! That's what you are! That's exactly what that murderin' greaser wants you to do! Step outside that door and you're dead meat!"

Oscar scrambled to his feet, fear evident in his wan features. "Yeah? Well, what are we if we stay in here much longer? We're gonna die of dehydration pretty soon! And even if one of us could get to the creek and bring water without bein' snagged by Murieta, we're gonna starve to death in a few more days!"

"Aw, a man can go over a month without food before he dies!" said Lang, standing up.

"Well, I can't!" Oleson retorted sharply, his fear of Lang becoming less of a factor. "I'm leavin' as soon as it's dark!"

Lang's big hand lashed out, slapping the man hard with an open palm. "Get a hold on yourself, Oscar! You're actin' like a dumbfool crazy man! I'm telling you…you go out that door, and Murieta will have you within half a minute!"

Oleson blinked his eyes, rubbing the stinging cheek, and showed his teeth in a grimace of anger. "Big man, ain'tcha, Lang? If I was your size, I'd take you on."

Wheeling, he pulled his gun from its holster and stomped to the door. Jerking it open, he looked back and said, "I'm goin' right now. You with me, Ben?"

Wiggins said, "Let's wait till dark."

"I'm goin' right now. I'm gonna go out there and make peace with that greaser."

"Make peace?" echoed Wiggins. "What are you talkin' about?"

"Hey, the man's got a heart somewhere down in that body of his. Maybe if we tell him we're sorry for what we did, he'll let us go."

"Yeah!" Wiggins grinned. "Sure! We should've thought of that before! Let's go."

Lang looked at Walt DeFoe. "You goin', too?"

DeFoe was torn. He wanted to make peace with Joaquin Murieta in order to save his life, but he was not sure it could be done. He swallowed hard. "Naw. I'm stayin' with you."

"Every man to his own poison," said Oleson. "C'mon, Ben. Just do like I do."

Eagerness to end the nightmare, like a powerful shove, sent Oscar Oleson out the door and across the porch. Ben Wiggins was on his heels. The western sky was still aglow with purple light as Oleson stopped a few feet in front of the cabin and held his gun high over his head by the barrel. "Joaquin Murieta! I know you're out there! Listen to me! I'm sorry for my part in hangin' your brother! Honestly sorry! If I could turn back the calendar and change it, I would! I'm askin' your forgiveness! I'll do anything you want! I have several thousand dollars in gold buried in a secret place over by the mine! It's yours if you want it! Please don't kill me!"

Wiggins held his gun overhead in the same manner and repeated almost the identical words at the top of his voice.

All was still. There was no sound except for the soft breeze whistling through the treetops.

Taking a deep breath, Oleson cried, "Murieta-a-a-a!"

The word seemed to hang between Oleson and the edge of the forest as if he was in a tunnel, deep and hollow.

There was no response.

"Murieta! Please! I want to make peace with you!"

"Me too!" cried Wiggins. "Please come out and talk to us!"

When all they got was silence, Oscar said, "Ben, he ain't out there. Now's the time to light out. Let's get on our horses and go!"

"Let's do it!"

Suddenly, Bill Lang's voice boomed from the cabin door. "You stupid fools! He's only lurin' you out there so's he can kill you!"

"He ain't here, Bill!" called Wiggins. "C'mon. You guys go with us! Now's your chance to get away!"

"Go on, you numbskulls! It's your funeral!" Thinking on what he had just said, Bill added, "Only you'll be like Alf and Emmett out there in the privy! You won't get a funeral!"

Lang watched the two men make a dash for the spot within the trees where the horses were kept. When they dissolved into the shadows, he turned to Walt DeFoe and said, "Murieta's out there, all right. He just suckered them two into his clutches."

Closing the door and shoving the bolt home, Lang stood close to the window that faced the rope corral and waited for the sound of pounding hooves, but it never came. Turning to DeFoe, who was a mere shadow in the darkening room, he said, "He got 'em, all right. They never even made it to the horses."

"Maybe they just led them a ways before mounting."

"Is that what you'd have done? You bet your boots, you wouldn't. Soon as you could be in the saddle and gallopin' away the better. Nope. Murieta got 'em, sure as shootin'."

Cold terror crawled across Walt DeFoe's skin, lifting the hairs on his arms and tingling his scalp. "Bill, what are we gonna do, now? It's just you and me. We're trapped!"

Disguising his own rising fear, Lang held his voice steady. "Since Murieta's been right here with us for several days, Steffen ain't found him. That's for sure. Maybe he'll think about it and figure where the bloody Mex might be. If Steffen and that big posse came ridin' in here at sunup, we'd be safe. Ain't no way Murieta's gonna take on that many men. And even if all Steffen and his posse did was hold

Murieta at bay, we could get away with the posse and have 'em put us in protective custody."

DeFoe could barely make out the form of Lang in the dark. Straining to see him, he asked, "You mean put us in jail with the idea of us bein' safe?"

"Yeah. Keep us in the jail till they can catch that murderin' skunk."

"Wouldn't work," said DeFoe, croaking on the dryness of his throat. "He'd find a way to get in there and kill us."

"Maybe not."

"Yeah? Are you forgettin' what the man's accomplished so far? If, indeed, he got Ben and Oscar, we're the only two left. Remember what Murieta's message was? He'd get all of us, then he'd get you. He's come mighty close to fulfillin' his prophecy, Bill. No jail, nowhere, could protect us from him."

Lang knew DeFoe was right. He crossed the room in the dark and sat down on the cot. "Well, maybe Steffen and the posse will show up. Some of 'em could at least stay right here and protect us while the rest of 'em track Murieta down."

"I appreciate your optimism, Bill." DeFoe felt for the wall. Putting his back to it and sliding down to a sitting position, he added gloomily, "But let's face it. We're doomed. The mangy greaser is gonna kill us."

"No, he ain't!" Lang thundered. "We're gonna get out of this thing alive, Walt! Now, don't let me hear no more talk about us bein' doomed."

The duo spent a sleepless night, mumbling to each other periodically.

When the sun peeked over the Sierras the next morning, DeFoe rose to his feet and looked at Lang, who was on the cot. "Bill, I gotta have water. I'm dehydratin'. You gotta be thirsty too. Let's go to the creek together."

Thirst was rampant in Bill Lang's mouth and throat, but he feared exposing himself to Joaquin Murieta. Sitting up on the cot, he feigned dizziness, holding his head. "Whew! My blood must be dryin' up, Walt. The whole room is whirlin' around me. I gotta have water, but I don't think I could walk as far as the creek. Would… would you go dip us some water?"

The coppery taste of fear filled DeFoe's dry mouth. He almost refused, but he knew Lang was staying put. If there was going to be any water in the cabin, Walter J. DeFoe was going to have to fetch it. His own need for water was desperate, so there was no choice. Picking up the bucket—which had been relieved of Nick Roma's ears—he went to the door, slid the bolt, and pulled it open. What he saw at the edge of the clearing near the rope corral froze him in his tracks. A slight gasp escaped his parched mouth.

Hearing the gasp, Lang spoke from his horizontal position on the cot, "What is it?"

"Better come and see for yourself," DeFoe said weakly.

Grunting with the effort, Lang sat up, paused briefly, then rose to his feet. Stumbling to his partner's side, he focused on the ghastly scene. It was Lang's turn to gasp.

Ben Wiggins and Oscar Oleson were hanging earless by their ankles from tree limbs, a few feet apart. Lang swore and took a backward step, panting. "Shut the door!"

Walt DeFoe slammed the door and shoved the bolt in place, then fell to his knees and broke into childlike sobs. A look of stark horror was in his bulging eyes. Though his body was dehydrating, there were tears on his cheeks.

Lang sagged onto the cot and stared at him, saying nothing. Walt crumpled in a heap and wept hard for several minutes, mumbling that they were in for the same kind of death Ben and Oscar had suffered. Still Lang remained silent. He only stared toward the door, wondering where Joaquin Murieta was at the moment.

DeFoe lay on the floor, pulled himself into a fetal position, and cried intermittently for the rest of the day. As the last rays of sun were penetrating the dirty window on the west side of the cabin, he rose to his feet and stood over Bill Lang, who lay quietly on the cot.

Lang focused on DeFoe's haggard face as the man said in a strangled whimper, "I can't stand the waitin' any longer. I'm goin' out and get it over with."

Turning about and moving like a zombie, he went to the door, calmly slid the bolt, and turned the knob.

"Wait a minute, Walt," croaked Lang. "As long as we're alive, we got hope. Don't—"

"There ain't no hope," retorted DeFoe, jerking the door open. "I'm gettin' it over with."

Lang rose up on his elbows and watched the last remaining member of his bunch grope his way across the porch. With effort, he left the cot and shuffled to the door. DeFoe was staggering like a drunk man, calling out with thick tongue, "Murieta! Here I am! C'mon! Kill me! Get it done!"

Bill Lang ejected a shrill whine, slammed the door, and bolted it. Pivoting on his heels, he braced his back against the door and stood there, teeth clenched, sucking air between them. After a long moment, he stumbled to the window beside the door and looked out. Walt DeFoe was gone.

Lang moved falteringly across the floor to the cupboard. Hunger was gnawing at his stomach. The food supply had run out two days before, but maybe somewhere in the cupboard they had overlooked something edible. Swinging cupboard doors and leaving them open, he searched vainly for any type of morsel. There was nothing.

He made his way to the cot and lay down. Because of his extreme exhaustion, he fell asleep.

Bill Lang awakened when the sun thrust its brilliant rays through the windows on the east side of the room. The wind was kicking up outside. It gave off a haunting sound at the eaves, prodding the fear that was running through his veins like melting frost. He jerked at a thumping sound on the roof. Suddenly one of the west windows crashed and splattered broken glass across the floor. With instinctive reaction, Lang leaped to his feet, drawing his gun. Thinking that Joaquin Murieta was going to gun him down from the window, he fired through it twice, catching sight of some kind of form through the cloud of powder smoke. Terrified, he blasted away until the hammer of his revolver slammed down on an empty cartridge.

Adrenalin flowing, Lang stood there staring at the window as the thick blue-white smoke slowly cleared. Hanging upside down and staring at him through the window was the corpse of Walt DeFoe. A rush of wind swayed DeFoe's lifeless body. It was displayed in the rectangular frame from the middle of his naked chest, which now bore six bloodless holes. Above the bulging, sightless eyes,

DeFoe's mouth was wide open, teeth bared, in a silent, frozen scream. His throat was slit and his ears were gone.

Bill Lang's breath was locked deep in his chest. His lungs were compressed in a shell of thick-ribbed ice. The cold emptiness of despair congealed in his brain. His thoughts were slow, but deliberate. True to his word, Murieta had killed the other nineteen men who had hanged his brother and left their leader till last. Not one of the others had escaped the vengeful man in black. Bill Lang was not going to escape, either.

Glaring at Walt DeFoe's vacant eyes and realizing the horrid, unthinkable death Murieta had put on him, Lang slowly backed toward the opposite side of the one-room cabin, each step a razor edge of terror. "No-o-o-o!" he screamed. "You're not gonna do that to me, you bloody greaser! I won't give you that satisfaction!"

Blind panic suddenly wiped away all reason. Sweat beaded on Lang's brow as he raised the revolver in his hand, cocked it, and stuck the muzzle in his mouth. His eyes fluttered as he pressed the trigger with his thumb. There was only a hollow, metallic click.

He'd forgotten that he emptied the gun into Walt DeFoe's upside-down body at the window. Whimpering like a distraught woman, he stumbled toward a front corner of the room where his long-barreled rifle stood against the wall. Taking a deep, shaky breath, he picked up the rifle and cocked the hammer. With one hand, he grasped a broom that hung on nails near the door. He placed the butt of the rifle on the floor, and bending over, opened his mouth to the muzzle. He pressed the tip of the broomstick against the trigger and escaped the wrath of Joaquin Murieta.

Within a few seconds after the rifle roared, a dark, handsome face appeared at the window beside Walt DeFoe's dangling form. Murieta smiled to himself, turned, and walked toward the black horse that waited in the shadows of the forest.

He was satisfied.

CHAPTER NINETEEN

Having completed his first project, Joaquin Murieta returned to Sonora to set up operations for retaliation against the California legislature for imposing the unfair tax on his people. His brother Claudio and Rosita's brother Reyes Feliz joined him wholeheartedly in his task.

Joaquin's popularity accelerated among the Mexican population as he held rallies in towns and mining camps up and down the foothill range of the Sierra Nevada. Always beside him were Claudio and Reyes. The Mexican people were ready to join ranks with Joaquin and fight the dominating gringos and their government. Training camps were set up where Joaquin and other former conquistadores instructed men and teenage boys in guerilla warfare.

On December 11, 1850, Joaquin's preparations for conflict were intensified when the news came that the California legislature had passed the dreaded Greaser Act. The Mexicans of California would now have their property taken from them by the state. They could in turn lease residential property from the state at an extremely high price, but they could no longer own commercial property nor mine claims. Without the income from the gold mines, very few Mexicans could afford the exorbitant cost of the leases. Under young Joaquin Murieta's leadership, they made ready to fight for their right to own land and to mine gold.

News of Murieta's rallies and preparation for retaliation soon spread to the ears of state government officials in Sacramento. The legislature held an emergency meeting to deal with the situation. The governor called for permission from the legislature to authorize county sheriffs and town marshals in northern California to form posses from their white citizenship to put down any Mexican uprisings.

The legislature was basically in favor of the move but it had to be discussed at length, and proper procedures had to be followed, which resulted in an indeterminate delay while the Mexicans openly continued to make preparations for battle if it became necessary.

Unwilling to wait for the government to act, Mexican-hating Anglos quickly formed vigilante bands and made it known that they would shoot any greasers who caused trouble over the Greaser Act. Upon learning of the vigilante threat, Joaquin Murieta, along with Claudio and Reyes, held more rallies. Joaquin explained to the people what was happening and made sure they understood that the Mexicans would not be aggressors in the situation. They would only fight the gringos when the government officials tried to remove them from their homes and claim sites.

On the morning of January 1, 1851, a vigilante band of three dozen men led by forty-four-year-old Jason Baer met in Baer's barn just outside of a settlement known as Angel's Camp. Baer's two lieutenants were Slim Wyatt and Darold Canady, both ten years his junior.

Well-armed and ready to fight, the vigilantes gathered at Baer's summons. Everyone knew that Baer had a special hatred for Mexicans because his young son had been maimed and crippled for life while fighting in the Mexican-American War three years previously.

Facing the collection of men inside the barn, Baer hooked his thumbs in his gun belt. "Slow as the government is on this Mexican thing, pals, they won't put their posses together till Joaquin Murieta is telling his great-grandchildren how he defied the good citizens of California and won the fight. I say it's time to act right now. I have word from a reliable source that Murieta is holding a rally this afternoon at the Mexican mining camp over at Cucumber Gulch. Seems to me these dirty greasers need a little fear put into 'em and I figure we're just the guys to do it."

The vigilantes waved their hats and shook their fists. They were ready to show the Mexicans who was in charge.

When the noise subsided, Baer said, "We're gonna bust in on Murieta's little rally and tie a tin can to his tail," said Baer. "If we can make him run, the people will lose confidence in him, and this whole resistance movement will die. Then we can send all the greasers back to Mexico with their tails between their legs."

There were more shouts as the fever against the Mexicans grew hotter. Slim Wyatt and Darold Canady flanked Baer. When the noise died down again, Wyatt turned to Baer and asked, "Just how rough do we get with 'em, Jase?"

"We'll be ready for anything," came the quick reply. "My plan is to make a fool of this Murieta dude by makin' him show some fear. If any of those greasers try to resist, we'll give 'em hot lead!"

The vigilantes whooped it up once more. Jason Baer had them ready to make life miserable for the Mexicans.

It was just after two o'clock that afternoon when Baer and his pack rode up on the rally at Cucumber Gulch. A hundred or so Mexican men, women, and children were gathered around a young Mexican who was making a rousing speech, inciting the people to resist the "greedy gringos" and to fight for what was rightfully theirs.

When the Mexicans saw the heavily armed Anglos ride up, they looked at them with scorn. The dark-skinned man who was speaking broke off his words and glared at the vigilantes. He noted the man on the lead horse and shouted, "This is a private rally, mister! You have no business here!"

Jason Baer gave a hand signal and thirty-six rifles were quickly cocked and aimed at the crowd while the vigilantes remained in their saddles. Pulling his revolver, Baer lined it over the heads of the crowd, cocked it, and aimed it between the speaker's eyes. "This rally is over, Murieta!"

Showing no fear, the speaker held his gaze. "You are looking for Joaquin Murieta?"

Raising his eyebrows, Baer gusted, "Ain't you him?"

"My name is Reyes Feliz. Joaquin is holding a rally elsewhere."

Jason Baer's jaw tightened. "You're lyin'! I got it on good word that Joaquin Murieta was holdin' this rally. You're Murieta, all right! You're just such a yellow-bellied coward you're afraid to admit it!"

An older Mexican man who recognized the vigilante leader stepped close to his horse and looked up. "This man is not Joaquin, Mr. Baer. He is telling you the truth. His name is Reyes Feliz."

Baer's features darkened. "What's your name, old man?"

"Mario Velazquez."

"Well, Mario," Baer said insolently, pointing the gun down at him, "why don't you tell me where this Murieta dude is holdin' his rally."

The old man's eyes widened. "I…I do not know."

Pushing his way through the fearful crowd, Reyes came up beside Mario Velazquez, and set his black gaze on Baer. "What is it with you gringos? You think you own the world, do you? Well, I have news for you. We have as much a right to this California land as the gringos do! If we want to hold a rally, that is our business. Now I am asking you politely to put your gun away and leave. Take your wolf pack with you."

Frustrated that Joaquin Murieta was not on the scene, Baer rasped, "Don't be mouthin' off to me, greaser!" As he spoke, he pointed the gun at Feliz's face. "One more word outta you, and I'll blow your head off!"

"Big tough hombre, aren't you, Jason Baer?" said a Mexican woman who stood on the fringe of the crowd. "You're real brave with all of these gun-packing hounds behind you! Hah! You are the one with the yellow belly! Our Joaquin Murieta could make you crawl on that yellow belly and eat dirt! He is a real man!"

Darold Canady turned around in his saddle. "Shut up, sister, or you'll get your head blown off too!"

Next to the woman was her twelve-year-old son. Irritated at Canady for the way he spoke to his mother, the boy bent down, picked up a fist-sized rock, and hurled it with all his might. The rock struck Canady solidly on the temple, knocking him from the saddle.

In the heat of the moment, Jason Baer swore, swung his gun on the boy, and fired. Women screamed, men shouted, and twelve-year-old Alejandro Cruz fell dead. His mother wailed and fell on top of him, screaming his name.

When the Mexican men looked like they were going to charge into the vigilantes bare-handed, Jason Baer fired a shot into the air. "Hold it! If you want to die, just make a move and my men'll mow you down!"

The ominous black muzzles of three dozen rifles held the crowd in check. Slim Wyatt dismounted and helped a stunned Darold Canady to his feet. While Wyatt was boosting him back into the saddle, Canady mumbled, "We oughtta kill every one of 'em. Dirty greasers!"

Baer spoke to the crowd loudly, "That kid would be alive if you stupid greasers hadn't had this rally! If you follow Joaquin Murieta's insurrection against us, there'll be more bloodshed!"

"Gringos bleed when they are shot, too!" Reyes Feliz said, a jagged edge in his voice.

Eyeing him with contempt, Baer snapped, "You just tell Joaquin Murieta he'd best rally you all back to Mexico! Otherwise there'll be plenty of Mexican coffins planted in California soil!"

With that, Jason Baer led his vigilantes away at a gallop.

Three hours later, a furious Joaquin Murieta stood over the body of Alejandro Cruz as it lay on the bed in his room. Teresa Cruz sat in a chair beside the bed, weeping. Reyes Feliz, Claudio Murieta, and elderly Mario Velazquez were in a semicircle at the foot of the bed.

"Mario, where does this Jason Baer live?" Joaquin asked.

"Over at Angel's Camp."

"He's a dead man," Joaquin said icily.

"He may not be easy to find, Joaquin," said Teresa. "His wife died a few years ago. He doesn't stay home a lot. Seems to have plenty of money. Roams around a lot with those two friends of his, Darold Canady and Slim Wyatt. It was Canady my boy hit with the rock."

"I want the description of all three of them," Joaquin said evenly. "I will find them sooner or later."

Word spread quickly amongst the Mexican towns and camps of Alejandro Cruz's brutal death. Jason Baer learned that the Mexicans were out to get him. To save his life, he holed up in an old abandoned barn near San Andreas, which was some fourteen miles north of Angel's Camp. Slim Wyatt and Darold Canady led the vigilante band and periodically brought food to Baer.

Vigilante bands began attacking Mexican mining camps and quickly met with stiff opposition. Joaquin Murieta had trained them well and much Anglo blood was being shed.

Murieta and his own band of fighters engaged in battle with no less than a dozen vigilante bands in January and February of 1851. Ten of the gringo bands were shot up and crippled so badly that they disbanded.

By early March the California legislature had commissioned lawmen to form posses, deputize them, and go after Joaquin Murieta and his growing army of resistors.

Mexicans up and down the Sierra Nevada Range were elated at Murieta's successes. So far, they were still in their homes and were continuing to dig gold from their mines. They owed this to their leader, and soon dubbed him El Patrio: The Patriot.

Making Sonora his home base, Murieta and his several bands of resistors rode up and down the length and breadth of the San Joaquin Valley robbing stagecoaches, stores, and banks. The Anglo population was paying dearly for its legislature having passed laws against the Mexican people.

On March 12, a stagecoach was wending its way along the rocky, winding road between Stockton and Valley Springs. Just as the coach was topping a steep incline and rounding a curve at the same time, a rider on a black horse darted from the dense forest, wielding a revolver. "Hold it!"

The driver drew rein and the shotgunner turned white. Passengers inside the coach looked out the windows to see four other riders quickly draw up and flank the vehicle on both sides.

The rider in front of them was dressed completely in black, including a black serape. While his four partners held guns on crew and passengers, the leader dismounted, and smiled at the shotgunner. "I have a request, sir. Throw your sidearm and your shotgun down."

As the shotgunner complied, the man in black smiled at the driver. "You will please drop your rifle to the ground, along with your sidearm."

While his men picked up the guns to take with them, the man opened the door of the coach, smiled, and said to the passengers, "You will please give me your purses and wallets."

One of the men pulled his wallet from his coat and said tartly, "The way you're smiling, you must really enjoy this."

"I really do not enjoy it, sir," replied the robber, collecting the aforesaid items. "I wish I did not have to do it at all, but your gringo politicians in Sacramento have forced me to it. By robbing stagecoaches, stores, and banks, I am trying to get people like you to put pressure on those stuffed-shirt politicians to revoke the laws they have enacted against my people. When the laws are off the books and they let us live in California like other human beings, the robberies and all the other trouble will stop."

One of the young women said excitedly, "I know who you are! You're Joaquin Murieta, aren't you?"

He removed his black, flat-crowned hat and bowed. "Yes, ma'am, I am Joaquin Murieta."

"Oh, Daddy!" she said, gripping the arm of the older man sitting beside her. "Isn't this something? Wait'll I tell my friends at home that I was robbed by Joaquin Murieta, the smiling bandito!"

Appreciating her attitude, Joaquin showed her an even broader smile and extended her purse toward her. "Here, young lady. You are so nice. I will not take your purse."

"Oh no! Take it! How can I tell my friends you robbed me if you give it back?"

Shrugging, Murieta backed away and closed the door. Looking up at the driver, he said, "Be sure to tell your superiors that I robbed their stagecoach because of what the California legislature has done to my people."

Sullen-faced, the driver snapped the reins and put the coach in motion.

"Just think of it, Daddy!" the Mexicans heard the young woman say, "I was actually robbed by Joaquin Murieta, the smiling bandito!"

From that day, Joaquin Murieta became known far and wide as the smiling bandito. He was even becoming a champion to much of California's Anglo population.

With each report of the counterattacks against the posses and vigilante bands and the robberies boldly committed by the polite, smiling bandito, the politicians in Sacramento were infuriated. They called a special session and agreed to offer a reward to the sheriff's posse or vigilantes who captured or killed Murieta. Though unspoken to the public, their preference was that he be brought in dead. Whoever accomplished his capture dead or alive would be awarded a thousand dollars.

The offer of money for Murieta's capture or demise stirred posses and vigilantes to work harder. In the weeks that followed, the manhunt was the topic of newspapers and conversations all over California. Before the state could remove the Mexicans from their homes and mines, El Patrio would have to be eliminated. In March and April alone, posses and vigilante bands thundered into Sonora in violent attempts to trap Murieta, but he was either not there at the time or successfully escaped from under their noses. Each time the gringos were fired upon and being outnumbered by Murieta's followers, had to run for their lives. The Mexican men fought with the expertise of conquistadores.

Joaquin Murieta remained a thorn in the side of Anglo government, counterattacking the bands of well-armed men. Law enforcement agencies enlarged the size of their posses and armed them to the teeth, but the well-trained Mexicans continued to kill and maim them. After six months of men coming close to apprehending Murieta—but always ending in failure—the governor of California dubbed him the elusive Ghost of Sonora.

On May 2, the *California Police Gazette* carried a front page story of how the slippery Ghost of Sonora was making fools of lawmen and vigilantes. Sometimes he had even been seen in his black outfit on his black horse, but was gone before the eager men could trap him. The story went on to call the massive manhunt posses and vigilantes the "Engine of Terror," explaining how the Anglo bands attacked Mexican towns, villages, and mining camps, killing even women and children in a desperate attempt to surface Murieta and force him into a showdown. The story went on to tell how vigilante leader Jason Baer had killed the Mexican boy, Alejandro Cruz, at Cucumber Gulch, and for fear of Murieta, had decided to disappear.

In the following issue, the *Police Gazette* carried a front page continuation of the story, telling how the Ghost of Sonora and his guerilla bands had met the gringo "Engine of Terror" head-on and had made the San Joaquin Valley a virtual graveyard. More Anglos had been killed than Mexicans by far.

The story quoted journals of the mining forty-niners referring to Murieta's attacks on the Anglo population as "acts of revenge." It also quoted Caleb Dorsey, district attorney of Tuolumne County, who seemed to understand Murieta's plight. Dorsey said, "I have admiration for the black-clad smiling bandito. He never raised a finger against the Anglos until they first passed laws against his people, and never fired a shot against them until a vigilante leader named Jason Baer shot down a twelve-year-old Mexican boy who was trying to defend his mother. Joaquin Murieta is quiet-spoken and a gentleman. In my humble opinion, the man is a reluctant revolutionary."

So many copies of the *Gazette* were sold because of the Murieta story, that a third issue carried more information on the front page. The article pointed out that Joaquin Murieta had turned twenty-one on February 8 and to date was attributed with killing sixty-four men. After giving the names of the men Joaquin Murieta had sent into eternity, the article closed with a question: "Cannot the law enforcement agencies of the sovereign state of California track down and capture the youthful Ghost of Sonora?"

As the story of Murieta's crusade spread to Mexico, many Mexicans came to California to aid in the fight. Some were notorious Mexican outlaws. The meanest among them was a heartless killer named Three-Fingered Jack, who had lost the thumb and forefinger on his right hand in a knife fight. Other members of the hardcore group fresh from the old country were Luis Vulvia, Joaquin Valenzuela, Juan Senate, and Rafael Escobar. Arriving at the same time, but not part of the hard-cores, was Joaquin Murieta's old friend, Chico Herrera. Chico was stunned to learn of the deaths of Rosita and Carlos. This made him even more eager to join the fight against the gringos.

With the arrival of the hard-core Mexicans, Murieta's army reached its peak in size and strength. Each of the hard-core men directed a full company of desperadoes under Joaquin Murieta's command, operating simultaneously over a hundred-mile front.

Hiding out in a Sierra Nevada canyon, Joaquin and his band of forty men were sitting around a campfire on a warm night in late May. Joaquin and Chico Herrera were in conversation with Claudio Murieta and Reyes Feliz. They talked of old times in Mexico. After a while, Joaquin looked at the others by firelight and said, "All of this talk has made me homesick. Things are in control here. My forces are accomplishing my desires. I think I will take a little leave of absence and go home to Mexico. I want to see my parents. They have a right to know that Carlos is dead and Rosita's parents must know of her death too."

"You want I should go with you?" asked Claudio.

"No need." Joaquin waved him off. "It is better that I travel alone." Pondering on it for a moment, he added, "I have a good friend down in San Jacinto that I want to stop by and see too."

"Who is this, Joaquin?" queried Chico Herrera.

Joaquin told him briefly of Marshal Colby Cullins and how

they had become friends, saying he wanted to see how things were going for Cullins in San Jacinto.

Joaquin Murieta was gone from California until the first week of July. Upon his return, he found his guerilla army still making the gringo Californians pay for what they had done to his people. Reporting to Claudio and Reyes, he told them that both sets of parents were doing well. They, of course, had taken the news of Rosita's and Carlos's deaths very hard. Joaquin had been able to spend some time with Don Miguel Gonzales, who now owned the Gonzales ranch. Don Jose had died in May. He had also seen his friend Colby Cullins, who was still wearing the badge in San Jacinto.

Because of Murieta's strike force, the general public was living in fear, not knowing when or where the Mexican guerillas would strike next. People all over the state were asking the governor to revoke the Greaser Act and to kill the unfair tax law against the Mexican miners. People wanted a truce with Murieta. However, the governor and the lawmakers who sat safely in their state houses would not back down. They must save face. They insisted that Murieta would be captured soon.

In the town of San Andreas, Jason Baer had been talked into leaving his hiding place and having lunch with his two pals, Slim Wyatt and Darold Canady. They had just come out of the café and were picking their teeth in the bright sunlight when a lone Mexican rode along the street and took note of them.

Joaquin Murieta had memorized the description of the man who had gunned down young Alejandro Cruz along with the descriptions of his two companions. He recognized them the moment his eyes happened to stray their direction. He was not wearing his black outfit, but was clad in a bright-colored shirt and fancy sombrero. Angling the Arabian gelding he was riding toward the spot where they stood on the boardwalk, he hauled up directly in front of them.

Casually laying his hand on the butt of his revolver, he pushed the sombrero off his head, allowing it to dangle against his back. Smiling warmly, he centered his attention on Baer, who stood between the others. "Good afternoon. I believe you are Mr. Jason Baer, correct?"

Baer regarded the dark-skinned man with open derision. "So what's it to you?"

"I just thought you would like to know my name."

Baer flicked a glance at Wyatt and Canady. "Why should I care who you are, greasebucket?"

Murieta's smile vanished. "Does the name Joaquin Murieta mean anything to you, child killer?"

Baer's face blanched. "Y-you're Murieta?"

"In person."

All three men clawed for their guns, but were too slow to act. Both of Murieta's weapons were out and spitting fire before they cleared leather. Leaving them lying on the boardwalk, Murieta quietly rode away.

The next day, a local newspaper, the *Alta Californian,* reported:

On Thursday a lone Mexican gunman rode into San Andreas and singled out three innocent Americanos. Pulling guns on them, he identified himself as Joaquin Murieta, then shot them down in cold blood. The Ghost of Sonora is a crack shot. All three men took slugs through the Adam's apple. Bystanders who heard the killer identify himself as Joaquin Murieta said he laughed while shooting down the innocent men. Dead are Jason Baer, Darold Canady, and B. K. "Slim" Wyatt, all of Angel's Camp.

Midafternoon the following day, Edgar Price, the *Alta Californian*'s editor, was at his desk, concentrating on an article he was writing when he suddenly became aware that someone was standing over him. Looking up, he focused on a dark-skinned man who was dressed in black. This time there was no serape, but Price knew the identity of his visitor without asking. His face drained of color and shock dropped his jaw.

"My name is Joaquin Murieta, Mr. Price. You printed some lies about me in yesterday's paper."

Price shook his head. "N-no, Mr. Murieta. I…I didn't. The eyewitnesses are th-the ones who—"

"Then they lied!" Murieta banged the desk with his fist. "You should not print something unless you verify the facts, sir."

"B-but…I—"

Murieta leaned down close. "You will print a front-page article in tomorrow's paper correcting those lies, mister! First of all, those men were not innocent. Over a hundred witnesses saw them shoot down a twelve-year-old boy. His name was Alejandro Cruz. Secondly, I identified myself to those men before I pulled my guns. My weapons did not come out of their holsters until they went for theirs. They were slow. That was their fault, not mine. And thirdly, I did not laugh while shooting them. Do you understand what I am saying?"

Quivering as if he were in an icy gale, Edgar Price said, "M-Mr. Murieta, it is too late in the day to make any changes in t-tomorrow's edition. All the type has been set."

"Then reset it!"

"Y-you don't understand," Price said, "it just can't be changed this late. It…it will have to wait until the next day's edition. There's just no way—"

Murieta's hand moved quicker than a blink and seized the editor's shirt. Dragging him halfway out of his chair over the desk, he showed his teeth in a grimace of anger. "You will correct your lies in tomorrow's paper, Mr. Price…or the next Adam's apple to collect a bullet will be yours!"

Warning Price that he would be back the next day if the correction was not on the front page, the Ghost of Sonora left the office.

When the *Alta Californian* came off the press the next morning, the correction was printed in bold letters on the front page.

CHAPTER TWENTY

As Joaquin Murieta's forces grew stronger and bolder, towns throughout the San Joaquin Valley posted squads of armed guards around their communities. The stagecoach companies refused to operate unless their stages were accompanied by heavily-armed guards. Anglo miners abandoned their claims, which were quickly taken over by Mexicans. Tax collectors who were supposed to collect from Mexican miners had long since given up their jobs. State authorities who would remove them from their land and properties had been frightened off by Murieta's army.

Citizens in many towns and communities of the Mother Lode country became weary of waiting for the law to stop Murieta. Giving up on the frail efforts of law enforcement agencies, they merged with vigilante bands and formed their own army of over five hundred men and divided into companies. Taking courage in their large number, they had but one objective: to capture and hang the elusive Ghost of Sonora.

The determined new army of vigilantes began to take a toll on the Murieta forces. Until September 1851, the Murieta army had suffered relatively few casualties, though the killings attributed to his guerilla force were in excess of three hundred.

On September 15, two of Murieta's men were trapped in Sonora by a company of the citizens' army and killed on the spot. On September 18, another was caught and hanged in Mokelumne Hill, and two others met the same fate a day later in Angel's Camp.

An infuriated Murieta sent out word to his troops to intensify their attacks. In the days that followed, there was more killing and bloodshed as the citizens' army fought back. At Chaparral Hill, Joaquin was leading his own band toward the town when they were suddenly ambushed. Chico Herrera was slightly wounded, but six Mexicans were shot from their saddles and killed. Murieta barely escaped with his life.

A band of citizens' army vigilantes from San Andreas picked up

Murieta's trail and followed it to a mountain town called Yaqui, which was populated entirely by Mexicans. The band was composed of a hundred and sixty-five men, who were blood-hungry and bitter. They held the populace at bay and entered every building. Joaquin Murieta and his band were nowhere to be found. Angry because the Ghost of Sonora had eluded them again, they demanded that the people tell them where he had gone. When they refused, a hundred and sixty-five guns fired and every citizen of Yaqui was killed.

Upon returning to San Andreas, the Anglo band was still in a mood for Mexican destruction. Shouting words of hatred, they burned out the entire Mexican section of the town, sending hundreds of Mexicans homeless and destitute into the foothills of the Sierra Nevada.

The sizable victory gave impetus to other bands of the citizens' army. Within the next few weeks, several of Murieta's individual bands were tracked down, cornered, and wiped out.

The Ghost of Sonora knew his army was now vastly outnumbered and learned of more gringos joining the fight every day. This did not dampen his desire to fight, but it did cause him to retreat for a while and take stock of the situation. Using runners, he spread the word to his army to pull back into the hills and wait for further instructions. Claudio Murieta and Reyes Feliz were put in charge of those troops hiding in the hills.

After spending a few days in San Jose, where he had gone to enlist more Mexicans for his army, Joaquin sent word for his troops to travel quietly to Los Angeles, where he figured to have fewer problems from the citizens' army. They would rendezvous in a designated ravine among the hills between Los Angeles and nearby San Gabriel on October 12.

When the rendezvous day came, Joaquin welcomed his men as they arrived, band by band. It was dark when the final band rode in, led by Juan Senate. A fire had been built, and by its light Joaquin saw that Senate's band had picked up five women along the way.

Approaching Senate as he dismounted, Joaquin said firmly, "Juan, you know how I feel about having females in our camps. It is not good. They always cause trouble."

Grinning, Senate said, "Not these women, Joaquin. They are singers on their way to work in Los Angeles hotels and saloons. We are simply escorting them to see that they arrive safely. Besides, one of them is very eager to meet you." Turning away, he called to a woman who was just being helped from her horse. "Antonia, come here!"

Wearing a black riding outfit and low-crowned hat, the beautiful woman came hastily. She was tall for a Mexican woman, five feet seven inches. When Senate introduced Antonia La Molinera to Joaquin, she smiled warmly and extended her hand. Though he was annoyed that Senate had brought the women into the camp, Joaquin took Antonia's hand, bowed, and kissed it. "I am happy to make your acquaintance, señorita."

"Thank you. I have long been an admirer of yours, Joaquin, and I am extremely happy to finally get to meet you." Pausing for effect, she swept her hands from her black hat to her black boots. "You will notice that I am dressed like the Ghost of Sonora, except for a serape and the guns, of course."

"Yes, I noticed." He turned to Juan Senate. "When are the ladies going into Los Angeles?"

"Tomorrow morning."

Displeasure showed in Murieta's dark eyes. Pointing to a particular spot in the ravine, he said, "The women will sleep over there. I want no men anywhere near them. Understand?"

"I understand."

Two hours later, when all were in their bedrolls, Joaquin Murieta sat on a fallen tree by the fire, engulfed in thoughts of Rosita. His heart ached for her. Seeing Antonia La Molinera had stirred memories of Rosita, for in some ways, she resembled Rosita.

A soft breeze sifted through the ravine, causing the flames to crackle. Just before she drew up beside him, Joaquin heard footsteps. He turned to see who was coming, and wished Antonia La Molinera had stayed in her bedroll.

Wrapped in a shawl, she looked down at him and smiled. "May I sit down?"

It was not in Joaquin Murieta to be impolite to a lady. "Of course."

Antonia placed herself quite close to him. "I noticed you sitting here alone and thought you might like some company."

"You ought to get your sleep."

"I will, shortly. But…but…well, I just wanted to take advantage of a private moment to tell you that though we have never met, I have admired you greatly."

"You said something like that earlier."

"I know, but now that I have met you, I admire you even more. You are a very attractive man, Joaquin. I have known a lot of men in my twenty years of life, but I have never known one like you." Sliding closer to him, she breathed, "I think you would like me too, if we could get better acquainted."

"I do not dislike you, Antonia, but—"

"Do you think I am beautiful?"

Rising to his feet quickly, Joaquin replied, "You are very beautiful, Antonia, but it is time for me to get into my bedroll and like I said, you need to get your sleep, too. Good night."

Temper flared in Antonia La Molinera. Jumping up, eyes flashing, she snapped, "I have never been cold-shouldered by a man before! How dare you brush me off like this!"

Without another word, Joaquin turned and went to his bedroll. Antonia stood by the fire, seething.

The next morning, as the women were preparing to ride into Los Angeles, Antonia set her eyes on Joaquin Murieta, who was standing near the rope corral, talking to his brother and Reyes Feliz. Joaquin had not spoken to her at breakfast and there was fire in her black eyes.

She was approached by Chico Herrera. "May I speak with you, señorita?"

Lips drawn tight, she snapped, "What about?"

"Joaquin."

"Yes?"

"I was awake last night when you two were by the fire. I saw and heard everything, and there is something you need to know."

"I am listening."

Chico quietly told Antonia about Rosita Murieta's violent, untimely death, then explained that Joaquin had not gotten over it yet. When Chico was finished, she thanked him and walked away.

Moments later, when the women were mounting up, Antonia approached Joaquin. "I owe you an apology."

"For what?"

"For the way I acted last night. Chico talked to me this morning and told me about Rosita. I am truly sorry for your loss. Please forgive my angry outburst."

"You are forgiven," he replied in an amiable tone. "It was nice to have met you."

"Could…could we be friends?"

"Certainly. We will meet again sometime."

Antonia's attraction toward Joaquin Murieta was genuine and strong. As she rode away from the camp, she told herself she would wait until Joaquin's mourning over his dead wife had subsided, then she would make her play for him.

When the women were gone, Murieta sat his men down and mapped out a new plan to harass the gringos. They would rob stagecoaches going in and out of Los Angeles and hit stores and banks all over the area. The California legislature would still get the message. When the citizens' army came after them, they would move elsewhere.

Murieta sent one band into Los Angeles to rob a couple of stores. Three-Fingered Jack would head up the band. Chico Herrera would be his right-hand man. The other bands would hit stores and banks in San Gabriel and other outlying towns. Joaquin's band would take on a couple of stagecoaches.

That night Murieta's army rode into the ravine and assembled around the fire to give reports to their leader. Much loot was brought in and all had gone well. There was one thing to worry about, however. Three-Fingered Jack's band had not yet returned. After supper, Joaquin told his men that he would take half a dozen riders and go into Los Angeles. They must find the missing band.

Mounting up, Murieta and his chosen six rode out of the ravine. They had gone only a mile when they met up with Three-Fingered Jack and his band. Joaquin saw immediately that one man was missing and that two others were seriously wounded. The missing man was Chico Herrera.

As they hurried toward the camp to give aid to the wounded men, Jack told Joaquin that when they were robbing the third store in Los Angeles, they were set upon by a Los Angeles deputy sheriff named Harry Love and a posse of mean-eyed men who had learned that Murieta's army was in the vicinity. A gunfight broke out. In the midst of it, Chico had been shot in the leg while running across a wide street. Deputy Love could have taken him prisoner, but purposely shot him through the heart instead. The rest of them managed to escape and had been hiding out, waiting for darkness to fall.

Murieta was inflamed with wrath toward Deputy Sheriff Harry Love. The next day, dressed in bright clothing and riding a bay horse, he rode into Los Angeles, bent on killing Love. As he rode into town, he noticed a billboard in front of the Chaparral Hotel advertising Antonia La Molinera as their star singer.

Three blocks farther down the street, the Ghost of Sonora reined in at the Los Angeles County sheriff's office. At the same time, a young skinny deputy emerged from the office. Jack had given Joaquin Harry Love's description. This badge-toter was not Love. Speaking in broken English to throw the deputy off, Joaquin asked if Deputy Harry Love was in. The skinny lawman informed him that Love was out of town looking for Joaquin Murieta and would not return for several days.

Disappointed that he could not level revenge on Harry Love immediately, Joaquin thanked the deputy and headed back out of town. As he drew near the Chaparral Hotel, he noticed three dark-haired women standing on the boardwalk in conversation. Just as he was drawing parallel with them, he recognized Antonia La Molinera. At the same instant, her line of sight fell on him. Excusing herself to the women, she stepped into the street and waved, calling, "Joaquin!"

Veering toward her, Murieta smiled and touched the brim of his flat-crowned hat. "Hello."

Reaching up to offer her hand, she smiled, "It is good to see you again, Joaquin."

Squeezing her hand, he said, "It is good to see you again, too." Swinging his leg over the saddlehorn, he dropped to the ground and felt the warmth of her personality. Though his heart was still clinging to the memory of Rosita, he did find Antonia attractive. If she did not push herself on him as before, he would allow them to become friends.

They chatted for a few moments, then Antonia said, "You must come and hear me sing sometime, Joaquin."

"I would like that. As you know, I have to be careful that the law does not recognize me. It would be best if I come when the crowd is the largest."

"Then that would be tonight. Saturday night always brings in the largest crowds."

"I will see what I can do."

"Oh, I would love to sing for you! Please make it tonight!"

"We will see," Joaquin said, not willing to give her any false ideas.

Antonia La Molinera was midway through her first song that evening when she spotted the handsome face of El Patrio near the back of the large room. She sang three more, then for her finale, she dedicated the song to "a very special friend in the audience" and sang like a lark to please Joaquin Murieta.

As the audience was filing out at the close of the performance, a young page boy drew up to Joaquin and handed him a note. Antonia's message said she would meet him at a side door in ten minutes. When she stepped out the door as promised, the dark space between the hotel and the next building was dimly lit by a street lantern some forty feet away. When she asked how he liked the song she had dedicated to him and Joaquin replied favorably, she moved close and wrapped her arms around his neck.

She felt Joaquin stiffen and inched back, leaving her hands locked behind his neck. "I'm sorry to be so forward, Joaquin, but I must tell you, I meant every word in the song I dedicated to you tonight. I...I love you, Joaquin Murieta."

Joaquin pulled her arms from him. "Antonia, you are a very beautiful woman. Most men would melt if they were in my boots right now. But please let me explain something."

Antonia listened as Joaquin bared his heart and told her of the great love he had felt for Rosita and how her memory was still so fresh in his mind. He was not ready to fall in love again, and was not sure if or when he might be. Saying that she understood, Antonia vowed to make him fall in love with her, asking if they could see each other often.

He explained that he must continue to be a thorn in the side of the California legislature until they succumbed to the pressure and revoked the tax law against their people and did away with the Greaser Act. This goal would dominate his time, but he would come and see her as often as possible. With tears in her eyes, Antonia told him she would always be there for him and would live for the day he would say he loved her. She watched him ride away, then went to her room in the hotel, happy that he had left the door open for something to develop between them.

In the days and weeks that followed, Murieta tried to get to Deputy Harry Love, but he found it impossible because of the well-organized posses that swarmed the area. He was finding it much more difficult to operate around Los Angeles than it had been up north, which was a disappointment. The stiff resistance, however, made him vow to fight harder.

As time moved on and Joaquin continued to harass the Anglos, the city of Los Angeles placed a five-thousand-dollar reward on his head. A deputy sheriff in Santa Barbara named Robert Wilson heard of the cash reward, and knowing that the notorious smiling bandito was hiding somewhere in the Los Angeles area, he rode south to see if he could garner the reward.

Arriving in Los Angeles, Wilson let it be known that he was looking for Murieta. He would share a portion of the reward with anyone who would give him a lead on where to find him.

Early on the morning of his third day in town, Wilson was in his street-side ground level room at the Bella Union Hotel. He heard a fracas just outside his window and pushed back the curtain to get a look. Two Mexican men were swinging punches at each other, and a crowd was gathering to watch the fight. Though the Mexicans did not seem to be doing much damage to each other, the crowd chose sides and cheered them on.

Wanting to get a better look at the fight, Wilson made his way out to the street. Standing alone, he noticed a Mexican riding down the street wearing a big sombrero and slouching lazily in the saddle. To his surprise, the man rode up and reined in, facing him.

The two combatants were still flailing at each other in the street.

The Mexican pushed his sombrero to the back of his head and smiled, saying in broken English, "I see you are wearing a badge, señor. Do you happen to be Deputy Sheriff Robert Wilson?"

"That's right," clipped Wilson irritably.

"I understand you are offering a reward to anyone who can tell you where to find Joaquin Murieta."

Wilson's face lit up. "Yes, sir! Can you tell me where to find him?"

"Si, señor. He is right here on this street."

The deputy's eyes widened. "Really? Where?"

"He is sitting on a horse."

Swinging his head back and forth, Wilson said, "Where? Where?"

"Right in front of you. I am Joaquin Murieta and you are a dead deputy."

Wilson's mouth wagged and his hand streaked for his gun. He was too slow. He died on his feet with his gun half out of its holster, a bullet through his Adam's apple.

As soon as the deputy went down, the two Mexicans stopped fighting, ran to their horses, leaped in the saddles, and galloped away with Joaquin Murieta.

Deputy Robert Wilson's death at the hands of the Ghost of Sonora inflamed the minds of the posses around Los Angeles. They declared war. In the next few days, many of Murieta's men were shot down or captured and hanged. Murieta retaliated, wiping out two entire posses in two days by ambush. Posses and vigilantes learned that to infuriate Joaquin Murieta was costly.

This was emphasized on the night of November 21, 1852. One of the most prominent members of the Murieta-hating vigilantes in Los Angeles was General Joshua H. Bean, a former general of the California State Militia. On that cool November night, Bean was leaving a government building in San Gabriel after an important meeting with several hundred vigilantes. He was the last to leave.

Pulling the door shut, Bean locked it, and started down the street toward an old Spanish mission building where he had temporary quarters. The mission was a half-block away.

As Bean drew near the mission, he was startled by a mysterious man in black who stepped out of the shadows and faced him. His upper body was veiled with a black serape. The general stopped, frozen with fear. "Wh-what d-do you w-want?"

"Was your meeting profitable tonight, General Bean?"

Bean had trouble finding his voice. His entire body was shaking.

"When are you going to close in and capture me, General?"

Bean felt cold sweat bead up on his forehead. Terror was gnawing at his insides like a hungry rodent. In a desperate move, he plunged his hand toward the shoulder holster under his coat. Three shots ripped into his chest, the sounds echoing along the dark, empty street. Murieta decided to leave his old calling card. He cut off the general's ears and stuffed them in his shirt pocket.

The reaction to General Bean's killing was fierce among the vigilantes. For three days they swarmed like angry bees all over the San Gabriel area. On the third night, they found the Murieta camp in the ravine and ambushed the Mexicans as they were sitting around the fire.

In the melee that followed, guns roared and men fell on both sides. Joaquin, Claudio, and Three-Fingered Jack emptied their guns, killing four vigilantes, and ran to their horses in the dark. They heard others around them galloping away, also.

At sunrise, Murieta's army gathered in the hills east of San Gabriel and counted their losses. Fourteen men were missing. Taking a lowland route to the ravine, they found nine dead men, and assumed that the other five had been taken as prisoners. Among them were Reyes Feliz and Juan Senate.

Murieta located another spot for their camp and told his men to rest. He was going into Los Angeles and see where they were keeping Feliz, Senate, and the other three men. If it looked feasible, they would go in that night and free them.

Arriving in Los Angeles at seven-thirty that morning, Joaquin found that the vigilantes, along with the Los Angeles County sheriff, had hanged his five men in the town square at midnight. Newspapers were already on the streets telling the story. The screaming headlines told of the vigilantes' daring raid on the Murieta camp. The bold-print article that followed boasted that the vigilantes had killed nine Mexicans at the campsite and brought five in for hanging. Among the five were two of Murieta's generals, Reyes Feliz and Juan Senate. All five had been hanged in front of a small crowd at the town square at midnight.

The article went on to say that seven vigilantes had been killed in the gunfight at the ravine, and two wounded. The sheriff's hangman, Lester Frye, had pulled the lever on the multiple gallows to drop the Mexicans to their deaths.

Upset especially over the death of Reyes Feliz, Joaquin returned to his men and made the sad report. He told them he had decided that they should leave the Los Angeles area and regroup somewhere up north, but before they left he wanted to do two things. He would pay Antonia La Molinera a visit, and he would settle a little score with the hangman who dropped his five men to their deaths.

The next morning, citizens of Los Angeles were stunned to find Lester Frye hanging on his own gallows with his bloody ears pinned to his nose.

The Ghost of Sonora took the remnant of his army and headed north. An earless town marshal was found dead near Santa Barbara. At San Luis Obispo, three local lawmen were found dead in a ditch, their ears stuffed in their mouths.

Rumors soon circulated across the state that Joaquin Murieta was rebuilding his bloody army. Citizens from Los Angeles to San Francisco prepared themselves for another siege of terror. Songs were being written and sung about the elusive Ghost of Sonora. The best of lawmen and vigilantes could not catch him. Mexicans far and wide cheered El Patrio.

Many more earless victims were left dead in the next several months in central and northern California. The lawmakers had still not ventured into the goldfields and mining towns to tax the Mexicans or force them from their properties.

Rewards for Murieta's capture across the state were up to a total of forty thousand dollars, and the governor added another five thousand to the man or men who brought the Ghost of Sonora in dead or alive.

Shortly thereafter, Deputy Sheriff Harry Love traveled to Sacramento and made a proposal to the California Assembly that he be allowed to form a private company of tough and able men with the authority of the state behind it. They would hunt down the crafty man in black and capture him. Love would need state funds to do so, but he assured the Assembly he could rid the world of Joaquin Murieta.

The Assembly granted Love's request, limiting the size of his company to twenty men. Love must hire the best and they had only ninety days to complete the task. If they had not done it by that time, there would be no more funds allotted. If Love and his men brought Murieta in dead or alive, all the rewards would be theirs. The Assembly gave Love's company the name California Rangers.

The recruiting took place at San Jose. It took two weeks to sort through hundreds of men, test their abilities, and begin making the final choices.

On the last day, a tall, slender, well-dressed man walked into the Rangers' temporary office and spoke to the thick-bodied man who sat behind the desk. "Good morning. I am looking for Harry Love."

Eyeing the man suspiciously, Love said, "You've found him. What can I do for you?"

"You must hire me as one of your rangers."

Love ran his gaze over the man. Unimpressed, he said flatly, "Can't use you."

"I said you must hire me as one of your rangers."

Love sighed and leaned back in his chair. "Now just why is that?"

"How many of the men you have hired have seen Joaquin Murieta?"

"Huh?"

"How many of the men you are making California Rangers would know Murieta if they saw him?"

Love rubbed his heavy jaw. "Well, I…uh…I guess none of 'em would."

"Not even yourself?"

"Nope. I've never laid eyes on the dirty greaser."

"How are you going to know when you've caught him?"

Love cleared his throat. "Well, to tell you the truth, fella, I hadn't thought about it. Who are you, anyway?"

"My name is Bill Byrnes. I used to be a business partner of Murieta's. I know him well. That is why you must hire me. You need someone who can positively identify him. Otherwise, even if you catch up with the whole gang of them, how will you know for sure which one is Murieta? He doesn't wear the black outfit nor ride the black horse all the time. His men will cover for him if they can."

Love conceded and Byrnes was hired. A boot camp was set up, and Love thoroughly trained his rangers. Plans were made to begin the hunt on June 1, 1853. On May 30, a saloon owner named Hubert Reynolds ran into the office and informed Love that he had seen a band of well-armed Mexicans in the Santa Cruz Mountains near San Jose. He was sure they were part of Murieta's army.

Having learned of the forming of the rangers, Joaquin Murieta had a few of his men casually moving about San Jose to gain as much information as possible. When his men informed him that it was Harry Love who was heading up the rangers and that the unit was being put together for the single purpose of bringing about his demise, he was furious. He was holding a grudge against Love for the useless killing of Chico Herrera to begin with but the second fact doubled his fury. Murieta was also told about the report Hubert Reynolds had made to Love.

The California Rangers were bivouacked in tents on a vacant lot next to their temporary headquarters. On the night of May 31, they bedded down with excitement, knowing that at sunrise the next morning they would be riding into the Santa Cruz Mountains after Joaquin Murieta.

At dawn on June 1, Harry Love stepped out of his tent and stumbled over a crumpled body that lay next to the flap. It was Hubert Reynolds. His throat had been slit and his ears were stuffed in his mouth. The brazen act angered Harry Love. He led his men out of San Jose toward the mountains with a dogged determination to see Murieta hanging at the end of a rope before the day was out.

After riding hard all day and searching diligently, Love's hopes of hanging Joaquin Murieta before sundown were dashed. They had combed many a square mile, but the Ghost of Sonora had eluded them again. The sun was lowering, and they were about to stop and set up camp when one of the rangers spotted fresh hoofprints leading southward, blazing a trail off the beaten path. Dismounting, Love examined the tracks. "It's them, boys. Has to be. There's nobody else runnin' around these mountains in a pack like this."

"Can you tell how many are in the pack?" asked another ranger.

"Not yet," came the reply. "They were a little too bunched up when they rode along here." Looking toward the lowering sun, he said, "We've still got over an hour of daylight left. Let's follow 'em. I'll be able to tell more farther on, I'm sure."

The rangers were quickly in hot pursuit. As they rushed head-long behind their eager leader, the adrenalin flowed. When they had captured the Ghost of Sonora and put a rope around his neck they would be famous…and rich.

The last rays of the sun were dying out over the mountain tops to the west when Harry Love drew rein, skidding to a halt. The rangers halted their mounts as Love slipped from the saddle, looking at an object hanging from a tree limb directly overhead. One of the rangers commented, "Hey, look, fellas! It's a dead skunk hangin' from that limb!"

Focusing on the lifeless form above him, Love said, "This is Murieta's work. The skunk's ears have been cut off and stuffed in its mouth. There's a piece of paper pinned to its body. Kyle, climb up there and cut it down."

Ranger Kyle Evans hastily climbed the tree and moved out on the limb with his hunting knife between his teeth. Balancing on the limb, he took the knife in hand as he read the words on the paper. Looking down, he said, "Harry, you ain't gonna like what this note says."

"What's it say?"

Evans cleared his throat. "Only two words. Harry Love."

The ranger leader got the message loud and clear. Red-faced, he swore vociferously and stomped his feet. "Forget it, Kyle! Leave the thing up there!"

As Love examined the tracks in the soft earth in the fading light, his loathing for Joaquin Murieta grew more intense. By the tracks he knew that Murieta was traveling with seven other men. He wondered where the rest of the greaser's army had gone, but he really did not care. He was after one man…the bloody Ghost of Sonora.

CHAPTER TWENTY-ONE

L earning of the California Rangers' southerly pursuit of Joaquin Murieta and his small band, newspaper reporters rode after them in an attempt to keep up with what was going on. Though Harry Love was irritated at their intermittent appearances, he kept them abreast of the pursuit.

As the state's newspapers reported periodically on the chase, it had the attention of people all over California. On June 6, the *California Police Gazette* reported that a man answering Murieta's description was seen talking to a tall, slender Mexican woman at the stagecoach station in San Luis Obispo. The beautiful woman boarded a stage heading south after talking to the man.

The next day a posse in Santa Barbara reported having chased the elusive outlaw and his seven men into the Santa Monica Mountains outside of Los Angeles before losing them. Three days later, reports were given to law enforcement agencies that the Murieta gang was seen camping in a gulch near the town of Santa Ana, south of Los Angeles.

Harry Love and his rangers stormed into the gulch the next day. They found where the gang had camped, but they were gone. Following their trail due east, the rangers lost it at sundown near the thick San Bernardino forest. They set up camp on the edge of the forest and built a fire. After eating supper, they sat by the fire and talked. Harry Love looked at Bill Byrnes and asked, "What do you know about Murieta's link to Marshal Colby Cullins over here in San Jacinto?"

"How'd you learn about that?" Byrnes queried with surprise.

"It's my job," replied Love, evading the question. "I asked you what you know about Murieta and Cullins."

"Only that they became friends when Joaquin and Rosita were coming into the state from Mexico. Joaquin told me that he had saved the marshal's life, and the deed gave birth to a strong friendship. That's all I know. Why?"

"Well, we lost the trail right here. San Jacinto is only a couple miles east. If they're friends, maybe Murieta has contacted him. Think you and I will ride to San Jacinto in the morning and talk to Cullins."

At eight-fifteen the next morning, Marshal Colby Cullins sat behind his desk, looked impassively at the two rangers, and said in a level tone, "Nope, I ain't seen Joaquin since he rode through here on his way to Mexico several months ago."

Harry Love leaned close and pressed him. "You're absolutely sure of that, Marshal?"

Cullins remained poker-faced, but there was fire in his eyes. "You questionin' my honesty, deputy?"

Love flicked a glance at Bill Byrnes and rose from his chair. "Sometimes friends will help friends in spite of what's right."

"I think this conversation has reached its limit."

As the two rangers trotted away from the San Jacinto marshal's office, Love said, "Bill, why do I get the feeling the man is lying?"

"I don't know. Why do you think he's lying?"

"Because I can't feature Murieta's getting this close to his friend without contacting him. I just got a feelin' that since Murieta saved Cullins' hide once, maybe Cullins is repaying the debt by savin' Murieta's."

Suddenly they looked up and saw one of the rangers coming at them at a full gallop. Skidding to a halt as Love and Byrnes drew rein, the ranger reported that the town marshal at San Juan Capistrano had sent a runner to find the rangers. He had information for Love and wanted to see him as soon as possible.

Sending Byrnes back to the camp with the ranger, Harry Love rode hard to San Juan Capistrano and arrived just before noon. He tied the horse to the hitching post, crossed the boardwalk, and entered Marshal Barry McClelland's office. After identifying himself to McClelland, Love said, "What did you want to see me about?"

"I want you to take a walk with me over to the stage office," replied the marshal.

Three minutes later, the two lawmen passed through the door of the stage office and Byrnes saw the marshal look quickly around the room. There was no one in the office but the elderly agent. McClelland stomped to the counter. "Where is she?"

"I don't know," replied the old man, shrugging his shoulders. "I stepped out for a few minutes. When I came back, she was gone."

McClelland swore.

Love said, "Will you please tell me what this is all about?"

McClelland quickly explained that he knew about a friendship Joaquin Murieta had struck up several months previously with a singer named Antonia La Molinera. It happened when Murieta was operating in the Los Angeles area and Antonia was singing at the Chaparral Hotel. McClelland's oldest daughter, Alicia, worked as a maid in the hotel and had heard the singer talk about it. Antonia had quit her job quite suddenly the first week of June. Alicia had not seen her until by chance they found themselves on the same stage-coach yesterday, heading south. During the ride, Antonia had told Alicia she was going to San Diego to look for a job in a hotel down there.

When McClelland had met his daughter at the stage station at dawn this morning, she quickly told him the story, knowing that the law was after Murieta. Alicia figured Antonia might know where Murieta was, or where he was headed.

Quickly McClelland cornered Antonia, who was waiting in the station for the next stage to San Diego. She admitted knowing Murieta, but said all she knew about the chase was what she read in the newspapers. McClelland wanted Harry Love to talk to her, so he made her promise to wait right where she was until he could get Love there. The stage from San Diego, which turned around in San Juan Capistrano, was not due in until two-thirty in the afternoon. It would pull out at three o'clock.

Love told McClelland that he knew about the connection between Murieta and the singer, and suggested that they look for her in the town. Possibly she had decided to take a walk.

A quick, thorough search was made for Antonia, but she had disappeared. They were about to mount up and ride through the surrounding countryside for further search, when another ranger galloped in and told Love that a rancher had found the ranger camp and reported that he saw the Murieta gang ride into Cantua Arroya Canyon in the mountains just southeast of San Juan Capistrano at sunrise.

More eager to catch Murieta than to run down Antonia La

Molinera, Love took his ranger and galloped out of town.

Love met up with his men and headed for the mountains. As darkness was falling, they were at the northern edge of Cantua Arroya Canyon. Just before dawn on June 13, 1853, the California Rangers moved cautiously into the canyon on foot. As the sky began to lighten, they smelled smoke.

"Campfire's still burnin'," Love whispered to his men as they followed the sinuous floor of the canyon. "They've got to be there."

Guns ready, they proceeded on tiptoe. Harry Love motioned to Bill Byrnes, wanting him by his side. When Byrnes flanked him, Love whispered, "Stay close to me. I want you to point out Murieta the instant you see him."

Byrnes nodded.

Nerves stretched tight, the rangers came to a sharp bend in the canyon floor with the smell of wood smoke strong in their nostrils. Love was the first to see the campfire with five Mexicans huddled around it, seated on the ground. A sixth was standing over them, drinking coffee from a tin cup. Their voices were low as they conversed in Spanish. Another was a few yards away, tending to an Arabian gelding.

Quickly, Bill Byrnes stabbed a finger in the direction of the Mexican beside the Arabian and whispered, "Harry, that's Joaquin Murieta!"

At that instant, one of the Mexicans at the fire spotted the rangers and shouted a warning. Dropping their cups, plates, and utensils, the Mexicans drew their guns and dived away from the fire, shooting at the shadowed figures at the bend in the canyon.

The rangers fired back, spreading out and taking cover. While gunfire racketed through the canyon, the man pointed out by Byrnes leaped on the Arabian and galloped away. A ranger named William T. Henderson dashed along the canyon's edge, hopped on one of the Mexicans' horses, and gave chase.

The gunfight at the camp was short. The well-trained rangers, by far outnumbering the Mexicans, killed four of them and took the other two as prisoners. None of the rangers was hurt.

As soon as the prisoners were secured, Harry Love ran to one of the other Mexican horses, and leaped into the saddle. "Four of you get on these other horses! We've got to help Henderson get Murieta!

The rest of you stay here with the prisoners!"

The rangers closest to the remaining animals obeyed and rode out in a cloud of dust behind their leader.

A ranger named Cal Tracy stood before the two prisoners, who were tied with ropes. "What are your names?"

Luis Vulvia and Rafael Escobar knew it would do no good to refuse an answer. They told Tracy their names.

Tracy then pointed to the dead Mexicans that lay in a row on the ground. "Now, I want to know who these men are."

The dead were identified as Three-Fingered Jack, Julio Martinez, Edwardo Gallardo, and Claudio Murieta.

One of the rangers chuckled. "Claudio Murieta, eh? He Joaquin's brother?"

Rafael Escobar nodded silently.

"Well," spoke up another, "looks like we'll get us two Murietas today!"

There was a round of laughter, then one of them said, "Yeah, and a few days from now, we'll pick us up the reward money!"

Suddenly Cal Tracy said, "Wait a minute! I just thought of something! There were eight men in this gang when we started trailing them in San Jose." Turning to Vulvia and Escobar, he demanded, "Where's the other one?"

The prisoners eyed each other, then gave Tracy a defiant look.

Face flushed with anger, Tracy spouted, "I can make you talk, you know! A little torture will loosen your tongues!"

Luis Vulvia said, "The eighth man is of no consequence, señor. His name is Pedro Hablia. He became ill while we were camping near Santa Ana. He told us to go on without him, so we did."

"If I find out you're lying to me—"

"He is not lying, señor," spoke up Escobar. "We hesitated to tell you because we do not want you hunting Pedro down."

"He's not important," Tracy said. "Our men will bring the important one back here shortly."

Some forty minutes after Love and the others had ridden away, they returned, along with William T. Henderson, leading the Arabian gelding. Draped over the Arabian's back was the bullet-riddled body of a handsome young Mexican man. The rangers began to shout and fire their guns in the air.

Dismounting, Harry Love said, "Okay, Bill. Take a good look at him and tell me for sure if he's Joaquin Murieta."

Luis Vulvia and Rafael Escobar looked on wide-eyed as Bill Byrnes stepped up to the dead man, took hold of his hair, and raised the face to look at it. Nodding, he let the head drop. "Yep. That's your man."

There was more rejoicing among the rangers. Their horses were brought in and whiskey bottles removed from the saddlebags. While the bottles were being opened, Cal Tracy brought up the subject of the eighth man to Harry Love. At first the leader was stunned that he had not thought of the eighth man. When Tracy told him that the prisoners named him as Pedro Hablia, explaining that he had become ill and that they had left him near Santa Ana, Love was concerned. Confronting the prisoners with it, he told them that they were going to hang at San Jose anyway so they might as well be truthful. Both men assured him they were telling the truth.

With a little uneasiness prickling the back of his neck, Love led the Arabian to where Vulvia and Escobar stood and lifted the face of the dead man into full view. "Tell me, is this Joaquin Murieta?"

Bill Byrnes stepped up and rasped, "Hey, what is this? I told you it's Murieta, Love!"

Ignoring him, the ranger leader spat at the prisoners, "I asked you a question! Is this Joaquin Murieta?"

Vulvia and Escobar stared at him insolently, their mouths clamped tight.

Bill Byrnes eyed them with contempt. "What's the matter with you two? What's it going to hurt if you tell the man your leader is dead?"

"Let him wonder," Vulvia said through tight lips.

"Hey!" Cal Tracy laughed. "What's all the fuss about, Harry? Bill knew Murieta well. He says the dead greaser is him! That's good enough for me. Let's celebrate!"

Love broke into a laugh and agreed. Whiskey flowed freely as each ranger talked about what he was going to do with his share of the reward money. When that subject was exhausted, they discussed their trip to Sacramento, where they would have to turn in the body in order to collect the reward. It was nearly five hundred miles. It would take them at least ten or eleven days. The body would begin to decompose. Bill Byrnes suggested that they leave the body and just take the head. They could probably obtain a sizable bottle in one of the larger towns. If they put the head in the bottle and filled the bottle with salt water, the flesh would be preserved.

Harry Love liked the idea and the others agreed. Byrnes used his bowie knife to sever the head from the body and slipped it in a gunnysack.

On the return trip the bottle was procured and the head was sealed in brine. The third day out, the procession was climbing through a mountain pass. Harry Love heard his two prisoners whispering to each other. He heard enough to learn that they were terrified at the prospect of a public hanging in San Jose. At one point, while the column of riders was moving along the edge of a high cliff, Luis Vulvia and Rafael Escobar leaped from their horses and jumped over the edge of the cliff.

Taking a look over the edge, Cal Tracy saw their broken bodies on the rocks four hundred feet below. Harry Love laughed, saying the world was better off with two less Mexicans.

On June 25, 1853, Harry Love and his rangers were paid the reward money in a formal ceremony conducted by the governor. The governor made a short speech, saying that the state legislature was most grateful for what the rangers had done in ridding California of its worst enemy. On the spot, he asked for a vote from the state lawmakers that the rangers be given another five thousand dollars to divide amongst themselves for a job well done. It was granted.

William T. Henderson's reward money was augmented by a tour of the state, bearing the head in the bottle. Henderson had pumped six bullets into the fleeing Mexican's body before the other rangers had caught up to him. As the hero who had killed Joaquin Murieta, Henderson collected a fee of one dollar apiece from each person who viewed the head in the bottle.

While displaying the bottled head in the Rusty Gun Saloon in Stockton, Henderson's heroic deed was put in question when three Mexican men paid their dollars and moved behind the chest-high curtain where the bottle sat on a table.

Upon examining the head, one of them looked at Henderson and said in front of some thirty people, "Hey, this is not El Patrio! I knew Joaquin Murieta very well and this is not him!"

His partners avowed that they knew Murieta too and declared that the head was a fake. It was some young, good-looking Mexican, but it was not Murieta.

Henderson was visibly shaken.

Others quickly paid their money and in viewing the head, argued that it was indeed El Patrio. Still others agreed with the first three, saying the whole thing was a hoax.

Word of the dispute quickly made its way to Sacramento, and Harry Love was ordered by the governor to prove that the head in the bottle had once been on the shoulders of the notorious Joaquin Murieta.

Upset at this development, Love assured the governor that he would produce Bill Byrnes, who had been Murieta's business partner. Byrnes would swear it under oath and the matter would be settled. However, Bill Byrnes was nowhere to be found. He had sold several businesses that he owned and no one had any idea where he had gone. A search was begun by Love and several other former rangers. Byrnes must be found and swear to the authenticity of the head or the governor would demand the return of the reward money.

While the search was going on, and in spite of the shadowed doubts and lack of confirmation, the bottled head was sold as that of Joaquin Murieta at an auction for thirty-five dollars. William T. Henderson no longer wished to be associated with it.

The new owner moved the bottle about from place to place all over northern California and the story was told time and time again of the California Rangers' triumph over the Ghost of Sonora. Scoffers who doubted the authenticity of the head spoke loudly, insisting it was a hoax. They laughed, saying that Joaquin Murieta put one over on Harry Love and his men by planting his close friend Bill Byrnes among them. The whole thing was preplanned. Byrnes identified the wrong man while Murieta was nowhere in the camp. He had actually been the eighth man. Murieta had eluded the rangers and returned to Mexico. The scoffers capitalized on the fact that there had been reports out of Mexico that he had been seen recently high in the mountains of the Sierra Madre with a beautiful young Mexican woman. However, no one could confirm the report.

Those who believed the head was that of Joaquin Murieta insisted just as loudly that the scoffers simply could not admit that their hero was finally outfoxed, tracked down, and killed.

The bickering was suddenly quieted when two responsible citizens of Angel's Camp reported a spine-tingling incident that happened to them on the night of July 2, 1853. They were driving their wagon home through the forest from visiting with friends who lived in Sonora when they heard hoofbeats pounding up behind them. The rider was on a black horse. Their flesh crawled when he drew abreast of them and they saw by the moonlight that he was dressed in black, including a black serape, but had no head. A haunting wail came from deep within him as he cried, "I am Joaquin Murieta, and I want my head!" The rider then galloped away and disappeared into the night.

Newspaper reporters from all over the state rushed to Angel's Camp to get the story firsthand. Before the first ones arrived, there were numerous other reports of responsible citizens in the area seeing the same apparition and hearing the same blood-chilling cry. Others all over San Joaquin Valley reported to law enforcement agencies that they were hearing the wail coming from out of the hills and canyons, accompanied by thundering hoofbeats.

Headlines across the state screamed that the Ghost of Sonora had returned as a headless horseman. Citizens from Bakersfield to Sacramento lived in terror. Children awakened their parents in the night, insisting that they saw the headless horseman outside their windows.

With San Joaquin Valley in an uproar over the dead Joaquin Murieta riding at night and frightening people out of their wits, the governor gave up on demanding the return of the reward money from the rangers. Harry Love also gave up on ever finding Bill Byrnes, who seemed to have vanished from the face of the earth.

As the weeks passed, more sightings of the headless horseman were reported—on the average of five a week. Political and religious leaders worked at calming the populace down, saying that the people were letting their imagination get the best of them. Those who had seen and heard the Ghost of Sonora insisted that it was not their imagination. The headless horseman story gained a greater stronghold when on the same night two respected Stockton clergymen and three of their laymen all reported seeing the apparition and hearing the haunting wail in the woods outside the town while driving from a church meeting. In spite of it, other religious leaders tried to convince their followers that such a thing simply could not be true.

After the Stockton incident, there were no more reports of seeing or hearing the headless horseman for over a month. The populace was beginning to settle down, hoping the terror was over.

Then it began to happen.

The men who had been in Harry Love's California Rangers were dying mysteriously. In a matter of a few days, they were killed violently, one by one. Each was found with his ears cut off. Eighteen died in this manner. Harry Love was suddenly shot to death in the aftermath of a domestic fight before the mysterious killer could get to him. Nineteen of the twenty rangers were dead and Bill Byrnes had strangely disappeared.

Californians were left with many puzzling questions: Did the eighteen rangers die at the hands of the headless Ghost of Sonora? Or were they killed by some deranged madman who wanted everyone to think so? Or was Joaquin Murieta actually still alive and doing the killing? Did Murieta and Bill Byrnes pull off an ingenious scheme with the help of Marshal Colby Cullins, or was the head in the bottle once on the shoulders of El Patrio? Where was Antonia La Molinera? She certainly could tell the public if the head in the bottle was Murieta's. But alas, lovely Antonia had also disappeared without a trace, and this mysterious disappearance climaxes the song as guitar-strumming Mexicans in the western United States and in Mexico to this day sing "The Ballad of Joaquin Murieta."

CHAPTER TWENTY-TWO

The wheels of the swaying train clicked in even rhythm as Don Miguel Gonzales handed the last page of the manuscript to his grandson and removed his spectacles. His eyes glistened with tears. Young Don Pablo Gonzales had been reading each page after his grandfather finished it. There was a look of awe on his dark face as he read the last few lines.

"Well, Don Miguel," said Allen Bartlett, "did you find any discrepancies in the story?"

The old man thumbed away the tears that now stained his wrinkled cheeks. "No, I did not. Of course the majority of the story took place out of my presence. But for the part I know about, you are quite accurate. You have done your work well."

At that moment the conductor came through the car announcing that the train would be in the San Francisco depot in ten minutes. It was already slowing down.

Don Miguel swallowed the hot lump in his throat and looked out the window. Nostalgia was clawing at his heart. Reading Allen Bartlett's manuscript had surfaced tender feelings he held for his old friend, Joaquin Murieta. Through the mist that was still in his eyes, he looked at the hills of San Francisco. They were alive with a bright orange hue in the glow of the setting sun.

Pleased at the old gentleman's comment, Bartlett said with a sigh, "Well, I guess it'll be ready for the publisher then, after I write the last chapter."

"You can go to work on the last chapter tomorrow," put in Don Pablo, "after Grandfather looks at the head in the bottle."

"Am I ever excited about that!" said the reporter.

The bell on the big engine was clanging as it chugged into the depot. The hiss of steam drowned out the sound of the excited voices of people who stood along the platform. Brakes squalled abreast the coach and the train rumbled to a halt.

Don Pablo pointed through the window. "Look, Grandfather,

there's a group of people out there holding a sign!"

Don Miguel and the reporter both viewed the small group and the sign that read:

Welcome DON MIGUEL GONZALES!
California Historical Society

Don Miguel and his grandson were greeted warmly by ten representatives of the Society, and told that a surrey awaited them that would take them to their hotel. They would be wined and dined that evening by the officers of the Society.

Several reporters were looking on, some who recognized Allen Bartlett and spoke to him. Bartlett excused himself to Don Miguel and Don Pablo, saying he would see them at the hotel in the morning. He expressed his deep appreciation for the old man's help, then disappeared into the bustling crowd.

Joaquin Murieta's old friend and his grandson were guided to the surrey. Three officials rode with them. As the surrey made its way up and down the steep, narrow streets, the officials explained that at ten o'clock the next morning, Don Miguel and his grandson would be met by them at their room on the fourth floor of the Barbary Coast Hotel and escorted downstairs to the ballroom on the first floor. At the same time, armed guards would be placing the bottled head on a table in the ballroom and covering it with a heavy cloth.

At precisely ten-thirty, Don Miguel would view the head with a large crowd of Society members looking on. It would be an historical moment. Don Miguel Gonzales would settle once and for all whether the head had ever been on the shoulders of the notorious Joaquin Murieta.

Soon the surrey made a left turn on to a broad street and young Don Pablo pointed off to the right. "Look, Grandfather! There's the Silver Slipper!"

A large sign over the double doors displayed a silver-colored woman's low-cut dress shoe above fancy lettering: SILVER SLIPPER SALOON.

On the wall next to the doors, a giant billboard with a hand-painted picture of the bottled head and bold lettering invited the public to come inside and see the head of Joaquin Murieta, California's famous Ghost of Sonora.

Don Miguel eyed the place without a word.

"Why don't we pull over and go in right now, Grandfather?" asked Don Pablo. "The curiosity is killing me! I would sleep better tonight if I knew whether or not the head was Joaquin's."

"One more night won't hurt you," replied the old man. "It would not be right for me to look at the bottle now, then make a pretense when I view it in the morning as if I had not seen it before."

"I guess you're right," Don Pablo said in a dull tone.

The Society officials agreed.

One block east of the Silver Slipper, the surrey pulled up to the curb in front of the Barbary Coast Hotel. They checked into their room, freshened up, and were joined in the hotel dining room by the president, vice president, and secretary-treasurer of the California Historical Society.

That night before retiring in their double-bedded room, Don Pablo was sitting on a chair pulling off his shoes as the old man finished brushing his teeth. "Well, Grandfather," he said, smiling, "you must be very excited about tomorrow. I am sure it will mean very much to you to settle in your own mind the fate of your friend, Joaquin Murieta."

Don Miguel smiled back without comment, placing his toothbrush in a small leather bag. Already in his long johns, he crossed the room and climbed into his featherbed, sighing.

"You're tired, aren't you?" said the younger Gonzales, peeling down to his own long johns.

"That I am, my boy."

Don Pablo blew out the kerosene lantern and settled into the other bed. He lay there for a moment in the darkness, then said, "Grandfather, correct me if I am wrong, but I have been getting a growing impression that your viewing the head in the bottle is for the sake of everyone else, and not for yourself. Am I correct?"

"I am too weary to talk anymore, Don Pablo," the elderly gentleman said sleepily. "Good night."

The young Mexican lay awake for a long time, listening to his grandfather snore. He was wide awake and his imagination was stirred. Did Joaquin Murieta, Bill Byrnes, and Marshal Colby Cullins actually devise and pull off a cunning scheme? If so, did Joaquin really die of loneliness for Rosita in Cucurpe? Or was the rumor true that Allen Bartlett had mentioned in his manuscript, that Joaquin was seen in the Sierra Madres with a beautiful Mexican woman not long after the California Rangers killed the young Mexican at Cantua Arroya Canyon? Was that beautiful woman Antonia La Molinera? Were they now living as elderly husband and wife in Mexico?

Don Pablo's curiosity was a gnawing, living thing in his stomach. Or did Bill Byrnes actually turn traitor on his friend and betray him? Did the mysterious blackclad headless horseman kill the eighteen rangers and cut their ears off? If so, the Ghost of Sonora was still riding the dark hills as some people say and the head in the bottle really was once on the shoulders of Joaquin Murieta.

After a while, Don Pablo felt himself getting drowsy. The last clear thought he had was about his grandfather. The dear old man was indeed acting a bit strange about the whole thing. Or was it just Don Pablo's imagination? One thing for sure, he told himself, at ten-thirty in the morning, on April 18, 1906, Don Miguel Gonzales would clear up the mystery once and for all. Then the whole world would know the truth about the Ghost of Sonora.

Dawn was only a hint on the eastern horizon in San Francisco when at 5.12 A.M., a deep rumbling was heard beneath the city and the earth began to rock to and fro in powerful undulating movements. Buildings commenced to tremble, and people were pulled instantly from their slumber. In a matter of seconds, the whole city was in the grip of a violent earthquake.

At the Barbary Coast Hotel, Don Pablo Gonzales jerked awake as the building swayed and groaned around him and his bed rolled across the floor. Sitting up in a half-daze, he peered through the dim light and saw his grandfather up on one elbow, trying to stay on his rocking bed. The frightened young Mexican managed to leave his own bed and staggered over the shifting floor in an attempt to get to the old man. Suddenly plaster and dust fell from the ceiling and the walls began to rip apart. Don Pablo's feet went out from under him and he fell flat. He was trying to get up when one of the walls collapsed on top of him. Something heavy struck him on the head, and a dark curtain settled over him as he was swallowed into a black abyss.

Don Pablo had no idea how long he had been unconscious when he came to, but the building around him was no longer in convulsions. His head ached something fierce as he thought of his grandfather and began to struggle against the weight that was holding him down. He could hear people screaming and shouting somewhere nearby as he raised out of the dusty heap into the early morning light that shafted through the gaping spaces where solid walls had been. While coughing dust and trying to clear his vision, he was aware of horses neighing down on the street and fire bells clanging loudly.

The smell of smoke met his nostrils and he could hear the crackling of flames as his dizziness subsided. "Grandfather!" he cried, shocked at the sharp sound of his own voice. Fear was rampant as an icy swell in his chest as he took a deep, shuddering breath and groped his way over a pile of rubble toward the last spot where he had seen the old man.

"Grandfather!" he shrieked at the top of his voice while throwing aside broken boards and shapeless chunks of plaster. Suddenly he found dust-covered flesh and hair. A wordless wail escaped his lips when he realized what he was looking at. A huge, broken ceiling beam had fallen on the old man, crushing his head. It had killed him instantly.

As the young man was weeping and making an attempt to free the lifeless body, two firemen plunged through what was left of a door frame and hurried to him. One of them took hold of his shoulders. "You've got to get out of here fast, fella! The building's on fire!"

"No!" retorted Don Pablo. "I've got to get my grandfather out!"

The other fireman took one look at the caved-in head of Don Miguel Gonzales. "He's dead, son. There's nothing you can do. It would take too long to extract the body. We've all got to get out of here or we'll die! C'mon!"

Don Pablo obeyed the firemen and allowed them to lead him out of the blazing hotel. They no sooner got to the ground level and out onto the street, when the entire building collapsed in a roaring, blazing heap. When the firemen were sure the young Mexican was all right, they left him for another burning building less than half a block away.

When his head had cleared completely, Don Pablo realized he was sitting there on a small shipping crate in his long johns. There was a partially demolished clothing store a few yards down the street. People were running every direction, and no one seemed to notice him as he made his way to the store and entered through a hole in the front wall. There was no one in the place. It went against his grain to take clothing without the owner's permission, but he had no choice.

Moments later, he emerged from the store fully clothed and wearing a pair of hightop shoes. Weeping over his grandfather's death, he made his way down the street westward. He had to find out if anything had happened to the head in the bottle. Wiping tears, he weaved his way among huge piles of wood, stone, and brick, leaping across the yawning, craggy fissures in the broken earth, and made his way to the spot where the Silver Slipper Saloon once stood. The size of the jagged-edged crater that lay before him took his breath. He stopped weeping and wiped the tears from his eyes. Not only was the Silver Slipper gone, but three adjoining buildings had also been swallowed by the convulsing earth.

Don Pablo noticed a tall, blond man standing at the edge of the crater, looking down at a large piece of the saloon's sign that lay partially buried in rubble at his feet. A portion of the silver-colored woman's shoe could be seen and a few of the letters.

Wan faced, Allen Bartlett slowly turned and set his bleary eyes on the young Mexican. When he greeted Don Pablo, he asked where his grandfather was.

Tears surfaced again as Don Pablo told him how Don Miguel had died. Bartlett put his arm around Don Pablo's shoulders and offered his sympathy. Holding that position, he looked down into the crater. "The head in the bottle is gone, Don Pablo. Gone forever. Now we will never know."

Don Pablo nodded sadly and replied in a tight voice, "That is right, Señor Bartlett. Now we will never know."

Other books by Morgan Hill:

DEAD MAN'S NOOSE

Safely to the Gallows…

"You may put a rope on my wrists," the captured outlaw Duke McClain taunts Sheriff Matt Blake, "but you'll never put one on my neck." A death sentence awaits McClain in Tucson for his robberies, massacres, and senseless murders—but it lies across miles of unforgiving desert, full of cruel traps and bloodthirsty villains. Although Blake is determined to bring the outlaw to justice, a single thought echoes in his head with every thirsty step: A lot of things could happen before they reach Tucson…

ISBN 1-59052-277-X